T0244932

FURIES RISING

Book One: Hollow Valley

ANDREW LYONS

Print ISBN: 979-8-35094-421-1
eBook ISBN: 979-8-35094-422-8

Printed in the United States of America

For my daughters,
who asked for this . . .

Day is done,

gone the sun,

from the lakes,

from the hills,

from the sky.

All is well,

safely rest,

God is nigh.

—"Green Trees and Taps"

PART I

PROLOGUE

Randy really didn't want to wait.

The line for gas at the Costco was longer than he liked, and he was already behind schedule.

He was supposed to be back at the camp by 2:00 p.m. But his special order of twenty-five chickens had been delayed, and it was already one thirty. If he stopped for gas, he'd be an hour late and that wasn't ideal, especially with three giant coolers' worth of chickens in the back of his SUV in the middle of the summer.

On the other hand, he was down to a third of a tank of gas. If he didn't fill up, he'd be close to empty by the time he got to the camp, and considering that there were no gas stations within twenty miles of the place, that seemed like a bad idea.

The decision was made for him when three cars pulled out of one line in quick succession. He immediately slid into the open spot and told himself that this was a sign that his luck was changing.

As he waited to move forward, he glanced at himself in the rearview mirror. His shaggy brown hair was getting long. It was on the verge of moving past hipster cool into plain old sloppy, which wouldn't go over with the gal he was hoping to win over.

He knew it was a long shot, but he was still hoping that Marta, the counselor for the oldest girls' bunk, might be willing to trip the light fantastic tonight. Yes, the big dance was mostly for the kids, and as the camp handyman, he wasn't even officially invited to attend, but the session was almost over and he hoped the rules might be loosened enough for him to impress her with some of his moves.

His little daydream faded when another car pulled out and he was rewarded with an available tank. He pulled into the spot, hopped out, and used the camp credit card to pay. He knew from experience that filling the tank was a good five-minute process, so he pulled out his earbuds, clicked on a song on his phone, and worked on his dance moves in the narrow space between the tank and the vehicle.

The woman at the tank in front of him gave him a disapproving stare, but he didn't care. There was a reason people called him Rowdy Randy, and it had a lot to do with his carefree, devil-may-care attitude. He wasn't going to let some uptight suburban chick ruin his vibe.

Randy closed his eyes and let the beat take over. In the background of the song, he thought he could almost hear people cheering for him. That was a good omen. After a few seconds, he opened his eyes and noted that the tense lady was no longer looking at him nastily. In fact, she was nowhere to be seen. He found that a little odd, since she'd left her driver's side door open.

Movement off to the left caught his attention. What he saw was befuddling. The woman from the car was running up the small hill away from the gas tanks. She glanced back briefly, and he was startled to see a look of panic on her face before she turned away again.

He turned off the song. Surprisingly, the cheering he'd heard in the background continued. Then it occurred to him that it sounded less like cheering than . . . screaming.

He turned back in the direction of the sound. What he saw in front of him made him blink multiple times. It didn't make any sense. Rather than try to comprehend it, he did the only thing that he could think of.

Leaping across the driver's seat of the SUV, he opened the glove compartment and pulled out the small pistol that he kept for emergencies but had never actually used. He took off the safety as he stood back up and turned to face whatever that thing was.

It was much closer now, and now Randy noticed that it wasn't only one. As people streamed past him, running away from the store and toward the road, he held his ground. Lifting the gun, he aimed as best he could, despite his shaking hands. Then he fired.

He landed a direct hit, but it didn't seem to make any difference. The thing kept coming, and then, before he even understood what was happening, it was on him.

CHAPTER 1

Lukas tried to quiet his palpitating heart.

He wiped his sweaty palms on his shirt and reminded himself to breathe. His stomach was one giant twisted knot, and his fingertips tingled slightly.

Everything told him that what he was about to do was a huge mistake, one that could ruin relationships and leave him a quivering mess.

But he'd been after this for weeks, and he was running out of time. After tonight, there would only be Sunday and Monday left; the buses would arrive early on Tuesday morning to take everyone back to their respective cities.

If he was ever going to take this chance, now was the time.

Steve Sailor, the bushy-mustached sleep-away summer camp director, stood on a bench and gave the brief obligatory warning about behaving responsibly. Then the music started up again, and the bravest kids swarmed across the tennis courts to match up with their intended targets.

Lukas decided to throw caution to the wind and started walking across the court, his gaze fixed on Juliana Goldenson. She was dressed for the end-of-session 80s' dance party as tennis star Gabriela Sabatini.

Admittedly it wasn't the most creative costume ever. Juliana was wearing a tucked-in crewneck Hollow Valley camp t-shirt and a tennis skirt. But to Lukas, it seemed like an inspired choice, setting off her long dark hair and showcasing her tanned arms and the muscular legs that had led her to victory as a mere junior at the state cross-country championship last spring.

Juliana, or Jules as she was known to everyone, felt someone's eyes on her. She glanced up, made eye contact with Lukas, and gave him her patented half smile. He started walking, brimming with unearned confidence.

He was halfway toward her, his prop eyeglasses and fishing cap both in danger of falling off, when someone grabbed him by the arm with a vise-like grip. He almost fell as he tried to maintain his balance. Looking up, he saw it was Aubrey West, one of the girls from the Lumens, the oldest girls' bunk.

She was wearing a full-length hot pink leotard and had a massive bow in her hair, which she'd curled into endless ringlets. She sported earrings that dangled down to her shoulders. Short and sinewy strong with cocoa skin and blazing brown eyes, she looked like she was about to deck him.

"Want to make a quick five bucks, Lincoln?" she asked. For some reason, she always called him by his last name. Lukas assumed it had something to do with her dad being a colonel in the military.

"What?" he asked, still not sure if she was angry at him for some unintended slight.

"Emily Satterfield offered me twenty dollars if I could get you to dance with me before you humiliated yourself by asking Jules. I agreed. If you go for it, I'll cut you in for 25 percent. Easy money for you—one dance, five bucks, no crushing rejection at the hands of an older woman."

"How did you know I was going—" Lukas began to ask, feeling his face start to flush.

"Everyone knows, dude," she said, cutting him off. "You're like a little lost puppy. It's embarrassing."

He pushed right past the substance of her comment, unwilling to process the consequences of "everyone knowing" at this moment, and focused instead on her tone. "This is how you ask me to dance— by insulting me?"

"I'm trying to help you, man," she insisted. "You'll come off less hopeless if you wait at least a few songs before hitting on my counselor, who also happens to be two years older than you and, in case your forgot, your brother's girlfriend."

Lukas set aside the unspoken judgment in her voice. He'd beaten himself up enough over his feelings lately. He wasn't going to do it tonight too.

Still, he had to admit Aubrey was probably right. He might be better off waiting a bit to ask Jules. It was less obvious, although apparently everything he'd been doing all summer was obvious to just about everyone.

"One song," he said reluctantly. "Five dollars?"

Aubrey nodded.

"We have a deal," Lukas said.

He began swinging his torso to a-ha in what he hoped was a rhythmic manner.

"Not this song," Aubrey said, aghast. "It has to be a slow one."

"You never said that!" Lukas objected.

"You think Emily would give me twenty dollars to bounce around for three minutes? That's no dare. It has to be a legit 'arms around the waist, swaying slowly' song."

"Then I get half."

"Half what?" Aubrey asked, though she clearly knew what he meant.

Still, he spelled it out for her. "I get ten bucks. You're taking up two precious songs and one of them is a slow dance."

"That hardly seems fair," she said unconvincingly.

"Take it or leave it. You can make ten dollars or lose twenty. It's up to you, West." He smiled, proud of his snarky quip.

The song changed, and "Take On Me" was replaced by Madonna's "Crazy for You."

"I'll take it," Aubrey said, her eyebrows raised, as if challenging him.

Refusing to back down, he wrapped his arms around her waist and began rocking from side to side. Slightly surprised, Aubrey took a second before joining in the motion. It continued like that for another minute or so, the two of them moving robotically back and forth, barely making eye contact.

"Who are you supposed to be, anyway?' he finally asked.

"You're kidding, right?" she asked, astounded.

He shook his head.

"I'm Whitney Houston, dumbass! Who the hell did you think I was?"

Lukas shrugged.

"I should ask you the same question," she said indignantly.

He opened his mouth to reply but she cut him off. "I was being sarcastic, Lincoln. I know who you are. You're Lucas from the movie *Lucas*. A little on the nose, don't you think?"

"I love that movie."

"Of course you do," she said, shaking her head pityingly, "because it's older, just like Jules."

The song ended, and the two of them quickly separated.

"Emily will give me the money when we get all our stuff back on Tuesday morning," she said brusquely. "We'll settle up then."

"You're lucky I don't charge interest," Lukas said.

"You're lucky I don't kick your ass," she retorted, turning on her heel before he could reply.

It took him a second to regroup from the indignity. Shaking it off, he glanced in the direction where Jules had been earlier. As the first strains of Cyndi Lauper singing "When You Were Mine" came over the speakers, he saw her.

She was still in the same spot, but now her arms were locked around Caleb's neck as she stared up into his eyes. As everyone near them hopped around, she and his older brother stood in place, barely moving, oblivious to everything around them.

Lukas, sensing the eyes of the entire camp on him, decided now would be a good time to get some fruit punch.

CHAPTER 2

For a while the next morning, Lukas pretended not to be bothered by what Aubrey had said. But it was short-lived. At breakfast, over dried Froot Loops, he kept his head down, refusing to make eye contact with anyone.

"We don't get powdered eggs this morning?" Stephen, who was sitting next to him in the dining hall, asked incredulously. "Not even milk for the cereal?"

Caleb, who was not just Lukas's older brother but his counselor too, responded. "Rowdy Randy still hasn't come back from his grocery run to San Antonio yesterday, and no one can get a hold of him," he said from the head of the table. "Steve is actually really worried about him. So please don't make it worse by complaining. He sent Lloyd to Kerrville for an emergency supply run this morning. He should be back in the next hour or so."

"Maybe Randy ran off the road or something. It wouldn't be the first time," Lonnie said, concerned. "Did Steve call the cops?"

"He did," Caleb said. "But they've got their hands full with some rioting in San Antonio, and Rowdy Randy isn't at the top of their priority list right now."

"Rioting?" Trevor asked. "What's that about?"

"That's not anything you boys need to be worrying about," Todd said, going into parental mode.

Todd Kemp, the senior counselor of the oldest boys' bunk, the Toros, was a smallish guy with curly light blond hair. He was headed into his final year at Southern Methodist University in Dallas where he was majoring in child development. He wanted to be a school guidance counselor, so this was the perfect summer gig for him.

Lukas didn't mind Todd even though the guy consistently forgot that he was dealing mostly with fifteen-year-olds and not preteens. He was constantly "checking in" to see how each of them was doing. But his heart seemed to be in the right place. Still, Lukas wasn't in the mood this morning. He tuned him out and returned his attention to his Froot Loops.

Javi nudged him and gave him a questioning look.

"What is it?" Lukas asked, mildly annoyed.

"You're not very chatty this morning. And you barely said a word last night after that dance with Aubrey. Did she steal your breath away? Your heart maybe?"

Lukas didn't take offense at the teasing dig. Javier Mendez was his best friend at camp. And though he was half a head shorter than Lukas, he made up for his lack of height with his out-sized personality and personal style. His long brown hair was swept to the side like the girl from that 1990s show *Friends*. While he'd never asked, Lukas was pretty sure that was by design.

Lukas put his spoon down and leaned over.

"Is it totally obvious to everyone at camp that I'm into Jules?" he whispered.

Javi looked at him with a mix of reticence and sympathy. "Not *everyone*," he said slowly.

"Like who?" Lukas demanded.

"The Dandelions don't know."

"The only people at camp who are unaware of my feelings are the seven-year-old girls' bunk?" Lukas hissed.

"To be honest, man," Javi said, trying not to laugh, "some of them might know, too."

"What about *him*?" Lukas asked, not smiling as he nodded imperceptibly in his brother's direction.

"Yeah, Lukas," Javi said quietly, "I'm pretty sure Caleb knows. He's a smart guy, and you're not exactly Mr. Subtlety. But I wouldn't sweat it. I don't think he cares that much."

"Why not?"

"For one thing, I doubt he can blame you. Jules is hot. He probably thinks you have good taste."

"And the other thing?"

"What?" Javi asked confused.

"You said 'for one thing.' That implies a second thing."

"Oh yeah. Well, the second thing is, Lukas, your brother is pretty damn hot, too. I mean, like go-down-to-the-creek-at-free-swim-just-to-watch-him-in-his-trunks hot."

"Okay, Javi, I get it. You've told me about your crush on my brother many times. What's your point?"

"My point is," Javi replied, enjoying watching his friend squirm, "I think he mostly doesn't care because she's with *him*. So it doesn't really matter how many longing looks you send her way, you know?"

Lukas nodded. He did know.

Caleb Lincoln didn't have to sweat much these days. He was headed off to Brown University after the summer. He could have stayed closer to home and gone to either Pepperdine or Loyola Marymount, both in Southern California, both of which had offered him full basketball scholarships.

Caleb had the same brown hair as Lukas, but at six foot three and two hundred pounds, he was a full five inches taller and fifty pounds heavier than his little brother. He was also a beast on the court. But instead of accepting an offer from one of those schools, he'd chosen an Ivy League university on the complete other side of the country that didn't even give out athletic scholarships.

Lukas tried not to take the decision personally. He knew Caleb was trying to escape their parents, especially their mom, who treated his extracurricular activities like a second religion, who never missed a game or anything else he ever did.

But deep down, Lukas also knew there was another reason Caleb wanted to move far away, one that had scarred their family for a decade, one neither of them would ever acknowledge out loud. Lukas pushed his Froot Loops away. He wasn't hungry anymore.

CHAPTER 3

After breakfast, they all returned to the cabin for bunk cleanup. They traipsed along the dusty path, pretending not to notice that it was already ninety degrees at eight in the morning. Lukas distracted himself by listening to the Moore twins argue just ahead of him. With Mike's short fuse contrasting Mark's more chill state, they were always arguing about something.

"At least she talks," said Mark, the devil-may-care taller thinner half of the fraternal twin brothers. "Yours is mostly mute."

"Yeah, well," said his more intense shorter barrel-chested brother, Mike. "I'd rather that than a girl who never shuts up, ever."

When Lukas realized they were talking about their camp girlfriends, his interest waned. Luckily, there was another distraction. In the distance, they could hear the loud yells from the top of Hollow Hill.

"Who is it this morning?" Lonnie asked, squinting into the sun.

"I think it's the Billy Goats," Mike said. "They sound pretty amped."

The Billy Goats were the second youngest boys' bunk, mostly eight- and nine-year-olds, so their enthusiasm made sense.

At some point during the session, every bunk got to climb Hollow Hill. It was a tradition. If it was your day, you woke up early—well before dawn—went to the dining hall to get single-serving boxes of cereal and cartons of milk, which one of the counselors stuffed in a backpack, and then trekked up the hill.

The hike took between a half hour and forty-five minutes, depending on the route chosen and the age and energy level of the group. The quickest route, usually only attempted by the older bunks, required navigating some sketchy steep terrain and scaling a few large boulders. Lloyd, the nature study counselor who was currently making the emergency grocery run to Kerrville, was said to have once made it to the top in fourteen minutes, but that was unofficial.

Once there, everyone would get their cereal and spread out on the summit, which was surprisingly flat and covered in slabs of cracked rock. As people walked around in the valley below, it was customary to shout down to them, with echoed greetings along the lines of "Morning, Steve!" or "Billy Goats rule!" Then the bunk would pack everything up and return down the hill in time for the first activity.

Lukas turned his attention away from Hollow Hill and back to the trail leading to the bunk. The path was notorious for horse manure, and if one wasn't careful, things could get messy, which would make him late for the first activity. Each day, every bunk was assigned to three activities, two before lunch and one after. That was followed by free swim in the late afternoon. For the Toros, the first activity today was riflery.

Lukas would be happy when they got there. The riflery range was set away from the main camp, in a dried-out ravine with overhanging trees. It was always cool, even when it was well over hundred degrees everywhere else at camp.

He hadn't gotten to shoot as much as he liked this summer because of "Wilderness Week," during which the oldest boys' and girls' bunks spent three full days of the session in remote corners of the ranch that the camp was located on. The week—really half a week—involved long hikes each day, training in survival skills and first aid, team-building exercises, and setting up a campsite every night, including dinner prep and water filtration.

Lukas had been looking forward to it for months. When it actually came last week, he both loved and excelled at it. And considering how dire things had looked for maintaining a functional society just a few years ago—what with closed schools, shuttered businesses, and millions of people in quarantine—the skill set seemed unexpectedly practical these days.

But spending all that time doing Wilderness Week had come at an unexpected cost. He hadn't realized how much he would miss swimming in the creek, horseback riding, and even cheesy evening programs like Western Night and the talent show. He almost felt like he'd been robbed of part of the camp experience.

Now that they were back, he was trying to maximize every second he'd missed at the activities. Plus, he was a good shot, easily the best in the bunk and among the most accurate in all of camp. Aubrey, his hostile dance partner from last night, was more consistent, but her dad had been training her to shoot since she was a toddler. Lukas had never fired a gun other than at Hollow Valley.

As he dodged a particularly impressive pile of horse crap in the middle of the path back to the bunk, Lukas silently mused that there were a lot of things he never did outside of Camp Hollow Valley, the summer camp he'd been attending for years now (minus a temporary pause because of the pandemic.) Over time, he'd come to view camp as an oasis, a place where he could set aside the concerns of his normal life and be someone else, not a *different* person exactly, but a different side of the person he usually was.

Tenth grade classmates and friends of the Lukas Lincoln from El Segundo, California, would have been shocked to discover what he was capable of. They knew him as the kid with more enthusiasm for basketball than skill at it, who had read every *His Dark Materials* book but still couldn't get an A in English. They knew him as the friendly guy they had no objection to but no strong affinity for either. They knew him as Caleb's little brother.

With his medium build, middling height, carefully modulated tone of voice, inoffensive brown wavy hair, and blue but not *bright* blue eyes, he knew he was perceived as the epitome of mild-mannered, bordering on boring.

His friends back home had no idea that he was reasonably adept at archery or that he could fire a .22 long rifle with impressive accuracy; that he could start a fire with nothing more than loose brush and flint in less than two minutes; that he could ride a galloping horse, even if it always made him a little nervous; that he was a genius at Capture the Flag; that he could hike for hours without ever getting tired.

Unfortunately, Lukas admitted something to himself that he'd never say out loud: almost none of the skills that made "camp Lukas" so impressive were useful in the daily life of "home Lukas." And he was pretty sure that most of the people at his school would roll their eyes if he ever tried to talk about them. So he kept that stuff to himself.

Back at the bunk, he did his best not to fixate on his shortcomings and instead poured all his attention into the task at hand. His bunk cleanup assignment today was mop duty, and he happily embraced it, hoping that the monotonous job would allow him to shut off his brain for at least a few minutes.

It didn't work.

CHAPTER 4

An hour later, Lukas was still hoping for a distraction that would ease his self-consciousness.

If there was any place where he could set aside all those anxieties, it was on the riflery range. He focused on the paper target ten yards in front of him, his finger gripping the trigger of the .22 rifle. The younger campers used .177 air rifles. But the Toros went straight for the .22s.

All the guns were stored in a weapons locker in the lodge, as were the bows and arrows for archery. The senior staffer in the lodge, usually camp founder Aunt Winnie or camp director Steve Sailor, unlocked the locker. Then the weapons had to be physically signed out by the instructing counselor.

Lukas fired. He wasn't in top form today. Whether it was malaise associated with camp drawing to a close or anxiousness about how many people were aware of his crush on Jules, he only got bullseyes on about half his shots. Usually the percentage was closer to three-quarters.

The day's second activity was archery, and he was equally unsteady. One arrow missed the target completely. It didn't help that Caleb was one of the instructing counselors. He raised his eyebrows at the misfire but said nothing. In fact, while walking to lunch later with Javi, Lukas realized that Caleb had barely spoken to him at all during the activity.

They had to forego the traditional Fried Chicken Sunday Lunch because Rowdy Randy, who was supposed to have brought back two dozen chickens from San Antonio, still hadn't been heard from. Instead, they had a selection of turkey and roast beef sandwiches. Some of the younger kids were upset about missing out, but their counselors were reluctant to tell them the reason.

At one point, Lukas stepped out of the dining hall to go to the restroom by the back kitchen and noticed Steve outside by the main office talking to a man in a uniform marked "Bandera County Sheriff's Deputy." The deputy was tall and broad shouldered but didn't look to be much older than their counselor Todd. Lukas managed to shuffle over behind a supply shed to get close enough to catch what was being said.

"…lots of missing persons calls, too many to investigate," the sheriff's deputy was saying.

"And they're all related to these riots?' Steve asked.

The camp director was alternately rubbing his ample belly and tugging absentmindedly on the mustache he hadn't trimmed since camp started. Between the two features, Steve looked like a cross between a Hell's Angel biker and a portly teddy bear.

"No one's sure, sir," the deputy answered. "It could be related to so much communication being difficult right now. Cell towers are overwhelmed. Last I heard, whole sections of the city were being cordoned off. A person might be physically fine but trapped in a part of town where they can't reach out or might want to stay hidden. There just isn't the manpower right now to track down everyone. It'll probably be a while. I know the president was considering calling in the National Guard. But that's a big step and it wouldn't just happen here."

"This is going on other places?" Steve asked, incredulous.

"Yup. There was a major incident in Colorado and one near Atlanta," the deputy said. "There might be more I don't know about."

"And you don't know what everyone's rioting about? It's not related to another COVID breakout, is it?"

"I'm not sure, sir," the deputy said, then added in a quieter tone that suggested he was sharing something secret. "I've heard on the radio that it might be related to a quarantine of some sort. Word is there *is* some kind of virus going around, something different than last time, and they don't want it to spread. But that's not confirmed."

Steve was quiet for a second, as if letting that possibility settle into his brain. Lukas wondered if his grandparents were okay. They lived in a gated community on the outskirts of San Antonio. He and Caleb were staying with them for the week before and after camp. It was miles from the heart of the city, but he was worried nonetheless.

"What am I supposed to do with all these kids?" Steve asked, with a level of concern in his voice Lukas had never heard before. "A bunch of them live in the San Antonio area. Am I supposed to just send them there on buses, not knowing what they'll be facing? With all the phone lines down, I'm having trouble reaching parents."

"I don't know, sir," the deputy replied. "Though I would say that, if you can get authorization to keep them here a little longer, that might not be a bad idea. Whatever's going on, they're probably safer way out here, away from all the craziness in the city. Right now, being so off the radar, this may be the best place for them."

At that moment, a fly buzzed in front of Lukas's face. He involuntarily swatted it away and accidentally hit the edge of the tin shed, causing it to echo.

"Who's there?" he heard Steve ask.

Lukas darted back inside and hurried through the kitchen, hoping Steve wouldn't care enough to follow him. Once in the dining hall, he glanced over his shoulder and saw that the camp director was nowhere in sight.

He returned to his table, trying to look as casual as possible, unsure whether he should mention what he'd heard to the others. He was pretty certain that, if he repeated it to anyone other than Javi or Caleb, word would get around camp within minutes.

He decided to stay quiet for now. He didn't know what was true and what was rumor. But that wouldn't matter to the little kids who'd surely get scared that they might not be reunited with their parents in two days.

Though most of them were too young to remember the details of the pandemic, they all still moved through the world with a shared lingering anxiety. No matter what was said to reassure them, they were bound to panic. He didn't want to be responsible for forty-eight hours of children crying.

Under normal circumstances, he would just try to call his family to find out what was up. But Camp Hollow Valley, located on a ranch deep in the Texas hill country, had a strict "no devices" policy, not that you could get much of a signal out here anyway.

Each phone, tablet, and other device was collected by a counselor as the camper stepped off the bus at camp for the first time. The items would be logged and then taken to a large safe kept in the lodge where they would remain untouched for the duration of the session.

He decided his best bet would be to talk to Caleb about it later tonight. Even if his brother didn't know what was going on, he was respected by the older staff and could probably convince Steve or Aunt Winnie to let him contact their grandparents or maybe even reach out to their parents in California.

Lukas could keep it a secret until then.

CHAPTER 5

Despite what Lukas had learned at lunch, the world around him seemed oblivious. The rest of the day passed in a leisurely haze. Sundays were always casual, but this last one of the session was even more so.

After siesta concluded, the third activity began. Today it was free choice. Everyone gravitated toward their favorite game, location, or counselor. For some, it was one last chance to play softball on the main valley flat. Others tried to escape the heat with an extended free swim in Wallace Creek. A few chose dance in the pavilion. Lukas went to the radio shack where he could help deejay the songs to be played over the PA system and maybe get some news from an AM radio station.

When he arrived, Richard, a curmudgeonly balding counselor who ran the radio club, was already settling in, preparing to play one of his awful classic rock bands. For a guy in his mid-twenties, he acted like he was two decades older than that. He was the kind of dude who thought playing a Jimi Hendrix album at a party would impress the girls. Before Lukas could object, the tiresome sound of Steve Miller Band's "Take the Money and Run" began blasting across camp.

There was already a crowd of campers clambering around Richard, writing their song choices on the clipboard beside him in the hope that they would get to introduce them at some point during the hour. Lukas knew better. For every camper preference Richard allowed, he'd play two or three of his own. These kids were in for a lot of the Doors and Led Zeppelin.

Instead of wasting his time trying to get a selection, Lukas moved to the back of the shack, turned on a small forlorn transistor radio, and scanned the dial. It was always hard to get anything FM in Hollow Valley because of the hills surrounding the camp. Even AM stations were a challenge.

As Lukas flipped around, it quickly became clear that the problem today wasn't interference. It was that no one was broadcasting. Almost every station was playing the same message from the Emergency Alert System. The Tejano station was running it in Spanish. It was frustratingly vague.

"This is a message from the Emergency Alert System. Due to a potential health hazard in the greater Bexar, Comal, and Medina counties area, all citizens are instructed to remain in their homes or places of business. Leaving your current location is inadvisable. Interacting with those outside your current location is *highly* inadvisable. Please await further instructions."

That was it—the whole message. About five seconds after ending, it would repeat. The process continued uninterrupted. Lukas kept waiting for someone to break in with some kind of live announcement, but it never happened. He listened to it drone on again and again, almost hypnotized, only shutting it off when a little blue-eyed, tousle-haired blond boy of about eight named Nate wandered over.

"What was that?" the kid asked.

"Nothing," Lukas said quickly. "Just boring news stuff."

"It sounded kind of scary," Nate said, his eyes big.

24

"News always sounds scary," Lukas said casually, before trying to change the subject. "What song are you hoping to play?"

"Hello Mudduh, Hello Fadduh," Nate answered. "But I don't think Richard's going to get to me in time."

"Oh, that's a good one," Lukas said approvingly as he led Nate back to the front of the shack. "Richard might be into it because of the kitsch factor. Let's see what we can do."

"What's the kitsch factor?"

"It kind of means it's silly in a fun way, like you, Nate."

He mussed up Nate's already unruly hair. By the time they got back to everyone else, the kid was giggling and had completely forgotten about the scary sounding news. But Lukas hadn't.

*

He still hadn't found a chance to talk to Caleb about what he'd heard Steve Sailor discussing with the sheriff's deputy. But a discovery at dinner assured him that he'd have a good opportunity later.

Because the kitchen staff had the night off, Sunday was always picnic dinner night. The meal was comprised of burgers, hot dogs, bags of chips, and watermelon. It was a good thing too, because it seemed to Lukas that they were running out of food for a conventional meal. At this rate, they'd all be eating dried Froot Loops exclusively by tomorrow.

Lukas and Javi sat quietly at the edge of the picnic area, eating their burgers and taking in the late summer aroma of meat on the grill as it mixed with the nearby chaparral and the occasional whiff of horse manure from a nearby trail. To Lukas, that scent was the essence of camp. Even though the session wasn't over, he found himself preemptively missing it.

But amid all the screaming kids playing tag and spitting hot dog buns at each other, Lukas noticed something else. The oldest girls' bunk, the Lumens, was missing.

"Where are they?" he asked Javi as they ate their burgers.

"Their overnight is tonight. It's at Sasquatch Toe. They left about an hour ago."

Sasquatch Toe was the local nickname for a section of Wallace Creek that ran through the camp property and had a massive rock indentation that, if looked at just so, resembled the shape of a big toe. Because it was a good twenty-minute walk from the main camp, the Toe gave the illusion of seclusion and was often used for cookouts and overnights.

Every bunk was allowed one night apart from the rest of the camp population. The younger kids had cookouts before returning to camp in time for lights out. The older bunks had overnights that included cooking dinner over a fire pit, singing songs, telling ghost stories by firelight, sleeping under the stars, waking up on dewy ground the next morning, having breakfast, and returning to camp in time for the first activity.

Because of Wilderness Week, the Toros had voted to forgo the overnight this year. But apparently the Lumens had decided they still wanted to do it for nostalgia's sake. And if the Lumens were having an overnight this evening, then that almost certainly meant the Toros would be raiding their camp later.

It was a tradition even under normal circumstances. But with one of the Toro counselors dating one of the Lumen counselors, it was a guarantee. Darkness, a campfire, and oblivious campers would allow Caleb and Jules to sneak off for some private time without worrying about Steve Sailor calling them out.

For Lukas, this was good and bad news. The good news was that he'd almost certainly have time to talk to Caleb about what was happening in San Antonio on the long walk out to the campsite. The bad news was that, when they got there, Caleb would likely disappear into the woods with the girl Lukas dreamt about most nights.

"You know what that means," he said to Javi, voicing aloud what he was dreading.

"It means you're going to have to keep very busy tonight playing campfire games so as not to fly into an unjustified jealous rage?"

"I was just going to say we'd be raiding their overnight," Lukas lied. "But thanks for painting the evening in the least flattering light."

"What are friends for?" Javi asked, smiling wide as he shoved another piece of hot dog into his face.

They were finishing up, waiting patiently for the watermelon line to die down (each slice was cut individually on camper demand), when a heavyset kid named Sal from the second-oldest boys' bunk, the Desperados, cut in front of Nate, the young camper from the radio shack, knocking him to the ground with a rough shove.

"Back of the line, small fry," Sal jeered at the smaller boy as he snagged a slice of watermelon from the plate of a little girl walking by. His prominent front teeth and small beady eyes gave him a rat-faced look that Lukas thought fit just right.

Nate popped back up immediately. "You took my spot," he protested, trying to wriggle back into his original position.

Sal shoved him hard in the chest with an open palm, sending Nate to the ground a second time. "Stay down, loser," Sal ordered, "or next time I won't be so gentle."

It took only seconds for Lukas to close the distance from his picnic table to Sal.

"Go for it, Sal," he said, placing his body in front of Nate. The smaller boy was being helped to his feet by Javi who had arrived a half second later.

Sal looked briefly surprised by the turn of events. But it didn't take long for his expression to change into a nasty sneer.

"You must be sad," he said to Lukas out of the blue, his words hard to understand because his mouth was stuffed with watermelon.

"What are you talking about?" Lukas asked, annoyed.

"Because your dream girl isn't here tonight," he said in a tauntingly singsong tone. "Her bunk is on an overnight so you're all alone."

Lukas took a step closer. He could smell Sal's rancid breath. The younger Desperado had about thirty pounds on Lukas but was easily four inches shorter than him. Lukas looked down at the kid who was chomping his fruit like it was a cud.

"It's one thing to say that stuff behind my back, Sal," he said, moving closer again so that their noses were only inches apart. "But saying it to my face is something else. Maybe you forgot that I'm not a little Billy Goat you can knock to the ground. I'm not going to take crap from some punk with breath like a dumpster and watermelon between his teeth."

"What are you gonna do?" Sal asked, puffing out his chest, despite the quaver in his voice and his anxiously darting eyes. "Call in your big brother?"

"No. I'm going to gather some of my friends, sneak into your bunk tonight, hold you down, and smear horse crap all over you and everything you own. You won't know when I'm coming, so I wouldn't fall asleep if I was you."

He stared at Sal with a half smile. The other kid clearly didn't know how seriously to take him.

"Anything else you want to say?" Lukas added, deciding to take an extra little dig. "Or do you want to turn around now and go back to the kids' table?"

Sal looked torn between aching to spit out a comeback and not wanting to antagonize a guy he feared might really follow through on his threat. He settled for a dismissive grunt and turned away, skulking back to his table.

"One more thing," Lukas called out. "Apologize to Nate."

Sal looked like he was about to protest but managed to stop himself when he saw Lukas's jaw clench.

"Sorry," he muttered unconvincingly before spinning on his heel and trudging off.

"You okay?" Lukas asked, turning his attention to Nate.

"Yeah, thanks."

"Why don't you hop back in line? Watermelon always tastes best after a victory," Lukas said, smiling as he ruffled Nate's already messy hair. It was becoming a habit.

Nate gave him a huge smile. After they all got their watermelon, he returned to his table and Lukas and Javi went back to theirs.

"I liked your nighttime manure idea," Javi said when Sal was out of earshot. "If we can find some plastic gloves, I'm in."

"I would be, too," Lukas said, staring Sal down as he returned to his picnic bench. "But I think we have other plans tonight."

CHAPTER 6

They didn't leave their bunk until well after lights out. When Caleb had originally broached the idea of a raid on the Lumen camp a few hours earlier, there had been near unanimous approval. Only Kellen actively opposed the proposal, but then again, he opposed everything.

Perpetually sullen and resentful at being shipped off by his parents to a ranch camp for three weeks in the summer, Kellen Washburn made an art out of being nonparticipatory. His long black hair dyed with streaks of red usually hung over his skeptical eyes. His perpetually wrinkled brow and downturned nose served as his permanent mask when interacting with the rest of the world.

Todd clearly didn't want to go either, but he kept quiet about it. He apparently didn't want to be viewed with as much disdain as Kellen. Besides, even though he was the senior counselor, he probably suspected he would be overruled.

All the guys moved silently as they passed along the dirt road that ran through the main camp. They each knew that voices echoed on the main flat and could easily be heard by a restless camper in a younger kids' bunk. The thick warm night air had them all sweating even at their deliberate pace.

If they were caught by the wrong senior staffer, they might be sent back. What they were doing was technically against the rules, and while enforcement was generally lax for overnight raids, some higher-ups were sticklers.

As a result, all eight Toros and their two counselors were cautious as they walked through camp, their shadows slightly illuminated by the full moon. It wasn't until they were well past the bunks and on the trail to Sasquatch Toe that they began to whisper and turn on their flashlights. Lukas hurried to catch up to his brother so they could talk privately. Neither of them liked to have sibling-centric encounters with others around.

Caleb especially seemed to make a concerted effort not to treat his little brother any differently than the other Toros, calling him out occasionally but never personally. In fact, he had a pretty laissez-faire approach to camp counseling in general. Unless the guys in the bunk started fighting or picking on the little kids, he pretty much always let them do their thing.

Lukas suspected his brother's relaxed, borderline indifferent attitude had a lot to do with his ever-present awareness that, in just over a month, he'd be living in a dorm in Providence. It might also have had something to do with the fact that most of his non-counselor time was consumed by his girlfriend.

After a few seconds of jogging, Lukas sidled up next to Caleb who was leading the group and, as casually as possible, initiated the conversation he'd been meaning to have.

"How's it going?" he asked.

"Okay," Caleb replied, not breaking stride. "What's wrong?"

"Nothing's wrong," Lukas said defensively. "Why does something have to be wrong?"

"You almost never start a conversation with me at camp unless you want something or there's a problem."

"That's not true," Lukas insisted.

"Okay, my bad," Caleb said, short-circuiting the conflict. "Did you just want to chat, then?"

Lukas was quiet for a second. He thought he sensed a hint of hostility in his brother's voice but not enough to be certain. He wondered if he was just being hypersensitive about the whole Jules thing.

Caleb glanced over at him and raised his eyebrows in bemusement.

Unable to think of a good way to start, Lukas just dived in. "Actually, now that you mention it, I think there is something wrong."

"What is it?" Caleb asked, thankfully not rubbing it in, though he did seem to quicken his pace. Lukas tried to keep up with his brother whose long legs and obvious desire to get to his girlfriend had him moving at a near-panting pace.

"I overheard Steve Sailor talking to a sheriff's deputy at lunch, and it sounds like things are way worse than just Rowdy Randy being missing. Have you heard about any of that?"

Caleb didn't seem especially troubled by the question as he sidestepped a fallen branch.

"I heard there was some rioting in San Antonio, and they were putting sections of the city under martial law. Is that what you mean?"

"Partly," Lukas said, trying to keep his voice down so the others wouldn't hear. "But the deputy also said they were worried about some kind of virus outbreak. He didn't know specifics, but he mentioned that it had happened in other places too, like Atlanta and Colorado. And every radio station I checked today is just playing the same prerecorded emergency message telling people to stay in their homes. It sounds like more than just riots to me."

Caleb looked over at him, his brow now furrowed and his brown eyes wide. It was clear that he hadn't known much of this until right now. "Have you mentioned this to anyone?" he asked.

"No. I was worried it would get out, and I didn't want to cause a panic. But Steve sounded concerned. He wasn't sure if he was going to be able to send the kids home on Tuesday, and the deputy didn't have much in the way of suggestions. Are you saying the staff hasn't been given any kind of update?"

Caleb sighed, fidgeting with his fingers in a way that typically indicated he didn't love what he was about to say. Lukas knew he was debating whether or not to take him into his confidence and tried not to be offended that it was apparently a tough call. Caleb finally decided to open up.

"We had a staff meeting this afternoon. Steve and Aunt Winnie said there was some unrest in town, and it was possible that some parents might want to pick up their kids early. They warned us that, if that happened, the other campers might have questions and that we should try to reassure them. If they were still upset, we should send them to Aunt Winnie for a heart-to-heart. There was no mention of a virus, which doesn't surprise me. You know how that would go over. They're not going there unless they know something for sure."

They continued on silently for a few seconds. Lukas got the sense that, at least for the time being, this conversation was finished.

When they reached the makeshift rock bridge that stretched across the section of the creek separating them from Sasquatch Toe, they crossed over. Caleb went first, then Lukas, both trying to keep their sneakers as dry as possible. They waited for the others, both of them shining their flashlights on the rocks to give everyone a view of where they were stepping. Lonnie Milliner looked a little hesitant as he crossed, and Javi offered his arm for support.

Lonnie had cerebral palsy and walked in a slightly stiff, her-ky-jerky fashion. His left leg often dragged behind his right. Sometimes basic tasks like buttoning a shirt took him extra time.

He said that he had it easy compared to some kids he knew. Many others his age had difficulty walking, talking, even swallowing. He didn't have any of those issues yet. Still, simple tasks like getting dressed in the morning were slow, deliberative processes.

But no one felt that sorry for him. That was partly because he never seemed to feel sorry for himself. It was also because Lonnie had compensated for his limitations through constant physical therapy and relentless working out. As a result, he was actually freakishly strong and had developed serious endurance.

But he knew his limitations—balance among them—and graciously took Javi's arm as he navigated the slippery rocks. Once they all made it safely across the stream, they formed a tight huddle.

"We're getting closer, less than five minutes away," Caleb whispered to the group. "In a minute or two we should all stop talking. Voices carry out here, and we don't want to tip them off."

"They've got to know we're coming, right?" Trevor piped up, pushing the blond hair out of his eyes.

Lukas knew what the guy was thinking. Trevor Bertrand didn't want to piss the girls off. Other than his breezy good looks, much of Trevor's popularity around camp stemmed from winning people over, not alienating them. Agitating the entire oldest girls' bunk clearly wasn't something that enthused him.

"They'd have to be idiots if they didn't," Kellen hissed.

"That's not the point," Caleb said, pretending to ignore Kellen's tone, though Lukas could tell he was annoyed. "Even if they suspect we're coming, they don't know when. They can't stay on guard all night. At some point, they'll relax. And that's when we'll get them."

"This is so lame," Kellen muttered.

"You're lame, Kellen," Lonnie retorted, his normally enthusiastic voice filled with irritation. "And that's coming from someone who is actually, literally physically lame. Quit whining. Pretty soon you'll be back home in your McMansion with your butler and your five iPads. Until then, can you stop ruining it for the rest of us?"

"Enough," Todd injected, "or we can turn around right now. Is that what you want?"

Though that would have likely made Todd happy, he didn't say so. Everyone shook their heads, and Caleb continued.

"Jump out on my signal. Now remember—after we attack, give them a moment to regroup and catch their breaths before joining them. Some of them might really be freaked out. Got it?"

They all nodded. Caleb led the way again, and Lukas fell into step beside him, hoping to finish their conversation from before. He had yet to bring up the issue that had been eating at him.

"I'm worried about Grams and Gramps," Lukas said, voicing the concern that had been needling at the back of his head all afternoon. "I could see them going to get groceries, being totally oblivious, and getting caught up in all this."

He pictured his grandfather, Robert Lincoln, who was once a formidable trial lawyer. But the thought of him now, almost eighty and with slowed reflexes, trying to navigate through a chaotic grocery store parking lot full of people hoarding supplies, was not reassuring.

He imagined his grandmother, Betsy Lincoln, formerly a high school principal used to herding thousands of kids a day. But she was seventy-five years old herself, still fiery but white haired and fragile. He could easily visualize her desperately pointing out people and vehicles that Gramps should avoid hitting.

"They're old, Lukas, not clueless. They watch the news. They know what's going on in the world. Remember, they were extremely

cautious during the pandemic. I'm sure they wouldn't do anything risky."

"But what if there is no news?" Lukas countered. "If all the TV
stations are down, they might go out just to find out what's happening. Who even knows if the internet is working? We certainly don't
have a clue up here."

Caleb thought quietly for a moment as they continued to walk.
Lukas knew he was remembering the last time they'd both been
helpless to do anything for someone they both cared about. Finally,
his brother looked back over at him.

For a fraction of a second, Lukas thought Caleb might actually
bring up the tragedy that had haunted both of them since they were
little, that had made one of them hyper-protective and the other borderline reckless.

His mind flashed back briefly to the car, to the raised voices,
to the sudden sharp movement as a flash of light blinded his view,
to the deafening screech of tires merging with the sound of mangled
metal. But he was wrong. The moment passed. And when Caleb did
speak, it wasn't about that.

"Listen; calm down," he said. "First thing tomorrow morning,
I'll talk to Aunt Winnie and check on all that. She's got a desktop in
the lodge, and she'll let me check my phone if I ask. We'll get to the
bottom of this. Cool?"

"I guess," Lukas said reluctantly.

With that subject apparently closed, he briefly considered
addressing the Jules issue. But then he saw Broken Tree, which, as
the name suggested, was basically a huge fallen log in the middle of
the trail. He decided to hold off. They were too close to the Lumens'
campsite now to have any real discussion. And this didn't seem like
the ideal time to broach the topic anyway.

Almost immediately after stepping over Broken Tree, the sound of music became faintly audible in the distance. Caleb faced everyone, held his index finger to his lips, then led them down the trail another fifty paces where the light from the campfire became visible.

The sound of female voices was now clear, though words were hard to make out. Caleb motioned for everyone to form a semicircle around the camp, then held up two fingers to indicate they would jump out at the conclusion of the song after this one.

Everyone scurried off to their self-appointed spot. Lukas held back and waited for Lonnie who would likely need a bit of extra assistance. Together, they moved off the trail and into the thick brush that dominated the landscape from their current spot all the way to the campsite. A new song started playing.

Lukas still couldn't hear what the girls were saying, but he could see them now. They were all in a circle around the fire, some sitting, some lying on their sleeping bags. Whatever they were discussing had everyone's attention as the whole group seemed engaged.

The song, some dreamy techno-noir thing, started to fade out, and Lukas looked over at Lonnie who nodded back. Both of them tensed up, knowing the moment was close. The song got fainter, and Lukas was pretty sure it had ended. But he didn't want to jump the gun, so he waited for Caleb to take the initiative, as he so often did.

It wasn't long. A second later, he heard the loud, familiar shout of his brother. At that point, he jumped out, yelling at the top of his lungs, already mostly drowned out by the sound of half-shocked screams.

CHAPTER 7

There was only one injury. Stephen Mills had stepped in a small hole and turned his ankle. While the other guys were bouncing around, with faux menace, enjoying the happy squeals of the Lumens, Lukas saw him roll over and clutch his foot.

Other than that, the raid was a smashing success. It was pretty obvious the girls had been expecting them. But as Caleb had suspected, they had no idea when. They seemed to have been genuinely startled.

Lukas noticed some of the girls pulling on sweatshirts despite the warm air and the fire. Emily Satterfield, the blonde, golden-skinned bitingly sharp-tongued girl who had paid Aubrey to dance with him, and her best friend Fiona Wiley, a quiet petite brunette in full makeup, were hurriedly checking their faces in their compact mirrors.

They apparently wanted to look good for their boyfriends Mark and Mike Moore, respectively, who were politely avoiding joining them until they knew the girls were ready. Mark, who never seemed troubled by much of anything, appeared happy to watch the water gurgle along the creek until asked over. But Mike, his older (by three minutes) but smaller and more restless brother, kept glancing their way, waiting for the all clear. When Emily finally nodded their assent, he tapped his oblivious sibling and reminded him that there were two girls waiting to cuddle by the fire with them.

Jamie Winters, who was almost six feet tall and an all-district volleyball player as a freshman last season, seemed unaware of everything around her. With her shortish light-brown hair in a ponytail, she rolled over on top of her sleeping bag, and Lukas was stunned to realize that she was actually asleep.

Sarah Kree and Elena Gutierrez, permanently joined at the hip, were already pulling marshmallows out of a grocery bag and passing them around to everyone. The other girls—Gina, Courtney, and Jen—stayed near the fire, whispering among themselves. Aubrey, who didn't strike Lukas as the whispering type, sat off to the side, quietly watching everything unfold.

Lukas walked over to Stephen, who was still holding his ankle, and kneeled down beside him.

"Turned it?" he asked sympathetically.

"Uh-huh," Stephen more like grunted than said.

"Let me get Martie," Lukas said. "I know she's dealt with this stuff before."

He walked over and got Martie's attention, carefully avoiding eye contact with Jules who was sitting beside her. In addition to being the senior Lumen counselor and Aunt Winnie's daughter, Marta "Martie" Korngold, was the infirmary backup when the nurse was off. She got the gig primarily because of her medical training during her time in the Peace Corps.

She got up and headed over to Stephen. Lukas watched, marveling at how she was able to remain perspiration free while wearing jeans and a long-sleeved shirt. That was on top of her long, curly brown hair, which cascaded wildly down her back. In her mid-twenties, Martie often seemed like she might have been born in the wrong era. Her vibe was more 1960s Woodstock than twenty-first century.

"I'm not sure I should help you," she said when she knelt down beside Stephen.

"Why not?" he asked through gritted teeth.

She pointed at his black t-shirt, which had a picture of politically incorrect 1980s stand-up comedian Andrew Dice Clay on it and the words "Dice Man" in big white letters. "Not a fan," she said drily. "Maybe you deserve to suffer a bit."

Despite being in obvious pain, Stephen forced his grimace into a smile. "You know you love the Dice Man, Martie," he managed to mutter. "You just don't want everyone else to know."

Small in size but not in voice, with blonde, almost white, hair, and a smattering of freckles across his cheeks, Stephen considered himself the bunk's resident comedian despite the fact that no one else thought he was very funny. His favorite hobby was to recite old stand-up routines from actual 1980s comedians like Eddie Murphy and his hero "The Dice Man."

He'd already been called to Aunt Winnie's lodge twice for repeating material that was, in addition to not being especially funny, both misogynistic and homophobic. He'd been warned that another lodge visit would get him sent home early, even if camp was almost over.

Despite her disparaging comment, Martie consented to treat Stephen. She had him move his foot this way and that for a moment before quickly determining that it was only a mild sprain. She wrapped him up in an elastic bandage and declared him fit to return to camp, whenever that happened.

With that resolved, everybody settled in comfortably beside the fire, sharing long tree twigs for roasting marshmallows as they discussed the imminent end of camp. They watched as the fire crackled near them, sending embers up into the air briefly before they disappeared. The scent of burning cedar enveloped them all in its warm embrace. No one mentioned riots or viruses. Everyone seemed untroubled by whatever was going on beyond Hollow Valley.

Lukas finished warming his marshmallow and sat down at the foot of an unoccupied sleeping bag to enjoy it. Seemingly out of nowhere, Juliana Goldenson plopped down beside him.

"How's it going?" she asked nonchalantly.

"Okay," he answered, feeling his cheeks get suddenly warm and not as a result of the fire.

"That was nice of you to help Stephen out," she noted, glancing in the direction of his bunkmate who was milking all the sympathy he could out of his injury.

"Thanks," Lukas said quietly, looking over at her briefly so as not to make the situation even more awkward.

In just that fraction of a second, he took in the ponytail holding her raven-colored hair, the ruddy cheeks that suggested she'd only just recently wiped the makeup from her face, and the slight hint of mint on her clearly recently brushed teeth. He quickly returned his gaze to the fire. It crackled loudly, shooting several small sparks skyward like miniature fireworks.

In that moment, Lukas knew this was it—his last real chance to make any kind of connection with Jules before camp ended. The dance had been an epic fail. If he didn't try now, he doubted he'd ever get another chance.

CHAPTER 8

He gulped hard.

A trickle of cold sweat rolled down the small of his back, and despite the heat of the campfire, he shivered slightly. He felt his throat start to clench up. He desperately tried to remind himself that this didn't need to be a moment of crisis.

After all, it wasn't like he thought he could steal Jules away from his brother. That wasn't even really his goal. Caleb and Juliana had been together for two years now, though they weren't a traditional couple. The Lincoln brothers lived in Southern California, and Jules was from Houston. And Lukas knew that both of them had a few school boyfriends and girlfriends while they were officially together.

But somehow they didn't let that get in the way. Caleb had even gone to visit Jules for a few days over winter break. Lukas didn't dare ask about it but he suspected they had some kind of plan for how to make it work once Caleb left for college.

Of course, Lukas had a plan of his own.

It was unrealistic and borderline disloyal, but he was going for it anyway. He hoped to establish some kind of online connection with Jules so that, once they went back to school, they could stay in touch.

He knew that she'd probably agree to it, mostly just to be polite to Caleb's little brother. But he suspected that deep down, Jules might also be worried that, once Caleb went off to college, he'd lose interest in a girl who still had a year of high school left. Maybe she'd consider getting tight with Lukas as a way to maintain a connection with the Lincoln family and as an excuse to reach out to Caleb without seeming desperate.

With that foundation laid, once Caleb was at Brown and maybe really *did* start to lose interest, Lukas would make sure to be there for Jules as a sounding board, a long-distance shoulder to cry on, and a potential way back into Caleb's heart.

By next summer, if all went well, Caleb would have moved on. Jules would have come to terms with it just as she was returning to Hollow Valley, somehow drawn to the Lincoln brother who reminded her of her old boyfriend but offered a different, perhaps deeper, connection.

Lukas had thought it out thoroughly, considering all the angles, just as he did with everything else in his life. He knew it was a long shot, but it was better than just coming out and saying, "I know you're dating my big brother, but I'm into you. Like me instead please."

Of course, for any of that to happen, he had to talk to her for longer than thirty seconds without other people around. And the perfect opportunity had just presented itself without him even trying.

"You enjoy camp this year?" she asked.

He looked back at her. Her green eyes glinted in the firelight, and her mouth was upturned into a slight smile.

And then, without any reason other than he wished it to, the anxiety stopped. It was as if his mind had ordered his body to simply stop all the ridiculousness and his body, out of sheer embarrassment, had listened.

"I did," he said, impressed at how normal he sounded. "But I think I'm a little burned out on the camper side of things. Even with

Wilderness Week, you can only go to so many activities before it all starts to blend together, you know?"

"Absolutely," she agreed, nodding vigorously. "I was just reaching that point too around your age. Then I became a CIT. Having responsibility changes how you look at things. It gave me a fresh perspective on everything. All of a sudden, I was more focused on keeping everyone safe, trying to prevent arguments, checking that no one felt left out. It added a whole new element. Are you going to be a CIT next year?"

"I was planning on it," Lukas said. "I'm also hoping that, if I make varsity basketball, I'll be able to go to a summer camp for that. I think I can make my schedule work to fit both in. But that's jumping the gun."

"What do you mean?" she asked, leaning in a little closer in case whatever he said was sensitive.

He felt his stomach do a little flutter at her unexpected proximity. "It's just that there's no guarantee that I'll make the team."

"I've seen you play," Jules said. "You're good."

"Thanks. I guess I can hold my own against the Hollow Valley crowd. But I'm not sure that's a good test of how I'll do back home. The coaches might have unreasonable expectations, based on other folks in my family."

Jules smiled sympathetically, clearly getting the reference. "I don't think they expect you to be your brother, Lukas," she said reassuringly. "Just give it all you can, and whatever happens, happens."

He gave her a bit of side-eye despite his best effort not to. "Good advice from the Texas state cross-country champion," he said in what he hoped was only a mildly sarcastic tone. "Is that what you did, just gave it all you had and let whatever happened happen?"

"No," she said, leaning in conspiratorially and whispering in his ear. "I poisoned the competition—it works every time."

Lukas laughed, even as he felt the hair on the back of his neck stand up in reaction to her hot breath on his ear. "I may have to consider that tactic," he said.

"Can I tell you a secret?" she asked quietly.

He nodded without speaking, not sure he'd even be able to answer her as the slight scent of lavender radiated off her skin.

"Obviously the poisoning thing is a tad much," she assured him. "But I am a competitor, just like I know you are, Lukas. I find that folks forget that about people like us. All they notice is a pretty face or a kind spirit. They don't see the steel underneath, so they underestimate us. But we both know that looking hard and being hard isn't the same thing. Am I right?"

"Yeah," Lukas managed to say, surprised at this sudden turn in conversation. "I just didn't realize your worldview was so dark."

"I'm not all sweetness and light. We each face darkness from time to time."

"What darkness have you faced?" he asked playfully.

When Jules turned to face him directly, he saw that she wasn't smiling.

"When sorrows come, they come not single spies, but in battalions."

Though he got the reference, Lukas had no idea how to respond to it. "Good to know," he finally said before pivoting awkwardly. "How has camp been for you?"

She looked at him closely, as if deciding whether to let him off the hook for now. After a moment she made her decision, and the intensity left her eyes, replaced by the familiar warmth he was used to. "Good," she said, her smile fading slightly. "Bittersweet."

He nodded. She didn't have to explain why. And he didn't really want her to. He recognized there was no way he was going to be able make an impression on her in her current state. And somehow even trying felt wrong.

Very soon, she'd be starting her senior year of high school and Caleb would be going off to college thousands of miles away. The idea that Lukas could distract her from that reality, and whatever other realities she was privately confronting, seemed almost ludicrous as he sat next to her now. Suddenly feeling profoundly inadequate, he stood up, anxious to extricate himself from the situation.

"You want another marshmallow?" he asked.

"No, I'm good," she said, her thoughts clearly elsewhere.

He nodded and wandered over to the other side of the fire without another word, noticing Caleb move in the other direction to take his recently vacated spot.

"How did that go?" a voice asked from near his left leg. He jumped slightly, startled.

It was Aubrey who was sitting cross-legged on the dirt, a dark blanket draping her shoulders, camouflaging her. She looked up at him with a mix of amusement and curiosity.

"How did what go?" he replied, pretending not to get it.

"Your big chat with your dream girl, the conversation you've been itching for all session? Was it everything you hoped it would be?"

Lukas opened his mouth, about to offer a snarky reply. But none came to mind, and he wasn't really in the mood anyway. Instead, he sat down beside her and glanced at her empty hands.

"Not in a marshmallow mood?" he asked, ignoring her question.

"Gelatin and sugar? I'll pass," she said dismissively.

"I thought there were egg whites in there, too. Those are healthy, right?"

Aubrey turned to him, ready to offer a withering comeback, when she saw him smiling and realized that he was messing around.

"Touché," she said. "Anyway, we don't have any graham crackers or chocolate for s'mores, so I figure every marshmallow is precious."

Lukas could guess why they were short on s'mores fixings but decided not to comment on it.

"Hey," he said, trying to change the subject, "what were you guys talking about before we jumped out to scare you? It seemed pretty intense."

"You didn't scare me," Aubrey said defensively.

Lukas didn't feel like arguing, so he tried again. "Hey, what were you guys talking about before we jumped out and *didn't* scare you? It seemed pretty intense."

Aubrey was quiet for a second before finally replying. "We were talking about Rowdy Randy. You know, no one's heard from him in over twenty-four hours. People are really starting to worry about him."

"Yeah, I know," Lukas said, still keeping what he knew to himself. Aubrey didn't strike him as the type to panic at bad news, but it seemed unwise to mention martial law or virus breakouts with so many ears around.

"It feels like they should be doing more," Aubrey said, sounding frustrated.

"I know Steve reached out to law enforcement. I think they're doing everything they can. They just don't want to worry people, so they're keeping tight-lipped about it."

"Well, all the secrecy is making it worse, if you ask me," she said. She looked like she was about to say something else but stopped suddenly and glanced in the direction of the trail. "Do you hear that?"

"What?" Lukas asked. He couldn't hear anything above the talking, music, and the crackling fire.

"It sounds like footsteps," she said hesitantly, "lots of them. Like a herd of something."

And then Lukas heard it too.

CHAPTER 9

He saw it moments after he first heard it. But it took Lukas a few seconds to process what he was seeing. Coming at them from the same direction they'd taken to the girls' campsite were hundreds of what looked to be mice and rats.

Before he could say anything, the creatures were on them or, more accurately, through them.

The animals didn't seem interested in attacking anyone. They barreled past the crowd of people, almost oblivious to them as they dashed through the campsite, climbing over and around anything in their way. Some even darted through the fire itself. The screams of Lumens and Toros didn't faze them as they stormed by, seemingly desperate to get away from some unseen threat.

And then, less than ten seconds later, they were gone. They'd disappeared as quickly as they'd come, with the pattering of thousands of feet fading quickly into the distance.

"What the . . ." Javi asked the stunned assemblage before stopping, unsure how to finish the question.

"Turn off the music," Martie ordered.

Aubrey jumped up and hit the Off button on the portable speaker. Everyone was silent. The only sounds were the fire crackling near them and the gurgling stream in the background.

"Usually," Martie said slowly, "a bunch of rodents running in one direction means they're being chased by something. Does anyone see anything out there?"

Everyone peered into the darkness, holding their collective breaths. But it was pointless. It was impossible to see anything other than shadows beyond fifty feet, even with the full moon.

Lukas turned on his flashlight and pointed it back toward Broken Tree. Within seconds, a half dozen other flashlights did the same. But it didn't help. If there was something out there, it wasn't making itself visible.

"I don't know if it was a coyote or snakes or what," Caleb said. "But I'm going to suggest the Toros remain here for a while longer, if that's okay with you, Martie. I'm not excited to head back that way and run into whatever spooked them."

"That's fine," Martie said, sounding more composed than Lukas thought possible under the circumstances. "Stay all night if you like. Just make sure everyone behaves appropriately. And let's not mention it to my mother."

Lukas was surprised at her willingness to let a bunch of teenage boys spend the night with her teenage girls. Despite her causal demeanor, Martie must have been really concerned.

This was a woman who had worked for the Peace Corps in Africa during Ebola outbreaks, who had navigated tribal fighting and survived drought-induced famines. The fact that she was this unsettled by a collection of galloping rodents was not reassuring. He looked over at Aubrey and something in her expression told him she was thinking the same thing.

As everyone settled back down, Lukas saw Martie gather Caleb, Todd, and Juliana in a small group and talk to them quietly for a few moments. When the meeting broke up, each counselor ambled away in a suspiciously casual style and took a position around the camp-site in a formation like the points of a diamond.

"That can't be good." Aubrey muttered under her breath.

Lukas agreed but said nothing.

*

Lukas didn't remember falling asleep. But when he woke up the next morning, the sun was just coming up and there was a slight chill in the air, which he knew wouldn't last for long.

He was lying on his back and propped himself up on his elbows to assess the situation. The fire was almost out. Though the smoky scent lingered, just a few sad flames hung on, clinging to a couple of smoldering black and gray logs. The morning was foggy, and he couldn't see more than thirty or forty feet in any direction.

Glancing around the campsite, he noticed that most people were still asleep, including "guards," Juliana and Todd. Stephen was up, rewrapping his ankle, and Aubrey was sitting cross-legged, read-ing a book. Caleb and Martie were in the same spots as last night, though both were now sitting down and looked pretty worn out.

Lukas got up as quietly as he could and walked over to his brother, trying to avoid stepping on anyone. It was difficult as he was in the middle of the tightly packed group. He counted the total num-ber in their group as he navigated his way among torsos and splayed-out arms and legs: eight Toros, nine Lumens, and four counselors.

It was a lot of people, and he wondered if there would be enough food for all of them. He doubted it and suspected that he and the rest of the guys would have to go back to the dining hall for breakfast, though he was reluctant to go anywhere when it was so hard to see what was out there.

"Have you been up all night?" he whispered to Caleb when he finally extricated himself from the mass of body parts.

Caleb nodded but said nothing.

"See anything?" Lukas pressed.

"Nothing. I thought it would get better when the sun came up, but then this fog rolled in just before sunrise."

Lukas peered into the mist, hoping he might see something his brother hadn't. But it was all one big impenetrable white wall.

"I guess it will burn off eventually," he said.

"Yeah," Caleb agreed. "But the question is when. It could take hours. And I don't want us walking back in that stuff not knowing what caused that rat stampede."

"Should we just eat here and wait it out?"

"We may have to. I never thought I'd say this phrase, but we might have to ration the girls' Cheerios."

Lukas chuckled and Caleb smiled slightly.

"Can I ask you something?" Lukas said.

Caleb gave him a look that suggested he wasn't entirely sure that was a great idea, but Lukas proceeded anyway.

"What did Martie tell you in that little counselors-only meeting you had last night?"

Caleb seemed relieved by the question. "She said the only time she'd ever seen anything like that thing with the rats was in Africa when she was up on a hill looking down at a river. A group of crocodiles leapt out of the water and chased after some gazelles that had been grazing nearby. It freaked her out because they seemed to be operating as a unit. There were four of them, and they all teamed up to corner one gazelle and take it down. But before that, when they were in chase mode, she said it sounded like a herd of buffalo, what with the crocs and the gazelles all moving at once. She said that, as it happened, every rodent in the area scurried away, all in the same direction and all at once. She said it looked like a rolling gray and brown wave. So she figured that whatever made the rodents here run like that had to be crocodile-level scary. She told us to take up spots at equal distances around you guys and keep watch just in case."

"But nothing showed up," Lukas said.

"Not yet," Caleb agreed.

"You don't think whatever it was would have come right away?"

"I don't know," Caleb admitted. "There's no telling where they started running from. They could have been moving for a while."

"But they came from the direction of camp," Lukas said.

"I know."

Before either of them could say anything else, someone in the crowd of bodies and sleeping bags began to cough loudly. Both brothers turned around to find multiple people stirring. Several of them began to talk before Martie walked over and shushed them. She looked over at the Lincolns and waved for them to join the group.

"Can I get everyone's attention?" she said quietly as heads popped up from under sleeping bags and sleepy eyes tried to focus on her.

"What's going on?" Kellen muttered irritably.

"Probably nothing," Martie said. "But we're going to take pre-cautions anyway. Those rodents running through camp last night were very unusual. It could mean they were trying to escape a pred-ator. We have a few of those here in the Texas Hill Country: bobcats, coyotes, that sort of thing. But they usually avoid populated areas, and they certainly don't strike fear in massive numbers of rats."

"So what is it then?" asked Jamie Winters, speaking for the first time since the Toros had arrived last night. Lukas was pretty sure she'd slept through the rodent stampede.

"I don't know," Martie admitted. "But I don't want to run into anything unexpected in this fog. So we're going to make the safe choice and hang out here until it burns off. Only then will we return to the main camp. And while I know this doesn't excite you, we're going to stay extremely quiet. If there is a dangerous animal out there, we don't need to attract any extra attention to ourselves. Does everyone understand?"

There were collective nods from the group.

Finally Javi asked the question that was on everyone's mind. "What about breakfast?"

"Always focused on the top priorities, huh, Mendez?" Caleb said, injecting a much-needed note of levity into the proceedings.

"You know you were thinking it too, man," Javi replied with a toothy grin.

"We've got mini boxes of cereal and a cooler with milk," Martie said. "Unfortunately, it was only intended for eleven people, so please be thoughtful as you divvy it up. We'll get more food for everyone once we get back to camp. But for now, this is all we have. Since the fog could burn off in the next hour or take all morning, we need to be responsible in how we handle our resources."

"In the meantime," Todd added, speaking for the first time that morning, "everybody should collect their stuff: sleeping bags, backpacks, etc. We want to be ready to roll as soon as the fog lifts. Let's get moving, everyone. And remember—do it quietly."

The process of eating and packing up took less than half an hour. An hour after that, around seven thirty, the haze started to break and visibility began to improve. Ten minutes later, it was as if there had never been anything but clear views the whole morning.

Martie threw her backpack over her shoulder and looked at the unimpressive collection of exhausted, surly campers.

"Remember—keep your voices down. Until we know what spooked those rats, we need to err on the side of caution. Let's go."

CHAPTER 10

Lukas and Javi lingered toward the back of the group, with only Caleb, who was supporting the limping Stephen, behind them. Lukas saw a solid-looking stick in the brush at the edge of the trail and gave it to Stephen who seemed to find it helpful.

Martie was up front, walking deliberately, her head constantly moving as she eyed the terrain in front of them. Behind her were Jules and most of the Lumens, followed by a small group of couples that included Emily and Mark Moore, and Fiona and Mike Moore. After that came the rest of the Toros, with Todd trailing them.

Lukas thought the entire valley seemed eerily quiet until he remembered that camp wake-up wasn't officially for another few minutes.

"How did your chat last night with Jules go?" Javi asked in a hushed voice as they reached Broken Tree and they were out of ear-shot of anyone else.

"With everything that's happened in the last twelve hours, *that's* what you want to talk about?"

"I'd rather talk about your romantic prospects than killer rat-scaring predators any day," Javi said definitively.

"Well, there's not much to talk about," Lukas said. "I will say that she's got an intense side I had no idea about. Beyond that, I realized about halfway through the conversation that I have pretty much no chance with her."

"Dude, don't be so hard on yourself. It's like a supermodel athlete was dropped into our little sleepaway camp. The fact that you had the guts to even think about making a move is pretty impressive."

"But she's my brother's girlfriend," Lukas reminded him.

"There *is* that," Javi admitted.

"I'm just going to leave it be for now. Who knows what will happen? Maybe they'll grow apart when he leaves for college. Maybe she'll see me differently next summer if I grow a few inches. Maybe I'll meet a *different* gorgeous cross-country state champion at school this year and Juliana Goldenson won't seem like all that. But for the rest of this session, I'm going to focus on not embarrassing myself and actually getting enough food to survive until we leave."

"I can't promise you'll have success with the first part," Javi said. "But I'm with you on the second."

They fell into a comfortable silence as they hiked the rest of the way back to camp. The lower flat cabins came into sight, along with the Lumen bunk. Gina, Courtney, and Jen were already headed in that direction.

Martie stopped everyone else in the middle of the flat and waved for them all to gather round. When they were all close enough that she could speak quietly, she reminded them.

"Let's be respectful of those who are still sleeping," she said. "We may have been up for a while but most campers haven't been. So keep your voices down until official wake-up. And let's not scare anyone with talk about the rat thing last night. I don't know what it was about, but we still have one more night of camp left and I don't need dozens of little kids who can't sleep tonight. Okay?"

Everyone nodded in understanding.

"All right," she continued. "As you can see, some of our fellow Lumens are returning to the bunk to wash up. I certainly understand that. But for those of you who still have the energy, Jules and I could use some help returning supplies to the dining hall. If you can leave your stuff here for now and put it up in the bunk later, you might be able to grab an early breakfast while we're there. Who's in?"

A few raised their hands, including Aubrey, Emily, Fiona, and Jamie.

"I'm starving," the latter said.

"You're always starving," Emily jeered. "That's what happens when you have the body of an Amazon woman."

"Thank you," Jamie said, pretending it was meant as a compliment. She was clearly long past being fazed by cracks about her size. Lukas wondered why Emily even bothered.

"Enough," Jules interrupted. "We appreciate the help. The rest of you can shower up and meet us after."

"Elena and I are just going to drop off our stuff in the bunk, wash up real quick, and catch up," Sarah said surprising no one with her declaration that they would be acting in tandem. "Will you save us something to eat? We're pretty hungry, too."

"Even after all those marshmallows you were scarfing last night?" Emily accused, apparently unable to stop herself from sniping.

"Emily Satterfield," Martie growled, "one more unpleasant word out of you and you're on solo kitchen patrol duty for the final banquet. Got it?"

Emily nodded without replying, looking mildly chastened.

"We're all tired, guys," Todd said, adopting his best guidance counselor tone. "But let's try not to take it out on each other."

Martie looked at him with the same expression of disregard that Lukas often felt. "Right," she said noncommittally. "Let's get moving. And remember—voices down."

The girls who were going to the dining hall dropped their sleeping bags and backpacks where they stood and stretched their sore muscles. Then the entire Toros bunk and the more ambitious members of the Lumens resumed their trek, passing the main parking lot and trudging up the hill to the dining hall.

As they slogged up the steep dirt road, Lukas noticed a still-wet puddle pooling in the dusty earth about halfway up the path. It looked like someone had dropped a bucket of water in one random spot in the middle of the road. But it wasn't water. It was more rust colored. He was about to draw Javi's attention to it when his friend pointed over at the lodge.

"Is Aunt Winnie waving us over?" he asked curiously.

They all looked in the same direction, toward the one structure at camp that looked like it had taken more than a few weeks to build. The lodge, a combination of wooden logs and stone roofing, was where the important stuff happened. The private high-level staff meetings were held there. The safe with everyone's electronics was there. It was where all the weapons for riflery and archery were secured. Campers rarely got to go inside.

But just as Javi had said, the regal gray-haired sixty-something camp founder and matriarch, Winnie Korngold, was standing at the front door, waving at them to come over. Strangely though, in between each wave she would hold her index finger up to her lips to exaggeratedly indicate silence.

"What the . . ." Mark Moore started to ask.

"Be quiet, Mark," Martie ordered under her breath, an odd quaver in her voice. "Everyone do what she's saying. Go to the lodge as quickly and calmly as possible. But don't run and don't make any noise."

CHAPTER 11

Lukas stared at her. Martie was looking all around camp, her eyes darting back and forth with an intensity he'd never seen before. He followed the others toward the lodge, registering what Martie must have already noticed. Other than Aunt Winnie, there was nobody in sight.

On most mornings, even before the official camp wake-up, there were usually lots of people milling about: the kitchen staff, counselors prepping for the day, campers who were bored lying around in their bunks and just wanted to get up and about. But apart from Winnie, the Lumens, and the Toros, there wasn't a soul to be found.

Martie gave another instruction as they got close to the white wooden board fence that surrounded the lodge. "Don't open the gate," she said to Trevor who was at the front of the group. "It creaks. Crawl under the fence."

They all followed her instructions, even Stephen, who was struggling with his ankle. Lonnie, despite his cerebral palsy, navigated the fence smoothly. Lukas scrambled under it, ignoring the dewy grass stains on his shirt and shorts.

When they passed through the yard and got to the front door of the lodge, Aunt Winnie beckoned them inside. She was wearing khaki slacks, a denim shirt, and had on her standard straw hat.

Her bifocals, connected with a necklace chain, had slid down to the bridge of her nose. She looked hyperalert and extremely troubled.

Up close, Lukas noticed something he hadn't picked up on before. There was a shotgun propped by the screen door. Aunt Winnie grabbed it and hurried the last of them into the lodge.

Lukas moved to the interior of the living room to make room for the others. He'd only been in here occasionally. He was usually so nervous about why he'd been called here at all that he hadn't taken the time to note the surroundings.

But now, as he looked at the lodge walls, he saw that it was covered in photos of Aunt Winnie's life with Uncle Ron, the co-founder of Camp Hollow Valley and her husband of thirty years. He'd passed away four years ago from cancer, and Winnie had forged on ever since as best she could.

He studied one picture of the couple that looked to be from before their marriage. They were both in their twenties. Robust and skinny, they were barely recognizable as the people Lukas knew them as now. He was leaning in to get a better look when someone bumped into him, jostling him back into the present. The sheer number of people in the room now made it too crowded to see much of anything anyway. There were a total of seventeen of them.

Only when they were all inside and she'd locked the door did Aunt Winnie finally speak. "No one talk above a whisper," she ordered in a hushed voice. "Something terrible has happened." Her voice was hoarse and choked with emotion. For the first time, Lukas noticed that her eyes were red, as if she'd been crying.

"What is it, Mom?" Martie asked.

"I'm still not totally sure," she answered, sounding bewildered. "It started last night, around 11:00 p.m., a couple of hours after lights out. Two men in military fatigues came onto the property. They were down by the main parking area acting strangely. They were grunting and sort of twitching. I called the sheriff while Steve went down to meet them. Lloyd and Richard joined too, a little ways behind. And then . . ." She paused, as if uncertain whether she should continue. She looked like she was about to tell them she'd seen a ghost and knew no one would believe her.

"Then what?" Todd pressed, his voice edgy.

"I'm just going to show you the video footage. It cuts off at a certain point, but you'll understand better if you see it."

She turned on the television and inserted an old school video cassette in the VCR machine. Aunt Winnie was a little behind the times when it came to modern security. After a couple of seconds of static, a grainy black-and-white image came on the screen. It was of several campers walking down the hill by the dining hall that Lukas and the others had just come up.

"What's so weird about this?" Kellen asked derisively.

"Just wait. The system is motion activated," Aunt Winnie said patiently. "It runs while there's movement. After thirty seconds of inactivity, it resets to record again when there's fresh motion."

"What's the point of that?" Emily wanted to know. "So you can get portions of a robbery?"

"It's an old system," Aunt Winnie acknowledged.

Just then the image changed. The screen showed what Aunt Winnie had been describing: the strange twitchy military men coming up the hill and Steve approaching them as Richard and Lloyd followed a little behind him.

Suddenly one of the men jumped on top of Steve and pinned him down. Everyone in the lodge gasped at the sight. The man seemed to be sniffing Steve, almost breathing him in.

Steve struggled to get free, but the other man was stronger. At one point it looked like he was spitting in Steve's eyes. Then both men started attacking Steve, just ripping and tearing at him.

"What the . . ." Javi whispered before trailing off.

No one else said a word. Lukas suddenly realized what the pool of rust-colored liquid he'd seen on the dirt road earlier must have been.

Lloyd and Richard ran over and tried to pull the men off Steve, but then the men turned on them and began attacking them too. It was awful. They weren't just beating them. They were biting them, tearing the skin off them.

Fiona gasped. Kellen made a retching sound.

"Jeez," Lonnie muttered.

Aunt Winnie looked over at them with concern and paused the tape.

"What just happened?" Emily demanded, her panicky voice rising well above a whisper.

"Shh, "Aunt Winnie reminded her. "You have to keep your voice down."

"What the hell *was* that?" Javi whispered urgently, finding his voice again.

Lukas looked around at the others. Everyone else just stared at the static-filled screen in open-mouthed shock.

"I'm sorry to have shown you something so graphic," Aunt Winnie said, clearly grief-stricken. She sounded like she was struggling to maintain control. "But you all need to know exactly what's happening. I can't sugarcoat this."

No one spoke for several seconds.

"It's okay, Mom," Martie finally assured her. "Go on. What happened after that? Show us everything."

Aunt Winnie nodded, though she looked reluctant. Eventually, she seemed to make some kind of internal decision and pressed Play again. Steve, Lloyd, and Richard were all writhing on the ground.

She began to narrate the events on the screen. "There's no audio, but Steve and the guys were screaming in pain and then they weren't. I thought they were dead. I was on the phone, trying to reach the sheriff, but the line was busy. I grabbed my gun and was going to go out and confront the men. I looked out the window and saw . . ." Her voice trailed off, and she squeezed her eyes shut as if she couldn't bear the thought of what she'd seen.

"What?" Todd asked. But then his attention was captured by movement on the screen.

Steve got up. But somehow, he didn't look like himself. He had the same herky-jerky motion as the first two men. And then, moments later, Lloyd and Richard got up and started moving the same way.

"I almost went outside," Aunt Winnie said, her eyes now open again. "But something held me back."

"It sounds like you made the right choice, Aunt Winnie," Jules said reassuringly.

"No, I was cowardly, paralyzed by fear. And things only got worse from there."

"What do you mean, Mom?" Martie asked.

"Some other people heard the screams," she said.

She didn't need to explain beyond that. Other counselors were now visible on camera. They had clearly come to see what was going on. The two men attacked them. Then Steve, Lloyd, and Richard joined in. They were like animals, chasing down anyone they saw, bringing them to the ground and ripping and gnawing at them.

"I thought it couldn't get worse, but it did," Aunt Winnie said quietly.

"This seems . . . not possible," Trevor said, almost to himself.

She didn't respond, and no one else said anything. It was as if they believed not hearing the rest of it might stop it from being true. Some of them looked at each other like they thought Aunt Winnie might have lost it.

Eventually Caleb broke the silence. "What happened then?" he asked.

"You can't see it because we only have the one fixed camera. But I saw."

"What did you see?" Caleb pressed as gently as he could.

Aunt Winnie looked him directly in the eye and sighed deeply before responding. "They went after the children."

"The campers?" Javi asked, horrified.

"And the same thing happened to them," Aunt Winnie said, staring off into the distance at the memory. "The kids, no matter how small, lay on the ground for a minute or two, as if they were dead. Then they got up and started chasing down others too. At least most of them did."

"This is crazy," Todd said suddenly, almost angrily. "This is . . . Are you sure that you didn't misunderstand what you were seeing, Aunt Winnie?"

"What did you mean 'most of them'?" Aubrey asked her, as if Todd hadn't said anything at all.

"Some of the kids never got up," Aunt Winnie replied, choosing to focus on Aubrey's question. "I don't know if their injuries were so bad that they couldn't. It seemed like the attacks weren't always intended to kill. Sometimes they would only go for extremities, like they were trying to wound or maybe . . ." Again she trailed off.

"Or maybe what?" pressed Aubrey.

"Infect?" Aunt Winnie said, almost like she couldn't believe the words coming out of her own mouth.

"Are we really buying any of this?" Todd asked, his voice rising dangerously above a whisper. "I mean this sounds like a psychotic break or something. No offense, Aunt Winnie, but what you're describing is not actually possible."

Lukas saw both Martie and Aubrey stiffen. Each looked like they wanted to punch Todd. He stepped forward, ready to short-circuit any physical conflict. But neither made a move, so he turned to Aunt Winnie. Though he hated to push her when she was in such a troubled state, a question had popped into his head, one he couldn't help but ask.

"Aunt Winnie," he asked, "where is everyone? Where did they all go?"

Aunt Winnie fast-forwarded the video for what appeared to be several hours and then resumed playing. The first hints of morning light were visible. "The dining hall," she said, "just before dawn."

The fog that had made seeing so difficult down by Sasquatch Toe was rolling in on the main flat too. But amid the mist, the two men in military fatigues who had started it all were visible walking into the hall. Then everyone else followed. They all walked in, slowly, half limping, like their batteries had run out.

"They all congregated in the dining hall, like they were called there or something," Aunt Winnie said. "They've been there ever since."

Kellen walked over and peeked out. "We didn't hear anything coming from there when we were walking up," he said skeptically.

"They don't seem able to talk after they've been attacked and . . . changed," Aunt Winnie said. "They just sort of grunt. All those children, just grunting as they walked in—it's hardly real."

"It's okay, Mom," Martie said, trying to hug her.

"No, it's not," Aunt Winnie hissed, shaking her off. "I failed these kids. They were left in my care and I cowered in this house as they were being torn apart. I'm a disgrace."

"That's not true," Lonnie told her with firmness in his voice that surprised Lukas. "If you had gone out there, you'd be dead or worse right now. And you wouldn't have been able to warn us. So we'd be dead, too. We're alive right now because of you, Aunt Winnie."

No one spoke for several seconds after that, letting his words sink in. And in that silence, they heard something quite unexpected considering what Aunt Winnie had said. They heard voices.

CHAPTER 12

Kellen glanced through the window in the direction of the sound. Lukas saw his expression change from confusion to panic in a split second.

"It's Sarah and Elena," he said. "They're walking to the dining hall. They're talking."

The whole group scurried to the window and saw the two girls walking up the same dirt hill they'd been on only minutes earlier. They were immersed in conversation, speaking in voices that, under normal circumstances, would be considered respectfully quiet. But now, their words seemed to echo through the whole valley.

"We have to get them in here now," Aunt Winnie said. "If we can hear them, then *they* will be able to as well."

Jules was already opening the front door. Lukas saw her waving desperately in the direction of the girls, but they seemed oblivious.

"Maybe someone should whistle quietly," Fiona suggested meekly.

Everyone was now crowding around the front door.

"Anything Sarah and Elena can hear, those others will hear, too," Martie said. "I'm surprised they haven't come out already. I'm going to have to go get them."

Todd shook his head vigorously. "By the time you get to them," he said, apparently now willing to believe Aunt Winnie's claims, "they'll already be to the dining hall."

Lukas saw that he was right. Sarah and Elena were already at the same spot, near the puddle of blood, where Javi had noticed Aunt Winnie waving. They were less than fifty yards from the back door to the dining hall.

Lonnie, who had been in the crowd of people by the door, stepped forward next to Jules and looked up at the sky. Then he took a few steps farther out away from the lodge.

"What are you doing?" Emily hissed. "You think *you're* going to catch them in time?"

Lukas was appalled by her comment, but Lonnie seemed unperturbed. He held out his left arm and began moving it around, twisting it at odd angles. Lukas was confused at first, but then he saw a glint of sunlight bounce off the wristwatch in Lonnie's hand and realized what he was doing.

As the girls got closer to the dining hall, Lonnie continued to adjust his movements until he got what he wanted. The reflection of the sun off his watch managed to flash in Elena's sight line.

She brushed at her face as if pestered by a fly. But Lonnie kept moving the beam of light around, trying to hit her in the eye again. After a few more seconds of frustration, she stopped and looked for the source of the blinding ray.

Everyone at the lodge began doing what Aunt Winnie had done earlier—alternately waving for the girls to come over and making the "shush" signal with their fingers to their lips. Elena grabbed Sarah by the arm and pointed. Sarah saw them all and started to open her mouth to call out to them. Elena clamped her hand over her friend's lips and shook her head.

Then Lukas thought he heard a soft grunt. He wasn't sure whether it had come from Sarah or somewhere inside the dining hall. When both girls looked in that direction, he had his answer.

Sarah and Elena looked back at Lonnie who was desperately waving at them to come over. They glanced at each other briefly and then, in unison, began to walk toward the lodge.

Jules ran out to meet them. She got about twenty feet when she saw the same thing the rest of them did. The main dining hall door opened, making its familiar groaning sound as the rusted springs stretched. She froze and stared, as did the girls walking toward her.

A man stepped out of the door and onto the step below it. At least Lukas was fairly sure it was a man. He was dressed in military fatigues, which were dirty and ripped. His close-cropped black hair was matted with something that looked a lot like dried blood.

He was well built, probably six feet tall and over two hundred pounds. His face, or what was visible under the grime and gore, was taut, with a firmly set jaw line and dark eyes that glowered with intensity. He was grinding his teeth and swallowing as if he was chewing something or wanted to be.

Though he gave off an aura of stillness, every few seconds his whole body would twitch slightly as if he'd been jolted with an electric shock. Lukas recognized him as the man who had first attacked Steve on the security video. But for reasons he couldn't explain, the soldier seemed strangely familiar, as if he'd seen him before today.

He looked around as a second man stepped out into the light beside him. He too was wearing the remnants of fatigues, though his were more rags than clothes now. He was larger than the first man, easily six foot four and 230 pounds. His nearly shaved head had wisps of blond hair but was also stained by filth. His eyes were as intensely focused as his comrade's, and he twitched even more violently.

Sarah and Elena looked at them and then at Jules, unsure whether to remain still or run. The first man, the black-haired one, made the decision for them. His gaze fell on them and he grunted loudly, looking toward the dining hall. Lukas heard a stirring inside and what sounded like dozens of other grunts. Then the man turned back to the girls, licked his lips, and broke into a run.

He was headed straight toward them.

CHAPTER 13

"Run!" Jules screamed.

The girls startled to life and began to sprint in the direction of the lodge again. Jules rushed to meet them at the gate.

Lukas stepped into the entryway to get a clearer view of the scene. What he saw made his blood run cold. In addition to the solider-like men, a swarm of people were pouring out of the dining hall entrance. He recognized most of them, though they looked nothing like themselves.

He saw Steve Sailor, the camp director, who was only identifiable by his mustache. His face was almost completely covered in muck. Flesh hung in loose dangling ribbons from his cheeks and arms. His eyes had the same look as the other men, like a hungry wolf searching for prey.

Flanking him out of nowhere were Richard and Lloyd. Richard's bald head was torn to pieces, exposing what looked to be parts of his skull. Lloyds's longish dirty blond hair hung limply, clinging to his forehead.

But they looked somehow different than Steve and the soldiers. Their eyes didn't have the same focused intensity. Instead they bounced around with a frenzied madness.

Lukas couldn't keep track of everyone streaming out of the dining hall. And his attention was drawn elsewhere as he watched

Sarah and Elena desperately running toward them. Jules was almost to the gate, but the girls were still a good thirty feet from reaching her. The soldiers were closing fast.

"Jules, stop!" came a voice from beside Lukas. He glanced over and saw that it was Aubrey.

Jules had reached the gate and was about to push it open when Aubrey yelled again. "Come back! They're not going to make it. And if you don't come back now, neither will you."

The counselor looked in the direction of her two campers. So did Lukas. It was clear that Aubrey was right. The first soldier would be on the girls in mere seconds. The second soldier was only steps behind. Steve and the others were closing in, too. They were about to be swarmed.

Jules seemed to process the same facts. She paused for a moment, as if unsure what to do, then opened the gate for her campers, turned on her heel, and began running back in the direction from which she'd just come.

"Hurry, girls!" she screamed back over her shoulder at Sarah and Elena.

Lukas realized he'd never actually seen the state champion runner in action. But it was a sight to behold. Her arms and legs pumped in unison, and she seemed to close the distance from the gate to the lodge in no time.

Sarah and Elena weren't so fortunate. Sarah was further away, so they got to her first. Soldier One leapt on her back, taking her to the ground like a lion catching a gazelle. As she collapsed under his weight, he stayed upright, leaving her for the others as he pursued Elena.

Soldier Two pounced on the sprawled-out Sarah and pinned her arms to the dirt as he dug his teeth into her neck. By the time

Steve and Lloyd arrived, he was already tearing the fleshy tissue away from her throat. Within moments, she disappeared under a mass of bodies diving and grasping at her.

Elena had just reached the fence gate when Soldier One got to her. She seemed to sense he was almost upon her and called out one desperate word. "Jules!"

The second it had left her mouth, he was there, throwing himself at her and smashing her body into the fence with brutal force. She slumped to the ground. Her neck was bent in an unnatural direction. Lukas saw her eyes, open but unmoving. She was dead.

He stood there, at the door to the lodge, and tried to wrap his head around what he'd just seen. A girl he'd watched roasting marshmallows only hours earlier was now lying lifeless only a front yard away from him.

It took Soldier One a few seconds to realize that. As he bit into her right cheek, Lukas looked away. But what he saw wasn't any less horrifying. The campers and counselors who couldn't get a chunk of Sarah had turned their attention to Elena and were rushing toward where she lay motionless on the ground.

It occurred to Lukas that at any moment they would all realize she didn't have any fight left and search for new prey. Jules was almost back to the lodge, but she wasn't the only one outside. He looked at Lonnie and Aubrey, who were still steps beyond the porch, staring in horror at the scene before them.

"Guys," he said quietly. "You need to get back inside now before they focus on us."

That seemed to snap them both out of their daze, and they scurried back inside right behind Jules. Lukas saw Soldier One's head pop up at the movement. He had obviously figured out that Elena was dead and now stared at his new targets.

His eyes seemed to lock on Lukas's as he squinted, as if he was trying to imprint him into whatever memory bank he still had left. Lukas felt like he was being targeted by a laser that was focused entirely and exclusively on him. Then, without hesitation, Soldier One got up and bounded toward the lodge.

CHAPTER 14

"Lock all the doors!" Martie yelled.

Lukas was already doing that to the front door the second after Lonnie and Aubrey passed him. He turned every bolt and pulled down the wooden barricade that had always seemed like overkill to him until this very moment.

"Close the shutters too," Aunt Winnie ordered. "They lock from the inside. We don't want them to get in through the windows."

After locking the front door, Lukas turned around to see action everywhere. People were running all over the house, looking for any entry point and securing it. The Moore twins were locking the shutters on the large front-facing window to the left of the front door. Jamie and Kellen were doing the same to the one on the right, but Jamie, who was taller, seemed to be having trouble getting the upper slide bolt into place.

"Hurry," Kellen yelled. "He's running right at us."

Lukas stepped over and, refusing to look outside, helped line up the shutters so the bolt could slide through smoothly. Jamie had just locked it into place when they heard the smash of glass directly in front of them and felt the weight of a body throwing itself at the heavy wooden shutters.

He could hear the solider vainly attempting to rip the shutters away, but there was nowhere for him to get a grip. After a few moments of that, he threw himself at the shutters again. They groaned but held firm, though it was unlikely they could withstand too many blows like that.

"We need to put furniture in front of everything," Lukas yelled to them all. "That first guy is body-slamming the shutters. Pretty soon we'll have dozens of them doing the same thing. The windows won't last for long like that. Shove whatever you can against them and the doors, couches, chairs, cabinets, bookshelves—anything to reinforce them."

Caleb was already single-handedly lifting a couch upright and onto its side before shoving it against the side door where counselors would typically enter the lodge to get to the rifle locker. Others were doing the same throughout the house with various pieces of heavy furniture.

As Caleb turned away from the couch to see where else he could help, Lukas saw it shift and start to tip back inward toward him.

"Caleb, it's falling," he shouted and dashed over to help his brother stop and reposition it.

"Thanks," Caleb said, offering something close to a smile as he hurried away to help elsewhere. "That could have been ugly."

Lukas nodded. He was about to head back into the main room to see who else needed help when his eyes fell on the padlocked gun locker. Next to it, also locked, was the cupboard holding all the bows and arrows.

He felt a shudder as someone slammed against the side door. Then it began happening everywhere. Slamming sounds echoed though the lodge, like a torrent of hail, as their former friends outside threw themselves at doors and windows, smashing glass, hoping to break through.

Lukas tried to slow his fast-beating heart, which felt like it might explode right out of his chest. He forced a long, deep breath, reminding himself not to panic. He paused for a second to think. At some point, whatever these people had become would get into the lodge. It was unavoidable. They would slam into every entry point until one of them gave way. When they did, it would be nice to have something to defend themselves with.

"Who has the key to the gun locker?" he yelled out to no one in particular.

While he waited for an answer, he looked around the main room. The Moore twins were going around with Trevor and Jamie, making sure the furniture against the various doors and shutters was secure. Kellen, Jules, and Todd were rechecking that locks were properly in place.

Caleb, Aubrey, Javi, Martie, Emily, Fiona, Lonnie, and Stephen were nowhere in sight. He assumed they were all locking down other rooms in the house. The various voices calling out to one another suggested as much.

After a few seconds, Aunt Winnie rounded the corner, flipping through her set of keys. "That's a good idea, Lukas Lincoln," she said, her voice calmer than he thought possible under the circumstances. "We'll load all the .22s and pass them out. I don't think it's worth it to get out the .177s."

"No," Lukas agreed. "They take too long to pump and wouldn't do much good anyway. But maybe we get out the bows and arrows. Some people are pretty proficient with them."

"Okay," she said as she unlocked both lockers. "Why don't you pass them out based on people's skill sets? Who is good with weapons that I can have help you?"

"Aubrey," he said without hesitation. "She knows who can handle what better than any counselor."

"I'll get her," Aunt Winnie said, smiling slightly. "Hold tight."

When she left, he began removing the guns from the locker and laying them on the ground facing toward the door. There were a total of six .22 rifles. He was just getting out the boxes of cartridges when Aubrey rounded the corner. She was holding Aunt Winnie's shotgun.

"Aunt Winnie told me your idea. Nice thinking, Lincoln," she said as she approached him, lifting the shotgun high. "I thought this might come in handy, too."

"Every little bit helps," he said, noting that she looked pretty comfortable holding the thing. "I figured you could help decide who was best equipped to carry what."

"Yeah, give me a second to think here," she said.

As she stood there, looking at the weapons and back at the people in the room, Lukas heard a noise that sent a shiver down his spine. There was a scrambling sound in the eaves and then the distinct thud of feet on the roof, running upward.

Lukas and Aubrey looked up and followed the direction of the footsteps. Both realized where they were headed at the same time. They looked at each other in horror before turning their attention to the far wall of the living room.

"The chimney," Aubrey said, speaking both their thoughts aloud. "One of them is going for the chimney."

CHAPTER 15

"Move away from the fireplace!" Lukas yelled to Trevor and Jamie who were closest to it.

"What?" Jamie asked, clearly confused.

"One of them is moving to the chimney," he said, waving them away from it.

Jamie and Trevor hurried away, and everyone got quiet as the sound of the feet on the roof got closer to the chimney. Their silence was broken by Javi who hurried in holding a lit kerosene lamp he must have gotten from another room. He tossed it into the fireplace, lighting up the half-burned logs lying inside. The flames rose for a few seconds before settling into a dull flicker.

"Do you have extra kerosene, Aunt Winnie?" Jules asked anxiously.

"In the pantry," the older woman replied.

"I know where she keeps it," Martie said. "Come with me."

Jules followed her around the corner. Caleb grabbed a poker from beside the fireplace as everyone else backed away. Above them, the footsteps stopped. No one moved. It seemed that all fifteen people in the room were holding their breath.

Suddenly there was a scurrying sound Lukas couldn't identify. But someone else did.

"It's getting in the chimney," Emily said. "I think it's about to drop down."

She was right. Something was bumping against the inside of the chimney walls as it moved downward. A second later, a body dropped into the mouth of the fireplace, sending smoke, ash, and sparks everywhere.

For a second, Lukas couldn't see anything. Then the smoke cleared enough for him to discern that the person in the fireplace was Richard, the radio club counselor. He was pulling himself out of the structure, dragging a leg that had been badly broken and was bent in the wrong direction.

He seemed oblivious to it. His face was set in a grimace and his teeth were clenched tight with the effort of lifting himself upright. A section of his skull was visible under the loose mangled skin of his head. Caleb stepped forward, holding the poker at his shoulder like a spear.

Richard looked at him with a wild-eyed hunger. He didn't appear scared by or angry at the teenager holding a metal weapon above him. He seemed ravenous, like a predator staring at its next meal.

Caleb hesitated, seemingly unsure what to do. Lukas understood. His brother didn't want to stab a fellow counselor with a poker. But was this even Richard anymore? Was this thing in front of him even human?

"Richard?" Caleb said slowly, voicing all those questions with just one word.

Richard looked at him, and for a second it seemed that the name registered somewhere in his brain. But then any recognition was gone and was replaced by a guttural growl that got progressively louder until it was nearly a roar.

Without any warning, he leapt at Caleb who wasn't expecting it and stumbled backward to the floor. Richard's momentum was sending his teeth straight for Caleb's midsection when there was a shatteringly loud *bang* and Richard's body was thrust backward, slamming into the mantle before collapsing in a liquid mess beside the fireplace.

Lukas, half-deaf from the blast, looked over to see that Aubrey had fired Winnie's shotgun. She took a shell from her pocket and reloaded as she stepped forward, waiting to see if Richard would get up again.

He didn't. In fact, most of Richard's torso was missing. He lay unmoving on the edge of the fireplace, his body twitching slightly as his frenzied eyes dulled and went glassy.

As Caleb scrambled to his feet, Martie and Jules rushed into the room, each holding five-gallon plastic kerosene containers. They looked at Richard, at Caleb, and finally at Aubrey. No one needed to explain what had happened.

Before anyone could say another word, they heard more scrambling in the eaves. This time it sounded like two sets of feet.

"Let's throw some of that wood in the fire," Lonnie said, pointing at the pile on the side of the fireplace. "Then you guys can douse it with the gas. Where are your matches, Aunt Winnie?"

Everyone seemed to snap into action at the same time, communally choosing not to address what had just happened in front of them. Trevor, Jamie, and Mike Moore each grabbed a couple of logs and threw them in the fire. Then Martie dumped half of her kerosene container over the wood.

"That should be enough," she said as Jules stepped forward. "Save the rest."

Aunt Winnie sidestepped Richard's shattered body as she grabbed several long matches from a box above the mantle, lit them, and tossed them in the hearth. Flames immediately shot up. This time they stuck around, filling the fireplace and sending a wave of heat throughout the room.

The sound of feet on the roof near the chimney stopped suddenly. Everyone stood still, waiting for the sound of another person climbing in and dropping down. But the sound didn't come. After a few seconds, they allowed themselves a collective exhale.

"Can I give you the shotgun back?" Aubrey asked Aunt Winnie. "Keep it trained on the fireplace while Lincoln and I load the guns and pass out the bows and arrows."

"Not a problem," Aunt Winnie said, taking her gun back.

Lukas and Aubrey began loading the guns and placing boxes of cartridges next to each. Caleb handed the poker to Martie and joined them, stringing the bows and placing an equal number of arrows next to each one. Everyone else just watched in silence.

"Am I the only one who thinks this whole thing is crazy?" Kellen finally demanded, breaking the stillness. "We're trapped in a lodge in the middle of nowhere, surrounded by flesh-chewing creatures that used to be our friends, like, last night? And we're preparing to defend ourselves against them with rifles and bows and arrows?"

"Do you have a better idea?" Aubrey asked as she loaded another gun.

"Yeah," he retorted. "How about we just lock ourselves in the cellar? If they only have one way in, it's easier to defend, right?"

"That would be a great idea," Martie said, tossing two more logs on the fire. "Only one problem—this lodge doesn't have a cellar."

"Nice try, Kellen," Trevor said. "Thanks for playing."

There was a series of sudden slams outside the various doors and windows, as if the creatures outside had gotten their second wind and were redoubling their efforts to break in.

"Guys," Caleb said as he strung another bow, "I can't believe I have to say this, but maybe a little less sarcasm under the circumstances? We need to be working together if we want to find a way out of this."

"There is no way out of this," Emily muttered.

"That's not very constructive," Todd said.

"I'm not trying to be difficult," Emily insisted. "I'm serious. We can load guns and build fires all we want. But that's all just delaying the inevitable. At some point one of those things is going to get past the fire or break through a shutter. And once one gets in, others will, too. And then it's over."

"Jeez, Emily," said her dismayed boyfriend Mark.

Another round of thuds made everyone jump as bodies slammed into the ever-creakier shutters.

"Moore twins, Stephen, and Trevor," Caleb instructed, "please go around to every room and make sure all the locks and bolts are still secure."

The four guys left the room, happy to get away from the pall that had fallen over it.

"It pains me to say this," Martie said, "but she's not wrong. Listen to what's going on out there. What we're doing might work for a little while longer, but we're talking minutes, not hours. We need to come up with a longer term solution to get ourselves out of this. It's not like the cavalry is coming."

Out of the corner of his eye, Lukas saw Aubrey cock her head and looked over at her. Something about that line seemed to have made a connection click in her head, as if she'd suddenly located a missing puzzle piece.

"Maybe it could be," she said slowly.

"What do you mean?" Jules asked.

"I mean, my father is literally in the cavalry, or at least the military," she said. "His base is just outside San Antonio. If we could reach him, maybe he could send some troops to help."

No one spoke for a moment as everyone considered this unexpected ray of hope. The expression on Aubrey's face was inscrutable as she appeared to debate whether to continue. Then she seemed to decide she would and was just starting to pick up again when Jamie interrupted.

"But the phone lines are down," she blurted out. "I checked."

"That's just land lines," Caleb told her. "Maybe cell service is still working. I know it's terrible out here, but we could unlock the safe with all our cell phones and try him or 911. It's worth a shot. How about it, Aunt Winnie?"

The crestfallen look on her face told Lukas that they shouldn't get their hopes up. "I already tried that with my cell phone," she said. "I called 911 and every law enforcement number I know. I couldn't get any connections. I'm happy to give you all your phones. Maybe you'll have better luck. But I think the system is just too overloaded."

She opened the cabinet door that hid the safe and punched in the combination. The door popped open, and she took out the baskets of phones for their respective bunks and put them on the floor for everyone to find theirs.

"Mine's dead," Javi said, pushing buttons. "Do you have a charger?"

"I only have one," she said. "It's in the kitchen."

"I should use it," Aubrey said, almost reluctantly.

Everyone turned to look at her.

"Why are you so much more important than the rest of us?" Emily demanded.

"If she can reach her father," Lonnie noted, "maybe she *is* more important than us."

"But her phone isn't going to work any better, just because of who her daddy is," Emily spat back.

"Actually, it might," Aubrey replied, looking down.

Lukas was surprised at how reticent she seemed even as she was apparently insisting on taking priority. "Why?" he asked. "What aren't you telling us?"

Aubrey continued to stare at the floor. But after an especially loud slam against the side door, she quickly raised her head. The look on her face suggested she'd made some kind of decision. "I'm not supposed to talk about this," she said, "but I don't just have my cell phone here."

A new series of thuds made everyone look around the room to make sure everything was still secure. The four boys sent to check the locks had returned.

"We're all good," Mike said. "Or as good as we can be."

"Aubrey," Jules said, trying to keep her voice even, "it's clear that you're uncomfortable. But we don't have time for that right now. If you have something that can help, please tell us."

Aubrey nodded and held out her left arm. She pointed to her wristwatch, which Lukas noticed was unusually bulky. "This isn't a standard smartwatch," she said. "It also works as a satellite phone. It's highly classified tech and I'm not supposed to have one. My father gave it to me for emergencies. I'd say this qualifies."

"Ya think?" Kellen said before he could stop himself.

Aubrey tossed him a withering glare before continuing. "The thing is, the watch operates on a normal battery, so it lasts for months, even years. But the sat phone component works like any cell phone. It dies if it isn't charged every day. It recharges superfast, but it hasn't been plugged in since camp started."

"How long does it take to charge it enough to work?" Todd asked.

"I've never tested it when it was completely dead, but my dad said it only takes minutes."

"Well, let's find out," Javi said. "Plug it in. Every second matters."

"Come with me, dear," Aunt Winnie said, leading her into the kitchen.

A new round of scurrying on the roof made them all look up.

"Let's throw a couple more logs in the fireplace," Martie said. "Then I'll douse them with some fresh kerosene. Lincoln brothers, now might be a good time to hand out those weapons."

Lukas nodded and began distributing the guns as best he could. He wasn't sure what level of skill the Lumens had, and with Aubrey in the other room, he didn't want to guess.

"I can't believe she didn't tell us about the watch until now," Emily muttered to Fiona as they walked over to get rifles.

"I forgot, okay!" Aubrey snapped, now suddenly back in the doorway to the living room. "There was a lot going on and I didn't think about it until Martie mentioned the cavalry thing. I guess blowing away one of our counselors with a shotgun threw me just a bit."

"Okay, everyone, chill out," Todd soothed. "We're in a better place now than we were two minutes ago. Let's embrace that."

"Enough with the therapy talk, Todd," Kellen said derisively. "Unless you can counsel us out of this lodge, then please just shut up."

Todd opened his mouth to reply, then thought better of it and held his tongue. Emily's hand was outstretched for one of the .22s. Lukas looked over at Aubrey with raised eyebrows. She nodded back at him.

"Give her one," she said. "The girl is a bitch, but she's a good shot."

Lukas handed over a rifle.

There was a beep from the kitchen, and everyone looked in that direction.

"I think your watch is charged, Aubrey," Aunt Winnie said.

"That was fast," Javi marveled as Aubrey returned to the kitchen. "I've got to get me one of those."

A new set of slams against the shutters and doors temporarily drowned out every other sound in the room. One of the shutters on the wall near the fireplace creaked loudly and seemed to buckle.

"Hey, Aubrey," Lonnie called out as he looked closely at the sliding bolt on the shutter. "You better make that call quick. I don't think this lock is going to hold much longer."

CHAPTER 16

He needn't have warned her.

Aubrey had punched the button on the watch phone before Lonnie finished his sentence. Instead of ringing, it emitted a series of loud beeps, like an old dial-up modem. After that there was silence.

"Didn't it work?" Stephen asked after a few seconds.

Suddenly a voice came on the line. "Aubrey?" barked a gruff male voice.

"Yes, sir, it's me," she replied, holding the watch close to her lips.

"Aubrey, I've been trying to reach you for twelve hours now. I thought the camp might have been overrun. Are you okay?"

"Ask him what's going on," Stephen whispered.

Aubrey looked daggers at him.

"Not the highest priority right now," Javi muttered.

"No, sir. I am not okay," Aubrey told him, her voice clipped and official sounding. "The camp *has* been overrun. A small group of us is holed up in the main lodge. We've barricaded the doors and windows, but they aren't going to hold much longer. Are you able to send help?"

"I wanted to do that already. But my superiors wouldn't allow it without proof of life. I'll be able to get authorization now. How many of you are there?"

"Seventeen," Martie told her quietly.

"What about the girls back at the cabin?" Fiona, normally so quiet, asked urgently. "There are three of them."

Everyone looked at her, most with expressions of shock or pity.

"I'm sorry, sweetie," Jules said gently. "But we have to assume they're gone. Even if they're not, we have no way to get to them."

"But—" Fiona started.

"There are seventeen of us," Aubrey said into the watch, cutting her off. "A few are older or injured."

"All right," her father replied with what sounded to Lukas like extremely controlled anxiety. "Here's what we're going to do. I'm having an aerial transport scrambled to your location now. It will be there in . . . thirty-one minutes. It will be able to accommodate your entire contingent."

"Sir, there is no way we can hold out for another thirty-one minutes at this site," Aubrey told him, pointing out what everyone else was thinking.

"That's okay because you need to find a different exfil location anyway. If I recall, the lodge is surrounded by trees and easily accessible by hostiles from multiple directions. The transport can't land there. It needs to set down at an elevated point where gunners can pick off the enemy and the pilot can evade quickly if need be."

Aubrey's face fell, along with those of everyone else in the room. No one said anything. The banging outside the lodge was now continuous.

"Aubrey, are you still there?" her father barked.

"I am, sir. We just don't know how to resolve the situation. We're trapped in here."

Lukas closed his eyes and tried to concentrate. Aubrey was right; they were trapped. But if they *could* get out somehow, where could they go that met Aubrey's father's criteria?

"Well, you need to come up with something," the colonel said sharply. "The transport will be in the air in three minutes. I need to let the pilot know exactly where to set down. Once those Furies see it in the air, they're going to swarm to its destination. You'll need a head start, and that comes from knowing where it will land."

Lukas's eyes popped open. He looked at Aubrey who seemed to sense he had an idea.

"What?" she asked.

"Hollow Hill," he said. "I don't know how we get there. But if we could, it would be ideal. It's elevated, and the rocks at the summit are mostly flat. A helicopter could land there without much trouble."

"That's true," Caleb agreed. "Assuming we got out of here in the next couple of minutes, which we need to do regardless, we could get up there in around twenty-five minutes or so."

"Maybe *you* could," Kellen said indignantly, "or your girlfriend, the track star. But I doubt I could. And I know Lonnie can't. Plus, Stephen doesn't stand a chance with his ankle."

"We don't have much of a choice," Emily said. "I don't know that I can get up there that fast either. But I do know we're all dead if we stay here."

"I'll make it," Lonnie said firmly. "And I'll carry Stephen if I have to."

"We're *all* going to make it," Caleb said definitively.

"Then you better get moving," Colonel West yelled over the watch phone. "That transport is up in one minute. That means it will be at that hilltop in around twenty-eight minutes. What time does your watch show, Aubrey?"

"I have 8:08 a.m., sir."

"Okay then," he replied. "Expect that bird to land at the top of Hollow Hill at 8:36 a.m. You need to be there waiting. It can likely only set down for about thirty seconds, so every one of them counts. Got it?"

"Yes, sir," Aubrey said. "Any suggestions for how to get us out of this lodge?"

"I'd say your best bet is a distraction of some kind. The Furies are drawn to loud noises and bright lights, at least temporarily. If you've got anything like that, it might do the trick. I have to go now, Aubrey. I need to let the pilot know exactly where he's going. He'll see you at eight thirty-six. Talk soon."

The line went dead before she could respond. Despite the constant battering outside, Lukas could almost hear the group's collective shallow breathing. Only the awful groan of the faltering shutter by the fireplace managed to snap them out of their shared anxiety.

"So," Javi said, looking at the now-buckling slide bolt, "we have about two minutes to come up with a distraction and implement it. After that, I don't think we'll have time to get up the hill. Any ideas?"

"What if we tossed out the second kerosene container and shot it?" Jules asked, pointing to the unused one she'd brought in from the pantry. "The explosion might do the trick."

"I'm not sure it would explode," Martie said. "Especially since it's not under pressure like a propane tank is. Besides, getting it out a door or window would expose us to those things getting in."

"Aubrey's dad called them Furies," Stephen noted.

"Whatever we call them, we can't let any of them get in or they might not focus on the distraction outside," Caleb said.

"We're running out of time," Emily said, clearly trying to stave off panic.

"I know what to do," a voice said from behind them. Everyone turned around. It was Aunt Winnie.

"What?" Martie asked her mom.

"We have some leftover fireworks from the Fourth of July celebration. If they're set off in the front of the lodge, it should draw their attention away from the back of the house, allowing everyone to sneak out that way."

"I know where they are. I'll get them now," Todd said, running out of the room.

"That's a great idea," Jules said. "But how are we going to light and shoot them off with all the doors and windows closed?"

Aunt Winnie pointed at a small window above the front door. About the size of a laptop screen, it was mostly decorative and too small to offer access or even much of a breeze. But a person could certainly toss fireworks through it into the yard beyond.

"That'll work," Caleb said. "Let's make this happen. We don't have long. Moore twins, go to the back door in the kitchen and remove the furniture blocking it. Jamie and Lonnie will use their body weight to help you keep it shut until we bail."

"You got it," Mark said, his normally sleepy eyes clear and alert.

"Javi," Caleb continued as those four ran off, "find a spot where you can see the back of the lodge so that we know when those things have cleared the area. Aubrey, you do the same."

Todd returned to the living room, short of breath but holding the fireworks.

"Great. I'll take those," Caleb said, reaching for them. "Fiona, grab a chair from the kitchen so we have something to stand on to access the window."

As Fiona darted off, Caleb pointed at Lukas.

"You and I are going to help support Stephen on the way up the hill. We'll each throw an arm over one of our shoulders. Help get him to the kitchen."

"I'm fine," Stephen insisted. "I can get over there by myself."

"Don't be such a tough guy," Kellen said. "Right now, Andrew Dice Clay would be crying like a baby."

"Do not blaspheme the great one, even under circumstances like this," Stephen replied. Then both he and Kellen started to laugh.

"Okay," Emily said, disbelieving. "I didn't expect that. Can we please focus? We have, like, a minute before it'll be too late to get out of here."

"Stay on task, everyone," Caleb shouted, before turning to Aunt Winnie. "You should go near the back door, too. It'll help to have a head start."

"You are a dear, Caleb Lincoln. But there's no need."

"Why not?" he asked, perplexed.

"Because I'm not going."

CHAPTER 17

Those still in the room stared at her, dumbstruck.

"What did you say?" Martie finally asked.

"I said I'm not going," Aunt Winnie repeated. "Someone needs to shoot off the fireworks for as long as possible to keep the attention of those poor things out there away from the hill. And let's be honest—there's no way I could make it to the top in the time we have. Give me double that and I'm there, but not in twenty-five minutes."

"I'll carry you," Caleb volunteered.

"You're already helping Stephen," she reminded him. "Besides, I'm still responsible for the safety of the campers and counselors under my care. That's you all. This is something I can do to help keep you safe. So I will."

"But—" Jules started.

"There's no time for this," Aunt Winnie said in a sharper voice than usual. "My decision is made. So here's what I need you to do. Jules, take your kerosene container and spread the fuel all around the living room so that it will light quickly. Do it now, young lady."

Without another word, Jules grabbed the can and began pouring the kerosene.

"Caleb," Aunt Winnie continued, "when I tell you, please reposition the couch that's against the front door so I can easily push it away by myself. When I'm out of fireworks, we'll need another distraction. I intend to open the front door and lure them in here. When they're close, I'll light the place up and take as many as I can with me."

"Mom, no," Martie pleaded.

"There's no point in arguing, sweet girl," Aunt Winnie said calmly, taking her daughter's cheeks between her hands and giving her a kiss on the forehead. "My mind is made up. If I'm going to kill some of the very people I was hugging just yesterday, it's only right that I be here with them."

"I can't let you."

"It's not your choice, Martie. And there's no time to argue. You should probably already be gone. Start assembling at the back door. Jules, leave a little bit of kerosene in the container and put it in the middle of the room. Caleb, steady the chair as I get up and start handing me lit fireworks when I say. Be careful not to drop any of them with all this kerosene on the floor. Everyone else, go to the kitchen and be ready to run."

Those still in the living room shuffled out so that only Aunt Winnie, Martie, and Caleb remained. Lukas lingered in the doorway.

"Go, my love," Aunt Winnie whispered to Martie as she squeezed both her hands. "These people are your responsibility now. I know you'll keep them safe. I love you."

"I love you, too, Mom," Martie said, her eyes filling with tears.

"Go now."

Martie turned and walked to the kitchen. Lukas stayed to the back of the group so he could still see into the living room.

Caleb helped Aunt Winnie up on the chair, which had been placed in front of the door. He lit the first firework as she opened the small window and reached out her hand to him. Caleb placed the first explosive in her palm. She clasped it tight, waiting until it was close to going off.

"Get another one ready! Keep them coming fast and furious!" she yelled, though her voice was barely audible over the relentless banging on the doors and shutters. It was as if the creatures outside could sense that something major was imminent.

When the firework was set to go off, she tossed is out of the window, as far from the lodge as possible. About five seconds later, they all heard a series of loud pops as the acrid smell of chemical smoke wafted through the lodge.

Outside, the loud sound of yelps and grunts could be heard. Aunt Winnie reached her hand down, and Caleb put another lit firework in it. He prepped a third as he looked over at Lukas.

"As long as you're here, you may as well help," he barked. "Help me light these things faster."

Lukas ran over, dug a rocket out of the can, and lit it with a match that Caleb still had burning. The sounds of pops and whistles were everywhere, mixed in with howls and occasional groans.

They were moving fast now, handing Aunt Winnie a new firework every few seconds. At one point Lukas saw a hand leap up into view near the window.

"Be careful, Aunt Winnie," he warned. "I think they're trying to jump up to block the window."

She nodded and made sure her next toss arced upward where no hands could reach it. A second later the slide lock on the shutter near the fireplace to their left snapped. The top of it careened inward a couple of inches, only staying upright at all because of the love seat lodged against it. Bloody fingers appeared near the top as the creatures tried to climb in.

"Lukas, shove the love seat closer to the wall to seal that gap," Caleb ordered, then yelled to the kitchen, "We're almost out of time up here! How's it looking in back?"

Lukas darted over to the love seat and slammed into it, making the top of the shutter rise up again and pinning several fingers between it and the window frame. He thought he heard squeals of pain as Javi appeared in the doorway.

"There are a few blind spots," he yelled over the pounding. "But we can't see anyone back there anymore."

"You have to go," Aunt Winnie instructed as she threw out another lit firecracker. "That shutter's not going to hold, and we're almost out of firepower. Toss the rest of the matches in the can and give it to me."

Caleb followed her instructions.

Javi looked at him, then at Lukas straining to keep the shutter upright. "Guys, grab your weapons," he yelled back into the kitchen. "We're about to bail."

Caleb looked up at Aunt Winnie. "You good?" he asked.

"I'm good," she assured him. "If you could just shove that couch away from the front door, then run like hell. You too, Lukas."

"Yes, ma'am," Lukas shouted as Caleb toppled the couch away from the door.

"You boys take care of my campers, and my Martie too. Promise?"

"Promise!" both brothers shouted in unison.

"Go!"

They nodded, and as Aunt Winnie threw one of the last fireworks out of the window, they both ran toward the kitchen. Once there, Lukas saw the whole group waiting. Everyone had something in their hand, whether it was a gun, a bow and arrow, a fireplace poker, or a kitchen knife.

"Weapons ready," Martie yelled when she saw the boys enter the room. "Todd, open the door in three, two, one, now!"

CHAPTER 18

Aubrey was the first out of the door, holding Aunt Winnie's shotgun firmly against her shoulder as she stepped out, looking to her right. Caleb followed her, looking left with his .22 pointed in that direction. Lukas stepped out next and trained his .22 in the area in between them. There was no one there.

"It's clear," he whispered loudly back to the others. "Let's go. Run for the hill trailhead near the infirmary. Try to stay along the tree line and out of sight as long as you can."

The group streamed out, sprinting to the spot just beyond the infirmary that marked the closest access point to Hollow Hill. When everyone was out, Martie, also holding a .22, stepped back into the kitchen briefly and called out as loudly as she dared.

"We're all out, Mom. I'm closing the door."

She didn't wait for a response. Lukas looked around. Up ahead, Emily was leading the group with her .22 raised and ready. Just behind her were both the Moore brothers. Mark also carried a .22, but Mike had a bow and arrow, as did Jamie.

Behind them was a second group that included Jules, also holding a bow and arrow, and Todd, wielding a long kitchen knife. They were followed by Trevor, Kellen, and Javi who all carried bows and arrows, too. Bringing up the rear of that group were Lonnie, who had the last .22, and Fiona, who held the fireplace poker.

That left Lukas's group at the rear, which comprised Aubrey, Martie, Caleb, himself, and Stephen who was holding a butcher knife as he stood gingerly, favoring his sore ankle.

"Let's go," Martie said in a quiet, urgent voice.

She took the lead in the group as the Lincoln brothers each let Stephen throw an arm over their shoulder. Aubrey stayed in the rear, alternating between running and backpedaling to keep an eye out behind them.

They were almost to the infirmary when Lukas noticed that the fireworks had stopped. He thought he heard a woman's voice shouting and pictured the creatures busting down the front door to find Aunt Winnie standing in the middle of the living room, holding an open container of kerosene in one hand and a lit match in the other. He told himself not to look back.

By the time their group reached the trailhead at the base of the hill, the others were all already scrambling up ahead of them, taking the fastest but most challenging route. Lukas stopped for a second to catch his breath. Stephen, who weighed more than expected considering his size, removed his arms from around the brothers.

"I can make it from here," he said. "It'll be easier for me going uphill with all the handholds. Besides, you guys can't climb and carry me at the same time."

"Okay," Caleb agreed. "Get going. We'll have your back."

As Stephen began the ascent, Aubrey reached them, still looking back. Lukas, Caleb, and Martie did the same. Smoke was clearly visible emanating from the lodge. They could no longer hear the female voice shouting. Martie stared at the scene for a second, her eyes brimming with tears. Then she shook her head, turned to the other three, nodded, and started sprinting up the hill. So did Caleb and Aubrey.

Lukas was about to follow when he felt a shiver down his back. Something he couldn't explain made him take one last look at the burning house. That's when he saw him. Just to the left of the house, staring at the three of them, was Soldier One.

His eyes locked on Lukas, and for a second the world stopped. The soldier's eyes burned with the same intensity as when he'd first seen Lukas standing on the lodge porch. And for the briefest of seconds, there appeared to be something else in those eyes: recognition. Then it was gone.

What was left of the man seemed to be taking his measure, as if deciding if the fifteen-year-old boy across the valley flat was anything more threatening than a piece of meat. His assessment didn't take long.

Without warning, Soldier One broke into a gallop toward them as he opened his mouth and roared unintelligibly. A moment later, Soldier Two appeared behind him, followed by a half dozen more Furies, and then all of them.

"They've seen us," Lukas shouted. "We have to move fast."

Caleb and Aubrey, just ahead of him, looked back and saw the same thing. Then, in unison and without a word, they all began running up the hill.

*

For a few minutes everything went well. Even at top speed, Lukas guessed it would take Soldier One ninety seconds to reach the trailhead. Most of the other creatures would probably need closer to two minutes.

With the slower members of their party already well ahead after their head start, he had hopes that they might get close to the summit before anyone caught up. By then, maybe the transport would be in sight.

"What time is it?" he whispered loudly to Aubrey who was just ahead of him.

"Eight twenty-four," she hissed back.

Twelve minutes—that's how long they had until the transport landed at the top of Hollow Hill. Lukas scrambled up the brush-covered trail, slipping occasionally on the parched, dried-out dirt as he wondered if they'd reach the summit in time. Of even more concern were the things down below, still out of sight but almost certain to catch up to them before long.

Lukas, Aubrey, and Caleb reached Stephen whom Martie was trying to help navigate the tricky spots. Just ahead were Fiona and Lonnie who, despite his pronounced limp, was dragging her with one hand while holding his .22 in the other. Up a little higher, he could see Todd and Kellen. The others were out of sight.

Lukas leapt over a narrow stream, scaled a large boulder, and was turning around to warn Caleb about a cactus growing near its edge when he heard the sound of footfalls on pebbles. As if on cue, a cacophony of shrieks rose up behind them. Lukas couldn't see anyone yet, but he heard hundreds of feet headed in their direction.

Before he had time to process anything else, a voice above them called out.

"Keep moving," Aubrey yelled. "They're coming."

CHAPTER 19

Lukas looked below him and saw that she was right.

Dozens of the Furies were streaming out of the shadows below. They moved slowly and jerkily, falling often as their bodies twitched involuntarily. A few hesitated when they came to the rivulet of water, seemingly unsure of what to make of it. Others, apparently unbothered, splashed right through and kept moving. They were coming, a wave of faces, many still recognizable as people he'd gone to a dance with two nights before.

He shook the thought out of his head and turned to resume his sprint back up the hill, with Caleb right behind him. Glancing up, he saw that Aubrey was about a half dozen paces ahead of them. Martie and Stephen were only steps ahead of her. Lonnie and Fiona were no longer visible, which he took as a good sign that they were well ahead.

Just as he scaled a series of stair-like boulders that marked the halfway point up the hill, he saw Stephen take an ill-advised step on a notoriously gravelly section. His foot slipped out beneath him, and he began falling backward. Martie reached out for his wrist and grabbed it briefly. But whether because of stress or sweat, she couldn't get a grip, and he tumbled down a dozen feet to a ridge below.

Under normal circumstances, it wouldn't be a big deal. This happened often on hill hikes. Lukas had seen it a couple of times himself. Usually the person who fell had a few cuts and scrapes but not enough to prevent him from continuing the hike.

But in this case, the tumble had dropped him a few feet to the right and just above the quickest Furies. Lukas recognized one of them as Lloyd, the counselor who had supposedly set the record for the fastest ascent of Hollow Hill.

Stephen pulled himself upright almost immediately but found that he was in a spot where it was impossible to climb straight up, even without the ankle injury. To get back to the trail, he'd have to go through a section where the creatures were now gathering. He looked up at the group above him.

"Any ideas?" he shouted at them, with a surprising lack of panic in his voice. He seemed to sense they wouldn't have any.

"Grab your knife!" Aubrey shouted from about fifteen feet up, pointing at the gleaming blade at his feet. "Use it to dig into the dirt above you and pull yourself up. We'll cover you."

Lukas aimed his .22 at the creatures, though he doubted it would do much good. They were converging fast, getting close to Stephen even as some of them lost their footing and toppled downward, taking out others below them like bowling pins.

Stephen looked at the creatures, then at the wall of rock he'd have to scale. His expression morphed from fear into something Lukas couldn't identify. He seemed to have made a decision. "Don't waste your bullets," he shouted. "I'm trapped. Keep going. I'll keep them busy as long as I can."

Even as the last words were out of Stephen's mouth, one of the Furies—Lukas remembered him as a camper from the Bandeleros, the third-oldest boys' bunk—leapt at him. Stephen swiped at him, cutting into the boy's arms even as the younger kid tore at his t-shirt, ripping it right between the words "Dice" and "Man."

Stephen collapsed backward, and the knife fell from his hand. It slid down the hill as the boy dug his teeth into Stephen's exposed chest. Lukas heard the beginnings of a scream that ended suddenly as Lloyd attacked his neck. Within seconds, a half dozen more were on him and he wasn't visible at all. It reminded Lukas of ants swarming the carcass of a dead insect. He stared at the scene in revulsion.

"Come on," Caleb said quietly, tugging at his shirt. "Let's move while they're all distracted."

It was true. Almost all the creatures were trying to get to Stephen, locked in some crazed collective thirst for his flesh and blood. They seemed to have temporarily lost interest in the others.

Lukas felt his brain trying to process one of his bunkmates being torn apart right before his eyes. It had happened so quickly and brutally that he wasn't sure it was even real. The creeping horror of the moment was just beginning to take hold of him when he instinctively shoved it back down. *Deal with it when you're safe*, he silently ordered himself.

He turned back up the hill and saw Aubrey, still conflicted, pointing her shotgun in Stephen's direction, her finger tapping but not pulling the trigger.

"Don't," he said as he reached her. "It won't help him, and it will draw their attention back to us. Just keep moving."

That seemed to snap her out of it, and she took her finger off the trigger, nodding slightly as she fell into line behind him. He was right below Caleb who had reached Martie. She was staring down at the scene below, a pained look etched on her face.

"Come on, Martie," Caleb said, putting his hand on her shoulder. "You can't do anything for him now."

"I was responsible for him," she muttered. "I had his hand and I lost it. It's my fault."

Caleb shook her shoulder roughly. "It's not your fault. He just fell. You have to keep climbing!"

He physically turned her toward the summit and gave her a shove. It worked. She began to trudge up the hill, slowly for a few steps and then with vigor, as if she were trying to outrun the memory of what was beneath her.

They moved quickly after that, running over the packed dirt wherever possible and yanking themselves up the increasingly large boulders when necessary. Within two minutes, they had caught up to Lonnie and Fiona. Todd and Kellen were only a few yards ahead of them.

Lukas could see Trevor and Javi in the distance, reaching the next crest. The others—Jules, the Moore twins, Emily, and Jamie—weren't visible and must have gotten even further along. He imagined that group would reach the summit soon.

They came to a boulder known as the Clasper. It was the unofficial indicator that they were two-thirds of the way to the top. Unfortunately, it was a bear to navigate—six feet of near-vertical rock that had to be climbed using man-made holes that had been chipped into the rock to serve as footholds and handholds. It was one of the reasons younger bunks never took this route up the hill.

Lonnie was just pushing Fiona up the last bit and digging his sneakers into the lower holes when the last group reached them. Unable to go any further until the Clasper was unoccupied, Lukas spun around to scour the ground below.

None of the Furies were visible, but the increasingly loud sound of grunts and snarls told him they were getting closer. He aimed his gun in the direction of the noise, as did Caleb, Aubrey, and Martie. They all formed a semicircle at the base of the rock.

"What time have you got?" he asked Aubrey.

"Eight thirty-one," she replied. "I'm sure nothing bad will happen in the next five minutes."

Lukas appreciated the gallows humor and chuckled despite the situation.

"I forgot to mention I have a flare gun too," Martie said, patting a pistol shoved in the back of her jeans that Lukas hadn't noticed before. She seemed to have mostly recovered from the Stephen incident. "We can use it to signal the transport when we reach the summit."

"Don't fire it unless you absolutely have to," Caleb said. "The way things are going, we might need it as ammunition."

"We're up," Lonnie whispered from above them.

Lukas looked up and saw that the Clasper was free.

"Go," Caleb said, patting Martie on the back. "Then Aubrey and Lukas. I'll go last. Once you're up top, cover us down below."

No one argued with him. Martie scaled the boulder in seconds and trained her rifle on the hill below as Aubrey started climbing.

"Do you think it's weird," Lukas asked Caleb as he kept his eye on the trail, "that the first soldier with dark hair wasn't chasing us?"

"What do you mean?"

"He was ahead of all the others at the bottom of the hill, but he wasn't in the group attacking Stephen. Where did he go?"

"Clear!" Aubrey said from above.

"I don't know," Caleb admitted as Lukas started climbing the Clasper. "Maybe he fell."

Lukas reached the top and turned around quickly to cover his brother as he started scaling the rock. He reached out his hand and grabbed Caleb's forearm, yanking him up the last little bit. When they were face to face, he looked in his brother's eyes and could see the worry there.

"Yeah, maybe he fell," he agreed hopefully, though neither of them believed it.

"They're close," Aubrey said from behind. "The grunts are getting louder. Let's worry about the soldier guy later."

She broke into a run right behind Martie, and the brothers followed. Lukas allowed himself some hope that navigating the Clasper might cause serious difficulties for the Furies whose hunger seemed more developed than their coordination.

The summit came into view as they reached the next crest. It was only a couple of hundred yards away. The first group, finally visible now, was nearly to the top. About fifty feet lower, Javi and Trevor were making good time. Todd, Kellen, Lonnie, and Fiona were now a middle foursome, exhaustedly trudging up the steep terrain.

As Lukas rushed to catch up to them, he saw something out of the corner of his eye, coming in from a brushy area to the right of the foursome above. It only took him a second to register what he was seeing—Soldier One.

CHAPTER 20

He moved so fast that he was almost on them before Lukas could say anything.

"Look out!" he yelled, just as Soldier One dove at the person closest to him, Fiona.

She looked up just in time to see him flying at her and lifted her arms in self-defense as she screamed. By the time the two of them hit the ground in a heap, he was already gnawing at the fleshy spot on the side of her neck just above the collarbone.

The two of them rolled slowly down the left side of the hill, her body clutched in his vicious embrace, only coming to a stop after about ten feet of tumbling. Lukas went from a run into a sprint, trying to reach level ground where he could take aim at the soldier. The others in his group were all doing the same thing.

Lonnie, who had looked momentarily stunned at the turn of events when Fiona suddenly disappeared from directly in front of him, seemed to have recovered. He was lowering into a kneeling position and preparing to fire. Todd and Kellen, just beyond where Fiona had been attacked, both stared open-mouthed at the events unfolding in front of them.

Lonnie fired. Lukas saw the soldier jerk back briefly, then look down at his left shoulder where he'd apparently been hit. He didn't seem hurt so much as annoyed and dropped Fiona's limp body, his eyes now trained on Lonnie.

He appeared about to attack when Lukas and the others reached the top of the ridge. The soldier's eyes darted to them, and he seemed to be making a calculation.

"Prepare to fire," Martie shouted, using the same phrase counselors were instructed to announce before campers were allowed to fire at the paper targets on the riflery range.

Soldier One seemed to realize that the cluster of four armed, gun-wielding people posed a credible threat. Without hesitation, he turned and darted down the side of the hill before leaping into what looked like a big chasm.

Martie hurried to check on Fiona, while Lukas dashed over to the spot where the soldier had jumped. He looked down the twenty-foot drop to the wooded area below and saw nothing. The soldier was gone.

He turned back to the others to find a chaotic scene. Martie was kneeling over Fiona, trying to coax her back to consciousness. The girl's head dangled loosely and blood streamed from her neck. Lukas couldn't tell if she was even alive.

"Wake up, Fiona," Martie begged.

Caleb was helping Lonnie back to his feet and whispering something to him quietly. Lonnie nodded but didn't speak. Aubrey had her back to the group, pointing her gun alternately between the direction of the Clasper boulder and the bushes from which the soldier had emerged.

Kellen and Todd both stood dumbly in place. Kellen was still holding his bow but seemed to have lost his arrows. Todd's kitchen knife was nowhere in sight. Lukas saw the fireplace poker Fiona had been holding on a rock nearby and scrambled to retrieve it, hoping one of the guys could make use of it.

As he bent down to grab it, a tingling sensation coursed through his body. He felt suddenly as if he was being watched, like he was prey being hunted. He turned around and saw that Soldier One, only ten feet away, was pulling himself up from whatever rock he must have been clinging to on the side of the gulch. His eyes were trained on Lukas. In one fluid motion, he landed on solid ground and leapt toward him.

Everything seemed to slow down. Lukas stared at the gnashing teeth and pitiless eyes, knowing he'd never get off a shot in time. Instead, he did the only thing that he could think of—he dropped the gun, gripped the fireplace poker tightly with both hands, and swung it in front of him.

His body slammed back as the force of Soldier One smashed into him, sending him falling to the ground. The weight of the bigger man's body pressed down on him as his chomping teeth came toward him. Then suddenly, shockingly, the man's momentum stopped.

Lukas blinked in disbelief. The soldier's face was contorted in what looked like pain. And then Lukas realized why. When Soldier One had leapt onto him, he'd been pierced by the point of the fireplace poker, which had jammed in the right shoulder socket area, hitting bone and preventing him from going any further. His upper body and head dangled above Lukas, just out of biting range.

But that didn't stop him from reaching out and, even with one damaged limb, grabbing Lukas's face. The soldier clutched it tight in his rough hands and held his head still. Lukas thought the man was about to snap his neck.

Instead, Soldier One leaned in as close as he could and breathed in deeply. It was as if he was actually trying to inhale Lukas's scent. His eyes gleamed with furious intensity and something close to intimacy. As their eyes locked on each other, Lukas felt a sudden burst of static energy shoot through his entire body, like he'd been zapped with a quick, sharp jolt of electricity. For a brief moment, the soldier's mouth curled unnaturally, and with coagulated blood between his teeth, he actually appeared to smile.

Then, his fingers began to pull at Lukas's left eyelids, forcing them open. He seemed to almost be gulping. Lukas flashed back to what Aunt Winnie had said about one of the soldiers seeming to spit in Steve Sailor's eye. He realized that was what Soldier One was preparing to do to him right now.

He desperately tried to close it but knew that was useless. Then he tried to tilt his head away, but Soldier One had it locked in place. Finally he tried to push up with the fireplace poker, hoping to force the man further away or at least mess up his aim.

But none of it worked. Soldier One's body was like lead, slowly crushing him. A strange tingling sensation coursed through his body, making it hard to concentrate, much less move. He could feel his grip on the fireplace poker beginning to slip. Saliva was visible between the soldier's pursed lips.

And then he heard a loud click, like a gun safety being removed. Soldier One heard it, too, and looked up. Whatever he saw made him freeze. The soldier looked back down at his prey and then, to Lukas's shock, he spoke.

"Meet . . . again," he growled in a hoarse barely intelligible whisper.

CHAPTER 21

Without warning, Soldier One threw himself backward, ignoring the fireplace poker that ripped at his flesh as he tore away. He took one huge hurdle and disappeared back down the gorge that Lukas had originally thought he'd tumbled into.

He craned his neck back behind him even as he began to breathe again. About ten feet away stood Aubrey, her shotgun trained on the spot where Soldier One had disappeared, her eyes darting back and forth with an intensity he'd never seen before.

He didn't have the energy to thank her. He feared he couldn't speak coherently anyway. His back was screaming, and his palms were ripped up from where the poker had cut into them.

The painful tingling that had come upon him so suddenly was still there, though it was starting to subside slightly. He barely had the strength to crawl back to his feet and grab the gun still lying on the ground beside him. He was just standing up when he heard another scream.

He looked up, gun in one hand, poker in the other, to see that the noise had come from Todd. The counselor was pointing at the brushy area where the soldier had originally come from. Two other people had emerged and were running toward the group. Lukas recognized them both.

The first was Steve Sailor, the camp director, who Aunt Winnie had said was Soldier One's first victim. He ran with purpose and a stern focus in his eyes. His face was more red than tan, and his bushy mustache was caked in blood, dripping like an over-soaked sponge.

Behind him was Soldier Two. He was silently running toward them, his muscles straining, his nearly shaved head glistening with sweat. His torso twitched intermittently as he ran, knocking him off balance.

Everything seemed to happen at once. Martie looked up from Fiona, lying limp in her lap. Aubrey whirled around to see what was happening. Caleb and Lonnie both tried to raise their guns, as did Lukas. But none of them could do anything before Steve reached his target, Todd.

The counselor screamed again at his former boss, now thundering toward him. And then, without seeming to even think about it, he grabbed Kellen, his camper, and shoved him forward into Steve's path. As he was thrust forward, Kellen's expression was more shock than fear.

Steve was happy to maul the substitute victim. Kellen's eyes went wide as he saw the mustached thing leap at him. He raised his bow to block the charge, but Steve slammed into him, knocking him down. Todd, behind them, collapsed to the ground, too.

Lukas wanted to fire his rifle but worried he might hit Kellen or Todd. Instead, he dropped the .22 and, ignoring the throbbing he felt in his back and hands, sprinted toward the group, raising the fireplace poker high above his head.

As he ran, he heard gunshots around him. But his attention was focused on Kellen, Todd, and Steve, and he didn't know who was firing where. He was about fifteen feet from them when he saw something briefly out of the corner of his eye. He glanced over just in time to see Soldier Two leaping at Caleb who was right behind him.

His brother didn't have time to protect himself as he was blind-sided from the right. Soldier Two's body slammed into his exposed ribs, and Lukas could almost see the breath escape his body. Despite that, as he fell to his left, Caleb simultaneously reached for Soldier Two's shirt and braced himself for the impact of hitting the ground.

He landed hard, but seemingly ignoring what must have been intense pain, he tugged at Soldier Two's clothes and yanked him away from his own body as they both rolled to the left down the slope. It worked. Soldier Two landed on top of him but quickly tumbled by him as a result of both Caleb's maneuver and his own momentum. His snapping jaws just missed Caleb's head as he rolled over him.

Caleb gasped for breath as he scrambled away from the former soldier. Lukas changed directions and ran toward them, releasing the poker and once again picking up the gun he'd just dropped. He saw his brother fixate on his own rifle on the ground nearby where it had fallen when he'd been hit.

He reached down to grab it as Soldier Two dived at him, grabbing his ankle. Caleb, rather than trying to take a shot in such close quarters, swung the butt of the weapon at the man, hitting him in the forehead and sending him backward.

Barely fazed, Soldier Two lifted his head and smiled. His mouth was stained red with blood. Several big pieces of what looked like skin were stuck in his teeth. He fixed his eyes on Caleb, regrouped from a crouched position, and leapt toward him a second time.

Lucas stopped running, aimed his gun at the man's head, and prepared to shoot. But just as he was about to pull the trigger, Caleb stepped into his line of fire.

His brother fired his rifle at point blank range, hitting Soldier Two in the throat, just below the Adam's apple, ripping off half his neck and spraying a mist of blood in a cloud behind him. The man collapsed forward, his chest hitting the barrel of Caleb's rifle.

Even then he tried to push forward, his legs spinning lazily in the dust until he finally came to a stop with his head only inches from Caleb's hands. His jaws were still snapping, though less ferociously.

Lukas stepped to the side to try to get a better angle for a shot when a gunshot rang out from somewhere to his right. It found its mark. A bullet slammed into Soldier Two's head, sending brain matter and blood everywhere. He finally stopped moving and slumped forward.

Caleb used the gun muzzle to push the creature away. His body toppled backward, and he landed in a lifeless heap at Caleb's feet. Both he and Lukas looked to see the source of the shot. Lonnie, kneeling, was still aiming the rifle in his direction.

A scream tore Lukas out of the moment and made him look to his left, reminding him that there was still another threat to deal with. Kellen, his eyes open in fixed terror, was lying unmoving on the ground. Dragging one of his legs uselessly behind him, Steve was crawling over him and toward Todd who was trying to scramble to his feet.

Aubrey was reloading her gun. Apparently she was the source of Steve's leg injury, though in the chaos with Soldier Two, Lukas must have missed the sound of the shot. Still the closest to Steve, he again dropped the gun, grabbed the fireplace poker, and, disregarding the pain in his hands and back, staggered toward the former camp director, trying to catch him before he got to Todd. The counselor, unarmed, could only kick at the approaching threat.

Steve, undeterred, dove at the smaller man and landed on top of him, diving straight at his head. Todd's face wasn't visible, but his curly blond locks bounced furiously as he tried to avoid the attack.

"Stop, Lukas," Aubrey yelled from somewhere behind him.

He was within touching distance of the two men but reluctantly followed the instruction. A second later another gunshot sounded, and Steve's back exploded. He collapsed on top of Todd and lay still.

Lukas, breathing heavily, slumped forward and looked over at Aubrey who still had the shotgun raised. She nodded that it was okay for him to move now. He staggered over and pulled what remained of Steve off Todd.

His counselor's face was a mess of loose blood-slicked flesh. His jawbone was exposed where Steve had ripped away the skin with his teeth. His neck was spurting blood in all directions like a hose with a leak. Todd was making a noise somewhere between a scream and a gurgle. His eyes were nearly bulging out of his head. Lukas looked around for something to stem the tide of blood, but there was nothing.

He felt a hand on his shoulder. It was Caleb, standing over him.

"We have to go," his brother said quietly.

"But he's still alive."

"Not for long," Caleb said. "And we can't do anything for him anyway. We have to be at the summit in two minutes and I'm not sure we can make it."

Lukas looked around. Lonnie was pulling Martie away from Fiona's body, which was twitching slightly. Aubrey had picked up the rifle Lukas had dropped and handed it to him.

"Your brother's right," she said. "My watch says eight thirty-four. We have to be on the summit ASAP. Besides, I can hear those things. I think some of them have cleared the Clasper boulder. That means they'll be in sight any moment. And then there's Fiona."

All three of them looked at the former Lumen whose body was now convulsing violently.

"If what Aunt Winnie said is true," Aubrey continued, "then she'll be turning into one of them soon. We have to go before that happens. I can't shoot one of my own bunkmates. I just can't. And I'm guessing you can't shoot Todd either."

As if in response, Fiona stopped shaking and a long, slow groan escaped her lips. Lukas feared she might get up at any second.

"They're coming," Lonnie shouted.

Everyone looked back down the hill. Some of the creatures had scaled the Clasper boulder and were lumbering toward them. There were easily a dozen of them.

And then Fiona sat up.

CHAPTER 22

They didn't wait for her eyes to open.

Instead, what remained of their group hurried up the hill with the little energy they had left. They could hear the sound of the grunting creatures behind them, more of them joining in every second.

They were approaching the final set of boulders, a series of large smooth rocks that typically took teamwork to scale. The boulders were protected by a wall of high brush that the group tore through, ignoring the sharp, thorny branches ripping at their skin.

Once there, Lukas feared they wouldn't have time to get up before the things chasing them caught up. He didn't know about the others, but he was limping, coughing, and operating on fumes. At least the prickling feeling that had consumed his entire body only minutes earlier was mostly, though not completely, gone.

When they arrived, Lonnie tossed his rifle over the rocks, gripped a boulder, and pulled himself up using just arm strength. Then he turned around and extended his arm to Aubrey who was scrambling up behind him. Caleb and Lukas helped Martie up the adjacent rock. She was almost to the top when Lonnie whispered urgently, "Hurry!"

Lukas didn't have to look back to know what was behind them. The rush of footsteps and rolling symphony of grunts told him the things were close. He tossed up his gun and began to clamber up one boulder, while Caleb did the same on the other.

Lonnie reached out an arm, and Lukas took it. To his surprise, his bunkmate yanked violently on it, pulling him off his feet as he toppled over onto the rocky ledge above. He looked back and saw why Lonnie had been so aggressive. The creatures were already at the base of the boulders, leaping inelegantly toward them. Only their ungainly aggression prevented their immediate success.

As everyone got to their feet and grabbed their weapons, the creatures began to scale the rocks through sheer volume of bodies, as they literally climbed up one another. Several were already on the cusp of the ridge. With so many of them so close, a sinking realization entered Lukas's head, one he suspected those around him shared—they weren't going to make it.

"Move!" Martie yelled, tugging at Caleb's shirt. Lukas could feel Lonnie doing the same to him and didn't fight it, using his friend's strength to help propel him upward, compensating for his own fading effort. He was just twisting around to face the summit when he heard a group of voices above them shout the same word all at once.

"Duck!"

He looked up to see seven people standing on the rise above them, all pointing weapons at the creatures crawling up the boulders. Emily and Mark Moore were holding their .22s, while Jules, Javi, Mike Moore, Trevor, and Jamie all had arrows strung in their bows. He dropped to the ground.

"Prepare to fire," Jules shouted and after a beat, yelled, "Fire!"

As they did, Lukas twisted back around and saw that most of them had hit a target. One unidentifiable creature lay face down at the top of one of the boulders. Two others had fallen backward, knocking over several more on their way down. For the moment, the area above the rocks was clear.

"Let's go, guys," Jules yelled to the group below. "The transport is close."

Everyone hurried to their feet and began running the last mostly flat stretch of rocks to the center of the summit. All of a sudden, Caleb stopped, grabbing Martie's shoulder. Lukas stopped too, perplexed.

"Do you still have the flare gun?" his brother asked.

Martie reached behind her and nodded. "But we don't need to fire it," she protested. "The transport knows where we are."

"Not to signal," Caleb said. "Fire it at the thick brush by the boulder. It might start a fire and make it harder for those things to get close."

"Good idea," she agreed as she pulled it out and rushed back down several steps to get a better view of the brushy area. She squinted.

"What's wrong?" Caleb asked.

"With all of them in the way, it's hard to get a clear shot at the scrub brush."

Aubrey stepped over to her. "Here," she said reaching her hand out for the gun. "Let me."

Martie handed it over without a word.

"What are you doing?" Javi yelled from ahead of them. "We just frickin' saved you and you want to go back down?"

"Just cover us," Lukas yelled back, raising his own gun to watch for anything that might somehow get up the boulder. A few were close already.

Aubrey was pointing the flare gun in that general direction, her arms steady, her breathing slow. After what felt like an interminable wait, she exhaled deeply and pulled the trigger.

The already bright day lit up with unnatural oranges and reds. Within seconds, the brush was on fire, flames quickly rising all around the base of the boulders. The grunts from those nearby turned quickly to howls and shrieks.

The group turned and ran the remaining way up until they had reached the center of the summit. When Lukas arrived, he saw the rest of what was left of their assemblage. They had begun the ascent with sixteen people. They were down to twelve now.

"Where's Fiona?" Emily yelled as she looked around for her best friend, apparently now realizing the difference in numbers herself. "Where are Todd and Stephen? Where's Kellen?"

Martie opened her mouth to say something, but then closed it, at a loss.

"They didn't make it," Caleb told her. "We'll deal with that later. Right now, we need to stay focused."

Lukas considered it good advice. The mental image of his friends being consumed by ravenous half humans was more than he could handle. Forcing the thought from his head, he looked up and saw that the transport was close now. He could see the words "U.S. Army" emblazoned on the side.

"Move to the west," a voice ordered over a speaker emanating from the helicopter. "We need more room to set down."

They hurriedly did as they were told.

"Keep your weapons ready," Aubrey yelled over the descending copter. "Form a semicircle around the area where the transport will land. Those things are still close."

They all did as she instructed, guns and bows raised, with their back to the fast-dropping helicopter. Lukas took a spot at the far left end of the semicircle. It sounded like the copter was almost on top of them, which may have been why Lukas didn't hear them coming.

CHAPTER 23

The first sign of trouble came when Lukas thought he heard more fireworks popping off behind him. Glancing back, he saw a gunner from the transport firing a huge mounted machine gun at an area to his right. He looked over to see multiple Furies rushing toward the people on that side of the semicircle. About a half dozen of the things had been mowed down, but three had gotten through, heading for the section manned by Mark and Emily. They were now too close for the gunner to shoot at without putting humans at risk.

Lukas swiveled, aiming his gun in that direction and screaming at those in his way. "Duck! Duck!"

Jules, who was two spots over from him, turned at the noise. She looked confused for a second, then apparently reading his lips, started to shout the same thing. The rest of the group began looking around, unsure what was going on. From their angle, none of them could see the approaching threat.

Lukas took two steps to his right so that he had a clear shot at the thing headed for Emily, the person most exposed. The creature, which looked a lot like the ceramics counselor Amy Crudow, was only steps away from her when he fired, hitting her in the face. She dropped at Emily's feet.

For half a second, Lukas considered reloading. But he knew the other two things would be on Emily and Mark before he could even dig out a cartridge. Instead he ran toward them. Emily had seemingly gotten over the shock and was already raising her gun to point it at one of the advancing creatures.

But before she could aim, it was on Mark who only saw it coming as it was leaping in the air toward him. He didn't even have time to raise his hands in defense. Within seconds, his face was being turned into ground meat. Emily aimed at the thing, oblivious to the third creature bearing down on her.

Lukas, running to stop it before it got to her, realized that he recognized it. The creature was Sal, the heavy camper from the Desperados bunk, the one who had bullied little Nate from the radio shack the night before at the picnic in the watermelon line and had teased Lukas about Jules. His already hateful eyes had an extra dose of malevolence as he zeroed in on Emily's exposed left side.

Lukas pointed the .22 at Sal and used it like a spear, ramming it into his gut just as he was reaching out for the girl who was only a step away. Sal grunted and fell backward with Lukas landing on top of him, the gun popping out of his hands from the force of the collision.

His momentum sent him rolling over the other camper and onto his back where he lay sprawled out and half-dazed. He only had half a second to regroup before he saw something bounding toward him. It was Sal, apparently unfazed by the gun to the abdomen.

Lukas raised his knees to his chest, managing to blunt the force of his smaller, heavier attacker as he slammed into him. Sal tried to claw at him, but Lukas grabbed the younger boy's forearms and lifted them up away from his body. Mad with frustration, Sal bobbed his head forward, snapping at Lukas's face with bloody drool-covered teeth. He was relentless, his eyes voracious.

The combined sound of the helicopter, gunfire, unintelligible yelling, and his attacker's grunts was deafening. Lukas sensed his body failing him. His ribs were screaming. His palms had blood dripping from them, little rivulets snaking down his wrists.

He felt his arms giving way as the sheer ferocity of Sal's attack overwhelmed him. Red saliva dripped from Sal's open mouth. Lukas closed his lips and eyes and turned his head for fear of being infected by whatever the younger boy had. He knew he was exposing his neck, but he had no choice.

And then suddenly, the unrelenting onslaught above him stopped. A moment later, the coiled tension of the body bearing down on him faltered, and he felt it collapse onto his torso. He opened his eyes to see Sal's shattered skull resting on his chest.

Behind him, Emily was lowering she gun she'd just used. Her expression was almost one of regret. To her right, the creature that had attacked Mark was unmoving, riddled with bullet holes. He lay still as well.

Caleb was there a second later, tossing Sal's body off to the side and pulling Lukas to his feet. "Are you okay?" he asked, his eyes wide with concern. "Can you walk?"

"I don't think so," Lukas heard himself say.

"Try. Because we have to go."

His older brother wrapped an arm around his waist and guided him to the helicopter, which was now resting on the rock summit of Hollow Hill. Lukas clutched Caleb tightly, uncertain if he could stay upright without assistance. He was being dragged more than walking on his own.

The gunner was still on alert, and two soldiers were at the chopper's door helping the others in. Jamie, Javi, and Trevor were already on board. Jules, Martie, and Lonnie were yanking Mike, who was screaming as he tried to get to his twin brother, toward the transport. Finally Lonnie, who was much stronger than the remaining Moore twin, just picked him up from behind by the waist, carried him to the chopper, and tossed him in.

Aubrey had run over and was tugging at Emily who continued to stare blankly at what used to be Sal.

"Help her," Lukas said to Caleb. "I'll be fine."

Caleb nodded and released him, going back to help Aubrey coax her bunkmate to the transport. Lukas stumbled the last few steps to the open door where one of the soldiers helped ease him inside. He crumpled into a heap and turned back around.

Aubrey and Caleb were still both trying to snap the unresponsive Emily out of her seeming trance, yelling words that disappeared in the rotors above Lukas's head. Aubrey looked away for a moment, and Lukas saw what had gotten her attention.

A swarm of former campers and counselors had somehow battled through the burning brush and cleared the boulders. Easily three dozen of them were storming toward the three remaining people standing on the summit. Lukas could see that many of them were running with burned strips of skin hanging loosely from their bodies, like streamers blowing in the breeze at a child's birthday party.

Aubrey yelled something at Caleb, and he nodded. Unable to wait any longer, he simply picked Emily up, threw her over his shoulder, and carried her across the rocks, with Aubrey close behind, her shotgun trained on the approaching masses.

The second they hopped in, the transport lifted off, rising with stunning speed. Lukas felt his stomach drop violently. Several of the advancing creatures were close enough that the gunner, fearing they might grab the landing strips, fired at them. They all dropped immediately.

As they rose up, Lukas saw the fire from the flare gun quickly enveloping the hill. His attention was drawn from the flames to one small creature that had been unable to scale the boulders and was madly trying to scramble up a steep dirt rise off to the side. As the copter passed over him, the creature looked up and Lukas realized who it was—Nate.

The little boy was barely recognizable. He was shirtless, with ripped shorts, red oozing wounds all over his torso, and a gaping space where his left cheek used to be. His eyes were still blue, but they didn't belong to the same gentle, worried kid he'd spoken to only yesterday. They were vacant of any thought other than the desire to consume whatever was within reach of his small blood-soaked hands.

And then he was gone as the transport sped through the sky, away from Hollow Hill, passing over the main flat of camp. It was only then that Lukas finally felt the last vestiges of the painful tingling sensation he'd experienced earlier completely disappear.

Below, he could see the charred, still smoking remnants of the lodge. Other than that, the rest of the place looked strangely peaceful and silent. No one was walking to breakfast. No one was saddling the horses. No one was playing catch on the softball field.

Suddenly, the transport banked sharply left, leaving Hollow Valley behind and speeding toward an uncertain future.

PART II

CHAPTER 24

For the first few minutes of their flight, no one spoke.

Lukas felt his body starting to shake from the overdose of adrenaline in his system and tried to force himself to take slow, steadying breaths. He refused to think about what had just happened, instead keeping his attention focused on the people in front of him. He studied the helicopter crew, which comprised six soldiers: the pilot and copilot, the two soldiers who had helped them onboard, and two gunners.

When he could no longer avoid it, he looked at the other survivors. Everyone from camp appeared shell-shocked. Most heads were down, as if no one could bear to look at anyone else because it might remind them of who wasn't there.

Trevor, Jamie, and Lonnie all had their eyes on the helicopter floor. Emily stared straight ahead, with Caleb and Aubrey on either side of her. Both of them looked wiped out. Neither spoke, but each had a hand resting on one of Emily's arms, as if preparing for the possibility that she might try to jump out of the helicopter. Mike was crumpled up in the corner of the transport, hugging his legs against his body. Jules was beside him, whispering something Lukas couldn't hear. Martie was there, too, an arm wrapped around him but staring into space, her mind clearly elsewhere.

Of the sixteen of them who had started up Hollow Hill, only eleven remained. And considering what had been after them, Lukas considered them lucky.

Flickering flashes of faces cycled through his head: Todd's fear as he pushed Kellen into harm's way, Kellen's shock at it happening, Stephen's resignation to his fate, Fiona sitting bolt upright after being lifeless seconds earlier.

His thoughts were interrupted by the pilot's voice on the helicopter's internal speaker. "We are en route to Joint Base San Antonio at Camp Tarris. We will arrive in approximately twenty-four minutes, at which time Colonel Huell West will assume custody of you."

The speaker cut out, and Lukas realized that was all the pilot intended to say. Since he was close to the cockpit, he leaned over and yelled as loudly as he could. "What's going on? How did this happen?"

"I'm not authorized to answer any questions at this time," the pilot yelled back. "Colonel West will be available to provide an update once we're on the ground."

Lukas settled back into his spot, unsatisfied but unsurprised. Left with nothing to ponder but his own thoughts, he tried to divert himself by looking outside for the rest of the flight.

His mind drifted to his parents in Southern California and what they might be doing right now. He knew they had planned a boat trip to Catalina Island, an hour off the coast. Had they already left?

If not, he imagined his mother desperately packing essentials and madly throwing them into a suitcase. She pictured her yelling at his father, so subdued and fatalistic in recent years, to get moving.

For a decade now, his dad had been living as if he was already half a ghost. The pandemic had only reinforced his sense that doom was inevitable. Would this new threat of potentially imminent death finally push him into rejoining the living? Lukas wasn't hopeful.

A sudden sharp turn to the right by the pilot jolted Lukas back into the present. He looked down. They were several thousand feet up, racing across the Texas Hill Country. Down below he could see occasional people running. But he had no idea if they were still human and trying to escape or if they had turned and were now hunting something.

There was something odd about what he saw on the ground, but it took him a while to figure out what it was. When he did, he realized it wasn't what he saw below, but what he didn't. There were no moving vehicles.

He saw cars and trucks everywhere, on the country roads and two-lane highways. But so far, he had not seen a single one that was actually in motion.

Eventually, as they got closer to San Antonio and passed over Interstate 10, the main freeway in the area, he saw a huge backup of cars that had been heading northwest out of the city. But they were all at a standstill, as if caught in the biggest traffic jam of all time. Some doors were open. He thought he could see what looked like bodies on the ground between some vehicles.

The helicopter banked softly left, and Lukas realized they were now passing over The Promontory, the exclusive gated community on the outskirts of San Antonio where his grandparents lived. He looked down, vainly trying to identify their home.

And then suddenly they were descending. It was only then that he remembered that Camp Tarris was just a few miles and one freeway exit away from The Promontory. He'd seen the signs for it every time his grandparents had driven by the base but never really given it a second thought. Now, as the transport began to land, he hoped it would be his safe haven.

But as they got closer to the ground, that sense of relief was almost immediately dashed. Camp Tarris was surrounded by a stone wall that rose about fifteen feet high. Just inside the wall was additional barbed wire fencing that rose about five feet above the top of the stone barrier.

It looked to have been hastily assembled, as it was uneven in sections and not fully erected yet in others. The reason for the extra fencing was immediately obvious. Just outside the walls, as far as the eye could see, were hundreds, if not thousands, of the Furies. Lukas couldn't help but feel a strange guilty sense of relief that he didn't immediately recognize any of the faces.

As they had when trying to scale the boulders on Hollow Hill, the Furies here were climbing mindlessly on top of each other, trying to get high enough to scale the stone barrier. So far, they seemed to be meeting with little success.

Even if any did, they would likely get tangled in the barbed wire fencing above and be shot by soldiers in the guard towers or by those patrolling the grounds. Still, Lukas couldn't help but wonder what would happen when multiple Furies got up and began to put pressure on the wire.

The helicopter set down before he had time to ponder it further. As the rotor blades slowed, he saw three people in fatigues emerge from a nearby temporary building. Two of them, a tall skinny man in his early twenties and a petite blonde woman who was slightly older, walked on either side of another man who was clearly Aubrey's father.

Colonel Huell West wasn't tall but even in his loose-fitting army fatigues, Lukas could tell he was jacked. His shoulders seemed like they might split his overshirt open, and his thighs were about as thick as his daughter's entire torso. The deep brown skin of his bald head gleamed in the sun as he approached them. He looked to be in his early forties.

Aubrey moved closer to the helicopter doors as he got closer but didn't get out. Only when the rotor blades had stopped completely did she jump up and run over to him. He embraced her tightly, leaning down and whispering something in her ear. She gave a thin smile, nodded up at him, and released her grip, standing deferentially to the side. The colonel looked at the rest of them as they slowly disembarked from the transport.

"Welcome to Joint Base San Antonio at Camp Tarris," he said, his voice loud but gravelly, with a slight hoarseness that Lukas suspected came from years of yelling. "I'm Colonel Huell West, an officer at this facility and Aubrey's father, as you all know. I'm sorry your visit comes under such unpleasant circumstances. Additionally, I understand that not everyone in your group managed to escape. For that I am also truly sorry. But we're glad to have you."

"Thank you for sending your people to help us," Caleb said.

"Of course," Colonel West said, not mentioning that sending no one would have meant leaving his daughter to die. "I'm sure you have a number of questions. And while I doubt I can answer all of them, I can probably help to some degree. I plan to hold a briefing for all of you momentarily. But before that, we'll need to take care of a few basics."

"I'm sorry to interrupt, sir," Javi said, interrupting. "But do any of those basics involve access to a restroom? I've had to go for quite a while."

"They do," Colonel West assured him, turning to walk back from where he'd come and waving for them all to follow. "Please come with me and I'll let you know the plan along the way. We've set up a triage center in the hangar over there. Inside you'll have access to lavatories and medical care. Personnel are waiting to attend to any injuries you have and also do preliminary assessments."

"Assessments?" Lukas repeated skeptically.

"Yes, son," Colonel West said as he led them briskly to a large hangar just beyond the temporary building. "I regret to be so blunt.

But we need to check you out. My understanding is that several of you engaged the Furies in close combat. If you were scratched deeply or bitten, you run the risk of infection and . . . transformation."

Lukas glanced over at Caleb who shook his head ever so slightly. Neither of them spoke.

"I'm not overly concerned," the colonel continued. "In our extremely limited experience, it takes much more than a surface wound or two for infection to set in. It seems the Furies have to get deep into the tissue for that to occur. And if any of you were at risk, you'd likely be showing overt signs by now. But we need to take precautions nonetheless. So you'll all strip down and undergo full body examinations. Appealing, I know."

"I'm not consenting to any kind of full body search," Jamie said defiantly, squaring up. At her full height, she was easily four inches taller than the colonel.

"It's not optional, miss," he said, politely but without a hint of conciliation. "But this is US military property. And to remain here, you're required to follow all army procedures. This is one of them. You can comply or be escorted from the base."

Jamie slumped slightly, realizing further argument was futile. "I assume the search will at least be done by someone of the same gender," she mustered.

"Of course," the petite blonde beside Colonel West interjected. "This is a safety and medical precaution, nothing more."

The taller male soldier held the door open for the group. Lukas was at the back and lingered as the others entered, looking around the base. Vehicles were moving everywhere all at once. Soldiers ran from one building to another with purposeful speed. Clearly, some kind of operation was underway.

When Lukas stepped inside the hangar, he found that it had been converted into a makeshift living space. There were multiple cots spread out across one half of the facility. Lukas noticed the petite blonde walk over to a soldier nearby and whisper something. He nodded and motioned to another soldier, saying something to him. They each immediately collected several cots and removed them from the area. After counting, Lukas saw that there were now eleven instead of seventeen, the original number Aubrey had given her father on the call from the lodge.

On the other side of the room, multiple people in scrubs stood waiting next to vinyl dividing walls. Colonel West led the group to that part of the hangar, and then turned to face everyone.

"I know this has been an ordeal," he said. "And unfortunately, there are more challenges to come. But take comfort in the knowledge that, after these exams are finished, the bulk of your obligations will be complete. We will reassemble in Strategy Room D at 1000 hours. That's about fifty minutes from now, at 10:00 a.m. At that time, I will update you on the nature of our situation to the best of my ability. Then you will be free to regroup. Does everyone understand?"

There was a general collection of nodding from the group, after which Colonel West gave a tight smile.

"Now if you will all excuse me, I have some pressing matters to attend to. But before that, if I might have a brief word with you," he said to Aubrey and, without waiting for confirmation from her, walked to a distant corner of the hangar.

She glanced over at the rest of them, her eyes falling on the Lincoln brothers in particular. They held a brief glimmer of hesitation. Then it was gone, and she followed her father who didn't stop walking until he was much too far away to be heard by prying ears.

CHAPTER 25

Lukas was concerned about his medical exam.

But apparently he needn't have been. After he changed into a hospital gown, the doctor who examined him treated the scratches on his arms—the ones Sal had given him—with alcohol and iodine. Then he bandaged his torn-up palms and put medical tape on the ribs that were the most bruised.

He said there wasn't much to do about the throbbing in his back other than wait. After offering that recommendation and a handful of ibuprofen, the doctor signed off on him. As he changed back into his dirty, sweaty clothes, Lukas didn't mention the intense tingling sensation that had temporarily overcome him during Soldier One's attack on him.

Caleb, who had been scraped up a bit in Soldier Two's attack, also got an all clear. Emily, who had been splattered with blood when the helicopter gunner fired on the Fury attacking Mark, was also free to go.

Lukas noticed that none of the doctors or nurses asked her why she was covered in blood but had no wounds. Nor did they ask why she seemed borderline catatonic. He also wondered what would have happened to him if he *had* suffered deeper wounds.

Things didn't go as smoothly for Mike. When a nearby nurse tried to swab a scratch on his forearm, he swatted the young man's hand away. He stumbled back, surprised. Two nearby soldiers immediately raised their rifles and pointed them at him.

"Do not touch the medical personnel," one of them ordered forcefully.

Mike looked at him with fiery eyes. "Don't touch me without asking first," he countered belligerently.

Jamie and Emily, who was still sitting on a nearby exam table, both stood up.

"He's not a piece of meat," Jamie protested loudly. Emily didn't speak but nodded in agreement.

"Back off, guys," Aubrey objected, coming over. "They're just doing their jobs. Don't take it out on them."

"Is that what Daddy told you to say?" Jamie demanded, showing more venom than Lukas had ever seen from her.

"My dad didn't tell me shit," Aubrey said coldly. "And you better watch your mouth. I don't care how big you are; I will lay you out."

Lukas and Caleb exchanged worried glances, unsure whether they'd have to get involved.

"You will consent to the medical exam, as ordered by Colonel Hunt, or you will be thrown in the brig," the other guard barked at Mike, ignoring the bickering around him.

"I thought I would get thrown off the base if I didn't," Mike shot back.

"Comply with the examination," the first guard replied, refusing to be baited. "Or you will be cuffed and forcibly examined."

Lukas decided that things were escalating too much and started to take a step forward. But before he could move, Trevor moved in front of Mike so that the weapons were now trained on him.

"Please," he pleaded, holding up his palms like stop signs. "Cut him some slack. He just saw his twin brother killed. He's really raw right now."

One of the soldiers lowered his rifle slightly. The other kept his up, seemingly unmoved.

"I'm sorry for his loss," he said crisply. "But we've all lost people we care about. That doesn't excuse violating orders."

"But he's not a soldier who's used to following orders," Trevor pressed. "He's a teenage boy who just lost his brother. He's not a threat. He's just upset. Please lower your weapons."

Lukas was impressed with Trevor's willingness to hold his ground. He'd always viewed the guy as more interested in being liked than doing the right thing. If anyone was likely to take the easy way out, he figured it would be the kid who viewed popularity as a form of currency. Seeing him stand up for Mike made him question that long-held assumption.

"Look," the first less strident guard said. "We're sorry to hear about your brother. But this exam is required to ensure you're not infected. It's for the safety of everyone on the base. Just let the medical personnel do their job. Then it will be over and you'll be able to move about."

Trevor turned to Mike who was still glaring at the soldiers, body taught, fists clenched.

"Come on, man," Trevor said. "Let's get this over with. I'll hang here with you until it's done. Okay?"

After several interminable seconds, Mike nodded. The nurse returned to his side and gingerly resumed swabbing his arm. This time he held still. Jamie, Emily, and Aubrey retreated to opposite corners of the hangar. The rest of the exam went without incident.

By the time everyone had been checked out, it was almost ten. Lukas walked over to where the rest of the group had assembled. No one spoke. They all still looked like they hadn't processed what had happened to them or what was going on now. He felt the same way.

"Do you think they'll let us make calls?" he asked as he slid over next to Caleb. "I'd like to know how Mom and Dad are doing, Grams and Gramps too. Maybe they could send a team to pick them up."

"They might let us call. But I think Grams and Gramps are on their own, unless they're hiding another one of Colonel West's kids at their house."

"I think she's an only child," Lukas said, aware that wasn't the point.

"There's your answer."

The back door of the hangar opened, and the petite blonde from earlier stepped inside and beckoned for the group to follow her. Lukas saw Caleb eyeing her and did the same, trying to discern what had his brother so interested. He squinted at her ID and saw that it read: "Cpl. K. Daugherty."

As they filed through the door into the long connecting hallway between the hangar and the adjacent building, Lukas tried to survey their surroundings. The hall extended as far as he could see, with offshoots spidering out in multiple directions from the main one. They were all lit by rows of bright fluorescent overhead lights that hummed softly as they illuminated the dull-green metallic-painted walls. The drabness seemed intentionally depressing.

Lukas was right behind Caleb and Jules.

His brother leaned over and muttered in his girlfriend's ear. "Don't be mad but I'm gonna try something," he said before picking up the pace to join Corporal Daugherty who was walking briskly ahead of the group down the busy low-lit hall.

"How's everyone here holding up?" he asked her in a surprisingly conversational tone, considering the situation. Lukas immediately recognized this as Caleb's patented charm mode. Daugherty looked up at him as she dodged one of the many soldiers hurrying through the hall. He was almost a full foot taller than her.

"We do what we have to do," she said noncommittally.

"I'm sure. It looked like it was a finely tuned machine out there. I don't know how y'all do it when things are this crazy."

"I don't know how someone from El Segundo, California, ends up saying 'y'all,'" she said sharply.

"Oh, my grandparents are from around here," he said sheepishly. "Hey, how did you know where I'm from?"

"Like you said, Mr. Lincoln, we're a finely tuned machine. Is there something I can help you with?"

"Actually, yes. I was hoping we'd get the opportunity to reach out to our loved ones after the colonel meets with us. Do you think that would be possible?"

"That decision is up to Colonel West, Mr. Lincoln, as is every other request you're likely to have of me. I recommend you take up your concerns with him. We're here." She pointed to the sign on a door, which read "Strategy Room D," then opened it and went inside.

"That went well," Jules murmured sarcastically as she brushed past him into the room. Lukas entered next, followed by Aubrey, who leaned over to Caleb.

"You're wasting your time. I know her. She's likely more interested in Jamie than you." She didn't stop as she passed by him, so she didn't see the scowl Caleb gave her.

"I'm trying to win her over, not ask her out," he muttered half to Lukas, half to himself.

Lukas knew better than to poke his brother when his ego had been bruised.

But Javi, who'd also seen the exchange, didn't seem to care. "Looks like you took the loss," he said, smiling impishly.

Caleb started to say something but then apparently thought better of it. Lukas was glad he held his tongue. It was nice to see his best friend smile, and he suspected his brother thought so, too.

As everyone took seats around the conference table, Colonel West walked in. He stood at the front of the room, in front of a large monitor. Lukas wondered if this was going to be a formal military-style presentation for a bunch of campers and counselors. It felt weird to be seated in high-backed chairs around a conference table with the same people he was used to seeing scarf up pancakes or do cannonballs into the river.

"It started about forty-eight hours ago," the colonel started, diving right in. "People in unrelated regions of the country began engaging in extremely violent attacks against loved ones and strangers alike. There was no logical reason. Quarantines were established, and for a short time, they seemed to be holding. But the sheer number of affected victims was just too overwhelming."

"What cities did it start in?" Trevor interrupted.

"Let him finish," Aubrey hissed under her breath.

"It's okay," Colonel West said, though his expression suggested otherwise. "If I don't answer all your questions in my initial rundown, feel free to pose them when I'm done. But to answer that one, as best we can tell, the outbreaks began in New York, Pittsburgh, Baltimore, Atlanta, New Orleans, Saint Louis, Detroit, Denver, Los Angeles, Portland, and here in San Antonio."

Lukas glanced over at Caleb to see if he'd also noted the reference to Los Angeles being an outbreak epicenter. His brother nodded imperceptibly without looking over.

"Outbreaks?" Javi asked, and then realizing he had interrupted, added, "Sorry."

"That's what we're calling them until we know more," Colonel West answered, then picked up where he left off. "After twenty-four hours, the focus turned from trying to control the situation and limit the damage to basic survival."

"Survival," Emily repeated softly, speaking for the first time since the summit of Hollow Hill.

"Things are bad out there," Colonel West said with emphasis, as if until now he'd been sugarcoating it. "From what I can tell, you all got a pretty brutal sampling of what has been happening. But you were in an isolated area so it took a while to get to you. You have to understand that, in the cities, as much as 75 percent of the populace was wiped out in the first day. There were no hilltops to evacuate from."

CHAPTER 26

He was quiet for a moment, letting the magnitude of the situation settle in.

"Did you say 75 percent?" Jamie asked, disbelieving.

Colonel West nodded. "And as you saw outside when you were landing," he went on, "the swarms in metropolitan areas aren't like the comparatively small population of a summer camp. They're the size of small towns, sometimes thousands of people hunting down one fleeing family. That's where the term 'Furies' came from. I think it's apt. They are just relentless, unstoppable flesh sacks, full of unbridled, unthinking rage."

Lukas silently took issue with the description. There was something offensive about referring to little Nate as merely a rage-filled flesh sack. Beyond that, at least a few of these Furies didn't appear to be unthinking at all.

Both the soldiers who began the attack at camp last night, as well as Steve Sailor, were clearly operating with some higher-level functioning. Soldier One had actually spoken to him. More than that, he seemed to have been strategizing to the point of ambushing them. It was almost as if he was targeting them specifically.

"Some of them seem to be acting on more than just instinct," he said before he could stop himself. "One of the soldiers who attacked the camp spoke to me directly. He was stalking a group of us. And based on what Aunt Winnie said, he did something to Steve, the camp director—spit in his eyes or something—and then Steve changed. But when he did, he was like the soldier, retaining some ability to think."

"We've noticed that, as well," Colonel West agreed, not addressing the "talking solider" point as he shifted uncomfortably from one foot to another. "We know that infection only occurs when deeper tissue is impacted. Surface cuts don't seem to cause the change, as you've discovered yourselves. And as to what Winnie Korngold described, fluid transfers, like saliva interacting with the viscous area of the eye, appear to have a more concentrated impact. We don't have clarity on why that is as of yet."

"So this isn't some mutated form of COVID?" Juliana asked, voicing the question Lukas felt sure was on many of their minds.

"It doesn't appear to be," Colonel West answered. "It's not a respiratory virus as far as we can tell. And it's not aerosolized. It seems to be something completely new."

He stepped aside and pushed a button on a remote control that Lukas hadn't noticed he'd been holding up to that point. The monitor behind him came to life, showing an image of North America.

Everyone else's attention focused on that. They all seemed to forget about what Lukas considered a deeply unsatisfying answer to his question. Colonel West had never actually explained *why* the soldiers or Steve had behaved differently from the others. In fact he had seemed to deliberately respond in a way that clouded the issue.

Lukas did notice Aubrey looking at him uneasily. When she saw him return her gaze, she quickly looked away and stared intently at the screen where an animation appeared, showing concentric circles expanding from the cities he'd mentioned to much wider areas.

"As you can see," the colonel said, "the outbreaks have expanded to cover most metropolitan areas. Some more isolated regions in the western states haven't been hit yet, and there are rural pockets throughout the country that are so far unaffected. Your camp was an example. Based on what my daughter told me, it wasn't impacted until late last night, almost twelve hours after most population centers had been overrun."

Lukas looked specifically at the areas around San Antonio and Los Angeles. In both cases, the circles extended well outside the city limits and encompassed both his grandparents' house here and his parents' home in El Segundo, a coastal suburban town just southwest of L.A.

"Weren't Mom and Dad planning to go to Catalina Island this weekend on Uncle Jim's boat?" Lukas whispered to his brother, trying to get clarity on the timing of their parents' trip. "Maybe they were at sea when all this happened."

"I hope so," Caleb said. "But that means reaching them will be almost impossible. Cell phones never work out there."

Lonnie raised his hand.

Colonel West noted it and pointed at him. "Yes, young man?"

"It looks like the circles stop at the borders. Have other countries been hit?"

"To the best of our knowledge, the outbreak is limited to the continental United States. Canadian and Mexican authorities both monitor our media closely, so they were aware something was happening. Once we realized the magnitude of the situation, we warned them, and both countries shut down their borders. In many cases they had to quickly erect fencing much like what you saw as you were landing. So far it all seems to be holding."

"How did this start?" Martie asked, ignoring the no-interruptions rule. "Was there some infection on a flight from overseas that passengers carried on to their hometowns? The outbreak areas are so widespread."

"To be honest, we just don't know yet," Colonel West replied. "We don't think it started outside the US as there are no reports of anything like this anywhere outside the country. But the source is . . . unclear."

He looked like he might be about to expand on that topic but then seemed to change his mind. "There's not much else I can share at this point. You're about as safe as you can be right now in this facility. Realistically, we're going to have to assume these things are going to get in at some point. Once that happens, the situation is likely to deteriorate rapidly. We're making contingency plans for that inevitability, but I don't have anything specific on that for you at this juncture."

Caleb raised his hand and waited as the colonel looked around the room, as if waiting for questions from anyone else. Finally he relented.

"Yes?" he said.

"Are we going to be provided the chance to reach out to our families after we're done here?"

West seemed to have anticipated the question. "As you can imagine, most of our resources are being used to communicate with other military facilities. Having said that, I've already set aside a room adjacent to the communications center for you to try to contact your loved ones. However, I should warn you—almost all cell service is down. Satellite communication is still viable, which is how Aubrey was able to reach me. But that won't help most of you unless your family has sat phones, too. Even then, connections have been buggy. Lastly, you should prepare for the likelihood that you won't be able to reach anyone. There may be no one left to reach."

"What do you mean?" Trevor asked.

"As I said, we believe close to 75 percent of the population in urban and suburban areas was killed or infected on day one. By the end of day two, that number was probably closer to 90 percent. These are obviously very rough numbers. Communication is spotty. Estimates vary wildly. It might only be 80 percent. In a best-case scenario, maybe even less. But even using the rosiest projections, chances are remote that the people you care about are still alive and functioning in any meaningful way."

No one spoke for several seconds as they let his words sink in. The enormity of it was too much for Lukas to process.

"Colonel," Javi finally said as he raised his hand perfunctorily, "let's say your worst-case numbers are accurate. You said 90 percent had been killed or infected. But what's the breakdown? Maybe the infected people could be saved with some kind of antidote?"

"That's a nice thought, young man," Colonel West said with unintended condescension. "It would be great if such a thing was possible. As to hard numbers on dead versus infected, we don't have any. All I'll say is that there seem to be more still bodies out there than moving ones."

The silence after that statement stretched interminably.

"I have to wrap this up, folks," Colonel West finally said. "Corporal Daugherty and Private First Class O'Connor will direct you to the communications center where you can attempt to contact family members. I'll let you know if there are any developments worth sharing. Otherwise try to make yourselves as comfortable as possible. And please, don't leave the secure hangar area without an escort for any reason. We don't need any overzealous trigger-happy soldiers mistaking you for Furies."

Then he turned on his heel and left. The rest of the group slowly got to their feet and gathered behind Corporal Daugherty. Lukas stayed in his seat, trying to put a name to the uncomfortable sensation that was eating at him. The fact that Aubrey kept giving him occasional sidelong glances only heightened his unease.

Colonel West hadn't directly answered Javi's question about an antidote, just as he had dodged Martie's curiosity about how the outbreak had begun and had nervously evaded Lukas's inquiry about why the two soldiers and Steve had acted differently than the other Furies.

Colonel West was hiding something. Aubrey's behavior suggested she knew it. And as Lukas stepped into line behind the others as they went to the communications center, he came to a decision.

He was going to find out what.

CHAPTER 27

"What makes you think Aubrey will tell you anything?" Javi asked.

"Because she seemed like she wanted to," Lukas answered quietly. "And it was clear that she knew her dad wasn't being totally honest."

They were sitting on cots back in the hangar that served as their makeshift home after returning from the communications center.

No one had been able to reach family members anywhere in the country, not even Mike, whose father was a civilian web engineer with the San Antonio Police Department's Northside Division, located less than ten miles south of here. A communications center staffer had helped try to reach him on the secure law enforcement channel but got only static in return.

Neither Lukas nor Caleb knew if their parents were at home, at sea, or on Catalina Island. But it didn't matter anyway, as the only contact numbers they had were their cell phones, which were unresponsive. Calls to Grams and Gramps never even connected.

"So what are you going to do?" Javi asked as they conferred away from the others. "Corner her and demand answers? I don't think that'll go over so well."

"No," Lukas muttered softly under his breath. "I think we need some more information before we approach her."

"*We?*" Javi repeated incredulously. "You've got to be kidding me. Did you see that girl when she was toting around that shotgun? I don't want to do anything to get on her bad side."

"Coward," Lukas said, grinning for the first time since this had all begun.

"'Savvy' is the word I would use," Javi countered before relenting. "So how are we going to get this additional information? I don't think Google is going to have the answers we're looking for."

Lukas looked around. The rest of the group was scattered throughout the hangar. A few, including Lonnie, Trevor, and Jamie, were at a card table playing a board game in an admirable attempt to create some sense of normalcy.

Caleb was sitting on a cot next to Mike Moore with his arm around his shoulder. They were talking quietly, though Mike looked very agitated. Martie and Jules were over in the hangar's medical section with a doctor and the still largely unresponsive Emily. With the brief exception of halfheartedly standing up in defense of Mike during his physical exam, she'd been in an almost trancelike state ever since Mark had been attacked. Aubrey was nowhere to be found.

"I had another idea," Lukas said. "Did you notice how all the personnel working in the communications center went quiet when we walked in and didn't start talking again until we were taken to that soundproof room in the corner?"

"I thought they were just being polite," Javi said sincerely.

"That's one possibility," Lukas replied, trying to keep the snark out of his voice. "Or they could have been waiting until we were out of earshot so they could go back to discussing stuff that we weren't supposed to hear about."

"Like what?"

"That's what I want to find out," Lukas said. "And that's why we're going back there."

Javi looked at him with a mix of shock and skepticism. "Are you joking?" he asked incredulously. "Did you see how those soldiers reacted when Mike slapped at that nurse? How do you think they'll respond if we try to sneak out of here in direct violation of Colonel Hunt's orders?"

"If we get caught, we can just act clueless," Lukas insisted.

"Is that before or after they shoot us? No way, man. I'm not risking pissing off these guys on your long shot hunch that we're being kept in the dark about some deep, dark secret."

"You're not suspicious?" Lukas asked.

"Not suspicious enough to get thrown in the brig or tossed over the wall," Javi said.

"You really think they'd do either of those things?" Lukas challenged, growing annoyed.

"It's not a chance I want to take."

Before he could stop himself, Lukas blurted out the comment he'd been trying to avoid. "You're all about not taking chances, aren't you, Javi?" he asked, sounding more bitter than he'd intended to.

"What the hell is that supposed to mean?"

"You know what it means. You're never willing to rock the boat. For example, you make a big deal out of being out, but does anyone outside of camp know even you're gay?"

Javi stared at him, dumbfounded, for several seconds before finding his voice. "Is this the moment you've chosen to call me out for not being loud and proud enough, Mr. Rich White Kid from the SoCal Beach Town? I didn't realize I was such a disappointment to you."

"That's not what I mean, Javi," Lukas insisted, backtracking quickly. "I just mean that, if there was ever a time to take a risk, this is it."

"Really?" Javi countered. "Because I kind of think this is the worst time to take a risk, when we could, you know, get shot for it."

They stared at each other silently, neither willing to concede. Lukas looked at his closest friend in the world, whose face was screwed up in wounded frustration, and decided to take a step back.

"I'm sorry I jumped down your throat," he said quietly, without excuses.

Javi's face unscrewed a bit. "I forgive you."

Lukas waited a beat, until he was sure they were cool, before continuing. "But we're not going to get shot," he insisted, trying to steer the conversation back to his original plan and away from more sensitive topics. "In fact, once we get out of this hangar, I think it will be mostly clear sailing."

"Get out of the hangar?" Javi repeated. "How do you propose we do that? Don't we need key card access to get anywhere? I see everyone around here swiping them to get places."

"They only need them to get from the door of this hangar to the rest of the facility. All the rooms beyond that were unlocked. Maybe they were more hardcore about that before. But I think that, with everything going on, they just want people to have quick access to everywhere they need to go. And as to getting shot, as long as we don't go around slapping at people, I don't think that a couple of curious teenagers are at the top of their list of concerns right now. I bet we could just slip into the hallway after someone else enters the hangar."

"Okay, when should we do it?" Javi asked, reluctantly warming to the idea despite himself.

"I say now. All it takes is for a few of those Furies to get over the fence and people are going to start turning in seconds. Let's not wait for that to happen."

"I'm okay with that," Javi agreed, setting aside his hurt feelings much quicker than Lukas could have. "Just one question—is that what we're calling them, Furies? I just wanted to know if that's our official designation from now on."

"I like it better than zombies, which doesn't feel real, or what Colonel West called them, 'flesh sacks.'"

"Yeah," Javi said. "That was kind of offensive. We're talking about some of our friends here. Maybe he hasn't lost anyone yet so it's not personal to him."

"Javi, I think everyone's lost someone, even if they don't have proof yet."

They both considered all the people they hadn't been able to reach earlier and knew that West had likely done the same hours ago, almost certainly without success. Lukas remembered the surprise in the man's voice when he'd answered Aubrey's call from the lodge. Until that moment, he'd surely assumed she was lost.

"Let's do this," he said, shaking himself out of the reverie. "Time may be short."

*

It was easier than they'd expected.

There was only a skeleton crew in the hangar, and they all looked like they'd rather be anywhere else. Lukas and Javi walked over to the restrooms, which were near the door to the hallway, and waited inside the men's room with the door slightly ajar so they could see out.

After five minutes, a nurse returned from the hallway carrying several cups of coffee. As the door closed, Lukas darted out, grabbed it before it locked, and held it open for Javi to zip past him. Then he followed behind. The whole thing took less than five seconds. Now they stood uncertainly in the long hallway that led to the rest of the administration building.

"Let's start moving," Lukas said, starting down the hall. "Act like we're supposed to be here. As long as we look confident, I don't think anyone will pay attention to us."

"Okay," Javi said as he joined him. "But if we get shot dead, I'm blaming you."

"Tough but fair," Lukas replied as they walked purposefully along the hallway, past Strategy Room D, until they reached the communications center.

"I thought this would be harder," Javi noted. "I figured we'd need invisibility cloaks or something."

"Don't get cocky," Lukas warned as he reached for the door. "Like I said, those things outside may have diverted their attention a little bit."

"Hold on," Javi said, grabbing his arm. "If we just walk in like we did before, they're going to clam up again."

"You're right," Lukas agreed, stumped.

"Let's loop around," Javi suggested. "I noticed the room where they had us make our calls had an exterior door. If it's unlocked, too, we can get in that way and listen from inside. They won't even know we're there."

Lukas agreed it was a good idea. They followed the hallway around, careful to look like they had a firm destination in mind, until it split in two. Javi chose the left path, which seemed to circle around the communications center. Sure enough, it led to a series of doors, all marked as conference rooms.

He opened the first one, peeked in, then looked back and nodded to Lukas. They stepped inside the darkened room, and Lukas immediately recognized it. There was the same bank of hard line phones along the back wall that they'd used to try to reach family. The door to the communications center was partly open, and they could hear the loud murmuring of multiple voices. They scurried over quietly and listened in.

At first it was difficult to discern any words among the multiple overlapping voices. But after a few seconds, Lukas realized it didn't matter whom he listened to. They were all essentially saying the same thing—the base was being evacuated.

After several minutes of eavesdropping, the basics of what was going on became clear. It had been determined that, even if the outer walls held, there were just too many Furies outside. Estimates were that, by climbing over each other, they would overtop the wall by tomorrow morning. The base commander had given the order to evacuate at dawn.

Lukas and Javi retreated to the conference room and closed the door.

"This is really bad," Javi muttered. "If the army can't hold a fortified base, I don't know where we could go that's safe."

"They must have some idea of where they plan to evacuate to," Lukas said. "Did you hear any mention of that?"

"No. But I did hear someone say there are limited air resources so most troops would be deployed via ground transportation."

"That brings up another question," Lukas said reluctantly. "If there's an involved plan to abandon the base, why hasn't anyone told us about it?"

"Maybe they've just been too busy," Javi offered hopefully.

"Maybe," Lukas conceded. "But Colonel West could have mentioned it in that meeting. If you remember, when he talked about the camp potentially being invaded, he only vaguely mentioned 'contingency plans.' That would have been the perfect time to bring it up. But he didn't, which was one of a few sketchy things he said, or rather didn't say. And when we all came in here to make our calls earlier, they shut the soundproof door. Why would they do that?"

"To give us privacy?"

"Is that what you really think, Javi?" Lukas asked, his eyebrows raised.

"What do *you* think?"

Lukas hesitated, reluctant to speak his suspicion aloud. "I don't think we're part of their plans," he finally answered. "I think they're just going to leave us here."

CHAPTER 28

They were heading back down the split hallway to where it merged again when Javi stopped suddenly. He grabbed Lukas's shirt and yanked him back around the corner.

"What?" Lukas demanded, stumbling a bit.

"I just saw the colonel in the other hallway. I was worried he was going to run into us. But he stepped into that last room there."

Lukas looked at the sign outside the room Javi was pointing at. It read "MedLab." He knew it was probably unwise, but he made a snap decision. "Why don't you go back to the hangar?" he suggested. "I'll be there soon."

"You're not going to call him out, are you?" Javi asked, horrified. "He seems like the kind of person who might shoot you if you rub him the wrong way."

"No way," Lukas assured him. "That guy isn't going to sweat anything I have to say to him. But maybe I can learn a little more if I play dumb and ask a few questions."

"I think you're wasting your time," Javi said. "And you're risking him getting pissed off and snapping you in half."

"Thanks for the support, buddy. I'll be okay. Just go back. I'll be there soon. And Javi, don't mention what we heard, okay? We need to figure out a plan before we freak everyone out."

"Couldn't agree more," Javi said before darting back down the hallway toward the hangar.

When he was gone, Lukas headed in the other direction. He moved toward the MedLab with what he hoped looked like self-assurance. He reached for the door handle as he looked into the room through the small square window at eye level.

Colonel West was indeed in there. He was standing with his back to the door and was speaking to someone seated across from him. As his weight shifted, the other person came into view. It was Aubrey.

Lukas ducked down quickly, hoping she hadn't seen him. Realizing a teenage boy crouched outside a medical lab on a military base might look suspicious, he straightened up. As casually as possible, he ambled over to the door for the room next to MedLab and confidently turned the handle, as if he had every expectation that it would open. It did.

He quickly stepped inside. Looking around, he saw that he was in what appeared to be a classroom-style lab. There was a door in the back corner connecting his room to the MedLab. He went over and found that it was closed.

As delicately as possible, he turned the handle, praying that the efficient army staff would keep every joint and hinge in this place properly oiled. Apparently they did, as it opened silently. He only propped it a crack, just enough to hear the conversation inside. The colonel was mid-sentence.

"… so there's no point in giving it to them if they can't come with us."

"Then let them come, sir," Aubrey demanded emphatically.

"I've already told you," Colonel West replied, clearly exasperated. "I can't get authorization for that. The only reason they let me send that transport to Hollow Valley was because *you* were there. It was an outrageous use of resources that served no strategic purpose. But they allowed it, as a favor to me. And they have consented to let you come to the secondary base because they know I would resign my commission on the spot if they didn't. But they are not going to permit ten additional civilians who can't defend themselves to go with us. The commander isn't willing to risk one army life unless it's for a legitimate purpose."

"First of all—" Aubrey began, her voice getting that peel-the-paint-off-the-walls tone that Lukas recognized.

"First of all, *sir*," Colonel West interrupted.

"First of all, sir," she repeated, only slightly chastened, "those ten civilians managed to make it up a boulder-covered hill with dozens of Furies chasing them. So they're not helpless babies. And second, I thought the whole point of the US military was to protect the citizens of this country."

There was a brief moment of silence, but Lukas couldn't gauge the colonel's reaction because his back was to him.

"Aubrey," he finally replied, clearly trying to remain calm, "if there is no military left, then how are we supposed to protect anyone? We have to be strategic in our decision making."

"That's a cop out and you know it."

"Listen, I'm not going to argue with you," he said, the calm quickly leaking away. "We did the best we could for your little camp friends. We can't be responsible for them any longer. Now they're on their own."

Aubrey stood up, her body still and her jaw set. "You haven't done the best you can for my *little camp friends*. Giving them the vaccine would at least let them have a fighting chance."

"We don't even know if it works! A vaccine usually takes twelve to eighteen months to develop. This was reconfigured from the remnants of an existing antiserum over just hours. It hasn't been properly tested."

"What's the harm?" she insisted. "You gave it to me."

"That was out of an abundance of caution. Besides, there are a limited number of doses."

"That's not true," she argued. "I saw lots more in the refrigerator. And I'm willing to bet everyone on this base has already gotten vaccinated."

"Aubrey West, I'm not debating this any longer," West replied emphatically. "As of tomorrow morning, your friends are on their own. We will leave them with food and water and secure the hangar as best we can. You need to be out of there by 0600 hours. I'll have someone wake you and escort you out. I don't want you drawing suspicion by leaving when they're awake. Evac begins promptly at dawn, which will be at approximately 0653 hours. Now please return to the hangar. You've been gone a while and I don't want you to have to answer too many questions."

"But, Dad . . ." she pleaded, calling him by a title Lukas had never heard her use.

"You're dismissed," Colonel West said definitively, then walked out himself.

As the colonel quickly left the MedLab, Lukas skulked away from the connecting door, making sure even his shadow wasn't visible. He remained in the adjoining room until Aubrey had left, too.

His head was swimming in a sea of churning thoughts. Eventually, he reminded himself that his presence would be missed in the hangar and decided to return. But he had no idea what he would say or do when he got back.

CHAPTER 29

Amid all the madness, the group at least got one semblance of normalcy: pizza for dinner.

As everyone sat around three card tables all pulled together to make a big one, Lukas silently noted that something close to routine had settled over the group. Lonnie and Trevor were telling dirty jokes and loving the fact that none of the counselors—not even Martie—were stopping them. Jamie and Javi were having a contest to see who could stuff the biggest slice into their mouth. Even Emily had consented to take a few bites.

Lukas stood a little apart from the others, appreciating but not fully able to participate in their valiant attempt to pretend like the world wasn't crumbling around them. Other than him, the only people who were visibly out of sorts were Mike who had an understandable permanent glower and Aubrey who smiled at the shenanigans but didn't participate. Lukas felt like they all had good cause for their reserve.

A little earlier, Javi had tried to get him to reveal what had happened in the MedLab. But at the time, Lukas didn't feel like he could grasp it yet, much less explain it, and begged off. But now, with dinner coming to a close and the evening creeping toward them, he felt obligated to reveal at least some of what he'd learned to the group.

However, with two guards wandering by the table periodically, he knew he couldn't be forthcoming. After a moment, he thought of an idea, one that would serve dual purposes. He stood up and approached the closest soldier who eyed him warily.

"Could I ask a favor?" Lukas said, trying to appear as open-faced and transparent as possible.

"What?" the guard asked skeptically.

"We haven't really had a chance to mourn our friends yet. Five people died on that hill today. I was hoping you and your colleague might allow us a few minutes of privacy. We'd like to have some kind of small personal memorial. Could you give us some space for a bit?"

The soldier looked briefly conflicted. But after seeing the pleading look in Lukas's eyes, he nodded and motioned for the second guard to join him on the other side of the hangar.

Lukas asked for the group's attention as they walked away. "Guys, I'm sorry to interrupt . . ." he said, waiting for the chatter to die down. When it did, he continued. "I was hoping we could take a moment of silence to remember the people we lost today, not just those who didn't make it up that hill, but also those who were turned against us through no fault of their own. I don't know about the rest of you, but I'm still having trouble processing what happened today. And while I don't understand it, I don't want to let the insanity around us prevent us from thinking about how special all those folks were and how it's our duty to fight on in their memory."

"Even Todd's?" Aubrey muttered bitterly under her breath.

Those closest to her looked confused by the comment. Only the survivors from the last group ascending the hill—Aubrey, Martie, Lonnie, Caleb, and Lukas—had seen Todd push his own camper into harm's way to protect himself.

Lukas felt the same ambivalence toward his former counselor but didn't want to sully the moment by addressing what had happened. Pretending not to notice the comment, he continued. "Could we all lower our heads?" he asked.

Everyone nodded their assent. Jules lowered hers first, and without a word, everyone else followed suit. Lukas did the same. But after about ten seconds, with his head still down, he began to speak softly.

"Please keep your heads lowered, guys. I have to tell you something else and I don't want the soldiers to hear. I'm sorry to use a moment intended as a memorial for this, but it's that important. Please don't react in any obvious way to what I'm about to tell you. We don't want to draw suspicion."

"Go ahead," Trevor said impatiently, his head bowed.

"The people here haven't been totally honest with us," Lukas said, deciding to divulge only some of the information he had learned rather than provide a data dump that might overwhelm them. "Javi and I snuck out a while ago and listened in to what they were saying in the communications center. The base commander has determined that the outer walls won't hold. He expects the Furies to overtop them by tomorrow morning and has ordered an evacuation at dawn."

Everyone was quiet for a moment, taking it in.

"How is an evacuation a bad thing?" Jamie eventually asked in a hushed whisper, her head down. "At least they know what's going on and have a timetable, right?"

"That's not the point," Javi piped in. "No one has told us this, despite having a perfect opportunity at that meeting. We're not part of their plans."

"That seems like a huge conclusion to jump to," Lonnie argued. "Maybe they hadn't made any firm decisions at the time of the meeting."

"Maybe," Lukas conceded, though he was skeptical. "But Javi and I overheard this hours ago. They've had lots of time to update us, and they still haven't done it."

"They've been kind of busy, Lukas," Caleb noted.

"What do you think, Aubrey?" Emily asked quietly, addressing her bunkmate with a deference Lukas had never heard before. "Maybe you could check with your dad to see what's going on."

Aubrey looked up and met Lukas's eyes. He could tell from her expression what she intended to say. "Amen," she intoned loudly before saying anything else.

Everyone realized what she was doing and repeated her amen. The soldiers heard the word but stayed at the other end of the hangar, apparently uncomfortable intruding immediately after the group had finished their makeshift service.

"I don't need to talk to my dad," she began, "because I already know—what Lukas said is true."

At first no one responded.

"How do you know that?" Mike finally demanded, his voice raw with emotion.

"I'll tell you," she assured him. "But you need to remember not to yell or freak out. Trust me—you're going to want to. But if you do, those guards are going to come over here and any chance to keep what we say private will be gone."

"We get it," Trevor said edgily. "Just tell us."

Aubrey sighed heavily, then began. "I know because my father told me straight out. They are planning a full base evacuation at dawn. They would do it in the middle of the night if they could. But because of satellite issues, they need daylight to operate effectively. But anything later than dawn and they worry those things will get inside. They're shipping out to a secondary base that's been set up on an oil rig in the Gulf of Mexico."

"What about us?" Jamie implored.

"They're leaving you," she said with bluntness that even Lukas found surprising. "Apparently you offer no tactical value. They believe that risking military assets to protect civilians who can't serve the larger mission is a waste of resources. You're to be left here in the hangar, along with some rations."

"I couldn't help but notice that you keep saying 'you,'" Mike accused.

"That's right," Aubrey said, looking straight back at him. "My father has gotten authorization for me to go with them. But not for any of you."

Nobody spoke for a moment.

"Maybe we could change his mind—" Jules finally said, trying to refocus the group away from glaring at the one person with a way out.

"It won't work," Aubrey interrupted. "It's not up to him. And besides, he's on board with it."

In the long silence that followed, Lukas debated whether to bring up the vaccines. He didn't want to confront Aubrey about it. She was already in an impossible position. Besides, she'd fought for them in the MedLab with her dad.

But that didn't change the fact that there was a potential form of protection in a refrigerator only several hundred feet away. If they were all going to be stuck here, they needed any additional defense they could get. He was about to suggest a plan to steal the necessary number of doses for each of them when Aubrey spoke again.

"There's more."

CHAPTER 30

"Jeez, you mean things can get worse?" Trevor asked incredulously.

"They can always get worse," Emily replied. "What is it? Is your dad ordering that we all be thrown to the Furies as a distraction while they escape?"

"Hey!" Jules hissed. "Cut it out. This isn't Aubrey's fault. She's telling us this stuff when she didn't have to. She could have just left us, and we'd never have known any of this. Now we at least understand the situation. Can you appreciate how hard it must have been for her to share this when she was probably ordered not to?"

"Is that true?" Mike demanded. "Did your dad tell you not to say anything?"

Aubrey nodded, her face a mix of guilt and obstinacy. In the quiet that followed, Lukas notice a strange humming sound, almost like cicadas chirping in a lower register. He was about to comment on it when Martie did.

"Does anyone else hear that?" she asked.

"I've been hearing it for a while actually," Javi noted. "I thought it was a helicopter or something. But that's not it."

"It's them," Lonnie said quietly.

"Who?" Javi asked.

"The Furies. It's that grunting sound they make. It's just that there are so many of them out there now that all the voices together sound like . . . something else. They must be close to clearing the walls."

"We can't worry about that right now," Caleb said sharply. "Let's focus on what we can control. Aubrey, you were saying you had more info to share."

"Yes, I was. This is actually a tiny bit of good news, if you can get past the fact that you weren't supposed to know about it. There's a vaccine."

Lukas stared at her, stunned and impressed that she was revealing this, though he wasn't sure what the point was.

"There is?" Martie asked, sounding hopeful.

"They have no idea if it works," Aubrey cautioned. "It was apparently developed on the fly in the last twenty-four hours. My father says it's a reformulation of an existing antiserum. The theory is that, if you get bitten, even if you're infected, it will prevent you from becoming a Fury. But it's just a theory; it hasn't been tested. And of course, none of you are supposed to get it, which is why I had to steal it."

Despite the instruction not to react to anything, a few people gasped involuntarily. One of the guards glanced over briefly before losing interest in them.

"Where is it?" Martie asked.

"Under the blanket on my cot," Aubrey said. "Each dose is already prepared in mist form. All you have to is inhale it through the nose."

"Don't they have to be refrigerated?" Lonnie asked.

"They were, as a precaution. And each dose is individually wrapped in a cold pack. But my father said they don't have any proof that refrigeration is necessary. Of course, like I said, they also don't have any proof that the vaccine works either, so draw your own conclusions."

Lukas looked at the group. From their eager expressions, it was clear that some had already determined that they should take the vaccine right away. But a few, notably Mike, Emily, Jamie, and Trevor, looked suspiciously at Aubrey, as if her lack of candor earlier put her current credibility in question. Lukas had to admit that, if he hadn't overheard her conversation with her father, he might be in that camp himself.

"So how should we do this?" Jules asked, obviously not troubled by those doubts. "I assume the sooner we take it the better, to let it circulate in our systems."

"I was thinking I would provide everyone with a dose and you could go into the restroom so you won't be seen."

"Then let's go," Emily said anxiously, apparently setting aside her doubts about Aubrey's credibility. "Who knows when those things will start overtopping the walls?"

"Before we do that," Caleb suggested, "I think we should take advantage of the guards being out of earshot to come up with a larger plan."

"A larger plan?" Jamie repeated.

"Yeah, we need to know how we're going to get out of here when this base is evacuated. We're sitting ducks if we stay in this hangar. They'll get in eventually, and even if we're vaccinated so that we don't turn into those things, it won't protect us from getting ripped to shreds."

"It sounds like you have an idea," Lukas said, recognizing the tone in his brother's voice.

"Kind of," Caleb said. "I have a thought for where we might go if we could actually find a way out of here."

"Where?" Javi asked eagerly.

"Our grandparents' house," he said, nodding at Lukas. "It's literally three or four miles from here. Their place is in a gated community near the top of a hill. As long as the house hasn't been hit yet, we could lock it down and stay there until we come up with a more permanent plan. I know how to get there and can drive us, assuming we can find a vehicle."

"I have a better idea," Mike interjected.

Even before he said it, Lukas knew where this was headed. So did Caleb apparently, as evidenced by the look of pained resignation on his face.

"What's that?" his brother asked reluctantly.

"We go to my dad's precinct," Mike said. "It's only a half dozen exits down the highway. And once we get there, it will be way more secure than some house with a gate at the guard house. There'll be a ton of weapons and probably a bunch of cops holed up there, too."

No one spoke for a moment, clearly reluctant to challenge Mike's passion.

"But you couldn't reach your dad in the communications center," Caleb finally reminded him gently.

"What difference does that make?" Mike protested, his voice rising. "You couldn't get hold of your grandparents either. That didn't stop you from suggesting their place."

"Keep your voice down, Mike," Martie chastened. "We don't need those soldiers getting curious."

"I get it, Mike," Caleb assured him, adopting his best warm but authoritative counselor tone. "Under normal circumstances, going to a police station makes the most sense. But six exits farther into the city is a major trek in this situation. And you saw the freeway when we flew in. It was clogged with stopped cars. There's no guarantee we could even get there. We don't want to get stuck out in the open on the street with those things everywhere. My grandparents' house is just one exit away. I guarantee we can access it, even if we have to drive across front lawns to get there."

Mike seemed momentarily uncertain.

But then Jamie jumped in. "How is it better to go to some unprotected house just one exit away from thousands of Furies all gathered together than to a police station designed to be secure? I say we go with the safer choice."

Lukas didn't know how to respond to this. It was like Jamie was willfully ignoring everything his brother had said.

"There's no guarantee it's any safer," Jules said, speaking for the first time. "Logic suggests that a military base like this would be pretty secure. But it's about to get overrun."

"I want to see my dad!" Mike blurted out, his voice echoing throughout the hangar. The soldiers all turned and looked at him. One of them looked like he was about to come over.

"He's just upset," Martie said loudly, hoping to assuage their obvious misgivings.

Neither Caleb nor Jules responded, apparently not wanting to exacerbate the situation. Lukas doubted anything they might say would change Mike's mind anyway.

"Regardless of where we decide to go," Aubrey said, trying to move past the disagreement, "I might have an idea on how to secure a vehicle, as well as how to snag a few weapons. I know where they keep both."

"Well, let's hear it," Lukas said, also eager to get everyone back on the same page. "Time is not on our side."

Two hours later, after they'd all been vaccinated and the guards on duty looked especially tired, they put their plan into action.

Over the course of several minutes, Lukas, Javi, and Caleb went to the men's room. The next time a staffer entered the hangar, Emily played her prescribed role. Without much coaxing required, she "succumbed" to a meltdown over Mark's death and ran into the women's bathroom, followed by the other girls. While everyone's attention was on them, Lukas, Javi, and Caleb escaped into the hall through the unlocked door as the staffer passed by, much as Lukas had done with Javi earlier.

As they watched through a small window in the door, Emily returned to the cot area, still upset and being tended to by Martie and Jamie, as well as Lonnie, Trevor, and Mike, who all gathered around supportively. While they all returned to the cots, Jules and Aubrey snuck out of the women's restroom and over to the hangar door, which was opened for them by the waiting brothers and Javi.

It all worked surprisingly well, though Lukas suspected that was more because of the guards' exhaustion and lack of interest than because of their group's collective cleverness.

Everyone who'd snuck out quickly followed Aubrey down the deserted hallway until they got to a room marked simply "Supplies." They entered and were met by rows of uniforms, all hung neatly on hangers.

"Find your size, Caleb," Aubrey instructed. "The rest of you come with me."

She led them to a small map on the wall with an "X" marking their current location. "This is the motor pool," she said, pointing to a large space down the hall and to the right. "I wouldn't be surprised if it's busier than usual, if they're gassing up vehicles for the evacuation. You'll need to find a truck at the very back of the line for this to work. We don't want anyone noticing what you've done. You all remember the rest of the plan?"

"Of course," Javi assured her.

"Make it believable. If they suspect anything, nothing else we do will matter. Got it?"

"Don't worry about us, Aubrey," Jules assured her. "We'll get it done. Are you and Caleb good?"

They all looked over and saw him finish buttoning the shirt of the uniform he'd selected. It seemed to fit perfectly.

"Remind me why he's going with you and I'm going with these two?" Javi asked.

"Because he's more believable as a soldier who might legitimately be allowed to check out multiple weapons. And you're more believable as a pathetic goober in need of assistance."

"Fair enough," Javi said, grinning broadly.

"I'm glad you're enjoying yourself, Mendez," she said, trying to fight off a smile of her own. "Make the most of it, because this is the closest you're ever going to get to playing G.I. Joe."

"I swear, Aubrey West," Javi replied, "if I was into girls, you'd totally be my type—so dynamic!"

"All right, you two," Jules piped in. "Let's get going. Those guards in the hangar might eventually realize we're gone, and we want to have all this done before then."

"Agreed," Caleb said, walking over and looking totally convincing as a member of the US Army. "We don't have a second to waste. We'll see you back in the hangar as soon as this is done. We ready?"

"Ready or not, this is happening," Aubrey said, her expression completely serious again. "Let's go."

She and Caleb walked out of the door. The other three waited thirty seconds, then followed. Jules stepped out first, then Javi, and finally Lukas.

He turned off the supply room light and stepped out into the hallway as he reminded himself to breathe.

CHAPTER 31

Just as Aubrey had warned, the motor pool was busy.

Initially, Lukas was concerned that one of the many soldiers running about might call them out. But it quickly became clear that no one cared about the three teenagers shuffling hesitantly among them. Despite Colonel West's warning to them, security had taken a distant backseat to expediency.

They moved as unobtrusively as possible to the back of the massive garage, passing rows of trucks, Jeeps, and Humvees until they saw what they were looking for. At the very end of one of the rows was a smaller flatbed truck with a canvas dome cover. It looked like it could comfortably hold all eleven people in their group.

The three of them shared an unspoken nod before Jules and Javi walked toward the far end of the garage. Lukas waited until they were halfway there before he followed Aubrey's preplanned instructions and began to approach the small closet in the corner marked "Information Center." There was no one around, but he was still reluctant to enter until the others had made their move.

"Hi," he heard Jules say in her most inviting voice, her usually mild Texas accent suddenly flowering into a honeyed twang. "Can you please help us?"

That was his cue. He stepped inside the closet and began rifling through a series of plastic signs attached to metal hooks. He found what he was looking for before the soldier Jules addressed had finished his sentence.

"What's the problem?" the young man said, trying to sound peeved but not pulling it off after seeing who he was talking to. "Are you even supposed to be in this area?"

"I don't think so," Jules said, her voice taking on the tenor of warm molasses. "We were told to go to the infirmary, but I think we got turned around. My little brother here isn't feeling too well."

Lukas stepped out of the closet and looked in their direction. As discussed, Jules and Javi had positioned themselves facing him so that they could see what he was doing and the three soldiers they were speaking to, who had their backs to him, couldn't.

Not discussed, but clearly part of Jules's unspoken plan, was making herself into eye candy to help distract the soldiers. Lukas saw that she had tucked her t-shirt into her jeans shorts so that her chest was more prominent than usual. And she was leaning in towards the soldiers in a way that made the phrase "come hither" pop into Lukas's head.

"What's wrong with him?" the first soldier asked distractedly about Javi as Lukas moved next to the locker that Aubrey had told him would have the vehicle keys.

"He has diabetes and he's been showing signs that his blood sugar is too low," Jules answered, rubbing her "brother's" back sympathetically. "He's been slurring his speech and having trouble walking. The last time this happened he started having seizures."

Javi looked over at Lukas who nodded at him that the time had come. Without a second's hesitation, Javi began to shake.

"I don't feel so good," he muttered and dropped to one knee.

"Oh God, I think it's happening again," Jules said in a worried hushed voice.

Just then, Javi toppled on his side and his whole body began convulsing. His eyes were clenched tight.

"What do we do?" the second of the three guards asked, panicked.

"Get a sugary drink," Jules ordered. "And you two help keep him from hurting himself."

They'd discussed this before, and even though no one was sure if that was the right medical move, it sounded credible, so they decided to go with it. As the second soldier ran off to the refrigerator and the other two bent down to help Javi, Lukas did his part.

He opened the key locker and searched for the one with the license plate tag that matched the truck they'd chosen. There were at least two dozen sets of keys and it was taking him longer than he liked to find the right one.

"Here's some orange juice," he heard the guard who'd run to get it say.

Glancing over, Lukas saw Jules pouring a bit into Javi's hard-to-access mouth.

"Is it working?" the soldier asked after a few seconds.

Lukas held his hand out with his thumb pointed down. He couldn't seem to find the matching key.

"Not yet," he heard Jules say. "Hold his head still so I can get more into him."

Lukas tried to ignore the scuffling behind him as he searched for the right key. Finally he saw it, near the bottom of the locker with the tag facing the wrong way. He snagged it, shoved it in his shorts pocket, and hurried over to the truck with two signs in his hands, both of which read "Out of service."

He hung one of them on the driver's door handle and was just placing the other on the front grill when one of the soldiers desperately asked, "What about now?"

Jules looked up, pretending to focus on the soldier but really looking beyond him to Lukas. He gave her the thumbs-up sign.

"I think it might be working," she said. "It feels like he's settling down."

Conveniently, at that exact moment, Javi's shaking began to subside slightly before coming to a complete stop over the next few seconds. As planned, Lukas rushed over when Javi finally opened his eyes.

"Hey, guys," he said as he ran over. "I got turned around looking for you. Is everything okay?"

"Javi had a seizure," Jules told him. "But these men helped him out."

"Thank goodness," Lukas said, sounding as relieved as possible. "How are you doing, buddy?"

"I think I'm okay now," Javi croaked, sitting up with the assistance of his "sister."

"Do you still want to go to the infirmary?" Jules asked.

"No. I think that juice did the trick. Maybe we go back to the hangar so I can lie down for a bit."

The soldiers helped him to his feet, and he swung his arms over Jules's and Lukas's shoulders.

"Thanks for your help," he said, offering a weak smile.

"No problem," the first soldier said, giving him a pat on the back.

"Yes, you gentlemen are just the sweetest," Jules added, laying it on extra thick.

All three soldiers stared at her, unable to tear their eyes away.

After an uncomfortably long pause, the third one finally managed to find his voice. "Sure thing," he said to Jules before turning to Javi and adding, "Take it easy, little man."

The three of them shuffled slowly to the motor pool exit but were still close enough to hear the second solider mutter under his breath. "I feel bad. Seizures are going to seem like a walk in the park for them in a few hours."

"Yeah, I especially feel bad for her," the first soldier said. "What a waste. But there's nothing we can do about it, so let's get back to work."

"Maybe there is something," the third soldier said before yelling, "Hold up."

Lukas felt his stomach tighten as he heard him jog over behind the three of them. They all turned around as he approached. For the first time, Lukas looked at the guy closely.

He was big, broad shouldered, and thick, with close-cropped blond hair and a tanned face that suggested he spent a lot of time outdoors. The concerned look from before had been replaced by something more predatory.

"What's your name, big sister?" he asked with faux familiarity.

"Becky," Jules lied, the name spilling out so easily that Lukas suspected this wasn't the first time she'd used it.

"Well, Becky, I'm sure you're aware that things are about to get pretty hairy soon. I was wondering if you wanted to take advantage of this last little bit of down time to . . . de-stress a bit?"

Lukas stared at the guy, stunned at his bravado.

Jules recovered far quicker. "Thanks for the offer, but I'm good," she said, feigning a lack of understanding. "Besides, I have to take care of my brother."

"It looks like his buddy there can handle that," the soldier said, nodding at Lukas as he smiled smarmily. "Come on; we could all be dead in a few hours. Let's help each other enjoy the time we have left."

"She said she's good," Lukas said loudly, standing up straight. "What part of that don't you get?"

The soldier gave him a dismissive smirk. "Now, young fella, is that any way to talk to a man who just helped you out?" he asked condescendingly as he took a step forward, the smile dropping from his lips.

Lukas knew he was in over his head, but he didn't care. He felt a strong urge to take a swing at the guy. "It seems like this is how I have to talk to get it through your thick head," he answered as he removed Javi's arm from around his shoulder and stepped forward to meet the soldier.

The man smiled again, this time with an overt menace he'd managed to hide before. Lukas noticed that the other two soldiers had conveniently moved to the other side of the motor pool where they could pretend not to hear the conversation.

The blond guy leaned in close and growled at him. "Maybe I break you in half and show the little lady the good time she didn't know she wanted."

Lukas rose on the balls of feet, ready to leap at the guy. But just before he did, Jules stepped forward, still "supporting" Javi's weight. "Conduct unbecoming or rape?" she asked briskly.

The solider turned back to her, confused. "What?" he asked.

"Oh, I'm just wondering if you want to be charged with conduct unbecoming or rape?" she asked with a steeliness in her voice that was new to Lukas. "Maybe both? Because I'm pretty sure abandoning your post while on duty to assault a seventeen-year-old girl fits the description of both of those crimes. But if you think I'm wrong, we can consult with Colonel West who brought us here and promised to keep us safe. Would you like to explain your current behavior to him, soldier?"

The guy stared at her with a mix of shock and contempt. After a long pause, he replied. "No," he muttered under his breath.

"Then I suggest you back the hell off, asshole. Otherwise I'm about three seconds from yelling 'rape' and having a bunch soldiers come over here who aren't as scared of you as your buddies seem to be."

The soldier glared back at her with surly defiance.

"Three," Jules began, "two—"

"Okay, okay," he said, holding up his hands. "I was just kidding around anyway. You don't have to be such a bitch about it."

"You're the bitch," she snarled back, her cheeks flushing as her eyes bore into him. "Now walk away."

After the man spun on his heel and trudged back to his buddies, Jules looked over at Lukas and Javi who had thrown his arm back over his friend's shoulder.

"Let's go," she said quickly.

Only when they were through the exit door did Lukas and Jules untangle themselves from Javi.

"Everyone okay?" Jules asked, her face now back to its normal shade.

"We're good," Lukas assured her. "How are you?"

"Fine, thanks to your chivalrous actions," she replied, sounding mostly sincere.

"Are you serious?" he said, having none of it. "I was about to get my butt kicked. You're the badass."

Jules smiled uncomfortably. She clearly wanted to move on. "Don't tell Caleb, okay?" she requested.

Both guys nodded in acquiescence. They all stood quietly for a second before Javi broke into a big smile.

"Don't get too cocky, Juliana Goldenson," he said in mock protest. "Your sisterly skills could use some work. You got orange juice all over my face and it dribbled down my neck. Now I'm going to be sticky."

"Sorry," she retorted, grinning. "I was just trying to keep up with your Oscar-worthy performance there, Pacino."

"You were emoting pretty hardcore yourself," Lukas noted, joining in. "I thought I'd stumbled into the middle of a performance of *A Streetcar Named Desire*, only with short shorts."

"I *have* always depended on the kindness of strangers," Jules replied, batting her eyes hammily. "Was I convincing?"

"You seemed to have those soldiers in the palm of your hand," Lukas said, regretting the comment immediately.

"I might have been a little too convincing," she replied softly.

"I know you had me all hot and bothered," Javi cracked, trying to lighten the mood.

They all laughed, Lukas louder than necessary. He was slightly embarrassed to admit that, in the middle of her Southern belle routine, she'd had an unintended effect on him. He could feel his face flushing at the memory and wondered if she noticed.

"Everything go okay on your end?" Javi asked him pointedly as they hurried down the hall. Lukas could sense that he was clearly trying to change the subject to help out his scarlet-faced friend. "I felt like I was shaking uncontrollably for a long time there."

"I had a little trouble finding the key," Lukas admitted. "But we're all good now."

They were rounding the corner to the last stretch of hallway when they suddenly heard footsteps. They only had a second to retreat before two people in uniform emerged from a side corridor. One of them was Corporal Daugherty.

"Oh no," Javi muttered. "We're screwed."

CHAPTER 32

They listened as Daugherty and another soldier hurried in their direction.

Lukas considered suggesting they run but realized they'd never get out of sight in time. If the petite corporal who served as Colonel West's right-hand woman saw them and subsequently started poking around, everything they'd just done would be for nothing. He was debating how to explain their presence to her when the footsteps stopped.

"Who was the idiot who moved them to a room without a working lock?" he heard Daugherty demand.

"I'm sorry, ma'am," the soldier with her replied. "We needed to put them in a lab environment. The brig wasn't workable anymore. I think the lock worked initially. It may just be jammed. If it helps, the interior cells are still secure."

"I'm not worried about them getting out, private," Daugherty chastised. "I'm concerned about people getting *in*."

"Yes, ma'am."

"I'm late for a status meeting with Colonel West so here's what we're going to do. You're going to go to the maintenance department instead of just calling them, and you are going to personally bring back a tech who can fix this lock. After you return, you will not leave this spot until you're relieved. Are we clear?"

"Yes, ma'am," the soldier said. "But that's clear across the base. It'll take at least ten minutes."

"Then you better get moving. When you return, you will confirm that the issue is resolved, then send the tech to inform me personally in Colonel West's office while you remain here. Got it?"

"Yes, ma'am."

"Okay. Then move out, private. No stopping. No sharing."

"Yes, ma'am."

Lukas heard two sets of footsteps return in the direction from which they'd come. One was running. The other walked briskly. When he could no longer hear them, he peeked around the corner again and saw an empty hallway.

"That was close," a relieved Javi said. "Let's get back to the hangar before we run into anyone else."

Lukas looked at him incredulously. "Don't you want to know what they're keeping in there?" he asked, pointing at the room marked "Lab #4."

"Bad people, I'm assuming," Javi replied, being intentionally dense.

"Bad people who needed to be moved from the brig to a lab?" Jules asked, equally stunned by Javi's lack of curiosity.

"I don't know, guys," he replied. "But whatever it is, it's not related to what we're supposed to be doing. We've already had one close call and I'm not even counting our run-in with Private Creepy McRapesalot. Let's not push it."

Lukas looked at his friend squirm uncomfortably and felt a twinge of guilt at what he was about to say, but only a twinge. "Javi, there is no way I am *not* going in that lab. You know that, right?"

"I was kind of hoping against hope," Javi said weakly.

"So we're all in agreement," Jules said. "We're going in."

"This is the exact opposite of us all being in agreement," Javi protested.

"Good," Lukas said, smiling at Jules as he ignored his friend's pronouncement. "Let's go, then. That private will be back soon."

He scampered over to the lab door and held it open for Jules and the despondent-looking Javi. Once inside, they saw that they were in a small vestibule that was walled off from a much larger room.

The larger room was a lab that had been partially converted. In either corner were two sizable self-contained cages, the kind that might be used to transport zoo animals.

One cage held a soldier dressed in badly torn fatigues, not unlike the tatters that Soldier One and Soldier Two wore. He was lying still on the base of the cage.

The other cell was occupied by a pleasant-looking woman in her late twenties. She wore a uniform, too. But hers was in good shape, still crisp and starched looking. She had darkly tanned skin, brown hair pulled up in a bun, and features that looked vaguely Mediterranean. She was sitting in the corner of the cell, reading a book. Or at least she had been until she saw the three of them walk in. At the sight of them, she smiled warmly and waved them into the main room.

"I think that's a bad idea," Javi muttered.

"Of course you do," Lukas said as he opened the vestibule door and stepped in.

"How's it going, guys?" the woman said casually. "I'm guessing you are all with the camp crew that I've been hearing about?"

"What makes you say that?" Jules asked with suspicion as she stepped into the lab beside Lukas.

"Come on," the woman said jovially as she stood up. "We may be in the middle of a potential viral apocalypse, but even that doesn't travel as fast as gossip. Everyone heard about the kids who were rescued from a hilltop because Colonel West's daughter was in danger. Besides, you're dressed in civilian clothes. Young lady, you even have a Hollow Valley logo on your t-shirt. I don't have to be Sherlock Holmes to figure this one out."

"You seem to have us at a disadvantage," Lukas said, pointedly not confirming her suspicions. "Care to tell us who you are and why you're in a cell?"

Just then, the solider in the other cage, who had been lying silently on the floor, leapt up. Sweaty and wild-eyed, he grunted unintelligibly as he began convulsing. When the shaking stopped, he started slamming himself against the bars. After several seconds of that, he collapsed to the floor again.

"Don't mind Corporal Vickers," the woman said. "He gets a little stir-crazy from time to time, that is every sixty to ninety seconds or so."

"What happened to him?" Javi asked, finally joining the others. "Is he infected?"

"Maybe a little bit," the woman said mildly. "Just wait until he really gets going."

"Who are you?" Lukas asked realizing she had never answered the question and starting to worry that time was slipping away before the private would return with the assigned tech.

"How rude of me," the woman acknowledged. "I'm Dr. Raina DiSanto. I'm a military physician here at Camp Tarris. I've been assigned to keep an eye on our intermittently hyper friend over there."

"Really?" Javi asked.

"No. Not really. She's lying," Jules said.

Dr. DiSanto glanced over at Jules with a bland smile, but her eyes suggested she wasn't all that amused. Suddenly her whole body shivered, a milder but still disconcerting version of what they'd seen from Corporal Vickers moments earlier.

"She's right," she admitted once it had subsided. "I've caught a bit of the bug myself. We decided it would be best if I was quarantined until we could determine if it was a mild case or . . . something more substantial."

"*We* decided?" Jules pressed.

Dr. DiSanto again gave her the cold-eyed smile. "It was decided on my behalf. Luckily, I seem to be doing much better than Shaky over there. Pretty soon, he'll be like the soldiers who invaded your camp."

"How do you know about that?" Jules demanded.

Dr. DiSanto smiled nastily. "I told you—gossip. There's not much else to do in here, and you'd be surprised how chatty the guards get when they're bored."

"Do you know what's happening, how this all really started?" Lukas asked, cutting to the chase.

"What?" Dr. DiSanto said, amused. "Colonel West didn't give you the 411 on how society collapsed into total chaos in less than three days?"

"Does he know?" Lukas asked.

"Of course he does, just like I do."

"Then maybe you can fill us in," Lukas said, trying to sound disinterested and failing miserably.

Dr. DiSanto stared at him, and her smile fell away. She was silent for several seconds before responding. "What's in it for me?"

Lukas wasn't stunned by her question. He'd suspected she was working up to it all this time. At least it was out in the open now. "What do you want?" he asked.

"How about unlocking the door to this cell for starters?" she suggested as if she was merely asking for the salt and pepper.

"I'm thinking that would be a bad move, Dr. DiSanto," he answered directly. "You're infected, right? What's to prevent you from jumping on top of me and trying to chew my face off? I think I've had enough of that lately."

"First of all, call me Raina," she insisted. "Second, do I look like I'm on the verge of face chewing? Vickers over there, sure. But do you really think I'm a threat? I mean, I'm a vegetarian."

It was Lukas's chance to smile before replying. "Still a hard 'no.' And all this chit-chat isn't helping you. There's going to be a soldier back here in a few minutes and then you won't be in any position to negotiate then. How about asking for something more realistic?"

Raina looked back at him. He could see her mind racing, but it wasn't providing her any answers. She looked like she was about to speak when Corporal Vickers suddenly popped up again. He didn't convulse or slam into anything. Instead, he stared at Lukas with focused red-tinged eyes. He opened his mouth and groaned. Then, shockingly, he spoke.

"We see you," he growled slowly, pointing at Lukas. "We are coming for you."

Then his eyes grew cloudy. His body began to shake briefly before he flung himself at the bars, reaching out in a fruitless attempt to reach Lukas who was halfway across the room.

"Looks like you made a friend," Raina said slyly.

CHAPTER 33

Lukas, shocked, stumbled back half a step.

Jules grabbed his arm to steady him. He stared at Corporal Vickers, not sure if he'd heard him correctly. The expression on the man's face was simultaneously foreign and unnervingly familiar.

Jules stepped forward, looking at Dr. DiSanto while simultaneously blocking Vickers's view of Lukas. The soldier found the move infuriating and moved to his left to get a better view. But the act of moving seemed to rile him up beyond control, and he once again resumed slamming himself into the bars. It only stopped when he shuddered violently and slipped into the now-expected brief stretch of unconsciousness.

"He's getting worse," DiSanto muttered under her breath, almost too quietly to be heard.

"Look," Jules said, ignoring what had just happened with Vickers. "Here's the deal we can offer, and it's not negotiable. You tell us everything you know about how this all started. I'm sure you know there's going to be an evacuation, and I seriously doubt you've got a seat waiting for you. If we think you've been straight with us, we'll come back when we're about to leave and toss you the key to your cell. You can let yourself out. I can't promise it will do you much good. But then at least you've got a chance."

"That hardly seems like a fair trade," DiSanto said.

"Listen, lady—Raina," Javi pleaded. "All of our friends back at camp are either unrecognizable, bloodthirsty creatures, or dead. Our families probably are, too. And with those things outside, we may be as well in the next few hours. So the least you can do is give us the truth about how this started. We deserve that, don't you think?"

DiSanto looked at him with curiosity. Then she glanced back over at Vickers in the next cage, temporarily hibernating. "You promise you'll come back and unlock the cell?" she asked, sounding vulnerable for the first time since their arrival.

"We promise," Jules said, speaking for all of them.

DiSanto stared at the three of them for several more seconds before replying. "Deal," she finally said, "though I think you may regret hearing this. Pull up a chair."

There were no chairs, and the three of them simply stood there waiting for her to reveal what they knew was imminent.

"No sense of humor," she muttered, before finally diving in. "Fine. Those soldiers you saw at your summer camp, the ones who wreaked havoc on the place, were from here, though not originally. They were part of a small contingent of Special Forces operators— Vickers over there included—assigned to this base a couple of weeks ago. We didn't know why at the time."

"Soldiers were assigned to your base without you knowing why?" Javi asked, mystified.

"It's not as unusual as it seems," DiSanto told them. "Secret missions go on all the time, and these men were placed here by a high-ranking general. I was curious but not in any position to question their transfer. Let me back up a bit, to give you a little more context. Do you remember the International Viral Task Force that was set up in the aftermath of the COVID-19 pandemic?"

They all nodded that they did.

"Well, the task force didn't just deal with respiratory viruses," she told them. "Have you ever heard of hemorrhagic fever?"

Lukas and Javi exchanged uncertain expressions, but Jules spoke up.

"Like the Ebola virus?" she asked.

"That's correct," Dr. DiSanto said. "There's that, as well as another virus called Marburg. Without getting into too much detail, imagine that the two are sibling viruses. Both are forms of hemorrhagic fever. Both are highly contagious and easily spread through bodily fluids like blood, saliva, vomit—even sweat. Both do terrible things to the human body. We're talking liquefying organs, blood seeping from every bodily orifice—really horrifying stuff. Both viruses have massive death rates, although Ebola is generally regarded as more lethal. Depending on a variety of factors, the mortality rates for these viruses range from 25 to 90 percent."

Lukas tried to process those numbers. They were as bad as what the current virus was doing. The only apparent difference was that people with Marburg and Ebola weren't actively trying to infect others.

"But I heard they created a vaccine for Ebola?" Jules said, thankfully tugging his thoughts back to the hopeful.

"That's true," DiSanto confirmed. "They did. And it's especially effective if taken at least ten days prior to potential exposure. Unfortunately, the virus mutated recently. There's a brand new strain out there. It's being called Ebola X, and the vaccine doesn't work on it."

Lukas, Javi, and Jules traded worried expressions, unsure where this was headed.

The doctor continued, undeterred. "You may not have been following the news lately, but there have been several large outbreaks of Ebola in West Africa over the last few years. All of them were eventually contained. But a new massive one erupted in Sierra Leone about six weeks ago. This time it was the new Ebola X strain. It's already killed nearly 15 percent of the country's population. Doctors and scientists from all over the world have been working around the clock to find a cure, a new vaccine, anything to mitigate symptoms or reduce the virus's infectiousness. Nothing seemed to work, that is until about three weeks ago." Dr. DiSanto stopped.

Lukas thought she was just taking a moment to catch her breath. But after she remained silent for several seconds, it became clear that she was reconsidering the wisdom of telling them anything more. Clearly she had reached some kind of turning point. Lukas could guess why.

Everything she had said so far was public knowledge that a close follower of the news would likely already be aware of. What she was holding back obviously wasn't. He was about to give a little nudge when Jules beat him to the punch.

"Dr. DiSanto," she said softly, "you're in a cell, infected with this thing. I think you can loosen your obligation to keep everything classified at this point, don't you? Besides, we deserve to know. We *need* to know."

DiSanto nodded, ready to share the secret information. "One of our doctors found an antidote."

CHAPTER 34

For a second, the three of them stared at her in dumbfounded silence.

"For Ebola X?" Javi asked excitedly, finally finding his voice.

"Correct," Dr. DiSanto said. "Details on all of this are vague. It's not as if reports were being issued army-wide. But here's what I understand. A nonmilitary scientist who consults for the army developed an antiserum from the blood of a survivor. They call it Product Ebola X 1, or PEX-1 for short. The testing was done at an isolated facility at a Marine base called Camp Pendleton."

"I know that place," Lukas interjected. "It's just north of San Diego. It's massive."

"Exactly," DiSanto said. "They felt confident they could do the testing there in a remote location without risking an outbreak among the personnel or nearby civilian population. And my understanding is that it worked . . . at first."

"At first?" Jules repeated with anxiety in her voice.

"Yes," she said. "Several American physicians from Doctors Without Borders were infected in Sierra Leone, and instead of being taken to one of the standard care facilities, a few agreed to go to Camp Pendleton for this alternative treatment. It proved shockingly effective. My understanding is that within forty-eight hours all signs of the virus were gone."

"But . . ." Javi said expectantly.

"But there were side effects. This isn't my area of expertise, but from what I've been able to glean, the antiserum works by artificially revving up a group of white blood cells in the body called lymphocytes. Once activated, the lymphocytes fight the filovirus particles that comprise the virus. The problem was that, once the lymphocyte cells had wiped out the virus, they didn't just shut down. They stayed aggressive, seeking out other perceived threats."

She paused for questions. There were none, and she was about to continue when Vickers woke up, rolled over, and got on all fours. He looked disoriented. But when his eyes fell on Lukas, his lips curled back, revealing his teeth.

Without warning, the corporal leapt at him, slamming his head into the bars. He slumped to the ground hard, having apparently knocked himself out. For a moment, everyone stared at him in dumb amazement. Then Dr. DiSanto picked up again as if nothing had happened.

"The rest is very sketchy," she said, speaking more quickly now, seeming to realize that time was getting short before the soldier would return and put her release in jeopardy. "Information is hard to come by, and I don't really get all of it anyway. But the short version is, the aggression of the lymphocytes began to manifest in external aggression from the patients. They got violent. They attacked their caregivers, in some cases killing them. Their strength was off the charts, and they seemed impervious to pain. Ultimately, security personnel had to take most of them down. However, a few were incapacitated and put in isolation."

"What happened to the caregivers they didn't kill?" Javi asked. "Did they get infected, too?"

"They did," DiSanto said with a wry smile that suggested this part of the story had special resonance for her. "They were put in isolation as well."

"So the virus was contained?" Javi said hopefully.

"It seemed so," answered the doctor.

"Were any of the doctors or the people they attacked like the soldiers who infiltrated our camp?" Lukas asked. "Could they think coherently, or were they just flesh sacks of unbridled, unthinking rage?" He found himself unable to keep the resentment out of his voice as he remembered the phrase that West had used earlier to describe the infected.

"They had no significant higher mental function and were operating on almost pure instinct," DiSanto answered, oblivious to the reason for Lukas's challenging tone. "Compared to them, Vickers here is a Rhodes Scholar, able to speak in somewhat coherent sentences and make conscious choices."

"How are Vickers and the soldiers from camp able to retain the ability to reason when the others can't?" Jules demanded.

DiSanto sighed deeply as if trying to will away the information she was about to share. Eventually, she replied. "Do you remember that general I mentioned who sent the soldiers here?" she asked, not waiting to hear if they did. "His name is Heath Bannon. Apparently he got the brilliant idea that having soldiers with super strength who didn't feel pain might be a significant battlefield advantage. And he theorized that, if the antiserum was given to men who weren't already infected with the virus—whose immune systems hadn't been weakened—they might be able to retain their cognition *and* get the physical benefits of the antidote."

"And people went for that?" Javi asked incredulously. "Injecting healthy people with a barely tested treatment that caused people to go on mindless killing sprees?"

"No," Dr. DiSanto said emphatically. "He proposed the idea, and it was shot down by his superiors. In fact, the doctor who had developed the treatment was so appalled by the idea that he took all his research, along with almost every dose he had of it, and went into hiding."

"That worked?" Lukas asked, surprised. "He was just able to up and leave?"

"Amazingly, yes. The doctor's identity was a secret to all but the most senior authorities, perhaps two or three people total in the entire government. No one knew his real name. He went by a pseudonym, Dr. Cary Gray. I've looked him up in all our databases. There are no photos, no biographical information—nothing. He never went to the Camp Pendleton facility himself but sent research assistants who only communicated with him remotely. It's believed he's based out of one of the Southern California universities. But even that's not certain."

"Then if he took all the samples, how did it go bad?" Jules asked.

"Because unbeknownst to Dr. Gray, not *all* of the samples were secured. One dose of the antiserum was stolen by someone on General Bannon's staff. It was replicated in secret. Bannon was already under threat of a court-martial for a variety of reasons, including a formal recommendation that the US Government simply erect fencing around the entire country of Sierra Leone and let the virus burn through the population until there was no one left. He was notorious for his . . . lack of enthusiasm for darker-skinned folks, especially in Africa, which he once called a 'backwater continent.'"

Lukas, Javi, and Jules remained silent, unsure of how to even respond to such a thing.

"Anyway," she continued, not expecting them to, "we didn't know any of this when Special Forces operators from one of his units were assigned here and to various other military bases throughout the country. We just accepted them with open arms, though I can't say they were reciprocal."

"They didn't spend time with people here?" Lukas asked.

"No. They mostly kept to themselves, though that wasn't unusual. Even under normal circumstances, these guys tend to be standoffish. Comes with the territory, I guess. I never spoke to Vickers here until we became cage roomies and he started grunting at me. In fact, I only interacted with one of them, a command sergeant major named Curtas, pleasant enough, even charming in a professional detached way. But he knew all about me, about everyone he dealt with here. He mentioned that his wife and son had died in an accident many years prior and that, ever since, he'd devoted himself exclusively to 'serving the army in the cause of liberty.' He said it saved him. That was pretty much the only personal information he ever gave me, other than to say he liked Scotch and that he'd specifically requested being assigned to this base."

"Did he explain why he wanted to come here?" Lukas asked.

"He wasn't exactly the explaining type," DiSanto said.

"Let me guess," Javi said. "Was this guy about six feet tall and two hundred pounds with short black hair?"

"That'd be him," DiSanto confirmed. "Why?"

"He started the attack at our camp," Lukas told her. "He seemed to be leading the other Furies, to the extent they could be led."

"And this Curtas didn't give you any clue as to his orders?" Jules asked, clearly wanting to move the conversation away from the attack.

"No. We didn't even know these guys were connected to Bannon at that time. Then about four days ago, the formal order for the general's arrest came down. That must have been when he gave the directive for his men to inject themselves with the antiserum."

207

"Without having tested it in a safe environment?" Lukas asked. "So he did this without having any idea what it would do?"

"It's possible that he felt he didn't have time for testing," DiSanto said. "Or maybe he just didn't care. My suspicion is that it was the latter."

"Why do you say that?" Javi asked.

"Because—" Dr. DiSanto started to say before being interrupted by an intense shivering that lasted a good five seconds. She clutched the bars of the cage to keep from falling.

"Are you okay?" Javi asked once it had subsided.

"Peachy," she said unconvincingly.

"How were you infected?" Jules asked. "I don't see any obvious wounds on you."

"Not every wound is visible, prom queen," she replied coldly. "Do you want my personal history or the virus's?"

"The virus," Lukas said emphatically.

"Smart choice. Where was I? I get hazy sometimes."

"You suspected the general didn't care if the antiserum was tested in a safe environment," he reminded her.

"Right. That's because from what we've been able to piece together, all his men took it when they were off base, on leave, in highly trafficked areas of major population centers. It seems that he wanted his men to conduct a field experiment in an unsecure environment where they couldn't be easily stopped. And it worked."

CHAPTER 35

Lukas, Javi, and Jules stood in stunned silence as they collectively tried to process what they'd just heard.

"This is what he *wanted*?" Jules finally asked, disbelieving.

"I don't know what his ultimate plan was," the doctor said. "But it's clear that he wanted to learn the impact of the antiserum without facing interference from military authorities. And it turns out his theory was half right."

"What do you mean?" Lukas asked.

"It seems that for whatever reason—maybe because they weren't already infected with a preexisting virus like Ebola—these soldiers were able to develop incredible strength and pain tolerance while preserving some measure of higher-level thinking. Unfortunately for all of us, they were also highly infectious. Worse, almost all of the people *they* infected lack that ability to think and are as animalistic as the original infected doctors were." She stopped talking for a moment.

Everyone in the room realized that Dr. Raina DiSanto was describing the origins of the nightmare they were currently facing.

"So could Dr. Gray maybe reverse engineer it?" Jules asked hopefully.

"That's a great question," DiSanto said. "And if anyone had a clue where he was, maybe they could ask him."

"But won't the vaccine that everyone on this base has been getting do essentially the same thing?" Lukas asked. "Isn't that why it was created?"

"No," DiSanto said emphatically. "And that's the key thing to keep in mind. The vaccine being distributed here at the base is not an antidote. If a person is already a Fury, it won't change them back."

"Then what's the point?" Javi asked.

DiSanto sighed impatiently, as if she was talking to a toddler. "The goal of the vaccine is to prevent you from being turned into one of these things if you are infected by them," she explained slowly. "Yes, it comes from the same source as the antiserum that turned these soldiers into killers. But the hope is that, by deactivating all the lymphocyte accelerators in it, it will offer protection from transformation rather than cause it."

"So you're saying that we've all been dosed with a variation of the thing that turned Vickers here into a self-concussion machine," Jules noted. "How do we know that we won't be turned, too?"

"You don't," DiSanto said with a resigned smile. "But at least you've got a better shot than me. Since I got infected *before* the vaccine was developed, it's of no use to me. I'm eventually going to turn into Mrs. Vickers, that is unless the mysterious Dr. Gray comes up with a real, honest-to-God antidote and gets it to me in the next few hours."

"Hold up," Javi interrupted. "Finding an antidote would be great. But it seems like all this could have been avoided. Didn't Bannon consider this scenario, that his super soldiers might not follow his orders once infected?"

"No way to know for certain," DiSanto said. "But I have my suspicions. In the chaos after the initial outbreak and before he was supposed to be arrested, the general went AWOL with a unit of men loyal to him. They killed seven Marines when they fled Camp Pendleton. Their current location is unknown. Some of the folks here believe this is all part of an elaborate coup attempt."

"To take over the country?" Jules asked disbelievingly.

"Unclear. But the current circumstances do lend themselves to the possibility. The nation is in turmoil. Leadership is scattered. Opposition is largely dead or infected with a virus that makes them thoughtless eating machines. Someone who anticipated this situation, with a sizable number of faithful troops at his disposal, would be a credible threat."

"But what's the point?" Lukas asked. "Even if that's true and his plan worked out, he'd be in charge of something closer to a zoo than a country. It seems crazy."

"I certainly agree," Dr. DiSanto said. "And I think it's quite possible that Bannon has gone mad. But madness doesn't equal stupid. The general has a reputation as a brilliant strategist. And if all this is by design, then it's possible that he planned for this contingency. Just because we don't understand his plan doesn't mean he doesn't have one."

"So what's being done to stop him?" Javi asked.

"Kid," DiSanto said with an almost apologetic tone, "that's the whole point. Right now there's nothing we can do about Bannon because all our resources are being deployed to save the people who are still alive. That's why they're preparing to depart this base before it's overrun."

A groan from the other cell made them all look in that direction. Corporal Vickers got up slowly and looked around the room until his gaze fell once more on Lukas. He ran at him half-speed before being knocked backward by the cell bars. The collision seemed to wake him up, and he rammed the bars a second time, with much greater force.

This time he clung to the bars to stop from toppling back. He pulled himself forward so that his mouth squeezed between two of the bars. It was as if he was trying to pull his head through a space half its width. When he realized it was not physically possible, he contented himself to repeat the same phrase over and over, louder and louder, like a crazed mantra.

"We see you! We are coming for you!"

Though he knew it was impossible, Lukas began to worry that Vickers might actually break through the bars.

"We should go," Jules said anxiously.

Lukas nodded, and they all rushed out. Just before the door closed, he heard Raina DiSanto's voice shout out, even louder than Vickers's.

"Don't forget me!"

CHAPTER 36

As the three of them headed back to the hangar, they were unsure just how much to reveal to the others.

"After everything that happened today, I'm worried it will send some of them over the edge," Lukas said. "Emily is borderline catatonic. Mike already looks like he wants to blow up the base all by himself. If they find out that all of this was a planned attack by part of our own military, and that the United States government is totally unequipped to handle it, I'm afraid the whole group will melt down."

"Maybe," Jules said. "But they deserve to know, just like we did. Everyone has the right to understand what we're dealing with."

"Besides," Javi added, "we have to tell Caleb and Aubrey. Hell, she might already know. So what, half of us will know the truth and other half stay in the dark? That's not realistic, man."

"Then we should be prepared for the blowback," Lukas warned. "It could impact how effective everyone is when we put this plan into action."

"I think it's a risk we have to take," Jules insisted. "There are so few of us left, Lukas. We owe it to each other to be honest from here on out. Maybe reminding them that we have a vaccine in our systems will help keep everyone calm."

"Wait—that's one thing I don't get," Javi said. "How did they develop the vaccine that we took, the one Aubrey stole? Dr. DiSanto told us that Dr. Gray escaped with almost all the antiserum samples and that General Bannon had the others. How did they get it at some random military base in San Antonio?"

"I'd love the answer to that question, too," Lukas said. "But we can't go back to talk to DiSanto right now. It's too risky. The only other person to ask is Colonel West. And doing that would mean revealing that we know there *is* a vaccine here at the base. I worry that he might get squirrelly about all the questions and just lock *us* in cells or something."

"So we have no idea if what we took will do any good?" Javi asked. "It could just be a placebo?"

"I doubt it," Lukas said. "DiSanto described it like it was legit. She had no reason to lie about that. Plus, there's a huge health science center in this city. I'm sure the whole medical community was tasked with solving this. Maybe that's exactly why they're holding Vickers. They might have used his blood to develop the vaccine. And don't forget—Colonel West gave it to his own daughter."

"Right," Jules added, "*and* he's been hoarding it like he thinks it's of value. There must be some level of confidence in it."

Lukas nodded in agreement. "Whatever we took," he concluded, "it didn't turn us into Furies, so that's a good start."

"Maybe we can ask DiSanto about how the vaccine was developed when we go back to let her out," Javi suggested.

Jules looked at him with a surprised expression. "Javi," she said, doing her best to keep her voice even, "we're not letting her out."

"What?" he asked, disbelieving.

Lukas, equally stunned, stood beside him silently.

Jules seemed puzzled by their reactions. "You don't think I would ever actually let someone infected with that virus out of a cell, do you?"

"But we promised," Javi said, sounding five years old.

"No, *I* promised," Jules said. "I made the deal with her. Neither of you were involved. So you don't have to feel guilty about it. This is on me."

"But she told us everything we wanted to know," Javi said, somehow seeming younger with each word.

Lukas listened to their back and forth with a mix of shame and relief. The guilt at not saying anything as Javi voiced his exact thoughts was easily overpowered by his desire not to have Jules see him as a naïve little boy.

"Yes," Jules said, glancing over at Lukas with a can-you-believe-this-kid look. "She was honest and straightforward with us. I appreciate it but not enough to let her out."

"She'll be ripped to shreds," Javi protested, looking over at Lukas for support.

"She can't be our top priority right now, buddy," Lukas replied noncommittally as they approached the hangar entrance. "We have to focus on the people we care about. We'll deal with Dr. DiSanto later if we have time."

"Her name's Raina," Javi said quietly.

Lukas didn't know how to respond, so he didn't say anything.

They reached the hangar door and stopped. None of them was sure what would happen when they walked in. But they knew one thing for certain: it wouldn't be pretty.

*

To their surprise, there were almost no interruptions as they filled the group in on what they'd seen in that lab, as well as what they learned from Dr. DiSanto, including what little she knew about Soldier One, or Curtas. Caleb and Aubrey, who had returned to the hangar before them, stayed silent, as well. Lukas cast periodic glances at Aubrey, trying to determine if she already knew most of what they were relating to the others. But her expression was inscrutable.

"None of this changes our plan," Jules said when they were done. "We thought you deserved to know. But it doesn't really affect any of us in this moment. It's all big-picture stuff we have no impact on. What we *can* control is getting out of this place and making it to our next destination safely."

"You mean my father's precinct," Mike added pointedly.

"Right," she agreed reluctantly. "That's where our focus needs to be."

Lukas glanced hesitantly over at the guards and nurses who were clustered in the far corner of the hangar, talking amongst themselves. He'd been worried that they might be suspicious of the camp crew having what was clearly a meeting of some kind. But it was obvious that the base staff had largely lost interest in their group. Maybe it was because they knew the campers were not a priority to the higher-ups. Maybe it was because they had their own concerns to deal with. Either way, it allowed for more open conversation.

"I'm sorry," Trevor said, "but I'm having a little trouble getting past the fact that the deaths of most our friends at camp, and possibly everyone else we love, were entirely preventable."

There was a general quiet grumbling that suggested he wasn't the only one who felt that way. Emily nodded vehemently.

"I can't believe my brother is dead because of some psycho general halfway across the country," Mike muttered.

After a moment, Caleb stood up and walked over to where Jules was sitting. He stood behind her, putting his hand on her shoulder in support as much as affection. She reached up and clasped her fingers in his.

"I get it," he said quietly, looking out at the rest of the group. "I feel the same way. No one expects you to get past it. But Jules is right. We can't do anything about that. Our primary concern right now is that there are thousands of creatures outside those walls that want to rip us to shreds. And no matter how angry we are at how we ended up here, it means nothing if we don't survive. So let's set aside being pissed off and focus on getting out of here in one piece. Okay?"

"Listen," Martie added with intensity in her voice. "My mother didn't sacrifice her life so that we would get caught up in some kind of blame game. She wanted us to live. That's what we need to do, no matter what."

"Yeah," Lonnie agreed. "When we were trapped in that lodge, what were the odds that we'd be here now? We've been given a second chance. Let's not waste it."

Everyone, including the previously hesitant Trevor, Emily, and Mike, seemed convinced. Trevor even glanced over at Lukas and gave him a thumbs up, which seemed borderline excessive.

"All right then," Caleb said, considering the matter closed. "Aubrey, you're up. Why don't you walk us through your plan one final time? At some point, those guards are going to get curious about our little huddle, so we should make it fast."

Aubrey got up and took his place. Caleb pulled up a chair beside Jules who still hadn't let go of his hand. Lukas forced himself not to notice.

As Aubrey gathered herself, it suddenly occurred to him that, since his return and throughout their recitation of what Dr. DiSanto had told them, she hadn't said a word. He wondered just how much more she knew than the rest of them and, even now, whether her loyalty was truly with them or her father.

Nobody slept much that night.

Lukas, despite the pre-bedtime dose of pain medicine he'd been given by the nurse, felt a near-constant throbbing in his palms, ribs, and back. He tried to ignore them all.

At one point, while drifting in and out of consciousness, he looked up and thought he saw that Trevor's cot was empty. But the next time he awoke, the boy was fast asleep. At another point, he could have sworn he heard voices arguing. But he was too tired to investigate it before sinking back into an uneasy slumber.

By 5:30 a.m., everyone was up. They were all already fully dressed, having gone to bed that way the night before, though they were covered in blankets to keep it hidden.

According to her father's plan, Aubrey was supposed to sneak out of the hangar by 6:00 a.m. in anticipation of the base evacuation just before 7:00 a.m. There were only two guards in the hangar at this hour, and one of them kept falling asleep.

They all watched as the second guard woke the first one to say he was going to the bathroom. Within thirty seconds of the door closing, the first guard fell asleep again. Aubrey gave an elaborate wave to the group. It was time.

Everyone got out of their cots as quietly as possible and scurried to the hangar door. Aubrey pulled out a security card she'd snagged during her weapon-securing mission with Caleb yesterday and swiped it across the door panel. It turned green, and they all heard the door unlock. Caleb was just opening the door to let everyone out when an earsplitting alarm went off.

"Is that us?" Jamie asked, her voice quivering with anxiety.

"No," Aubrey said. "It's the general intruder alert. It means the Furies have gotten over the wall."

CHAPTER 37

"Let's go!" Caleb ordered, waving everyone through the door as the guard who'd been sleeping, disoriented, fell from the chair he was sitting in.

"I thought they weren't supposed to overtop the walls until dawn," Jamie said as if the creatures had violated some pact. "This seems early."

No one responded. Once in the hall, they all turned to Aubrey for instructions.

"Okay, let's keep moving," she said. "We don't know where those creatures are. We're going to the motor pool where there's hopefully still a truck waiting for us. Lukas, Javi, and Jules know where it is and will lead you there. Caleb and I are going to collect the guns we stashed. We'll need a little help. Martie and Jamie, you come with us to help grab them."

"Why them?" Mike demanded.

"Because no one will question Martie, and Jamie looks old enough to be a young recruit," Aubrey replied.

"You think anyone's going to question us with everything going on?" Mike countered angrily.

"This is not up for discussion," Martie said, assuming the authoritative tone none of them had heard in a while. "I know you want to have a weapon, Mike, and you will eventually. But this arguing helps no one, and we don't have time for it. Follow instructions now; debate them later. Understand?"

Mike nodded reluctantly.

"Okay, everyone head out," Aubrey said. "We'll be about five minutes behind you. And stay alert. We don't know how many of these things have broken through. They could be anywhere by now."

Lukas took the lead, followed by a group that included Javi, Jules, Emily, Mike, Lonnie, and Trevor who looked especially stricken. Aubrey and Caleb headed down a separate corridor with Martie and Jamie in tow.

They rushed down the hall to the motor pool, passing occasional soldiers headed in unknown directions. None of them gave the group more than a passing glance. Despite their disinterest, Lukas felt anxious.

Every door that swung open, every sound of fast-moving footsteps set him on edge, fearful that the next thing he saw would be a bloody-mouthed monster. There were occasional announcements over the PA system, but the lingo was technical and Lukas didn't understand much of it.

When they reached the motor pool, he cautiously pushed open the door. What he saw inside was pure chaos. Floodlights lit up the space. There were people running everywhere. A line of soldiers with guns raised stood guard at the large motor pool entrance, stepping aside intermittently as vehicles pulled out with tires squealing.

"Our truck is at the very back with an 'Out of service' sign on it," Lukas yelled over the din around them. "Everyone get in the covered bed in back and stay out of sight. Jules and Javi will take lead. I'll bring up the rear."

They sprinted across the exposed motor pool, ignoring everyone around them. Lukas stayed close to Lonnie who was moving as fast as he could despite his limitations.

For half a second, Lukas thought the truck was gone. But his eyes followed Javi who confidently ran past a pickup that had been recently parked near the truck, partially blocking his view of it. He heaved a sigh of relief as Javi jumped in the back and the others followed, then opened the unlocked driver's door and got in, keeping low to avoid detection.

"Everyone good back there?" he yelled.

"We're good," Jules called back. "But there are no straps or belts, just wooden benches along the sides. It's going to be a bumpy ride."

"It'll be just like a supply run back at camp," Lonnie shouted before the realization that those were done forever settled over all of them.

"I'll let you know when the others arrive," Lukas said, moving quickly past the subsequent awkward silence.

In the brief respite that followed, he stared at the steering wheel in front of him, trying to ignore the gnawing sense of dread that wrapped around his midsection. For some reason, the thought that he might end up in the truck's driver's seat hadn't occurred to him. He'd just assumed Caleb would be driving them.

The idea that the six people in the back of the truck might have to depend on his skills sent a wave of nausea through him. The truth, which he hadn't shared with anyone at camp, not even Javi, was that he hated driving.

Technically he could do it. He'd gotten his learner's permit and was reasonably adept at the task. But when he sat behind a wheel, especially if there wasn't someone in the passenger seat expecting him to act calm and collected, a wave of panic inevitably rose in his chest.

Despite his best effort to control himself, his mind would invariably flash back to the years' old memory of him in the backseat of the family car, Caleb reaching across the seat to grab his stuff, his parents blasting an 80s' ballad to drown out the brothers' arguing.

Then all of that was replaced by the sound of crunching metal mixed with screams, the feel of warm blood on his skin, much of it not his own, the sharp pain in his left side that still returned when the memory surfaced. No matter how hard he tried to block it all out, bits and pieces would always leak through.

He briefly considered asking Jules if she wanted to drive. But that would require her to hop out of the truck bed and come around front. With the swarm of people all around them now, it might attract unwanted attention. Besides, if she had wanted to drive, she surely would have said something before now.

He clumsily fished the key out of his pocket and put it in the ignition as he peeked up over the steering wheel in the hopes of seeing the others. But the door they'd used to access the motor pool remained closed. He tried to orient himself to what was going on around him, but it was difficult.

Soldiers seemed to be running around randomly, though they appeared to know their direction and purpose. Every thirty seconds or so, the half dozen soldiers guarding the motor pool entrance would move to the side to let another vehicle pass, then close ranks again.

There were no Furies in sight. Lukas began to wonder if maybe only a couple had gotten over the walls and that all this movement was more preventive than reactive. He was just starting to allow himself to hope that might be the case when the shooting started.

He looked over to the entrance and saw all the soldiers on the line firing in the same general direction. Then there was a pause.

He heard someone shout an order he couldn't understand, and suddenly an additional half dozen soldiers joined the first group of six. They positioned themselves in a semicircle that extended just past the entrance, with every combatant's weapon pointed at a different section of the shadows beyond.

In the lull that followed, Lukas heard that same dull humming noise they'd noticed back in the hangar, the one that sounded like thousands of cicadas chirping all at once.

"Ten o'clock!" someone shouted, breaking through the relative quiet.

Immediately all the soldiers turned to their left and began firing. Lukas couldn't see anything beyond them in the predawn darkness. And then, all at once, they were everywhere.

Hundreds of bodies moved toward the men, like a massive wave crashing onto a beach. The guards continued to shoot, but for every Fury that dropped, three more took its place.

"Fall back!" an authoritative voice yelled over a loudspeaker, but it was too late.

Before he'd even finished the sentence, the Furies were on the soldiers, drowning them in a sea of flailing arms and chomping teeth.

"All vehicles move out," the disembodied voice yelled. "All vehicles move out immediat—" There was a scream and a gurgle. Then the voice went silent.

Trucks began streaming toward the entrance, slamming into Furies and humans alike, knocking them down like bowling pins as they tore off toward some unknown destination.

"What's going on up there?" Javi yelled from the back. "It doesn't sound good."

"It's not," Lukas yelled back as he clenched his eyes shut and turned the ignition. "Hold on back there. I may have to start moving before I wanted to."

He felt himself hyperventilating and ordered his body to breathe in and out slowly. There was no choice. If this vehicle was going to move, he was the one who had to make it happen. He put his clammy hands on the wheel and squeezed, hoping the feel of it would settle him down. It didn't.

"We can't leave without the others!" Jules shouted, poking her head through the window separating the bed from the cab. But when she saw the endless horde of Furies pouring into the motor pool she fell silent.

"I don't want to go, either," Lukas whispered to her, "but we can't wait much longer. Pretty soon the whole place will be overrun, and we won't be able to get out."

"Give it another minute," she pleaded.

A brief image of Todd shoving Kellen into the path of Steve Sailor in order to save himself flashed through Lukas's head. While he couldn't forgive the counselor for his actions, in this moment he could understand them.

"I will, Jules," he said sharply, forcing the picture from his mind. "It's my brother. I'm going to wait until we have no choice but to go. The problem is that probably means only another thirty seconds."

Just then a voice came over the base PA system. "Alert! Alert! All personnel, this is the base commander. The outer walls have been breached. Hostiles have entered the complex. Report to your assigned station for immediate evacuation. Repeat—we are in full evacuation. All personnel are to rendezvous at Checkpoint Zulu at 1100 hours. This will be my last communication. Godspeed."

The system went quiet, replaced by the increasingly over-whelming sound of guttural, voracious grunts. The entire front half of the motor pool was now consumed by Furies. Pretty soon, the door the group had used to access to access the motor pool would be inaccessible. Lukas decided he couldn't wait any longer.

"I'm going," he said.

"You're leaving?" Jules asked, her voice quivering.

"No. I'm heading for the door. That way, they won't have to run as far and I can block the Furies with the truck."

Pretending like it was no big deal, he put the vehicle in drive and hit the accelerator, gunning it harder than he intended. The sound of people slamming into each other in the back of the truck made him wince. He was almost to the door when it suddenly opened.

He had a brief moment of exhilaration before realizing that the two people who stepped out were strangers. But then he saw that he was mistaken. One was a new face, but the other was Corporal Daugherty, the petite blonde who worked for Colonel West.

She and the man with her looked to their left, their jaws drop-ping in horror as they became aware that they were only fifty feet from a throng of ravenous eating machines. Lukas opened his mouth to call out to her.

But before he could speak, they began running toward the closest Jeep, which was just starting to pull out. They hopped into the packed vehicle just as the Furies reached them, diving in and onto the jeep, covering it in undulating bodies in seconds. Within moments, Daugherty's blonde head disappeared in an ocean of snapping jaws and grasping arms.

Lukas forced himself to ignore what he'd just seen and focus on the task at hand. He had just pulled up to the door when it opened again. He held his breath as he slammed on the brakes. Sure enough, out came Caleb, followed by Martie, Jamie, and finally Aubrey.

The four of them, who all had weapons raised and back-packs on, froze in shock at the sight of hundreds of Furies rushing toward them.

CHAPTER 38

"Get in! *Now!*" Lukas screamed as the truck came to a stop in front of them. He shoved open the driver's side door for Caleb as the other three hurried toward the back.

The Furies were less than twenty feet away and heading straight for them as he hopped into the passenger seat and rolled up the window. Caleb got into the driver's seat just as the first Furies slammed into the open door. He used his legs to jam it open so they couldn't sneak by to get to the three people who had hurried to the back.

Lukas was about to check into his side view mirror to see if he could catch a glimpse of whether they had gotten in safely when a Fury threw itself at his window, causing a crack that went from top to bottom.

"They're all in!" Jules yelled from the back. "Move out now!"

Caleb moved his feet, allowing the door to slam closed as Furies pressed against it. His own closed window shook violently. He threw the car in drive and punched it.

"Lock your door," he ordered as he swerved to avoid an onrushing mass of creatures. Lukas did it, then glanced back through the small window to see how the others were doing. It was hard to tell who was who, but he could see at least four guns trained on the back opening of the truck.

A series of thumps made him face forward again. He saw that Caleb was headed for the motor pool entrance, mowing down anything in his path. Another much bigger truck was just to their right. They both approached the opening, and it looked to Lukas that there wouldn't be room for both of them to get out at the same time.

Caleb seemed to sense the same thing and punched the gas, moving ahead of the larger vehicle, which already had Furies on its hood and roof. The smaller truck shot out of the entrance, briefly going airborne as it hit a small speed bump.

"I have no idea where I'm going!" he shouted toward the back after they slammed back down.

"Just follow the other vehicles," Aubrey yelled back from somewhere in the bed of the truck. "The base exits onto Camp Tarris Road. You can take that to the highway."

Caleb got in line behind a row of other vehicles, all headed in the same direction. The fast-moving convoy made it almost impossible for Furies to get in between them. The few that did ended up getting squashed. Caleb took half a second to glance over at his brother.

"Can you get this backpack off me?" he said. "It's making it hard to drive. And maybe you can find a good use for this." He handed over the gun that was in his lap.

It was unlike anything Lukas had ever seen before. "What is this?" he asked.

"It's an energy rifle," Caleb said. "They were almost all out of conventional firearms so we took these. Aubrey says they're experimental, which is probably why they were still there."

"What do they do?"

"I have no idea," Caleb admitted. "I haven't fired it."

Lukas looked down, trying to figure out the gun. Just as he was locating what he thought was the safety, he felt a screech and looked up to see a wall of brake lights ahead of him. The trucks in line before them were slowing down.

"What's going on?" he asked.

"I'm not sure," Caleb replied. "I think there might be a bottle-neck near the exit."

"If we get much slower, these things are going to be able to jump on the truck."

"I know that, Lukas, but I'm not sure what choice I have."

Aubrey must have heard them, because she poked her head through the window. "There's a secondary exit off to the left. It's intended for visitors. It's smaller because it's only designed for cars. Humvees and large trucks can't squeeze through, but I don't think we're too wide for it."

"How do I get there?" Caleb asked.

"See that dirt road up ahead to the left," she asked, "the one that runs along the outer wall? Follow it for another few hundred yards, and you'll come up on the gate."

"But there are no other vehicles going that way," Lukas protested. "We'll be the prime target for every Fury in the area."

"It's that or come to a standstill waiting to get out the main gate," she replied. "I'd rather go fast, even if we're on our own."

"Not much of a choice," Caleb said. "Those trucks ahead are at a complete stop now. We're already going slower than I would like. We'll be swarmed if we keep going that direction."

As if to illustrate his point, something leapt onto their hood. It had clearly once been a soldier, but now it was a wild-eyed hunter with red saliva dripping from its mouth. It grabbed at the windshield, getting hold of a wiper blade before the thing broke off in his hands, sending him tumbling off to the side.

Caleb didn't need any more prompting and immediately veered left, driving over several hundred feet of parched, wilted grass before hitting the dirt road and yanking the steering wheel hard left. He was just straightening out when they heard a loud thump on the roof. "What the—" he started to ask.

Lukas looked out his window to see if he could figure out what was going on. What he saw made his blood run cold. "They're on the wall," he shouted. "They're leaping for the truck from the top of the wall. One of them must be on the roof."

At that moment, a series of additional thuds sounded, indicating that at least two more creatures had successfully landed on the roof. Suddenly Lukas heard a loud ripping noise. It only took a moment for him understand what had happened. One of the Furies had either fallen or leapt onto the canvas top of the truck bed and torn through it. The scream he heard from behind him verified his suspicion.

He looked back through the window to see a Fury sprawled on the floor of the truck bed but quickly getting up. Everyone in the back had moved away to create a circle of space around it. Just as the creature got to its feet, Lukas heard a blast and saw the thing drop lifelessly to the floor, a massive charred hole in its chest. Beyond it, Martie was holding one of the energy rifles.

The thumping on top of them suggested that at least a few Furies were still on the roof. Lukas worried that they too were about to jump down into the truck bed.

"Caleb, hit the brakes for a second so we can get rid of those things up top," he advised before shouting to the gang in back. "Hold on to something. We're going to brake hard."

Just as he said it, Caleb slammed to a stop. Three Furies flew off the roof, hit the hood in front of them, and tumbled to the ground below. Almost immediately, Caleb hit the gas again, rolling over everything beneath.

"You good back there?" Lukas shouted.

"Bumps and bruises," Aubrey said. "But we need to get to that gate fast. I see another crowd of those things on a section of wall up ahead."

"I can see the gate," Caleb announced. "We're less than a hundred yards away. Warn everyone that it's going to be sharp right in a few seconds."

Lukas was tempted to suggest his brother drive on the grass farther away from the wall, but then he noticed that, every twenty feet or so, there was a white wooden block embedded in the ground, about two feet high, preventing them from going off-road. Any attempt to do so would likely result in a blown tire or worse.

As they passed the section of the wall that Aubrey had noted, he saw a group of at least five Furies leap from it in their direction. One landed on the hood and rolled away. He felt a series of thuds on the roof and saw one creature skid over Caleb's door and land in the grass to the left. That left three that must have stuck the landing. The shouts from the back verified this.

He twisted around to see that two of the things had jumped into the truck bed. Both were near the cab window. Everyone in the bed had moved near the back of the truck to avoid them. Aubrey and Martie had their guns raised and looked ready to fire when Caleb shouted at them.

"Hard right coming now!"

Lukas felt the entire vehicle careen sharply as he slammed into his brother's right shoulder. The rifle he'd been holding slipped from his grasp and dropped to the floor near his feet.

There were screams and shouts from the back that he couldn't identify as either related to attacks or just general mayhem. As he tried to get his bearings, a fist coming from above slammed into Caleb's window, shattering it.

The hand, with glass sticking out of the back of it and bone exposed, grasped around desperately, trying to grab hold of anything. Caleb leaned right to avoid it. The creature grunted loudly, and the weight of its body banging against the roof sounded like thunderclaps.

Lukas reached down, grabbed the rifle from the ground, and whacked at the flailing hand with the butt end. It didn't seem to be any deterrent. They hit another speed bump. This one indicated that they were off the base and on a normal road.

"Don't worry about me," Caleb insisted as he yanked the steering wheel hard left. "Check the back."

Lukas twisted back around again. It took him several seconds to make sense of what he saw. Both of the Furies looked to be underneath a big section of the canvas tarp that had recently served as the truck bed's roof. Trevor, Emily, and Jamie had jumped on top of it to prevent the creatures from escaping. At the same time, Mike, Martie, and Lonnie were dragging the entire mass to the back of the truck. Aubrey, Jules, and Javi had guns pointed at it.

"Get ready to roll off the canvas in a second and shove them out," Aubrey ordered.

They held the material down as the three people on top of the canvas scrambled off the pile and began kicking at it, sending it tumbling out of the back with the creatures still under it. They were just getting to their feet with the assistance of the others when Lukas felt suddenly uneasy. Something was wrong. By the time he realized what it was, it was too late.

CHAPTER 39

The banging and grunting from the Fury on the roof had stopped. That meant it had either fallen off the truck entirely or . . .

"Look out!" someone in the back shouted as a thud rattled the truck bed. Lukas's view was blocked by the back of something that was hunched over. He flicked off what he hoped was the safety of the energy rifle and tried to aim it through the window next to him. Before he could get a clear shot, the creature lurched forward at the person closest to him, Emily.

She screamed as she tumbled backward and landed hard on the truck bed. As the Fury dove toward her, a shadowy figure slammed into it as a single word echoed through the night.

"No!"

Both the Fury and its attacker smashed into the cab wall before careening onto the floor. As they rolled over, Lukas saw who had leapt forward: Mike. Though he was smaller than the Fury, he made up for the size imbalance with his own furious anger. He was on top now and slamming the Fury's head into the floor using its hair.

The woman—for that's what the Fury had once been—flailed her arms wildly. The back of her right hand, with a large jagged chunk of window glass in it, swiped at Mike's face and cut him near the left eye.

Though he didn't cry out, the act seemed to startle him and he momentarily lost his grip. That was all it took for the woman to get the upper hand. In a flash, she was on top of him, her jaws snapping as he desperately tried to push her away. It was a losing battle.

Lukas regrouped and aimed his energy rifle at the woman's back. After one short exhale, he fired, unsure of what to expect. The kick wasn't terrible but he couldn't immediately tell what damage he had done. The woman was still moving, though more jerkily now. Then he saw the injury. Most of her right hip was gone.

Lonnie stepped forward and swung his rifle at her like a bat, connecting with her forehead. Lukas couldn't see her face clearly from his vantage point, but as she looked at her assailant, he thought she smiled.

He was about to pull the trigger again but Javi beat him to it, firing his weapon, a traditional handgun, at the woman's chest. She seemed unfazed, though now her attention was on him. She pulled herself upright on her one working leg and hopped in his direction. Lukas heard multiple guns cock, ready to fire.

"She's mine!" Mike yelled, freezing them all. He was rolling over and getting to his feet, his left eye seeping blood and some other fluid.

The creature half turned to him, unable to twist completely around due to the missing hip.

"We've got her," Martie said. "Just stay back, Mike."

Mike reached up to the side of his neck and noticed for the first time the same thing they all did—the female Fury had bitten a chunk out of him where his neck met the collarbone. The wound was deep and bleeding profusely.

Nobody spoke. Not even the Fury was grunting. They all seemed to process the reality of the situation at the same time.

Before anyone could say a word, he whispered quietly, "This is for my brother."

And then he ran straight at the Fury, body-slamming her as he lifted her off the ground. He kept his legs pumping, ignoring her swipes as he carried her to the back of the truck. No one had time to react.

Mike ran right out of the back of the truck with his arms wrapped around the Fury. They hit the ground together and eventually rolled to a stop a few feet from each other. Mike looked stunned, and his legs were crumpled below him unnaturally. The Fury didn't waste a second in crawling toward him.

"We have to stop," Jamie yelled. "We have to get him."

Even as she said it, they saw more Furies, at least a dozen, converging toward the scene. They would be on him in seconds.

"What happened?" Caleb asked from the driver's seat. "Should I stop?"

It took Lukas less time than he was proud of to answer. "No. It's too late. We can't help."

Even as he said it, the swarm of creatures was on Mike, tearing him to pieces. As the truck drove off and the mass of bodies receded in the distance, he thought he heard Mike scream, "Kill them all!"

But then the voice went quiet, and he wondered if he'd imagined it. He turned back around, facing forward, his eyes fixed determinedly on the road, trying to block out everything but the intermittently recurring straight white lines before him.

"We're clear," Aubrey said through the window. "You can ease up on the gas a little. Just go fast enough that nothing can jump in."

Caleb slowed down but only slightly. Lukas sat beside him quietly, watching as his brother approached the access road that ran parallel to the I-10 freeway. He recognized the area. They were only a couple of miles from their grandparents' gated community. If they turned right, they could be there in less than five minutes.

Caleb slowed the truck, glancing over at him. Lukas knew what his brother was thinking. Trying to get to Mike's dad's station was always a questionable idea. Now that he was dead, it made even less sense.

"What do you think?" Caleb asked him, the rest of his question obvious.

"We should go to Grams and Gramps's house," Lukas said without hesitation.

"No," someone yelled from the back. Lukas recognized it as Emily's voice. She sounded confused. "Tell them, Mike. We have to go to the precinct."

No one said anything. Lukas wasn't even sure he'd heard her correctly. For a few seconds, the only sound was the idling of the truck and the grunts of the distant but approaching Furies.

"We have to try," Caleb said. "We promised him."

"That's right," Jamie shouted from the back. "Besides, nothing has changed. It's still the safest option."

"It's not," Jules countered. "We have no idea what's waiting for us there. And look at the highway. It's choked with cars. We might not even make it."

Lukas looked ahead. It was true. The overpass in front of them was clogged with vehicles. It was still too dark to see much beyond that. But there was no reason to think it would be different as they headed toward the more populated part of town.

"You better decide quickly," Javi shouted. "Those things are catching up."

"Caleb," Jules said calmly, "Mike is dead. We need to do what's best for the rest of us."

"What?" Emily screamed, bewildered. "Who's dead?"

Lukas could hear Martie trying to calm her down with soothing words.

"Jules is right," Aubrey added, ignoring the chaos near her. "Go to the house."

"Don't be selfish," Jamie demanded. "You just want to see your family. A police station makes more sense than the home of some senior citizens. Keep your promise, Caleb!"

"Keep your promise!" Emily shouted, borderline incoherent.

Lukas saw Caleb's jaw clench, a sign that he'd made a decision. He looked ahead and punched the gas, heading under the overpass in the direction of the freeway entrance that would take them to the police station. Lukas sank in his seat, certain this was a mistake.

His concerns were borne out only seconds later. When Caleb tried to turn left to get on the freeway entrance, they saw that it was blocked by half a dozen unmoving vehicles, making access impossible.

"Damn it!" he muttered under his breath.

"Forget it," Lukas said. "Turn around and go back. We still have time to get to the house."

He couldn't see what was happening behind them and had no idea if what he'd said was true. But his brother needed support more than information right now. Caleb hurried through a three-point turn, as Emily's screeches of "Keep your promise" echoed through the morning darkness.

When they finally turned back in the direction from which they had come, they saw a stream of Furies coming toward them. They were still far enough away that the truck could outpace them. But the sheer number of them stunned Lukas. It looked like the entire population of a high school football stadium was converging on them all at once.

"I'm going to take the access road all the way there," Caleb said as he hit the gas hard.

Lukas nodded blankly. His brother went back below the underpass and veered sharply left. Within seconds the mass of Furies was left behind.

"You betrayed his one wish!" Jamie shouted from the backseat.

"Oh shut up, Jamie," Jules snapped. "We tried. And following his one wish almost got us all killed. There's a reason you're not in charge."

Jamie stopped arguing, but her silence was replaced by Emily, who had picked up on her last words, moaning "betrayed" over and over.

Lukas felt frustration rising in his throat. He opened his mouth and was just about to blurt out a demand for someone to deal with her when Aubrey beat him to it.

"Martie," she pleaded, "you've got to do something about her. Those things just have to follow her voice to find us. She's louder than the frickin' truck."

"I'm doing the best I can," Martie shot back, clearly at her wits' end. "It's just too much for her."

Lukas watched as Lonnie got up and moved over to sit next to them.

"Emily," he said soothingly, putting his hand on hers, "it's going to be okay. Just breathe. Breathe with me. Let's do it together, okay?"

Lukas watched as Emily locked her desperate, frenzied eyes on Lonnie's and mimicked his deep inhalations. Soon thereafter, her betrayal accusations ceased and were replaced by intermittent whimpering. Lukas was fine with the tradeoff.

During the short drive to his grandparents' place, small groups of Furies ran at the truck. But in the mostly wide open space of the unoccupied road, Caleb was able to avoid them all. In the back, they could hear people trying to help Emily regroup. Now that she was somewhat coherent again, she kept asking what had happened to Mike. No one would answer her.

It only took about two minutes to reach the main entrance of The Promontory. They turned right down the road that led to the guard station and security gate arm. Caleb switched off the headlights to avoid drawing attention. They weren't really necessary anyway as the first hint of the sun was just starting to peek over the hills in the east. Both brothers were unsettled by how quiet everything seemed to be. There wasn't anyone, human or otherwise, in sight.

"Maybe they all went to the base," Lukas suggested, answering their shared, unspoken question. "I'm sure those things could hear the crowd from way out here. There were thousands of them around those walls. Others might have been drawn in by the noise."

"Maybe," Caleb said, though he didn't sound convinced.

The area all around the gate arm was littered with empty cars, some of which were still running. Caleb had to weave his way in and out of the maze of vehicles to get by. The wooden security arm was still down, but someone had clearly ignored it, driving straight through and breaking it off so that only a short, now-jagged portion remained.

After they had navigated the obstacle course of cars, Caleb started down the main road in the neighborhood, Promontory Drive. As he picked up speed, Lukas heard a strange sound in the distance, one he couldn't identify. He was about to ask if his brother heard it, too, when a voice from the back hissed quietly.

"They're coming," Trevor said, "from the golf course."

Lukas looked through his window to the right, back at the eighteen-hole golf course, half of which ran along much of the south end of The Promontory community. Moving toward them across the first fairway in one giant mass were at least fifty Furies. The sound he'd heard was their collective grunting, louder and faster than usual, a result of running. They were still several hundred yards away but closing fast.

"Better pick up the pace a little," he warned Caleb. "We want to be well ahead of those things so they can't see where we're going."

Caleb didn't reply but apparently agreed because the truck immediately went from about thirty miles per hour to around fifty. Pretty soon, they had passed over a large hill and were headed down the other side toward the intersection that crossed their grandparents' street, Devonshire Lane. The Furies behind them were no longer in sight.

Caleb was just slowing down to make the right turn onto Devonshire when they appeared out of nowhere, not Furies but deer. A group of four of them darted out into the road, just yards ahead of the truck. Caleb, operating on years of driving instinct, veered hard right to avoid them.

Unfortunately the combination of a sudden swerve as he was already turning sharply in a top-heavy vehicle on a downhill slope while going about forty miles per hour was too much for the truck. The right front and rear tires lifted off the ground, suspended briefly in mid-air, before the truck landed on its left side and skidded to a stop in the exact middle of the intersection.

CHAPTER 40

Lukas realized he'd been holding his breath and exhaled slowly.

The crash happened so fast that no one even screamed as it occurred. But now that the truck had stopped moving, Emily began to make up for lost time. Martie immediately shushed her. Lukas considered it a good sign that he heard groans and not shrieks coming from the back. That likely meant any injuries weren't life-threatening.

"Is everyone okay?" Javi asked.

There were general sounds of confirmation as people clambered out of the truck. Lukas, who was still strapped into his seatbelt, dangled above his brother, who was now below him.

"You good?" he asked.

"Yeah," Caleb replied. "I slammed my left shoulder pretty hard but I'll live. Are you able to open that window and get out? I'm not sure how much time we have."

"Yeah," Lukas said, concerned about the same thing.

He pushed the button to open the window and was relieved when it worked. He hooked his right elbow over the door as he unbuckled his belt with his left hand. His body dropped forcefully, but he managed to cling to the door and hoist himself up on top of it.

From there, he could see that everyone was now out of the truck. Aubrey, Martie, and Jamie were swinging their weapon-filled backpacks onto their backs. The rest of the group seemed functional, though Trevor was supporting a woozy-looking Emily. Lukas glanced back in the direction of the hill they'd just passed over. There was no sign of the Furies.

Lukas heard a click and looked down too see his brother unbuckling himself. Caleb tossed up his own backpack, which Lukas grabbed and dropped into the arms of Javi, waiting below. Then Lukas lay down and braced himself on the outside of the truck door as he reached down to offer his arm. Behind him, he could hear the others talking quietly.

"Keep your eyes peeled," Aubrey warned in a loud whisper. "They can't be far behind."

"Do you smell something?" Javi asked.

"Yeah," Lonnie said. "I think it's gas. The truck might be leaking."

As Caleb got to his feet and prepared to leap up, Lukas held up his hand for him to wait and turned back to the group.

"Guys, while I get Caleb out, you should all head up the hill there on Devonshire. Our grandparents live in the last house on the left before the intersection. Follow the driveway all the way back to the garage and wait at the side door. It's out of sight from the street."

He returned his attention to Caleb who still looked like his shoulder was giving him trouble. "You able to do this?" Lukas asked, concerned.

"I can get up there. But I may need your help pulling me over the edge. I'm not at full strength."

"Let's hurry, then," Lukas instructed. "On three—one, two, three!"

Caleb leapt up and grasped the outside of the door with his right hand as Lukas wrapped his arms around his brother's chest and pulled him up the rest of the way. After some yanking and scrambling, they both lay safely on top, exhausted. They looked out and saw that everyone in the group, save for Javi, had begun the trek up the Devonshire hill.

"What are you still doing here?" Lukas asked.

"I thought y'all might like a hand getting down. Or are you too cool for school?"

"I could use it," Caleb admitted, swinging his legs around and preparing to hop down. "Grab me if I start to fall okay? My shoulder's a little hinky."

Javi nodded. Caleb dropped the approximately eight feet to the street with barely a wobble, no assistance required. Lukas was about to swing his own legs around when he noticed the energy rifle at the bottom of the truck.

"We forgot the gun," he said.

"There are lots more in the backpacks, Lukas," Caleb assured him. "We can dole them out once we're safely in the house. For now, we have to get there."

"Okay," Lukas said as he prepared to jump down. He was about to make the leap when he heard the same familiar grunting from a few minutes earlier. It was much louder now. Looking back up the hill of Promontory Drive, he still saw nothing but doubted it would stay that way for long.

"They're coming," he said as he hopped down, landing hard in something wet but managing to keep his feet without assistance. "We better move quick before they see us."

"Yeah, let's go," Javi agreed. "By the way, I think you just stepped in gasoline. So don't light any matches in the next few minutes."

Lukas was amazed at his friend's ability to maintain his sense of humor even under current conditions. "Thanks, buddy," he replied. "I'll keep it in mind."

The three of them began their ascent of the hill, which the others were already halfway up. As they passed the first house on the right, Lukas saw the four deer that had caused their crash. They all stood quietly, staring at them amiably as the three of them ran by, seemingly without a care in the world.

They had just reached the second house when the first Furies appeared over the ridge of the hill. Lukas was pretty sure he and the rest of the group were hidden from view by the house to the right. But he wasn't confident they'd make it to the security of their grandparents' driveway before they entered the line of sight of the fast-approaching horde.

"We should try to distract them," he suddenly said to Caleb and Javi, who were looking up the hill as well.

"How?" Caleb asked.

"Are there any flare guns in the backpack?" Lukas asked.

"I think so. But I doubt a flare is going to distract them for long."

"I don't want to fire it in the air," Lukas replied. "I want to shoot it at that pool of gasoline by the truck. I'll bet that would get their attention for a while."

"Okay," Caleb agreed. "But we have to make it quick. One shot only, okay?"

Lukas nodded, and they both rifled through the pack on Javi's back until Caleb pulled it out. He handed it to Lukas.

"I'm not sure about my aim with my shoulder," he said. "You better take the shot."

Lukas nodded and turned to face the overturned truck. He tried to locate the puddle of gas he'd stepped in, but in the half-light of the still-approaching dawn, it was difficult to find it. He decided to aim for the ground just below the passenger side door where he'd jumped down and hope for the best.

"What are you doing?" someone hissed from behind them. He turned around to see the rest of the group had reached their grandparents' driveway and was standing there waiting. Aubrey, who must have asked the question, had an incredulous look on her face.

With neither the time nor the inclination to explain himself, Lukas turned back around and tried to focus on his task. He'd never fired a flare gun before and had only seen one used once previously, by Aubrey, on Hollow Hill yesterday. He did as she had done, blowing one long, slow breath before pulling the trigger.

He knew immediately that his aim had been off. The flare veered short and left of his intended target, skidding along the road until it hit the bottom of the truck near the left rear tire.

His spirits were just starting to sink when a spray of sparks from the collision shot everywhere, lighting up a gas slick on the pavement next to the vehicle. The flames moved quickly, following a seemingly magical path to the spot where Lukas had hopped down. Suddenly the stream of fire turned into a pool of it, shooting up a concentrated inferno right in front of the truck.

"Let's go," Caleb said, tapping him on the shoulder. "That should work pretty well."

The three of them ran up the rest of the hill and arrived at the driveway. Lukas turned back briefly and saw that the fire had now fully engulfed the truck. An explosion had to be imminent. He could only hope that it didn't happen until a bunch of the Furies were close by.

He ran down the driveway after Javi and Caleb and found the others standing anxiously by the side door of the house, next to the attached garage. Aubrey and Martie had their weapons up, peering among the trees next to the driveway for anything unexpected.

Caleb ran past them and immediately pushed in on a brick in the wall next to the side door. The fake brick popped out when pressed, and Caleb scooped out the key hidden inside. He unlocked the door but held it closed.

"Have your weapons ready," he said. "But don't fire just because you see movement. My grandparents could easily be in there, and they might think we're looters or worse. Announce your presence."

"Wait," Lukas said, noting he was still holding the flare gun. "Let me trade this out."

He was just fishing a gun out of the backpack Javi was wearing when the truck down below exploded, sending a fireball into the air and making the windows of the house rattle violently.

"Let's get inside," Martie said. "That is going to attract a *lot* of attention."

Caleb opened the door, and they entered, with Aubrey taking the lead. Lukas waited for everyone to pass, then stepped inside as his brother closed the door, shutting out the popping and grunting in the distance.

CHAPTER 41

"Spread out and search the house," Caleb whispered once they were all inside.

Everyone nodded silently and dispersed in groups of two and three, each of them calling out quietly for "Gramps" and "Grams" to let the homeowners know they weren't total strangers.

It took less than three minutes for the ten of them to explore the entire downstairs floor, including the four bedrooms. There was no one there.

They reassembled in the breakfast room where they stood around the table, unsure of how to proceed. After a couple of uncertain seconds, Lonnie decided to take a seat. Others quickly followed. Trevor put down his gun and grabbed a sheet of paper lying on the table.

"I think it's a note for you guys," he said looking at Lukas and Caleb.

"What does it say?" Caleb asked pointedly not taking the paper himself.

Trevor looked at his counselor, making sure it was really okay to read it out loud. Caleb nodded at him.

"It says, 'Boys, the cars are gassed up. The keys are in the usual place. We love you. Grams & Gramps.'"

Lukas and Caleb exchanged glances.

"That sounds like a message that could have been left any day of the week," Jules noted.

"Maybe they wrote it before things got too bad," Lonnie offered.

"Or maybe," Aubrey suggested, voicing Lukas's suspicion, "they wanted to be cryptic so that potential looters wouldn't know where to look for the car keys."

"If they left both cars," Lukas said to Caleb, not commenting on the others' theories, "they probably didn't go anywhere."

"Right," his brother agreed. "It's possible they holed up with a neighbor. But they would have mentioned that. We should check upstairs."

Lukas nodded. He'd been thinking the same thing.

"Lukas and I are going upstairs to check their bedroom and study," Caleb announced in a hushed voice. "It's a small area so we can do it ourselves. Why don't the rest of you double-check every-thing down here? Make sure all the doors and windows are closed and locked, all the blinds are pulled. We don't want anyone to be able to see inside. Then make yourselves comfortable. Look around for some food. Just remember to stay quiet. Don't use any appliances. We don't know how close those things are. Once Lukas and I get back down, we can figure out a plan. Y'all good with that?"

There was a general murmur of agreement. As Lukas followed his brother up the stairs, he couldn't help but remember how Corporal Daugherty had given Caleb a hard time for being a California boy using the word "y'all."

Almost immediately his mind flashed back to the image of the young woman being overwhelmed as a dozen Furies converged on the Jeep that she'd tried to escape in, her blonde hair disappearing amid a multitude of limbs and teeth. He shook his head, literally trying to force the memory to go away.

When they got to the top of the stairs, Caleb pointed for him go right. "You take the bedroom and study," he said. "I'll check out the bathrooms and closets."

Lukas nodded and, with his rifle raised, passed through the hall into his grandparents' bedroom. The search didn't take long. Their bed was made, complete with fluffed up pillows. He continued to the adjoining study, which was also empty. He pressed on the false front of a wall that housed their safe just in case they were hiding in the small spaces on either side of it. They weren't.

He glanced out of the door that led to the balcony. They weren't outside, which was no surprise. But in the rising morning light, he could see hundreds of Furies moving toward the burning, smoking wreckage of the truck at the bottom of the hill. He wondered if the short-term advantage of distracting them with the flames might be offset by drawing so many of them nearby.

Even though he was on the second floor where the chances of being seen were remote, he pulled the blinds closed. Passing back through the bedroom into the hall at the top of the stairs, he met up with his brother who looked troubled.

"Find anything?" Caleb asked.

"Not Grams and Gramps. But I looked down below and the neighborhood is crawling with those things now. You?"

"No luck."

"Did you check the hidden room upstairs behind the pull-away cabinet unit in Grams's closet?" Lukas reminded him.

"Of course," Caleb said. "What kind of search would it be if I didn't check the panic room? We should get back down to the others."

"Okay. But I don't know where they would have gone. It's hard to imagine they wouldn't have told us where they were headed if they were leaving the house."

"I don't know Lukas," Caleb replied, sounding surprisingly testy. "But they clearly didn't want us to focus on that or they would have written more in their note than just gas tank information for the cars. They want us to get out of here if we can."

Lukas tried not to let his brother's sharp tone get to him. Everyone was stressed. "Yeah, well, we need a plan for that," he replied.

"Yes, we do," Caleb agreed. "Let's see if anyone else has ideas. And we should get you some food. As long as we have supplies, we should take advantage."

"You should eat, too," Lukas said. His brother suddenly looked unusually pale.

"I'm not hungry right now. Maybe later."

They returned downstairs where they saw the group had found some canned fruit and beef jerky. Most of them were still assembled around the breakfast table, nibbling unenthusiastically. Martie was sitting on the couch with Emily who seemed to have regained her senses. They were conducting what looked like some kind of concussion test on her. Aubrey was standing in the kitchen looking at her satellite watch, which she'd plugged into a wall socket.

"Any luck?" Caleb asked her.

"It's charging," she replied. "You guys still have intermittent power but it keeps cutting on and off, so it's taking longer than usual to charge. It doesn't have enough juice for calls yet. But soon, I think."

"No luck on your grandparents?" Lonnie asked.

Caleb shook his head. "We're on our own." he said.

"So what are we going to do?" Jamie asked. "We're safe for now. But that could change any minute. Don't we need a long-term plan?"

Everyone sat quietly, pondering their options. Lukas, who had the kernel of an idea, was about to broach it when Aubrey's watch beeped.

"It's connected," she said. "But it's only at 3 percent. It's going to take a while to fully charge. But I should be able to make a call now. Should I try to reach out to my father?"

"What's the point?" Emily asked bitterly, speaking with biting precision despite her recent hysteria and her bump on the head. "He wouldn't help us get out of there before. I doubt he's going to come looking for us now."

"One point would be to, you know, find out if my dad is still alive," Aubrey noted coldly.

"Must be nice to have a loved one who might not be dead or a rage zombie," Emily countered, not at all chastened.

"Hey, I understand you've been through a lot, Emily," Martie said quietly but firmly. "But we're not doing this right now. Everybody is struggling. Let's not start pointing fingers. We can do that when we're safe and sound."

"Not to be a jerk," Javi said apologetically, "but when do you see that happening? Because it looks kind of bleak out there to me."

"Maybe sooner than you think," Lukas said softly.

"What?" Emily asked incredulously. "Do you have some secret plan you've been keeping from the rest of us?"

"Not a secret plan," he responded, pretending not to notice her tone. "But I have an idea. And to see if it will work, we definitely need to contact Colonel West."

"What's your idea?" Jules asked.

Lukas looked around at the group, prepared for the mockery he would likely get when he voiced his suggestion. But he pressed ahead anyway.

"I want to drive to Mexico."

CHAPTER 42

There was total silence for several seconds before Trevor finally spoke.

"Why?" he asked, dumbfounded.

Lukas thought it would be obvious, but apparently it wasn't. "Don't you remember that briefing Colonel West gave us?" he asked. "He said that Mexico and Canada had closed their borders once they saw what was happening. Assuming that worked, it should be a safe haven for us—if we can get there."

"Is that even physically possible?" Trevor asked. "I mean isn't that a long way off?"

The rest of the group looked at him with disbelief.

Jules tried to respond diplomatically. "You're from Dallas, right?" she asked.

"Yeah."

"Well, it's a trek from there," she acknowledged. "But from here in San Antonio, it's only about three hours to the border, depending on the route you take."

"And a lot of it is pretty rural territory," Caleb added.

"How do you know that, California boy?" Jules asked, her eyebrows raised.

"I may have made the drive once with friends when I was visiting here last summer," he replied sheepishly before moving on. "The point is that it might not be as crowded with Furies as cities would be. We'd probably have an easier time dodging them."

"But what about when we got to the actual border?" Trevor persisted. "Assuming we made it there in one piece, would they even let us in?"

"That's why we need to contact the colonel," Lukas said. "He'd know better than most if that's realistic. If it is, maybe he could even call ahead to let them know we're coming."

Everyone fell silent as they all pondered the idea.

"So can I call then?" Aubrey finally asked.

"Go ahead," Caleb said. "It's worth a shot."

She hit the appropriate button on her phone and waited for the call to connect. When it did, they all heard the colonel's familiar voice. Lukas saw Aubrey's body visibly relax.

"Aubrey?" he barked anxiously. "Are you okay?"

"Yes, sir. What about you?"

"I'm fine," he assured her. "Our convoy is en route to Checkpoint Zulu. But I lost track of you. The guards in the hangar said your whole group had left."

Aubrey looked up at the others with apprehensive eyes. "We had to go," she half lied. "We heard the general alarm and were concerned that those things were about to bust in. We managed to get to the motor pool and secure a truck."

"I'm so relieved, sweetie," he said with a warmth Lukas hadn't heard before. "I sent Kim Daugherty to look for you, and when I didn't hear back, I feared the worst."

The image of the small blonde getting engulfed by Furies flashed once again through Lukas's head. He grimaced at the memory. Aubrey noticed and gave him a questioning look.

"I saw her in the motor pool," he whispered to her. "She didn't make it."

Aubrey paused before speaking again. "We must have somehow missed Kim in the chaos," she finally said to her father, pointedly not telling him the truth.

"Hopefully she'll check in soon," he said. "Where are you now?"

"We're holed up in the home of the Lincoln brothers' grandparents. They only live a few miles from the base. We're regrouping here before we make our next move."

"I would send help," Colonel West said, "but we don't have the resources right now. Every road vehicle is filled to capacity, and every copter and plane is spoken for. Your best bet may just be to hunker down there until things settle down."

Everyone looked at Lukas. If ever there was moment to broach his idea, this was it. He walked over and stood next to Aubrey.

"This is Lukas Lincoln, sir."

"Hello, Mr. Lincoln. I'm glad to hear your voice."

"Thank you, sir," he replied, pressing on. "I had an alternate idea, and I wanted to see if you thought it was workable."

"Let's hear it."

"Well, colonel, we probably can't stay here much longer," he explained. "Getting here was a messy undertaking. And the neighborhood is full of Furies. We're safe for the time being. But pretty soon, they'll be all over the place. Any loud or accidental sound will send them our way, and we'll be sitting ducks. Unlike the lodge at Hollow Hill, this house has tons of unsecured windows. It wouldn't take them long to get in."

"So what's your alternative idea?"

"Sir, my grandparents are gone but they left us two working, fully gassed up vehicles, one of which is a minivan. I think we could get out of the immediate area without too much trouble. The question is where we would go."

"I get the sense that you have somewhere in mind, son."

"I do, sir," Lukas answered. "I was thinking we could go to the Mexican border. I remember you saying it had been secured. But I have two questions. First, is that still the case? And second, if we made it, would they let us in?"

There was silence on the other end of the line. For a moment, Lukas thought they'd lost the connection. Then the colonel spoke.

"Sorry, Mr. Lincoln," he said. "I'm getting updates on those questions from my team right now. I'm being told that, so far at least, the Mexican defenses are holding. There are no reports of any Furies getting through."

"How can that be, colonel?" Caleb interjected. "They can't man the entire length of the border."

"I assume this is the other Mr. Lincoln?" Colonel West said.

"Yes, sir."

"Well, our friends south of the border made an amazing discovery when they were first addressing that very concern," Colonel West said. "Apparently the Furies aren't huge fans of water. Small amounts don't bother them. But it seems that, when it gets high enough to be noticeable, around the knees or so, they get skittish. They lose their balance. There have been reports of some of them falling in water less than waist high and drowning because they don't know what to do."

As Colonel West said it, Lukas recalled their desperate climb up Hollow Hill and how some of the Furies had hesitated when they came to the narrow stream that briefly cut across the trail. If that unimposing stretch of water had bothered them, then a real river ought to give them serious trouble.

"How does that help us?" Trevor asked, showing once again that geography must not be his strongest subject in school.

"I don't know who asked that," Colonel West replied, impressively keeping the condescension out of his voice, "but the answer is that it helps because virtually the entire border between Texas and Mexico runs along the Rio Grande River, creating a natural barrier. There are stretches where it is dried up or extremely shallow. But because those areas are so rural and unpopulated, the Mexican authorities know where the vulnerable spots are and have had time to reinforce them. That means that the bulk of the threat of a Furies' breach is in metro areas, at international border crossings, which almost all involve bridges. And bridges are more easily protected because they form a bottleneck."

"So," Javi joined in, "if we cross at an area where the river is deeper but we don't have to deal with Mexican officials, we should be good, right?"

"In theory, Mr. Mendez," the colonel answered, showing an amazing facility to keep track of the individual members of their group. "But that's a risk. There are roving patrols, and if they see a bunch of unidentified folks crossing without authorization, they might just open fire as a precaution. You're going to want their approval before entering their country."

"That was my second question," Lukas reminded him. "Will they give us that approval?"

"There's no way to know," Colonel West admitted. "Communication down there is spotty right now. And I don't personally have any contacts that could be useful. My best recommendation is find a high-water crossing, seek out the Mexican security personnel on the other side, and get their authorization to cross over."

"How are we supposed to do all that?" Emily piped in, her sharp tone revealing her residual animosity toward the colonel. "Especially if we've got a bunch of Furies on our heels."

"I would recommend trying to avoid them if possible," he replied drily. "And as discussed, you'd probably be well advised to find a less populated area to cross. That way, you'll draw less attention in general. Avoid major points of entry. No big international bridges. No population centers. Hold on a moment."

Everyone looked around at each other while they waited. Clearly none of them had any idea where that ideal crossing point might be.

"Do your grandparents have any maps?" Martie eventually asked.

Lukas was trying to recall where they were kept when the colonel came back on the line.

"Sorry about that," he said. "One of my guys was giving me some information that may be helpful. Based on your location, your best bet may be to head west, taking rural highways until you meet up with Highway 57. Follow that in the general direction of Eagle Pass. That's your closest border crossing that's reasonably accessible. If you try to cross the river north of town, you should avoid too many people but still be able to get the attention of the Mexican authorities. How does that sound?"

Lukas thought it sounded better than the plan they had up until then, which was no plan at all.

"It sounds good," Caleb said, speaking for the group. "But you don't think there's any way you can reach out to the border authorities at the Eagle Pass crossing and let them know to be on the lookout for us?"

"Frankly, I wouldn't know where to start," Colonel West said. "And even if I did, I'm not sure that the Mexican government is interested in putting any resources into keeping an eye out for a bunch of teenagers who may or may not show up at some point. Besides, we're approaching our checkpoint very soon. At that time, I will be required to go radio silent for security reasons. I won't be able to reach out to anyone. I'm afraid that from this point forward, you're on your own."

CHAPTER 43

No one balked when Aubrey unplugged the watch and walked to a back bedroom to finish the conversation with her dad. Most of them seemed to realize it might be the last time she got to speak to him for a long time, maybe ever.

In the meantime, Lukas hunted through his grandparents' travel drawer and found several maps of the state, along with an AAA guidebook that included information on Eagle Pass. Behind him, he could hear Lonnie and Jamie talking quietly about what they would do once they got to Mexico. He thought their planning was premature but said nothing. Aubrey came out of the bedroom hallway a minute later.

"How are you doing?" Jules asked quietly as she walked over and offered a hug.

"I'll get by," Aubrey muttered as she sidestepped the move and instead gave an appreciative but awkward smile.

Jules nodded, looking slightly embarrassed but saying nothing.

"I'm not even sure why I'm doing this," Aubrey said as she plugged the watch back in. "The chances that I'll need to use it again are pretty remote."

"Better to have it and not need it than the other way around," Martie reminded her supportively.

Aubrey nodded but looked unconvinced.

"Can I get everyone's attention?" Caleb asked in the loudest voice he felt comfortable using, which was barely above a whisper.

He was standing at the breakfast table, looking at a piece of paper he'd made notes on. The rest of them gathered around and waited. Lukas could see his brother was slightly nervous, again resorting to unconsciously fidgeting with his fingers, a sure sign that he wasn't excited about what he had to say next.

"Now that we know our situation and have something of a general plan, I think we need to start prepping—"

"Do we have a plan?" Emily interrupted. "Because if the plan is to drive a minivan through Fury-infested country in the hopes of making it to the border, I'm not sure I'm on board. Maybe we should take a vote."

Caleb seemed surprised that anyone would balk at what had been suggested. He was momentarily silent. Lukas saw from their expressions that Trevor and Jamie had similar reservations.

"That's not a bad idea," Trevor said, reinforcing Lukas's concern. "Maybe we should reconsider our options."

"Like you reconsidered your options last night?" Lonnie asked suddenly, speaking with a sharpness Lukas wasn't used to.

"What's that supposed to mean?" Trevor demanded.

"You know what it means. I saw you sneak out of the hangar last night. You were gone for close to an hour, Trevor. Where were you? Looking for a good hiding place when all hell broke loose?"

Everyone looked at Trevor expectantly.

"What's this all about?" Martie finally asked.

Trevor sat unresponsive for several seconds before responding. "It's no big deal," he replied defensively.

"If it's no big deal, then tell us what you were doing," Aubrey pressed.

Trevor looked at her resentfully. When it became clear that no one was going to let him off the hook, he answered. "Maybe I didn't have total confidence in your plan, okay? I guess I got cold feet for a little while. If I was like my mom, I'd just pop a Xanax and let it ride. But I decided to go a different route, so I just walked around for a while, looking for another option. Maybe I thought about stowing away in one of the other trucks. But in the end, I couldn't bail on everyone, so I came back."

"Was it that, or did you just not find a better option?" Lonnie asked derisively.

"Screw you, Lonnie," Trevor shot back. "I'm telling the truth. If you don't believe me, that's your problem, not mine."

Lukas looked at him, unsure of what to make of this revelation. Part of him couldn't blame the guy for temporarily losing his nerve. Still, he couldn't help but wonder if that was really the whole story. Regardless, at least he knew now that his half-asleep sighting of Trevor's empty cot wasn't just his imagination.

"It's hard to know if we can trust you anymore," Jules said with a self-righteousness that surprised Lukas considering how she'd so easily broken her own promise to Dr. Raina DiSanto.

For a brief moment, his mind flashed to an image of the doctor in the lab. Was she still alive, cowering in the center of her cage, trying to stay away from the grasping arms of the surrounding Furies? Or had they broken through the bars and either killed her or expedited her transformation into one of them? Either way, he felt a rush of shame as he realized this was the first time he'd thought of her at all today.

"I want to vote, too," Jamie said, ignoring the two guys glaring at each other on either side of her.

Lukas looked at the faces around the table, some terrified, some angry, all uncertain. He didn't feel any more confident than they looked, but one thing was clear to him: the path they were currently on was unsustainable.

Decisions had to be made, soon. And he trusted his own judgment more than most of the people he was looking at. So, fearing things might degenerate further, he stepped forward. He knew it might alienate some of them, but he didn't think he had much choice.

"There's not going to be a vote," he said quietly but firmly, completely sure of himself for the first time in a while. "If you don't want to go, no one's going to make you. You're welcome to stay in this house as long as you can hold out. Personally, I think that's just slow-motion suicide. But it's your choice. Having said that, our grandparents left those vehicles for Caleb and me, and we're in agreement—we're going to Mexico. So you can come or not come, but we're leaving."

Emily stared at him with an expression he wasn't used to seeing on her face. She looked defeated. She didn't even seem angry, just beaten down. Trevor and Jamie looked equally cowed. He didn't really care.

"You were saying, Caleb," he said, turning back to his brother.

"Thanks," Caleb said, looking mildly surprised. "I was saying that we should start prepping. I don't think it's realistic for us to leave today. We need to do a lot of organization. And I think we could all stand a decent night's sleep. My thought is that we should leave first thing tomorrow morning so we have as much daylight as possible in case something goes wrong. Plus, those creatures out there might have dispersed a little by tomorrow once the truck fire has burned off some more."

"Sounds reasonable," Martie agreed.

"Okay," Caleb said, visibly heartened by the support. "So between now and then, we have a lot to do. We need to check the weapons in those backpacks, make sure they're loaded and in working order. We should also charge up the energy rifles with whatever power we still have."

"I can handle that if I get some help," Aubrey offered.

"Great," Caleb said, then continued. "We should also load up on other supplies as a precaution. I'm pretty sure my grandparents have a first aid kit around somewhere. We should hunt down some flashlights and pack a bunch of easily transportable foods, high-energy stuff."

"And lots of water," Javi added. "Are there bottles?"

"Check the pantry," Caleb said. "I assume there are some. Then we should go over the route the colonel recommended so that everyone is on the same page. After we pack up the vehicles, we should lay low and try to relax. Have as many decent meals as we can today and really get a good night's sleep tonight. There are more than enough bedrooms for everyone to be comfortable. How does all that sound?"

"It sounds good," Jules said without hesitation, looking at Caleb with a mix of affection and pride.

"For those of you who don't want to come with us," he added, doing a solid job of keeping his voice measured, "we'll of course leave you weapons, food, and water. Like Lukas said, you can stay as long as you want. But we should get a head count so we know what we're dealing with. Who's coming?"

Caleb raised his own hand to get things started. Lukas, Martie, Aubrey, Jules, Javi, and Lonnie immediately did, too. After a moment Jamie raised her as well. Lastly, after sharing a look of uncertainty, Emily and Trevor did the same.

"All right then," Caleb said. "Now that that's decided, let's get to work."

CHAPTER 44

It didn't take as long as they thought.

Even moving slowly to avoid making noise, all of the tasks Caleb assigned were completed in under an hour. It wasn't even noon, and they had no idea what to do with themselves. Eventually most wandered off to check out the bedroom options for the night until Lukas realized he was alone at the table with Aubrey who was rechecking that all the rifles were in working order.

"Can I ask you something?" he said, deciding to bring up the question that had been eating at him since they talked to Colonel West.

"You can always ask, Lincoln," she said, not looking up from her work, "but I can't guarantee I'll answer."

"Okay. Why didn't you tell your father what I said about Corporal Daugherty not making it?"

Aubrey continued to study the rifle in her hands, checking the safety multiple times. Lukas was about to give up on getting any answer at all, but after a few seconds she replied. "Because he considered Kim to be kind of a second daughter. He was hard on her but respected how well she took it. He thought she had real officer potential. Her parents were pretty laissez-faire, so she embraced the discipline he provided. We had her over for dinner fairly often."

"You didn't resent that?"

Aubrey looked up, meeting his eyes for the first time in the conversation. "I did a little bit," she admitted softly. "But it seemed petty to show it. It wasn't her fault that he took an interest. And she never rubbed it in my face. I think she tried to be sensitive to how I felt."

"So you decided to protect him from the truth?"

Aubrey sighed. "He's already dealing with so much. I didn't want to add the extra burden of dealing with her death. Besides, if he doesn't know the truth, then he's still got hope for her. And the more people he has hope for, the more he believes that the people he cares about are still alive, the harder he'll fight. And I want him to fight."

Lukas nodded. Not sure what he could add, he returned his focus to the maps in front of him. After several minutes' poring over them, a distant creaking sound made him look up.

It was vaguely familiar, but he couldn't quite place it. Suddenly it got louder for a moment before quieting down again. That's when it clicked for him. Without meaning to, he gasped slightly.

"What is it?" Aubrey asked anxiously from behind him.

He waved her over as he walked to the breakfast room blinds and peeked out. When she joined him, he pointed to a metal gate in the backyard, on the other side of the pool. It was slightly ajar, swinging lazily in the gentle breeze.

"No one noticed that before, when were locking everything down?" she asked in a whisper.

"I guess not," he said. "I didn't even think of it until now."

"It doesn't seem like the sound is attracting any Furies," she noted, "but we should lock it to make it harder to access the house, don't you think?"

Lukas nodded. He knew where the key was and locking the gate was usually less noisy than the creaking noise itself. "Let's let the others know," he said.

"Or . . . maybe not," Aubrey suggested.

"What are you talking about?"

"It's just . . . we finally have everyone settled down. Emily's back to being obnoxious, which I'll take over hysterical any day. I think some people may even be sleeping. I'd rather not get everyone riled up if we can avoid it."

"So you want to go out there, just the two of us?" he asked skeptically. "What if something goes wrong?"

"You sound like your buddy, Javi," she replied, unable to hide her disdain. "Did you lose your nerve on the drive out here, Lincoln?"

Lukas looked at her, unsure if she was baiting him or being serious. Ultimately, he was too exhausted to care. "We'll need knives in case we run into any of them," he said. "Guns will attract the whole neighborhood. My grandma has a butcher knife on the kitchen island and a meat cleaver in a drawer."

"Now you're talking, Lincoln," she said approvingly. "If you had cojones like that at the dance the other night, maybes Jules would be sharing a bed with *you* tonight."

She seemed to realize almost immediately that she'd gone too far and was about to walk it back when he waved her off.

"Don't apologize. You can't help being cruel. It's just your way. Let's do this."

She waited silently as he grabbed the key and the knives, handing her the butcher knife and keeping the cleaver for himself. She looked like she wanted to say something more but held off.

He opened the back door slowly. Luckily, it made no noise. Looking around, he saw that at least so far, no Furies had discovered

269

the open gate. The yard was empty. He led the way, quietly walking around the pool, careful to avoid stepping on any of the dried leaves.

When they got to the gate, he poked his head around the stone wall and looked out onto the street. There were four Furies visible, all walking alone. They were barely moving, shuffling along slowly as if someone had pushed the extra-slow-motion button on a remote control. They seemed to need some kind of external stimulus in order to activate their aggression. He was reminded of Aunt Winnie's description of how, once they were out of targets to attack, the infected campers looked as if their batteries had run out.

"Be ready to run if they come this way," he whispered as he grasped the bars of the gate.

She nodded, tightening her grip on the knife. Lukas realized he was holding his breath and exhaled slowly. Then he closed the gate. It creaked slightly but no more than before. As carefully as possible, he put the metal key in the hole and turned it. The sound was negligible. He smiled at Aubrey and turned back to the house. That's when he saw him.

"What?" she asked, seeing his jaw drop.

He held his finger to his lips while pointing behind her with his cleaver hand. She turned around and saw what had caught his attention. Coming around from the corner of the yard where the water heater stood was a frail-looking, hunched-over Fury. Before he'd turned into one of them, he'd been an elderly man. In fact, he'd turned ninety earlier in the summer. Lukas knew that because he'd attended the man's birthday party.

"That's my grandparents' neighbor, Mr. Cronyn," he whispered.

Aubrey squinted at him, before whispering back. "How's his eyesight?' she asked hopefully.

"Not bad enough," he said.

The man's head was down and he hadn't yet seen them, but he would soon. And they couldn't get back to the door without crossing his path. Aubrey leaned over and spoke so quietly that even with her lips brushing his ear, Lukas could barely hear her.

"If he makes a fuss, all of the others outside are going to come running. We can't let that happen."

Lukas nodded. He knew what she was getting at, but he wasn't sure he was capable of doing what she was suggesting. She looked at her knife and his cleaver, then back at him, emphasizing her point.

Lukas remembered Mr. Cronyn as a sweet man, recently widowed but always smiling, with a twinkle in his eye. For his party, his daughter had gotten him a cake with ninety candles. He had spent a good five minutes blowing them all out, refusing any help.

But the thing in front of Lukas now wasn't Mr. Cronyn anymore. And if he got loud, everyone in that house would be dead in minutes. Lukas looked back over at Aubrey and saw the concerned expression on her face, as if she was unsure he could do what was required.

"Wait until he gets closer," he said quietly but with resolve. "The less time he has to make noise, the better chance we have."

She nodded. They waited several minutes, watching him shuffle aimlessly in their general direction, his eyes fixed on the ground in front of him. Though Lukas and Aubrey were silent, when he got within ten feet of them, Mr. Cronyn stiffened, seeming to sense that he wasn't alone. His head lifted and turned slowly in their direction. Lukas and Aubrey glanced at each other. Neither had to say a word.

They charged at him in unison. Mr. Cronyn saw them at the last moment and raised his right hand, claw like, as a low groan emanated from his mouth. The noise lasted less than a full second before Lukas swung the meat cleaver across his neck. He heard the sound of the man's windpipe being crushed. Still, a loud guttural sigh continued to linger on his lips.

Mr. Cronyn stumbled back and to the side, and then, as they watched in horror, he fell into the pool. As blood began to spread out from the open wound in his neck, he thrashed about violently, making splashing noises that sounded like crashing ocean waves to Lukas.

Aubrey looked at the scene, open-mouthed, and then, seemingly without thinking, jumped in the water beside Mr. Cronyn. Careful to avoid his slowly snapping jaws, she lifted the butcher knife high above the man's head and brought it down hard. Lukas looked away.

When he finally managed to turn his head back to the scene, Aubrey was climbing out of the pool, dripping in a mixture of blood and water. Mr. Cronyn silently bobbed in the water, the knife protruding from the top of his skull, his mouth still wide in a silent scream.

CHAPTER 45

Lukas waited for the sound of grunting, running Furies, but none came.

The noise of Mr. Cronyn flailing in the pool must not have been as deafening as he'd first thought. When they were sure that nothing was imminently headed their way, he and Aubrey got to work.

By the time they fished Mr. Cronyn's body out of the water, carried it to the corner of the yard, and covered it with the pool tarp, both of them were physically and emotionally drained. They each bent over, clutching their knees, barely able to stand.

Part of him embraced the exhaustion. If he was more alert, he'd have to process what he'd just done to his grandparents' neighbor. But at least for now, he could set it aside in an unoccupied part of his brain.

When they finally reentered the house and locked the door, the place was silent. Apparently everyone else had already found places to nap.

"I think it would be better if we kept this to ourselves," Aubrey said unnecessarily. "I don't see what good it would do to tell the others."

Lukas nodded, not wanting to discuss it any further. "You can check my grandmother's closet," he said, looking at her wet clothes. "There might be something clean in there that fits you."

She followed him up the stairs, and he pointed her in the right direction. While she changed, he sat on the chair at the top of the stairs. He could barely keep his eyes open and was startled awake when she came out in what might be considered active senior leisure wear, including thin green slacks and a golf-style shirt with vertical multi-colored stripes.

"Don't say anything," she growled. "I'm only wearing this until my stuff dries out."

"I would never," he assured her, raising his hands in surrender.

"I'm going to go rest on the couch downstairs," she said. "See you in a few hours?"

"Sure," he said and retreated to the nearby bed in his grandparents' room. He plopped down and curled up into the fetal position. He was asleep within seconds.

When he woke up, the sun was still fairly high in the sky, but he could tell they were approaching early evening. He guessed he'd been asleep for about two hours. He unfurled his body and rolled out of bed to peek outside.

There were still multiple Furies milling about down by the smoking carcass of the army truck, but very few of them had made their way up the hill to the house. He saw less than a half dozen, and none were closer than a couple of hundred feet.

He grabbed the extra clothes he'd put at the foot of the bed and wandered to the bathroom to shower. Unlike the others, he and Caleb were lucky enough to have left some stuff at their grandparents' place. He had a pair of jeans, a clean t-shirt, and a fresh pair of underwear, none of which were splattered with Mr. Cronyn's blood.

They'd already offered up anything else in the house to the others. But other than Aubrey and Martie, who took one of their grandmother's tops, no one else seemed interested. He walked into the bathroom and was about to get undressed to shower when Caleb popped his head in.

"I wouldn't do that," he said.

"Why not?"

"I'm not sure how much water we have available and I doubt any of it is hot. Maybe we should save it for cooking. Besides, we should think about the others."

"What do you mean?" Lukas asked.

"If you shower, they're going to want to, as well. We definitely don't have enough for that."

"I'm pretty grimy, man."

"Me too," Caleb told him. "But we're already dealing with a fragile situation here. I'd rather avoid anything that could exacerbate tensions even more."

"Okay," Lukas sighed, deciding it wasn't worth the argument. "Just give me a minute to get dressed. I can put on clean clothes, right?"

"Yes," Caleb said, ignoring his tone. "When you're done, meet me in Grams and Gramps's study. We need to discuss something."

Lukas didn't love the tone in his brother's voice. Still, he got dressed and made his way to the study where Caleb was standing at the top of a small stairwell that led to the balcony looking out over the hills. When he saw Lukas come in, he stepped back down and sat in their grandmother's chair. Lukas took their grandfather's.

"I wasn't honest with you before," Caleb said without preamble.

"About what?"

The second that Lukas saw his brother fall into his finger-fidgeting routine, he knew the news was bad.

"This is going to be hard to hear," Caleb said, "but Grams and Gramps didn't leave the house. I discovered them upstairs in the panic room. They're gone, Lukas. I found them sitting on the floor, hand in hand. I think they must have intentionally overdosed on some kind of medication. They looked . . . peaceful."

Lukas stared at Caleb who couldn't look him in the eye. It was clear that his big brother was worried that he'd be upset with him. But strangely, he wasn't entirely surprised to hear the news.

Something had felt off about Robert and Betsy Lincoln simply leaving their house unattended and going off to some unknown location. It made much more sense that they would have chosen to remain in their home and leave this world on their own terms.

"Why didn't you tell me?" he asked.

Caleb sighed. "We'd just escaped from Camp Tarris," he explained. "Mike had died. Emily was losing it. I just didn't want to throw something else at you in that moment, especially something that big. I wanted to wait until things were calmer, which I guess is now."

Lukas knew his brother was trying to protect him. But rather than appreciating it, he felt a familiar resentment bubbling up. Once again, the shared trauma that should have brought them together was threatening to rip them apart.

"This has to end, Caleb," he said heavily, surprising even himself with his directness.

"What does?" his brother asked, feigning confusion.

"It's been a decade, man. And you still try to protect me and everyone else as if you can somehow control what the universe doles out. We're in a frickin' zombie apocalypse and you're still trying to massage the situation."

"What are you talking about?" Caleb asked indignantly, though it was clear that he understood perfectly.

"She's gone," Lukas said simply. "And refusing to discuss it won't change that. You've had your head in the sand for ten years. You were even planning to move across the country to get away from the memories. Dad retreated into his work so much that he's basically more a shadow than a real person now. Mom clings to us as if letting us out of her sight will make us disappear. And I can't get behind the wheel of a car without having a panic attack."

His brother stared at him, either unwilling or unable to reply. His eyes were wet. Lukas felt certain he should stop now, but he couldn't.

"I get it, Caleb," he continued. "We all feel guilty. But don't you think that, at this point, when we're facing the end of the world, we can try to let a bit of that go? I mean you've known our grandparents were dead for hours and you're so concerned with protecting me that I only get to mourn them now?"

Something about saying the words out loud, hearing his own voice announce that Grams and Gramps were dead, broke the dam inside him, allowing the grief to pour in. Lukas felt a sudden ache in his chest, which rose quickly to his throat. He half gasped, half sobbed before he could stop himself. He inhaled deeply, trying to control the wave of anguish that seemed to suddenly threaten to swallow him up. The effort led to a bout of coughing that made his eyes water even more than they already were.

He stood up, trying to catch his breath, aware that he was making an uncomfortable amount of noise, considering their situation. Caleb looked at him anxiously but said nothing. Lukas took several more deep gulps of air.

The emptiness in his chest was still there, but the sense that he was falling into a dark pit had subsided. He tried to put himself in his grandparents' shoes: older, physically diminished, worried that they would meet an unceremonious end at the hands, and teeth, of creatures, possibly former neighbors and friends like Mr. Cronyn. He couldn't blame them for their choice.

"I'm sorry you had to find them by yourself," he finally managed to say.

Caleb looked at him with an expression Lukas hadn't expected to see—a combination of relief and appreciation. Without a word, his brother stepped over and wrapped him in a tight embrace. "Thank you," he whispered, his voice muffled.

"We're really alone now," Lukas whispered back. "Mom and Dad are probably gone. We're the last Lincolns. I'm so sick of mourning our family."

He knew his brother understood that he wasn't only referring to the people who had died in recent days, but to the other loss that, even now, despite his desperate plea, Caleb couldn't bring himself to acknowledge.

They stood like that for a long time, arms wrapped around each other, not speaking. Lukas would have let it go on forever, but at some point, Caleb felt the need to disengage. He wiped his own wet cheeks and gave a sheepish half smile.

"Is there anything we can do?" Lukas asked. "Some way we can respectfully deal with the bodies?"

"I already did what I could. We obviously can't bury them. I laid them down and put blankets over them. No matter what happens, I don't think they'll be found up there. That room will have to be their final resting place, at least until we can come back here."

Lukas looked his big brother in the eyes, trying to determine if he was sincere or just saying the appropriate thing. "Do you really think that will ever happen?" he asked.

Caleb looked at him closely. Instead of answering, he motioned for his brother to follow him up the steps to the balcony door, which he opened carefully. Both brothers stepped outside, careful to be as quiet as possible.

From this vantage point, they could look out on a wide swath of the Texas Hill Country without being seen themselves. Despite the heat, there was a slight breeze, which cooled the remaining tears still running down Lukas's face.

"You know," he said softly, "if you don't look down, if you just keep your eyes focused on the hills, it seems like just another beautiful South Texas day."

"Yeah," Caleb agreed. "The planet doesn't seem to care that we're destroying ourselves. We seem to keep trying. Whether we survive this plague or not, those hills will be there for millennia after we're gone. There's something reassuring about that."

They stood silently for a bit, soaking it in.

"Still," Lukas said, turning to face his brother directly, "I'd like to stick around for a while longer."

CHAPTER 46

The formal meal was Lonnie's idea.

Traditionally, on the last night of camp at Hollow Valley, a big banquet was held. Awards like iron-on patches, lanyard bracelets, and handmade belts were given out for everything from cleanest bunk to swimming certifications to multiple-session campers.

The big award was given to those who reached twenty sessions: a small smoothed-over pebble from the bottom of Wallace Creek, presented in a jewelry box like it was an engagement ring. Fewer than a dozen people had ever received one. Lonnie had been scheduled to get his this year.

"That's the real reason you want to do this fancy meal," Trevor teased.

But they all knew that wasn't the reason. If things hadn't gone to hell, the banquet would have been held last night. Instead, they had spent the evening on cots in an airplane hangar at a military base. It seemed appropriate to have it now, even a day late.

The electrical power was so irregular that they decided not to even try to heat the food. Candles were lit and put in the center of the table, flickering softly as items were passed around. Dinner consisted of cold black beans, canned corn, canned peaches, low-carb wheat tortillas that Grams was always trying to get Gramps to embrace, and bottled diet iced green tea. Dessert was reduced-calorie choco-late chip cookies.

They were all taking their seats when Lonnie pointed out a photo on the bookcase in the corner of the breakfast room. Everyone looked over. Lukas didn't need to. Despite Caleb's multiple requests, Grams had refused to take it down, the last time doing so with a hint of anger in her voice.

"Who's the little girl?" Lonnie asked.

It was a photo of three kids from a decade ago when Caleb had been eight and Lukas was five. The third child, in a sundress and smiling brightly, stood in front of the other two. She had chubby toddler cheeks and the same brown hair as her brothers.

"That's our sister, Rachel," Lukas said, knowing Caleb wouldn't speak. "That picture was taken a few months before she died. We were in a car accident. She was three."

No one knew what to say. Almost everyone looked down. Emily, however, was staring at Lukas, wide-eyed.

Finally Lonnie seemed to find his words again. "I'm sorry," he said quietly. "I didn't mean to pry."

"It's okay," Caleb said matter-of-factly. "We don't talk about it much anymore."

It wasn't okay. But despite everything Lukas had said upstairs, despite his pleas, his brother still wasn't willing to admit it.

Lukas saw the look on Jules's face and could tell from the mix of shock and hurt that his brother had never revealed this secret to her. He wanted to tell her not to take it personally, that with few exceptions, Caleb had not mentioned their sister's death to anyone in ten years.

He wanted to tell her that her boyfriend still considered him-self responsible for his sister's death. He blamed himself because he was yelling at Lukas at the time, during one of their many arguments over toys and games in the backseat of the family car. As Rachel sat placidly between them in her car seat, the brothers fought over a fistful of slime they both wanted to play with on the long drive up a mountain road to the idyllic resort town they visited every winter. "True," an 80s love song by the band Spandau Ballet, was playing, and his folks had turned the volume up high while they sang along, his dad horribly off-key, as they tried to drown out the bickering going on behind them.

Only this time, their father, at his wits' end, had turned around to order them both to pipe down, accidentally drifting across the center median. Unfortunately, he did so just as another car came around the bend toward them.

By the time their dad faced forward again, startled by the blaring horn and flashing lights of the approaching vehicle, the horror-struck face of the man driving the other car was dangerously close. Their dad veered sharply to the right, sending them careening off the two-lane road and down twenty feet before they slammed into a thick pine tree.

When Lukas woke up in the ambulance, he found himself strapped to a gurney. He was shirtless and had a large bandage covering the left side of his abdomen where the seatbelt buckle had slashed through a chunk of his flesh. Caleb was across from him on another gurney, seemingly unconscious. Their mother sat between them, a hand tightly gripping each of her sons'. Neither his father nor his sister was there.

"Where's Rachel?" Lukas remembered asking. His mother only shook her head, as silent tears streamed down his face. He sank back into unconsciousness, where he would remain until the next day when they finally told him the truth.

"Shall we eat?" Caleb asked, yanking Lukas out of the memory.

He looked around at the stunned faces of the others at the table. Everyone sat down, clearly still uncomfortable but not wanting to push a topic that was obviously off limits.

As they passed the bowls of food around, some semblance of normalcy returned. Martie, daughter of Aunt Winnie and the most tangible connection left to camp, took the lead in hosting the evening. She noted the longtimers, handing out belts gathered from Robert Lincoln's closet. Since it wasn't safe to go outside to get a pebble, she instead gave Lonnie a marble Caleb had found in his old play chest from when the brothers had visited their grandparents as little boys.

They all shared stories about mishaps involving poison ivy and stepping in horse manure and a whole bunk jumping out of the creek during a swimming class because of a possible water moccasin sighting.

They related talent show fails. They recounted the time that the Bandeleros bunk had managed to secretly hoist a San Antonio Spurs flag instead of an American one at flag raising. And they reminisced about the unfortunate dinner experiment a few years ago with jambalaya, which, it turned out, is difficult to spice correctly in large quantities.

Lukas wasn't sure exactly when the talk turned to from what they'd had to what they suspected they'd lost. He thought it might have been when Trevor mentioned how Stephen had once told an Andrew Dice Clay joke, forgetting that Aunt Winnie was in the room at the time.

"Luckily," he recalled, "it was one about an old lady who lived in a shoe. That was tame compared to some of them."

"How did she react?" Martie asked curiously.

Trevor smiled at the memory. "She made a point of clearing her throat," he said, "then walked out of the room without saying a word. I don't think Stephen spoke for a full ten minutes after that."

Everyone smiled until they remembered, seemingly all at once, that there wouldn't be any more embarrassing moments like that.

"I didn't think I would ever miss all those stupid jokes," Trevor said. "But I really wish he was here to tell one right now."

No one disagreed.

"I might have even let him," Martie said wistfully.

"I'd have loved to hear one just to watch Fiona's face turn red," Emily added.

"Yeah," Jamie agreed. "Everything embarrassed her. I remember she once even blushed when I referenced my bra."

"She was shy," Emily admitted. "But she had a good sense of humor. She just didn't like to laugh out loud because it would draw attention to her. She hated that. But she'd give other people all the attention they needed. She was a really good listener. Sometimes I thought she was the only one who really heard me. I miss her. I lost my aunt back during the pandemic. But this is different. It was just so . . . sudden."

Lukas didn't think he'd ever heard Emily even hint at something personal before. He didn't know what to say. Luckily Jamie filled the silence.

"My girlfriend, Lana, was the same way. She never got impatient with my whining about volleyball practices. She was so supportive. Actually, hopefully, she *is* so supportive."

"You think she made it?" Jules asked.

"It's possible," Jamie said. "She was on a trip to France with her family. She was supposed to get back yesterday. We'd made plans for her to meet me at camp pickup today. But I'm hoping that, if people in Europe saw what was going on here early enough, they would have cancelled all the flights. I had been dreaming about kissing her again when she arrived at Hollow Valley. But now I'm praying she's stuck in a Paris hotel somewhere."

"Be happy you got a kiss, girl," Javi said. "Some of us have never done even that."

"You've never been kissed?" Emily asked, shocked.

"I have," Javi said, his own cheeks turning crimson, "just not by a boy."

"I thought you were out," Lonnie said.

Javi shook his head uncomfortably. "I am at camp, but not back home. My parents are super-traditional and very religious. They would not have reacted well to that kind of revelation."

"I didn't expect that from you," Emily said, surprised. "I always considered you to be the most open person I know."

"We all play our roles, I guess," Javi replied. "That's one of the things I loved about camp. You get to try on new personas as often as new outfits and see how they fit."

"Well, hell, Javi," Trevor said, smiling mischievously, "I'm not into that kind of thing, but considering we're facing the apocalypse, I'll give you a smooch. Maybe it'll be the good deed that gets me to the pearly gates."

The rest of the group held their collective breath, waiting to see if this was some kind of truth-or-dare moment.

But Javi shook his head. "I appreciate the offer," he said, his voice lacking its usual playfulness. "And you're not a totally grotesque option. But I think I'll skip the pity kiss and wait for one from someone who really cares about me."

"You're running out of choices," Aubrey said drily. "Trevor may be your best bet for a while."

"I'll keep it in mind if I get desperate," Javi replied, before adding impishly, "Now if Caleb was feeling sympathetic . . ."

"He's taken," Jules piped up quickly. "Find your own man, Mendez."

Despite the possibility of 90 percent of America being wiped out and hordes of flesh-eating monsters meandering just outside their house, Lukas couldn't help but feel a twinge of jealousy. Jules glanced over at him apologetically, but he pretended as if he was oblivious.

After a little more reminiscing, they were all clearly tired and jointly decided to go to sleep early. No one spoke as they filed off to the rooms they had chosen.

Lukas waited until everyone had left the breakfast room before he blew out the candles, grabbed his rifle, and went up to sleep in his dead grandparents' bed.

CHAPTER 47

Lukas knew something was wrong the second he woke up.

At first he couldn't put his finger on it. He'd set his grandfather's battery-powered travel alarm clock at low volume and had awoken to it slowly. Even as he turned it off, he felt unsettled in a way he couldn't describe.

He sat up, and at the sight of his unusual surroundings, the realization of the overall situation hit him. But even after he recalled how humanity was mostly gone and that today his group planned to navigate a monster-filled wasteland in the hopes of reaching another country, he sensed there was something else amiss.

He rolled out of bed and tried to stand up, gasping involuntarily as the pain from the Hollow Hill attacks resurfaced. Even as the soreness permeated his body, he sensed that wasn't what had him on edge.

Once the discomfort subsided slightly, he became increasingly aware of another feeling, one that wasn't fading but growing stronger. His whole body was tingling. It was a more subdued version of the sensation he'd had on Hollow Hill and which had only dissipated after the rescue helicopter had sped away to Camp Tarris.

He couldn't help but wonder if this was a side effect of the scratches he'd suffered during his multiple attacks on the hill. Was it possible that the medical checkup he'd gotten at the base had somehow missed this? Was the tingling some kind of fast-acting infection? If so, why had it gone away for twenty-four hours, only to return now?

He got up and went to the bathroom, hoping the sensation would subside once he got moving. But it didn't, lingering like a fly that won't go away no matter how often you swatted at it. For a moment, he considered asking if any of the others felt the same thing but dismissed the idea, deciding that it wasn't worth freaking everyone out.

He tried his best to ignore it as he went to his grandparents' study and climbed the stairs to look through the blinds at the view from the balcony. Down the hill, the truck was still smoldering slightly, sending a thin wisp of smoke billowing into the predawn sky.

There were Furies visible everywhere. They weren't congregating in any large packs, but he could see them ambling aimlessly through the neighborhood in singles and occasional pairs, absent-mindedly looking for something to capture their attention.

After a few minutes of staring, he went downstairs to check on the others. The goal was to leave soon after daybreak, which was less than an hour away. A few people were up and milling around. Aubrey and Jamie were sitting at the breakfast table, nibbling on dry raisin bran.

Lonnie was pacing in the dining room as he noshed on a blueberry breakfast bar. Martie was in the kitchen, mixing what looked like protein powder into a glass of water. Trevor, Javi, Emily, Caleb, and Jules were nowhere to be found.

"Emily will be out in a second," Aubrey said, seeing him look around and guessing what he was thinking. "I think Trevor will too. I heard his voice. But I'm not sure about the other three."

"I can rouse Javi," Lukas said. "But maybe someone else can check on the others?"

"I'll do it," Martie offered, pointedly not referencing why Lukas might be uncomfortable with the assignment.

He nodded his thanks and went to the tiny back guest room behind the laundry room. When he opened the door, he saw Javi was completely out, still happily half snoring. He was reluctant to wake him from what looked like a pleasant dream to face their ugly reality, but time was short so he clicked on the light and gave his friend a gentle shove.

"Time for a trip to Mexico," he announced in the loudest voice he dared use.

Javi rolled away from him, groaning as he pulled the comforter over his head. But it only took a couple of seconds for him to sit bolt upright as the memory of their situation rushed back to him.

"It's morning?" he asked, his voice drowsy even if his eyes no longer were.

"It's morning," Lukas confirmed. "We need to get moving."

"Give me five minutes," Javi said.

Lukas left him and returned to the breakfast room where Caleb had joined the others at the table. He suspected Jules wouldn't be far behind.

"Sorry for oversleeping," Caleb said. "Maybe I shouldn't have taken that codeine last night. But everything was throbbing and I don't think I would have slept at all if I hadn't."

"Is your shoulder any better?" Lukas asked.

"It's getting there. I don't think it will prevent me from shooting straight or anything. How's everyone else doing? We going to be ready to go by seven at the latest?"

"I think so," Martie said. "Pretty much everything is already loaded in the vehicles—food, weapons, first aid kit, flashlights, extra clothes. Once we finish breakfast, I think we can head out."

"I looked outside from the balcony," Lukas added. "There are lots of Furies milling about but not in any kind of organized way. If that doesn't change, we should be able to get out of the neighborhood without too much trouble."

"Okay then," Caleb said. "I'm not really sure what else to say. Enjoy your meal. We leave in forty minutes."

As the others ate, Lukas went to the kitchen to see if he could find anything he'd be able to keep down. His stomach was unsettled, and the tingling sensation, which had only gotten stronger, was mildly disorienting.

He rifled through the pantry until he found some pretzels. He knew they weren't going to give him the energy he needed but doubted he could eat much else. He did find a few pieces of beef jerky, which he shoved in his pocket in case he was feeling up to it later.

He bit off tiny pieces of pretzel as he returned upstairs to wash his face and gather anything he'd left in his grandparents' bedroom. When he entered their bathroom, he glanced at the closed door to Grams's walk-in closet. He knew that beyond that was the secret door leading to their panic room where they were now silently lying side by side.

Lukas stared at the door for a long time. He had no desire to go up there, but he felt like he owed them some kind of moment of silence. For all of his fifteen years, Grams and Gramps had been a constant presence. Even though they lived in Texas, they would come to California at least twice a year to visit. And his family would come here every summer and again for Thanksgiving.

When he was four and Caleb was seven, they started visiting for a week during the summer without their folks. Back then, he thought it was because they were big boys who could handle being away from Mommy and Daddy. Only later did it dawn on him that the visit was actually to give Mommy and Daddy a break so they only had to care for one child.

Eventually, starting soon after Rachel died, the week extended to two. Once they started going to Hollow Valley, the same camp their dad had gone to as a kid, the stays lasted over a month. In the days just before and after the sessions started, their grandparents would spoil them relentlessly with endless trips to the swimming pool, to the movies, and to get frozen yogurt. Eventually, he grew to view this place as a second home.

And now the people who'd made it a home were lying dead upstairs, victims of a plague they likely never even understood. He hadn't even gotten to speak to them beforehand, to see them one last time. They died not knowing if their grandsons were safe.

He couldn't help but suspect his own parents had suffered a similar or even worse fate back in Southern California. He doubted their father's tenured professorship at UCLA or their mother's status as a partner at her law firm would do them much good when it came to escaping a city in meltdown. The thought of it all filled him with a bubbling anger, which he tried to force back down.

Eventually he tore his eyes away from the door. Grabbing his rifle and a baseball cap he'd pilfered from Gramps's closet, he headed back downstairs where everyone was assembling. There wasn't much left to collect. As Martie had noted earlier, almost everything was already in the vehicles.

Everyone was holding a gun, even those who weren't especially proficient with one. Aubrey had spent part of yesterday afternoon giving the uncertain among them primers in how to operate rifles and handguns. They had a few machine guns that hadn't already been commandeered from the armory at Camp Tarris, but she didn't want those in the hands of anyone inexperienced. That meant pretty much only she and Martie would be using them. Lukas had mixed feelings about that but kept that to himself for now.

They filed quietly into the garage as Caleb went over the plan one last time. He would drive the minivan, which would also carry Jules, Aubrey, Javi, Emily, Jamie, and Lonnie. Martie would drive the much smaller Audi, with Lukas in the passenger seat and Trevor in the back. That way, each vehicle would have someone who knew the area well.

Both groups had maps, but the goal was to stay close together and follow the same route from the house all the way to the border near Eagle Pass. The smaller, more maneuverable sports car would take the lead with the minivan following close behind.

But for all that to work, they had to safely navigate their way out of The Promontory. The first step in that process was to get out of the garage. But with the electrical power uncertain, they'd decided to open the doors manually, which meant they couldn't all be safely locked in the cars.

"Hold on," Lukas said as people were loading in.

He returned to the side door of the house they'd used to get in yesterday and peeked through the blinds. He couldn't see all the way down the driveway, but the area in front of the garage was unobstructed. Doing his best to ignore the prickling sensation that was growing stronger with each passing second, he returned to the garage and gave the all clear.

Everyone got in the vehicles except for Aubrey, Jamie, Lukas, and Trevor. As Aubrey and Trevor pointed their weapons at the garage doors, Lukas and Jamie prepared to pull them open using the manual release cords.

"Everyone ready?" Lukas whispered loudly. He saw nods and heard no objection. Checking one last time with Aubrey and Trevor to make sure they were good, he glanced at Jamie. "Let's do it," he said.

They popped the releases and opened the heavy metal doors. The noise echoed throughout the otherwise-silent neighborhood. Within seconds they could hear pounding footsteps coming in their direction.

CHAPTER 48

The Furies were close.

Lukas couldn't see any of them yet, but the sound of their greedy grunts was getting louder. Once the garage doors were open, he and the others darted back to the cars, jumped in, and locked the doors.

Caleb pulled out first. Since the driveway was long and they had to back out, they'd decided that the larger heavier vehicle would go initially, in case it needed to clear a path.

It turned out to be a good call, as the minivan slammed into half a dozen Furies as it sped backwards. Martie followed his route, using his wake to avoid any collisions of her own. Once out on the residential street in front of the house, she shifted into Drive and punched the accelerator.

"Don't go too fast," Trevor said from the backseat. "We don't want to lose the others."

Martie nodded, glancing in the rearview mirror as she sped down the hill toward the main road. When they reached the intersection at the bottom, they could see what remained of the army truck. There wasn't much, just a smoldering steel frame and an engine block, which was still coughing up a bit of acrid smoke.

She veered left onto Promontory Drive, dodging the occasional Fury that came running at her out of the trees just off the road. Lukas peered through the side-view mirror and saw that the minivan was right behind them.

"The exit is right at the top of that hill," he said, pointing her in the proper direction through pain-filled watery eyes. The tingling was getting worse, as if he was being prodded repeatedly by hot pointy fire pokers.

When they got over the rise and saw the guard house station, his heart sank. Since they had arrived yesterday morning, something had changed. There were now close to two dozen vehicles at the entrance and exit on either side of the guard house. They were spread out, almost as if they had been intentionally organized to create a barrier that would make getting out impossible.

Looking closer, Lukas realized that's exactly what it was—a wall of cars designed to prevent any vehicle from escaping The Promontory. How was that possible? How had these seemingly mindless creatures done such a thing?

"We can't get out that way," Martie shouted, snapping him out of his thoughts. "Where do we go?"

Lukas looked around. There was a street to the right just before the guardhouse. But going in that direction wouldn't help much. It led back into the gated community and was ultimately a dead end. To the left was the golf course.

"Go that way," he yelled, pointing at the first fairway.

"On to the course?" she asked, uncertain.

"Yes, the fairway for the first hole runs toward the access road," he told her, having trouble getting the words out because of the fire bubbling up under his skin. "You can just cut across it and get out on the road from there. The community's security gates don't extend that far."

She didn't need to be told twice, swerving hard left and jumping the curb, headed in the direction of the first tee and beyond. As she did, Lukas caught sight of a figure emerging from inside the guardhouse to the right.

Through tears of agony, he blinked, unable to believe his eyes. Staring back at him, with a face covered in dirt and blood, was Command Sergeant Major Curtas. Their eyes locked on each other in recognition. As the car tore away from him, Lukas could swear he saw the man's mouth curl into a malevolent smile.

Lukas tried to maintain eye contact but couldn't as the blazing fire under his skin made him gasp. It was like the pins-and-needles sensation he got when a foot fell asleep, only this was a hundred times worse and it consumed his entire body. He keeled over, only prevented from falling on the dashboard by his seatbelt.

"What's wrong, man?" Trevor asked from the backseat. "You don't look good at all."

Lukas breathed in deeply and on the exhale, muttered, "I don't know. My whole body feels like it's on fire. Everything stings. Did you see the soldier back there?"

"What soldier?" Trevor asked, confused.

"At the guard house," Lukas wheezed. "It was the soldier from—"

"Pull him back upright," Martie ordered Trevor, before telling Lukas, "Sorry to interrupt but I need you to direct me, no matter how much pain you're in."

He felt Trevor grab the front of his shoulders and yank him vertical. His bunkmate's fingers were like daggers jabbing into his flesh. Lukas tried to ignore it and focus on where they were headed as he took long, slow breaths.

It seemed to help. The pain eased slightly, and he felt as if he could concentrate a bit better. He opened his mouth and found that he wasn't in danger of screaming. "Veer right," he instructed, nodding in that direction. "Cut across the cart path up ahead and head for the flag on the first green in the distance. The access road is just beyond it, past that grove of trees."

Martie turned slightly, and he saw that she was on the right track. They careened over the cart path and headed along the fairway. Now on mostly level ground, without so much jolting, he could breathe close to normally. The sharp piercing pain was turning into more of a relentless prickling feeling.

That's when he noticed that Martie was headed straight for a bunker. From this direction, it only looked like an innocuous rolling hill. But Lukas, who had played this course with Gramps on several occasions, knew that on the other side of the hill's lip was a large sand trap that dominated the left side of the fairway.

"Cut right," he shouted as he pointed. "That's a bunker."

Martie yanked the steering wheel sharply to the right, fishtailing slightly on the dewy morning grass but narrowly avoiding the trap. She was just straightening out when they all heard a loud thud that made Lukas's heart sink.

He looked back through the rear window and saw what he'd feared. The minivan, which had been closely following them, had not managed to completely avoid the sand trap. The front was on the grass just ahead of the bunker and the right rear tire was also safe, but the left rear tire was embedded in the sand.

Lukas tried to set aside his frustration. Caleb had played this same course and knew its ins and outs. Had he forgotten the trap? Did it just look different from a car? Had he been distracted by something else? Whatever the reason, they were stuck and it was his brother's fault.

"Loop around," he told Martie who did so immediately.

Lukas looked off in the distance as she made the slow turn back to the bunker. In what was now broad daylight, he saw them coming—hundreds of Furies streaming toward them. Curtas was in the lead, moving faster than the others and easily twenty paces ahead of the next closest attacker.

Lukas's mind flashed back to the moment at the trailhead by the camp infirmary, just before they began the ascent of Hollow Hill, when the soldier had stepped out from behind the lodge, fixed his gaze on their group, and started running at them with dozens of campers and counselors right behind him.

This time, he and the others were still easily four hundred yards away but closing fast. Lukas forced himself to look away from them and fix his attention on the minivan. As the Audi pulled up next to the sand trap, he got a better view of the tire. It wasn't stuck horribly deep, but it was clear there was no way the vehicle would be able to get out if its current predicament on its own.

"I got distracted," Caleb shouted from the front seat. "How bad is it? Can we get out and push it up?"

"I think it's too heavy," Lukas said, deciding that now definitely wasn't the moment to ream out his brother. "Besides, there's not enough time."

"Can we get everyone in the Audi?" Jules suggested from the backseat.

"There's no way everyone can fit in here," Martie said. "Not even if we piled everybody in the back. It's just too tight."

"Maybe we make a run for the road," Lonnie offered. "There are bound to be other cars out there."

Lukas barely heard him. He was imagining a scenario in his head, trying to determine if it was plausible or ridiculous. Ultimately, he decided it was both and suggested it anyway.

"Listen," he said. "There's no time for any of that. This is what we're going to do. All of you move toward the front of the van. We're going to pull around again and come at you fast from the back. Martie is going to slam us into the rear of the van, popping you guys out of the bunker. Then the three of us will join you."

"You think that will work?" Jamie asked from the passenger seat of the minivan.

"I think it *could* work," he replied. "And unless you have a better idea, 'could' is better than 'won't.' Those things are less than ninety seconds from us."

"But if it doesn't work then we're all screwed," Aubrey said. "At least right now, you three can get away."

"I'm not interested in that," Lukas said, before turning to Martie and Trevor. "Are you two?"

"Hell no," Martie said.

"I'd be a real jerk if I disagreed," Trevor added, which Lukas decided to take as agreement.

"Then let's do this," he yelled. "You all brace yourselves. Caleb, hit the gas when you see us in the air. Martie, go now."

She punched the accelerator and looped around in a wide circle so she'd have lots of momentum when they rammed into the van. As they curled back toward the trap, slowing slightly, he glanced over at the Furies. They were now more like 250 yards away from the minivan. Curtas was even closer. Lukas bet they had less than a minute before they were swarmed.

When they had straightened out, Martie pressed on the accelerator again, softly at first and then slamming the pedal completely down. Looking at the speedometer, Lukas saw they were approaching thirty miles per hour. At this rate, they'd be well past forty when they made contact.

"Hold on to something," she shouted as they approached the hill again, this time intentionally.

Lukas gripped the center console with one hand and the door pocket with the other, knowing it was a futile gesture. He was just starting to notice the stinging sensation beginning to flare up again when they reached the hill and the car went airborne.

Martie had aimed well. The hood of Audi slammed into the back bumper of the minivan before entrenching itself in the sand below it. Lukas saw the minivan shoot out of the bunker just before he slammed forward to meet the airbag that punched him in the face.

For a few seconds, everything went quiet. He wasn't sure if it was the airbag muffling things or the force of slamming into it. He was vaguely aware of Trevor yelling at him from the backseat to open the door. He undid his seatbelt as he fumbled for the handle, managing to open it and push the door away before toppling out into the sand.

His head was screaming. He was almost certain he had a concussion. And yet, the pain in his head was nothing compared to the other feeling that was beginning to reassert itself. The excruciating tingling sensation was returning with ferocity.

He tried to push off from the sand he was lying in and stand up. But his limbs felt shaky, borderline useless. He managed to get to his knees before collapsing again. He saw Trevor standing over him, yelling something unintelligible before turning and shouting at someone out of sight.

Moments later, Jamie came into view. He saw her grab one of his arms as Trevor took the other. The sparks of pain he felt at their touch made him want to pull away, but he didn't have the strength to do it.

They dragged him over to the minivan where, with Martie's assistance, they lifted him and tossed him in. He was on his back now, splayed across the middle row of the van, with his head pressed against the rear of the driver's seat.

From this vantage point, he could see the mass of Furies advancing toward them in a lurching, uncoordinated frenzy. At the front of the group, now less than fifty yards away, was Curtas.

Lukas tried to call out and warn them, but his voice wouldn't work. He looked at Aubrey and, with his eyes, willed her to understand. But her expression, the fear etched across her face, suggested she was more concerned about him than the Furies. He wanted to make her understand, but he could barely keep his thoughts coherent as the searing agony that was consuming every muscle nearly made him retch.

"Let's go!" he heard her scream, cutting through the deafening silence that had consumed him until then.

He felt the van move. His eyes fluttered but remained open just long enough to see something fly at them. There was a thud on the roof and the sound of something sliding off it.

"What the . . ." he heard Caleb yell.

"Don't stop," Jamie shouted at him. "Just keep going!"

The voices receded again as Lukas strained to see how far behind them the Furies were. But soon, the overwhelming anguish consuming his entire body was too much. His eyes were heavy. His mind felt weak.

And then there was darkness.

PART III

CHAPTER 49

When he awoke, Lukas felt like he was encased in a shroud of molasses.

Everything sounded muffled and distant. He couldn't open his eyes. His entire body seemed beyond pain, almost paralyzed. As he slowly returned to consciousness, voices started to become distinguishable. He lay there, unmoving, trying to comprehend the situation.

The last thing he remembered was the minivan peeling out across the golf course as an army of Furies galloped toward them. Was that thirty seconds or thirty minutes ago? He had no idea.

The stinging pain was still with him, but it was as if his body had been so overwhelmed by it that it had just given up, too exhausted to fight back anymore. As long as he didn't move, that pain was just noise, and moving wasn't really an option anyway.

His torso was one big throbbing mass, with no part worse than or even distinguishable from any other. It was as if he was wrapped in some gauzy film that made everything less distinct and therefore less painful than it otherwise would be. Apparently there was one advantage to a head injury.

But he could feel the haze burning off. As the clarity of the words spoken around him began to sharpen, so did the pain. It was distant, but he could sense it strengthening with each passing second.

". . . our only choice," he heard Jamie say from the front seat. "According to the map, it's all tumbleweeds after this until we get there."

"But this is barely a town," Javi said from what sounded like the back row. "There's nothing here."

"We don't need much," Martie noted in a tone that suggested they'd covered this conversational terrain before. "As long as they have a gas station, we're good."

"I wouldn't mind a restroom too," Emily said from somewhere behind him.

"We may not have time for that," Caleb warned. "We don't know what we'll be facing. I'd just as soon have one person pump gas while the others surrounded the van with guns."

"Are we sure this is a good idea?" Trevor asked from somewhere in the back. "This town may be small but all it takes is one infected local to mess things up."

"We're down to less than a sixteenth of a tank," Caleb replied. "If we don't get more gas now, we might not make the border. We still have at least twenty miles to go."

Lukas tried to process what he was hearing. San Antonio was hundreds of miles from Eagle Pass. If they were only twenty miles from the border, they must have been driving for hours. Had he really been out that long?

"I see a station," he heard Jules announce from somewhere extremely close. From the sound of it, his head was in her lap. It occurred to him that he was likely still lying across the people in the middle row. He tried again to his open his eyes. They flickered but remained closed.

"Got it," Caleb noted. "Good. It looks like it's set away from the other buildings, so we should see anything coming at us."

"This place is so tiny," Lonnie said from nearby. "What's it called again?"

"McInnes," Aubrey answered from the back row. "The sign back there said the population was sixty-seven. But I'm guessing that includes farmers in the surrounding area too. I've seen less than a dozen structures so far and only about half look like homes."

"Okay," Caleb said. "We're going to pull in to the station but I'll keep the engine running for a bit until we're sure we're alone. Have your weapons ready."

As the car slowed, Lukas felt the bumpiness of the road settle down. The respite gave him the courage to try to open his eyes again. With all his might he willed his eyelids open. It worked.

Through mucky eyes, he saw light and then an image formed above him. It was Jules. He was lying on his back. His head, as he had suspected, was in her lap. She was sitting behind Caleb's driving position, her tanned face and green eyes framed by the black hair cascading around them.

To her right, in the middle seat, was Lonnie who was supporting the bulk of his weight. Next to him, near the sliding door, sat Martie. In the back row from left to right were Javi, Emily, Aubrey, and Trevor. Jamie was in the front passenger seat.

"What's happening?" he managed to groan, noticing that the tingling sensation, which he'd managed to keep somewhat under control until now, was flaring up again. It was as if the clearer his head got, the more the pain intensified.

Jules looked down at him, her face filled with joy and relief. For a fleeting second Lukas wondered if this was all he had to do to get her attention, merely fall into hours of unconsciousness.

"You're awake," she said, her eyes suddenly brimming with tears. "We were so worried. How do you feel?"

"Really . . . bad . . . actually," he answered, noticing that each word required effort if he didn't want to cry out in the middle of the sentence. "There's something wrong with me. I have this . . . pain that won't go away. It's like my body is burning from the inside out. It faded for a little bit. But I can feel it coming . . . back again. In a few minutes, it's going to be . . . unbearable."

Jules looked over at Martie in desperation. "Do you have anything for that in the first aid kit?" she asked.

Martie shook her head helplessly.

"Like what?" Emily asked snarkily from the back. "It sounds like he needs a dose of morphine or something. Do first aid kits have that now?"

Lukas saw anger flash across Jules's eyes, but she said nothing.

"He looked really bad back at the golf course," Trevor said. "He was doubled over in pain even before the sand trap thing. If it gets that bad again, I don't know what we'll do."

"I kept some extra codeine tablets in case my pain from last night came back," Caleb said, pulling them out of his pocket. "They might take a bit of time to kick in, but they could help."

He handed them back to Martie who opened two tabs and shoved them down Lukas's throat. "Swallow," she ordered as she poured water in his mouth.

For a moment he thought he would gag the big pills back up, but he managed to down them with one large tense gulp before collapsing back down on the legs of the people in his row. Unless the pills kicked in sometime in the next two minutes, he feared he'd be screaming soon.

The van eased to a stop, though the engine continued to idle.

"Everyone stay as quiet as possible," Caleb said. "Keep your eyes peeled for any movement coming from those buildings."

They all did as he instructed, though Lukas found it difficult to stay quiet. The sensation that his muscles were bubbling just below his skin was starting to return, and he doubted he could keep silent for long. Jules looked down at him worriedly.

"Shove something in my mouth just in case," he instructed her, wincing.

Jamie grabbed a fistful of tissues from a box near the center console and passed them back. Jules pushed them in his mouth more delicately than necessary. He clamped down hard, breathing through his nose, almost snorting.

"I see something," Javi suddenly said, pointing off to the left, "coming from that little house at the end of the street."

Lukas couldn't see anything from his vantage point lying on his back but did his best to gauge the situation on the basis of what was said.

"They don't look like Furies," Lonnie noted.

"No," Aubrey agreed, peering through a pair of binoculars that she'd somehow gotten hold of. "It's two women, maybe a mother and daughter. They don't look infected."

"They're coming straight for us," Emily said with concern in her voice.

"They look to be alone. But why are they running if there's no one around?" Jamie asked of no one in particular.

"Somehow I don't think they're alone," Javi said slowly.

"They're going to want to come with us," Trevor said. "Are we letting them in the van?"

"Are you kidding?" Emily demanded. "There's barely enough room as it is. This isn't an Uber, Trevor. We can't pick up every straggler we see."

"Oh no," Lonnie muttered.

Everyone else's head turned to look at what he'd seen.

"What?" Lukas managed to grunt despite the tissues in his mouth and the unseen knives piercing him everywhere.

"They're being chased," Jules told him. "About ten Furies, coming out of different buildings—they're gaining on them."

"They've got a good head start," Lonnie said. "Open the sliding door. They can jump in and we'll just take off."

"It's too risky," Emily protested. "The Furies could get in, too."

"We can't just leave them to die!" Trevor shouted, surprising Lukas slightly.

"We can if *we* want to live!" Emily shouted back. "We didn't go through all this just to get overrun within spitting distance of Mexico."

"Jamie, Aubrey, be prepared to shoot," Martie said calmly, cutting the argument short. "I'm opening the door when they get to us. Fire at anything else that gets close."

Lukas had no idea how far away the women were and could only watch the faces of others as their gaze followed movement to the left of the van, then in front of it, and finally to the right. He thought he heard shouts from outside but couldn't be sure if the noise was coming from other people or the increasingly loud anguished groans inside his own head.

Suddenly Martie yanked open the door. Two women stood in front of them, breathing heavily. Both were Latina. One, overweight and sweating profusely, looked to be in her forties. The younger one, fitter, with a ponytail holding her hair in place, looked to be closer to twenty. They were clearly related, with the same dark almond-shaped eyes and matching furrowed brows.

"Thank you so much," the older woman wheezed.

"Get in," Martie ordered.

Out of the corner of his eye, Lukas saw Aubrey visibly tense up at whatever she saw out of the window to the left. The Furies must be getting close.

"You first, mija," the older one said, waving for the younger one to get in.

The girl he assumed was her daughter hopped in as directed and then turned back, reaching out her hand to help her mother in. Suddenly Lukas felt an agony he'd never experienced before, as if someone was trying to split his entire body open right up the center with a chainsaw. Unable to move, breathe, or even close his eyes, he saw the expression on the older woman's face suddenly change from relief to terror as she looked down.

Lukas couldn't tell what she saw, but he could guess. He watched her abruptly disappear from sight as she seemed to be violently ripped to the ground. She screamed but only briefly.

"Mama!" the younger woman shouted, her face filled with horror, as she tried to leap back out.

Lonnie wrapped his arms around her and yanked her back so that she tumbled to the floor between the front and middle rows, right next to Lukas. Martie, with her eyes wide, desperately yanked on the sliding door handle, viciously banging it shut and slamming down the lock.

A second later, someone popped up. But it wasn't Mama. It was Curtas.

CHAPTER 50

The soldier looked at them through the window, his gaze moving quickly from one person to another until his attention landed on Lukas. He stared at him, transfixed.

Lukas, immobile and speechless, could only stare back. He could feel tears of pain roll down his cheeks from his uncloseable eyes. He took in the mix of dried blood and dirt that caked the man's face, like Halloween paint that had been spread on too thick. His eyes, blazing with intensity, were more red than white.

Lukas had a brief flash of this creature as the husband and father that Dr. DiSanto had described, a man destroyed by grief at the loss of his family, so devoid of hope that he was willing to participate in a mission that turned him into a flesh-ripping ball of virus. Was there anything left of that man? Was there any chance that he could go back to what he was before? The thing in front of him now seemed to be of a different species.

"Go!" he heard Aubrey hiss quietly at his brother, somehow cutting past the shrieks of anguish from the twenty-something girl in front of him.

That seemed to snap Caleb out of whatever state of shock he was in. He punched the gas as Curtas simultaneously punched the window, causing a starburst crack that looked like it might shatter at any moment.

They pulled away as Curtas leapt at the van, hitting it hard. His chest was pressed against the glass but his head wasn't visible. He seemed to be clinging to something up top.

"He's holding on to the roof rack!" Jules yelled as Curtas's body bounced against the sliding door.

As the soldier twisted sideways, Lukas saw his back and shoulders. They were torn up beyond recognition, with skin and sinew loosely flapping about. It was as if someone had taken a massive cheese grater to the entire back half of his body. The hole in his shoulder, where Lukas had stabbed him with the fireplace poker on Hollow Hill two days ago, was still oozing.

"Caleb," Martie said, her voice shockingly composed under the circumstances, "brake hard, then accelerate again. Hopefully he'll come loose. Everyone, brace yourself!"

Caleb slammed on the brakes, sending everyone careening forward. Only Lonnie's strong grasp prevented Lukas from smashing into the crying young woman in front of him. He groaned as Lonnie's tight grip cut into him, making him shiver involuntarily. Despite that, he looked up and saw that Curtas was no longer attached to the van.

"It worked. He fell off. Hit the gas!" Martie yelled even as Caleb was doing exactly that.

They sped off as a cloud of dust surrounded the vehicle, making it impossible for Lukas to see anything outside. He hoped his brother was having better luck.

"I see him back there," Emily shouted from the rear. "He's still running but we're pulling away."

For a long time, no one spoke. The only sound inside the car was that of their new passenger crying uncontrollably. Lukas wanted to say something to comfort her but couldn't think of anything, even if he'd had the strength to speak.

Trevor spoke from the backseat. "It's going to be okay, mija," he said in his most comforting voice.

"Mija means daughter, idiot," Javi said, with as much disdain as Lukas had ever heard from him.

"Oh, sorry," Trevor said, sounding genuinely apologetic.

"Hey, what's your name, sweetie?" Jules asked, putting her hand gently on the girl's shoulder.

Lukas noticed that she was crying so hard that her body was shivering as if she was in a snowstorm. Jules's touch seemed to help a little.

"Lauren," the girl whispered through her sobs.

"Lauren," Jules repeated. "I'm Juliana. I'm so sorry about your mom. That was awful. But please know that you're safe now. That's clearly what she wanted. That's why she had you get in first. We have a vehicle. We have weapons. And we're headed somewhere safe. You're going to be okay."

Lauren nodded. She was still crying, but the sobs had turned into whimpers. That was the only sound in the car for several minutes.

Eventually, Emily broke the silence. Her voice was eerily calm. "We're not going to have enough gas to get to the border," she noted quietly.

"No," Martie agreed. "We'll have to walk the last few miles. Caleb, I think we've got enough distance from that creature. Maybe throttle down a bit. We'll get better mileage if you go a bit slower."

Caleb nodded, and the car eased up a little, dropping from what felt like eighty miles per hour down closer to fifty. Very occasionally, he swerved to avoid random empty cars parked in the middle of the two-lane highway.

"Where did that guy come from?" Jamie asked.

"He looked like the main soldier from the camp," Lonnie said in disbelief. "But how could he have made it all the way out here? It's not possible."

"Wait," Trevor said, remembering something. "Lukas, didn't you say something about a soldier back when we leaving your grandparents' place?"

Lukas nodded, finding the act wasn't as painful as he'd expected. The searing misery of invisible shards of glass cutting him from the inside out was subsiding. It was replaced by a comparatively tame burning, tingling sensation. Under normal circumstances that feeling would be excruciating, but at the moment, it was a relief.

"Yeah," he said, surprised at his ability to both speak and think coherently. "It was the soldier from camp, Curtas, the same one who killed Steve Sailor and attacked us on the hill, who killed Fiona. I saw him at the guard house as we were pulling onto the golf course. I think he set up that roadblock so we couldn't get out."

Jamie shook her head from the front seat. "But there's no way he could have done all that," she said.

"Remember," Javi pointed out, "Dr. DiSanto said some of the original soldiers who were infected still had some higher-level thinking."

"No, I don't mean that," Jamie said. "How could he have found your grandparents' neighborhood from all the way out at camp? That's probably a sixty mile trip. How did he even know which way to go? And why would he go there?"

"Maybe he wasn't going there at all," Aubrey suggested quickly. "Maybe he was returning to Camp Tarris. He knew that place already, and it seemed real popular with the other Furies. It might just have been some kind of instinct to return to the spot he was most familiar with. It could be that he was just headed there, back to his home base, and saw the flames and smoke from our blown-up truck. Maybe he just made a pit stop and got lucky."

That seemed to satisfy some folks, but Lukas could tell from her voice that Aubrey didn't actually believe what she was saying. He wondered if she had the same theory he did, the same suspicions, about how Curtas ended up at The Promontory. If so, neither of them voiced them.

"But how did he end up in that little town?" Jamie pressed. "Did he chase us the whole way?"

Lukas could handle that one. "He must have been clinging to the undercarriage of the minivan," he said. "I saw something leap onto the roof and fall off as we were leaving the sand trap. He must have had time to crawl under and grab on to the undercarriage before we left. His entire back looked like it had been through a meat grinder. I think he was holding on below us that whole time."

"Jeez," Trevor said, almost marveling. "He's really got it out for us. I wonder why."

"There's no point in focusing on that right now," Aubrey said, pointedly changing the subject. "We need to figure out a plan for how we're going to get to the border when this van runs out of gas."

Lauren sniffled. Jamie grabbed a tissue and handed it to her.

"Thanks," Lauren whispered.

"No problem," Jamie replied, offering a sympathetic smile.

"Can I ask why you're trying to get to the border?" Lauren asked the group generally.

Everyone looked around at each other, surprised by the question. It took Lukas a second to realize why she'd asked.

"Guys," he reminded them, "she hasn't had access to the same information that we have."

"Oh, right," Trevor said. "Do you even get the news in that little town?"

"Yes," she replied sharply, mildly offended. "McInnes is small, but we have TVs and the internet. It's not like we live in the nineteenth century out here, using the Pony Express to get our information. Some of us have even been to other towns. I just finished my sophomore year at Texas Tech, if you can believe it."

"Sorry," he muttered, red-faced.

Lukas was relieved at her reaction. If she was annoyed, it gave her less time for despair.

"You really have a gift for stepping in it," Javi told Trevor before turning his attention to Lauren. "Tell us what you know and we'll try to fill in the gaps."

"Okay," she said heavily. "We saw the news about the infections and the quarantines. And then things got mostly silent. We went online, but at a certain point that seemed more like rumormongering than actual fact. Some people claimed it was the pandemic resurging. Others said it was something completely different. It was hard to know what was real. We saw video footage. But way out here, we didn't actually see anyone who was infected—until this morning."

"What happened?" Martie asked delicately.

"Some guy came into town, just walking. He headed for the General Mart. I was leaving my house to walk there myself. I saw him go in, shuffling, looking all herky-jerky. Then I heard screams. I had a bad feeling, so I ran back to the house. My mom was there. We watched through the window. A few people ran out, Mrs. Carstow, Jason Finch. The guy chased after them. He got her first, jumped on her right in the middle of the street. Then he went after Jason who made the mistake of running to his house. His wife and baby daughter were in there. The door was locked, but the guy just dove through a window. There was yelling. And then there wasn't. It deteriorated from there."

"But he didn't see you?" Martie wondered.

"No. After a few minutes, the people he attacked . . . changed, just like the news said they would. Those people started smashing into other nearby buildings. They broke into our house, but my dad had a special hidden room installed just in case. He was kind a of doomsday prepper. But he had a sense of humor about it."

"What does that mean?" Emily asked.

"It means he did a bunch of stuff to prep for emergency situations—natural disasters, nuclear war, Russian invasion . . . virus outbreaks."

"Sounds like he's a man ahead of his time," Lonnie admired.

"He wasn't totally serious. It was more like a hobby. It appealed to the darker side of his imagination. And he had fun building this secure room that could handle tornados or radioactive fallout. As it turned out, it was useful. Those creatures didn't even know it was there, much less try to break in. They scurried around the house for a while and then left."

"And you stayed in there the whole time?" Jules asked.

"It was only a few hours," Lauren said. "Then we saw your van pull up. The street was empty. We decided it might be our only chance to escape. So we went for it."

It was quiet for a moment as everyone recalled how that had turned out.

"What about your dad?" Jamie asked leadingly. "He wasn't there with you?"

"No," Lauren answered. She paused for a few seconds before continuing. "He died about a year ago."

"What happened?" Trevor asked, showing his usual sensitivity.

"He was a border patrol officer," she told him in a voice that sounded worn out, like she'd said the next part many times before. "He was on duty when his tire blew out. The Jeep flipped and crushed him."

There were several seconds of silence.

"I'm sorry," Jules finally said quietly.

No one else knew what to say.

"Me too," Lauren finally concluded before changing subjects. "But like I said, I don't know much more than that about what's going on. So what's with the whole Mexico thing?"

"Right," Javi said, glad to move on. "There's a long, complicated version, but the short one is that we've learned that Mexico and Canada closed their borders when they discovered what was happening. At least as of yesterday, there haven't been any outbreaks there. So we're hoping to find a place to cross the river. We need to find a spot where there aren't any people on our side but there *are* Mexican authorities who will let us cross and, you know, not shoot us."

"I see," Lauren said.

"And it's got to be pretty close to here," Caleb added from the driver's seat, "because I'm guessing we have about ten minutes' worth of gas left."

Lauren looked at Lukas who was the closest to her, lying down with his head only a foot from hers. He could tell she was coming to some kind of decision in her mind. She blinked slowly, and it was clear that whatever internal conflict she'd been dealing with had been put to rest.

"I might be able to help with that," she said.

CHAPTER 51

There was silence in the car as everyone looked at her with open mouths.

Aubrey was the first to recover. "I think we would be extremely grateful for any help you can offer."

"In that case, go right at the second dirt road you see in about two minutes," Lauren instructed, her voice sounding confident for the first time since they'd met her. "Look for a sign that says 'King Tank.'"

"Will do," Caleb assured her, sounding almost happy.

"Maybe you better explain what you have in mind?" Martie suggested.

Lauren did exactly that. Over the next few minutes, she detailed how her father used to take her to a fishing spot on the Rio Grande River that he'd first stumbled across accidentally while on patrol.

It was heavily guarded on the Mexican side because it wasn't far from a valuable oilfield. As a result, very few undocumented immigrants tried to cross there, which meant Border Patrol rarely had any reason to check the area. Because of that, it was quiet and pristine, perfect for fishing. It also meant the chances of encountering either humans or Furies were remote.

"How deep is the water there?" Lonnie asked.

"It gets close to twenty feet deep at some points in the middle of the river. And it's at least three to five feet in most places; you can stand in it to fish at some points," she answered. "Why?"

"Because the Furies—that's what we call them—supposedly don't do well in water," Lonnie told her. "So if it's a dry creek bed, that doesn't help us very much."

"This is the Rio Grande," she replied. "Even in the middle of the summer, that stretch of water has depth and a solid current."

"And you think law enforcement on the Mexican side will let us through?" Aubrey asked.

"That, I can't promise. But my dad was friendly with some of them. They talked back and forth across the river sometimes. They were generally pretty amiable. I suspect they'll be more receptive than if we went to an international bridge. They're pretty hardcore there."

"That's not an option anyway," Aubrey replied. "Any major crossing will be swarming with Furies."

"So how far away is it?" Caleb asked. "Because I think we're running on fumes here."

"Once you turn on the dirt road, we'll go about two miles north. That will get us past the closest neighborhood. Then it's about six miles west to the border. We can get part of the way there in the van, if it doesn't die before then. After that the road dead-ends and we'll have to walk."

"Back up a second," Emily said. "Did you say neighborhood?"

"Yeah. Why?"

"Because the whole goal here is to stay away from where other people are," Emily replied sharply. "It seems like going anywhere near a place like that is a bad idea."

Lukas felt the tension in the van suddenly escalate and silently wondered why Emily always had to be so curt, especially with someone who had just lost her mother. He looked over at Lauren who looked taken aback but unbowed.

"I get that," she replied, her tone equally edgy. "But the only access point to the trail we need to take runs along that route. Besides, it's an isolated community and we should be far enough north of it that they can't see us, whether they're still human or . . . something else. If you have a better suggestion, I'm all ears, Barbie."

Emily, stunned at the clap back, didn't respond.

"I think we'll follow your recommendation," Jules said, trying to calm the waters.

Lauren nodded and glanced up front.

"Here's your right," she said to Caleb who was already starting to slow down and veer right at the sign she'd mentioned.

The rest of the bumpy ride took place in silence.

*

Eight minutes later, the minivan coughed a few times before easing to an unceremonious stop three and a half miles west of Mexico. They were out of gas.

Everyone got out and gathered their things. As Martie and Lonnie helped Lukas to his feet, he found that he was surprisingly functional. He wasn't sure if it was the codeine or another factor that he was reluctant to acknowledge, but the prickling sensation had almost completely abated. He felt halfway normal again. There was still a dull ache hiding behind the medication, but it was like a low hum in the background that you eventually stopped noticing because it was always there.

Aubrey suggested they push the van behind a large bush just off the side of the road.

"Why?" Trevor asked.

"Then it won't be visible to anyone who comes by."

"You think a Fury is going to see it and start looking for us?" he asked dismissively.

She looked at him as if he was a toddler who needed to be taught why it gets dark at night. "I can think of at least one Fury who would both recognize the van and is already looking for us," she pointed out. "I don't want to make it any easier on him than necessary."

"You think he'll be able to find us on some random dirt road after we've been driving for fifteen minutes and he's on foot?" Lauren asked skeptically.

Aware that their new group member didn't have the whole backstory, Aubrey replied to her with less disdain. "I didn't think he'd be able to track us from the Hill Country to the outskirts of a major city. I also didn't think he'd cling to the undercarriage of our minivan for hours. I'm done making assumptions about this guy. I'd rather err on the side of caution."

Lauren seemed satisfied by the answer, and no one else was inclined to argue. So, with Jules behind the wheel steering them in the right direction, the rest of them pushed the van behind the bush. When they were done, it was still partially visible but didn't stick out as obviously.

"Okay," Martie said. "Let's finish packing up and get moving."

While they assembled their gear, Aubrey walked over and gave Lukas a sidelong glance. "How are you feeling?" she asked quietly enough that no one else could hear her.

"A lot better."

"How much of that do you think is the medication and how much is due to . . . other factors?"

It was now perfectly clear that she'd come to the same conclusion he had—in some inexplicable way, he was tied to Curtas. The closer in proximity they got, the worse Lukas's pain got. The more distance they had between them, the healthier he felt. Maybe, when it came to this soldier, there was more than one form of infection.

"I'm guessing it's about fifty-fifty," he admitted.

She studied him, seemingly debating whether to ask him the question that was clearly on her mind. In the end, she appeared to decide against it. "Then we better get moving, don't you think?"

"I think that would be wise."

"Everyone saddled up?" Martie asked, apparently thinking along the same lines.

It looked like they all were. Caleb, Martie, Jamie, and Trevor carried the heavy backpacks loaded with weapons. Lukas offered but was rebuffed, which didn't surprise him, considering his recent condition.

Aubrey, Javi, and Lonnie wore smaller backpacks loaded with food, water, and other supplies like flashlights and the first aid kit. That left the rest of them—Lukas, Jules, and Emily—holding only weapons, as was everyone else.

Aubrey walked over to Lauren and held out a rifle. "You want this?" she asked. "I'm assuming that, with your dad's job, you're pretty good with one."

"That's a safe assumption," Lauren replied, taking the gun and shoving a box of cartridges in her pocket.

"Good. Then we're all set," Martie said. "Lauren, why don't you take lead? And everyone remember to keep quiet. That neighbor-hood is already slightly visible in the distance. We don't want our voices to carry there. Also, just because we're in an isolated area doesn't mean there aren't stray Furies around. And as we've seen, all it takes is one to do serious damage."

Martie probably didn't realize that her comment was verbal salt in Lauren's wound. But Lukas saw her wince.

"We should probably move strategically too," he added quickly, hoping to refocus the conversation. "Maybe we put a couple of more accurate shooters up front and in the rear with the less efficient ones in the middle?"

"Good idea, Lukas," Martie agreed. "Why don't you and Emily stay up front with Lauren? Caleb, Aubrey, and I will bring up the rear. Lonnie, Jamie, Javi, Jules, and Trevor will be in between."

"Wow," Javi muttered. "Who would have thought a zombie apocalypse would mess with my self-image so much?"

"You're still valuable," Emily noted acidly. "If you die, your long lustrous hair will make me a gorgeous wig."

"It *is* pretty lustrous," Javi agreed rather than offer a comeback.

"Less talk, more walk," Martie said firmly, though she was smiling.

"That's our cue," Lukas said, walking over to Lauren who looked somewhat perplexed by the banter taking place under the circumstances.

Nonetheless, she shrugged and turned west toward the rolling hills in the distance. Between the van and the hills was a long stretch of mostly flat, dusty terrain with more tumbleweeds than trees. Despite the hundred-degrees-plus temperature, Lauren moved at a swift pace that Lukas had to hurry to match.

"I appreciate the whole saving-me thing," she said to him when he'd caught up, "but you are a weird group of people."

"That is unquestionably true," he admitted. "But you have to understand, we've been dealing with this situation for a few days now. Sometimes gallows humor is the only thing keeping us going."

"What happened to you all?" she asked. From her tone, it was clear she'd been itching to know for a while but just hadn't found the right opportunity to broach the subject.

Lukas thought for a second, trying to determine how best to distill the last two and a half days into one concise explanation. "You know what you told us happened in your town this morning?" he asked.

"Yeah."

"The same thing happened to us, only on a much larger scale. And with children."

CHAPTER 52

Lauren's expression made it clear that she didn't comprehend what he was saying. "I don't understand," she said. "Did you say children?"

Lukas nodded, searching for the perfect words to convey the horrors that he'd seen. Unable to come up with them, he just let the words tumble out of his mouth. "We were all at the same summer camp north of San Antonio," he began.

"Wait," Lauren interrupted. "Your whole group is from a summer camp? I didn't even know those things still existed."

"Yeah," Lukas assured her. "As corny as it sounds, it was actually pretty great."

Lauren gave him a sideways glance, as if she couldn't tell if he was serious. "I'm sorry," she said, apparently giving him the benefit of the doubt. "Please go on."

"Anyway, some Furies came into camp during the night and attacked. One of them was the same solider who attacked your mom. What happened to her happened to several hundred people there, counselors, campers as young as seven years old. We were the only survivors. We managed to get to a military base where we learned the thing about the Mexican border. Eventually we secured the van and managed to get this far."

"You're leaving quite a bit out," Emily said from behind him, "like how I lost my best friend and my boyfriend in the space of ten minutes and how his twin brother died less than twenty-four hours later."

"I think Lauren gets that we all lost people important to us, Emily."

Lauren looked back at Emily with unexpected sympathy. "I'm sorry for your loss," she said.

Emily seemed surprised as well. "Thank you," she said. "You too."

"Thanks."

"What was your mother's name?" Lukas asked, hoping he was doing more help than harm by bringing her up.

"Marisol," Lauren said quietly. "Marisol Ontivaros. She turned forty-one yesterday."

Lukas nodded, unable to think of anything more to say. Lauren didn't seem offended but rather content to have gotten the chance to say it. One thought eventually popped into his head.

"Can I give you a piece of advice, Lauren?"

"Okay," she said, though she sounded apprehensive.

"This is going to sound harsh, but until we get safely into Mexico, I'd set aside any mourning for her. As you saw, these creatures are brutal and relentless. And if you aren't totally focused on how to steer clear of them, you're vulnerable. Like Jules said back in the van, your mom sacrificed herself to keep you safe. Don't waste that."

Lauren seemed to take his advice to heart, letting it settle in before posing a question of her own. "Can I ask *you* something?"

"Of course," he replied.

"What's your name?"

"Oh, sorry," he said, realizing introductions had taken a backseat with everything going on. "I'm Lukas. You've met Emily. Behind her is Trevor. The tall gal is Jamie. The short dude behind her with the lustrous hair is Javi. Then there's Jules who you know—"

"Yes," Emily interjected significantly, "then there's Jules. That reminds me that I still owe Aubrey twenty dollars because of that bet at the 80s dance. Too bad American money is probably worthless now."

Lukas pretended to ignore the comment and the curious look on Lauren's face. "Behind her is Lonnie," he continued quickly. "Then we have Marta—she goes by Martie. Her mom, Winnie Korngold, ran the camp. She didn't make it either. She's followed by my brother, Caleb. Bringing up the rear is Aubrey."

"She seems serious," Lauren said, offering something close to a smile. For the first time since he'd seen her, the stress seemed to dissipate slightly from her face, and Lukas noticed just how pretty she was.

"Yeah, well, she is serious," he said. "Her father is military. He's a hard ass and it runs in the family. But if it wasn't for her, none of us would be here right now."

"You mean, if it wasn't for her dad," Emily corrected.

"No, I mean if it wasn't for her."

The terrain got steeper, and most conversation stopped. Lukas rediscovered the beef jerky he'd stuffed in his jeans earlier that morning and scarfed it down hungrily, suddenly aware of just how little he'd eaten today. He told himself it was helping a little as Lauren led them up a steep incline. Depending on one's perspective, the slope was either a huge hill or a small mountain.

"Do we *have* to go this way?" Emily gasped.

"Yes," Lauren answered, not at all out of breath. "If we go north of the hill, it will add a couple of miles to the hike. If we go south, folks from the neighborhood might be able to see us. This is the safest route."

Emily must not have liked either alternative, because she stopped complaining.

"Is it unusual that we haven't seen anyone, or anything, else out here?" Lukas asked.

Lauren squinted at him, blocking the brutal overhead sun with her hand. "Where are you from, Lukas?" she asked.

"The Los Angeles area," he answered, not sure what she was getting at. "Why?"

"LA, huh?" Lauren replied. "That's a pretty big city, so I understand how this might seem unusual to you. But it's not really. I've spent most of my twenty years on Earth in places like this. There's hardly anything around here under normal circumstances. So it's not that weird that those Furies wouldn't be around either. I assume they'd want to go to more populated areas where there are people to attack."

The logic made sense. It was, after all, the very reason they'd decided to try to cross the border in this part of the state in the first place. Nonetheless, Lukas stayed hypervigilant.

For the next forty-five minutes, they walked mostly in silence. He was glad the codeine was still coursing through his system. Otherwise the steep grade of the hill, the sharp thorns of the shrubbery, and the total lack of shade would almost certainly have done him in.

When they finally reached the top of the hill, Martie suggested a short break. As everyone caught their breath and took swigs of water, Lukas looked out over the surrounding landscape.

To the north was nothing but desolate desert. To the south was more of the same, broken up briefly by the isolated neighborhood

Lauren had mentioned, which he could now see clearly. It looked to be just a couple of hundred houses, all organized in a bland grid pattern. From his vantage point, there was no movement. Either the place had been abandoned, or whoever was still there was hiding inside.

He looked back to the east in the direction they'd come from. In the distance, he could barely see the van, visible behind the bush only because its windshield glimmered in the sunlight.

Finally, he turned his attention west, to Mexico. It was marked by the wide muddy Rio Grande River, which snaked from north to south as far as the eye could see. It was probably two miles away.

To get there, they'd have to make their way down the steep hill and through a stretch of barren desert until they hit a tree-lined area about a hundred yards from the river. After that, it was open territory for the last little stretch until they reached the riverbank. Cutting across the route, like a grey line on tan paper, was one dusty desolate road that came to a sudden dead end at the water's edge.

Across the river, he saw more trees on the other bank. Beyond that was a large fenced-off section of land with heavy equipment inside that he assumed was the oil field Lauren had mentioned.

"You see that tiny island in the middle of the river?" Lauren asked when everyone had joined them at the top of the hill. "We want to cross just north of that spot. That's where we did our fishing. There are almost always Federales patrolling the other side near there. They could be a real help, assuming they don't shoot us."

Lukas was trying to think of a clever quip when a sudden rush of adrenaline shot through his system, making all his nerve endings sting. He gasped involuntarily. Aubrey looked over at him with a mix of concern and expectation. A half second later her fears were borne out.

In the distance, a car horn began to honk.

CHAPTER 53

It was coming from the direction they'd just left, the east.

"That's so loud," Javi said anxiously. "It's going to attract the attention of every Fury in the area."

"I think that may be the point," Lukas muttered, trying to regroup.

After the initial burst of tingling, the discomfort had subsided slightly. But it was still there, far from incapacitating but definitely not comfortable.

Aubrey peered through the binoculars that had been dangling at her neck. It only took her a few seconds to locate the source of the noise.

"What is it?" Caleb asked, though his tone suggested he already suspected.

"Exactly what you think," she said. "It's the soldier, Curtas. He found the minivan. In between blaring the horn, he keeps looking south."

The rest of the group looked in that direction themselves. Though they didn't have binoculars, it was immediately clear what he was doing.

"He's trying to get the attention of whatever's in that neighborhood," Martie said.

"I think it's working," Lonnie added. "I see movement down there."

Aubrey refocused on that region, her head darting from spot to spot with the binoculars seemingly attached to her face.

"Lonnie's right," she confirmed. "They're coming out of the houses. And based on the way they're moving, I don't think they're human anymore. There's lots of stumbling and twitching. They're headed in his direct—no, wait. They've changed course. They're coming this way."

"That's because the soldier is too," Lauren said.

Everyone looked back toward the van. It was only then that Lukas realized the honking had stopped. That was because Curtas was running toward them, following the same path they'd taken.

"He sees us," Jules said breathlessly. "He's headed right for us."

"Those things see us, too," Aubrey noted. "They seem to be following his lead and trying to meet him here."

"That's great, guys," Emily said with impatience bordering on panic in her voice. "So maybe we spend less time chatting about what they're doing and get the hell out of here?"

"I think that's a solid suggestion," Caleb said. "Let's get going. Everyone head for the area just north of the island in the middle of the river that Lauren mentioned. If we move fast, I think we can get there in twenty to twenty five minutes."

"I'm not sure I can run for that long," Emily said as they started down the hill.

Martie looked over at her with grim determination on her face. "You don't a have choice," she said without a trace of sympathy. "Run or die."

Lukas had already made his choice, scrambling down the hill right behind Lauren who moved among the rock outcroppings with precision. He tried to follow directly in her footsteps as she maneuvered down what appeared to be the faintest outlines of a trail.

The burning sensation under his skin hadn't gone away, but it hadn't gotten worse either. He wasn't sure if that was a result of the codeine doing its job or his pace keeping Curtas far enough away. Despite the fact that he was going downhill and the soldier was going up, he feared it was the drugs keeping him functional.

After about ten minutes, they reached the bottom of the hill and were able to run full out on the level ground. Their primary obstacles were getting tripped up by blowing tumbleweeds or stumbling in the large cracks in the parched desert earth. Or so he thought.

"Watch out for rattlesnakes," Lauren yelled back over her shoulder from just ahead of him.

"That's just super," he managed to grumble between gasps of air.

He could see the tree line in the distance, about a mile away. Knowing that the river was just beyond that gave him a shot of optimism. But it was quickly dashed when he heard Martie yell from behind them.

"They've reached the top of hill. They're starting down. We need to pick up the pace if we want to make it."

"That was fast," Lauren said, looking over her shoulder.

"They don't get tired," Lukas pointed out.

"But I do," Emily panted.

Lukas noticed that she was no longer right behind him. She'd fallen back toward the middle of the group and seemed to be fading fast. Javi and Trevor, who had a heavy backpack filled with weapons, both seemed to be struggling as well.

"Do you want me to take the backpack?" he called out to the latter.

"No, I'm good," Trevor replied, before changing his mind. "Okay, maybe. My legs are rubber."

Lukas ran back to meet him as the others hurried by and made the mistake of looking up at the hill. A stream of Furies was pouring down, easily two dozen in total. Most weren't trying to stay upright on the steep grade. They would fall, roll for a time, then pop up and run briefly before losing their balance again and tumbling some more. They seemed oblivious.

Curtas was behind them but gaining ground quickly. He leapt down the hill, moving smoothly and only falling when his body periodically twitched. He too popped right back up as if toppling down the side of a rock-filled hill was no big deal.

Lukas reached Trevor who yanked off the backpack, tossed it to him, and kept going. He swung it over his shoulders as he turned back to the river. It wasn't comfortable, way too tight in the shoulders, but with no time to make adjustments, he snapped the waist belt in place and, trying to ignore the straps digging into his shoulders, attempted to catch up to the group.

Lauren was still in the lead, now more than fifty yards ahead of him. Jules was keeping pace with her. Despite her heavy backpack, Jamie was right behind them. Lonnie too, though one leg half dragging, wasn't far behind.

They were followed by Javi and Emily who were both clearly losing steam. The next group comprised Trevor, Caleb, Martie, and Aubrey who periodically turned around to see how fast the Furies were approaching. Lukas brought up the rear, about twenty yards behind them.

"How are you holding up?" Aubrey yelled back to him.

"I'm okay for now," he gasped back. "But Lauren doesn't have anyone covering her anymore. Should one of you get up front with her?"

"I would if I could," she replied. "But I don't think I can physically keep up with her."

"I'll do it," Caleb shouted as he extended his already long strides, closing the gap quickly. He looked at both Martie and Aubrey as he left them behind, adding, "Keep an eye on my brother."

Clearly he wasn't confident that Lukas was fully recovered. Nor should he have been. The combination of the medication, which made him feel slow, his existing injuries, his exhaustion, the heat, and the persistent tingling all had Lukas starting to wonder whether he would make the trees before the Furies caught up.

With each passing step, he became increasingly aware that the prickling was indeed getting worse. It had officially graduated to burning. Glancing back, he saw why.

Curtas had reached the bottom of the hill and was seemingly galloping as he passed the twitchier Furies around him. Lukas guessed that he was now only about half a mile back, a distance he could likely traverse in three or four minutes. Inconveniently, that looked to be about how long it would take Lukas to get to the river.

When he turned to face forward again, he noticed that he was getting closer to Aubrey and Martie who had obviously slowed down at Caleb's demand.

"Don't wait. I'm fine," he yelled at them convincingly, almost angrily.

Both of them looked skeptical but nonetheless resumed their original speed, putting distance between themselves and him almost immediately. His legs, heavy and sluggish, simply could not keep pace any longer.

He saw Lauren dash through a gap between two groves and quickly disappear, followed immediately by Jules and Caleb. Soon

Jamie and Lonnie were out of sight, too. By the time Javi and Emily reached the tree line, Martie and Aubrey had caught up to them.

As the desert floor turned to brownish grass and he neared the gap himself, Lukas thought he could hear the sound of winded grunting getting closer behind him. He cast one last glance back. Sure enough, an army of Furies was closing in, about two hundred yards behind them. And at the front of that group, pulling away from the others, was Solider One.

He gave no indication that he was tired or that the hours under the minivan had affected him. His arms pumped at his sides. His legs stretched across the dusty earth in huge strides, and his head remained still with his eyes focused directly on his prey.

Lukas turned back around and hurtled into the trees, doing his best to pretend that he wasn't on invisible fire. Forcing the thought of the full-body burning sensation out of his head, he crashed through the thick brush, trying to keep on the trail and not lose sight of those ahead of him.

But with each passing step, they seemed to get farther away. The backpack he wore, easily thirty pounds, seemed to be hammering him into the ground. His legs felt like they had weights strapped to them. The sensation that he was being stung by hundreds of fire ants all at once was impossible to ignore. He felt wobbly. Aubrey and Martie were no longer visible.

Unless something changed fast, he would never even see Mexico, much less make it there.

CHAPTER 54

Lukas made a tough decision.

Tucking his rifle under his arm, he undid the waist belt of the backpack and let the whole thing slide off his shoulders, dropping it to the ground behind him.

Almost immediately, he felt a renewed sense of energy and something else he desperately needed: buoyancy. His legs lifted higher as he ran, his pace quickened, and he no longer felt as if he might topple over at any moment.

They had just lost a quarter of their guns when he dropped the backpack. But if he was dragged down by Furies, they'd lose them anyway. He burst out onto the open stretch of dirt that was last part of America before he reached the Rio Grande River.

He saw a barbed wire fence and dove, rolling under it. As he sprang to his feet, he noticed that there were two more backpacks lying in the dirt. The people wearing them must have had to abandon them in order to clear the space below the wire.

Up ahead, Lauren, Jules, and Caleb, who still wore his weapons backpack, were almost to the riverbank. The rest of the group—Jamie, Lonnie, Javi, Emily, Trevor, Aubrey, and Martie—were getting close, as well. Neither Martie nor Jamie was wearing their packs now.

Not far away from them, an abandoned red pickup truck rested forlornly at the river's edge where the dirt road dead-ended. It was the only sign of civilization anywhere in sight. The little island they'd first glimpsed from the top of the hill was just to their left. They'd ended up exactly where they hoped to be.

Lukas scanned the other side of the river, hoping to see the Federales that Lauren had mentioned. But there was no one, just a sloping bank, reminiscent of a small beach. Then, out of the corner of his eye, he saw movement to the left.

Something had jumped out of the bed of the pickup truck and was lurching toward Lauren, Jules, and Caleb who were facing away from it. It was a Fury, perhaps once the truck owner, now a horribly sunburned creature, shirtless and sloppy but still wearing blue jeans.

Lukas started to call out and warn them even as he knew they wouldn't be able to react in time. The thing was only feet from Jules who was just starting to turn in his direction when a shot rang out.

The Fury's head disappeared in an explosion of red mist. The body, still upright, careened forward, and Jules had to step back fast to avoid it as it fell to the ground. Everyone else stopped running. No one was sure where the shot had come from or if there would be another.

Lukas felt the urge to stop, too, but the persistent grunting behind him told him that would be unwise. He continued to sprint toward the rest of them as he heard someone call out.

"Alto!" the loud male voice shouted. "Stop!"

Lukas wasn't clear of its exact origin, but it was definitely somewhere across the river. Regardless, he couldn't stop.

"We need to cross!" Caleb yelled back. "Please."

"No cross!" the voice yelled. "Mexico!"

Everyone in the group but Lukas had now reached the riverbank. He too would be there in another fifteen seconds. Glancing back, he saw that many of the Furies had gotten stuck in the barbed wire. Curtas, who he'd been sure was right behind him, was nowhere in sight. But instead of being reassuring, his absence was alarming. The burning beneath his skin had only grown stronger, which suggested the solider wasn't far off.

Lukas turned back around to the river and saw something that the others could not because of the high thick reeds growing at the water's edge. Streaming toward them from both north and south were countless additional Furies. They must have been loitering along the bank in hibernation mode, quiet and still, with nothing to catch their attention until this moment.

But now, the combination of noise and movement, the potential for meat, had them streaming in from everywhere. It was like two swarms of bees moving in from opposite directions. They were still a couple of football fields' distance away on either side, but they were closing the gap fast.

"They're coming from everywhere," he screamed, pointing madly in both directions as everyone turned around to look at him.

Ten sets of eyes opened wide, and despite the futility, everyone raised their weapons. Lauren spun back around to face the river.

"Do you remember me?' she pleaded with the unseen voice across the river. "I fished here with my father, Carlos. You joked with him then. Please help us now. We are not infected. Let us pass. I beg of you!"

After waiting a moment for response, she yelled what Lukas assumed were the same words in Spanish. But there was no response to those words either.

Lukas stopped, having reached the riverbank next to the others. He looked down at the fast-moving water, which was a brownish, silty color. There was no way to know how deep it was. The other side was a good fifty feet across at its most narrow point. He looked up again, hoping for a response from someone on the other side.

There was a long moment of silence where the only sound was the increasingly frenzied grunting of the fast-approaching Furies. Lukas looked behind him and saw that a half dozen of them had gotten through the barbed wire and were resuming their onslaught. They would be on the group in less than thirty seconds.

Then the voice from the bank yelled out in English. "Cross the river! They hate water!"

That was all they needed to hear. Martie began barking orders.

"Caleb, Aubrey, and Lukas, weapons ready. The four of us will backstop the others' crossing. Lauren, you lead the way. Everyone else follow her."

Lukas assessed what he was dealing with. Two more of the Furies had gotten through the barbed wire, bringing the total to eight. Curtas was still missing, but from the feeling that a hot poker was being run across his flesh, Lukas knew he couldn't be far.

He tried to ignore the agony and focus on aiming as he heard the sound of splashing behind him. Pointing the rifle at one particularly fast moving thirty-something male, he lined up the sight. He was just preparing to pull the trigger when a voice shouted from across the river.

"*Agachense!*"

Lukas didn't understand until he heard Lauren shouting. "Get down!"

The Fury who was lumbering toward him was only ten paces away, but Lukas chose to have faith in the people behind him and dropped to his stomach. Two seconds later, a fusillade of bullets rained from across the river, mowing down every Fury in front of them.

For several seconds, the air rang out with the echoes of gunfire. When it subsided, he heard something else.

"Come! Hurry!" the authoritative voice from across the river yelled, this time in English.

Lukas didn't need coaxing. He stood up and spun around, prepared to jump from the riverbank drop-off into the water. That's when he saw Aubrey struggling to get to her feet.

"What is it?" he asked.

"I tweaked my ankle when I dove down. Just help get me in the water and I'll be fine from there."

He nodded and reached out, deciding not to mention that his entire body was one big tweak. She grabbed his forearm as Caleb offered her his arm as well. They lowered her down to Martie who was already waiting in the waist-high water. After she got in and took Martie's hand, Lukas looked over at his brother.

"Youth before beauty," Caleb said, winking.

Lukas smiled despite himself and stepped down into the water. He tried to ignore the loud rumbling that indicated the nearness of the fast-approaching Furies coming at them from both directions along the bank. He was just fully immersing both legs in the water, holding his rifle high above his head, when he felt a shattering pain that burned through him, as if he'd been struck by lightning. Then, through tear-drenched eyes, he saw a flash of motion to his right.

He looked over to see Curtas dart out from behind the red pickup truck and run at the one person remaining on the riverbank—Caleb.

CHAPTER 55

His brother saw the look of horror on his face and immediately turned his head. Lukas saw him process the situation in a microsecond. When Caleb turned back to him, he had a look of resignation on his face.

"Go," he said calmly, even as he lifted his rifle in the direction of Curtas.

Lukas wanted to yell to his brother, to tell him to just jump in the water, but it all happened too fast. Before he could even open his mouth, the soldier slammed into Caleb, knocking him to the ground.

His gun fell away. He immediately began swinging his fists at the face of the creature on top of him. Lukas ordered himself not to go into shock, ordered himself to act.

His arms responded. He pulled his rifle down from above his head and aimed. But before he could shoot, Curtas dropped to the side, away from the riverbank. He pulled Caleb in toward him by the shirt so that there was no space between them, nowhere for Lukas to shoot.

He started back toward the bank, hoping to get out so he could aim down at Curtas and get a clear shot. But as he did, he noticed something. Caleb, who had been boxing the soldier's left ear repeatedly with his right fist, suddenly stopped. His arm gave one last weak punch and then slumped down at his side.

Curtas popped upright, swinging Caleb around and holding him up in front of him. He was using Caleb as a human shield as he scrambled backward toward the barbed wire fence and the tree line. His eyes gleamed maniacally. His body twitched violently. Red liquid dripped off his chin. Lukas looked desperately to see where it had come from.

Then he saw it. Caleb had a large mouth-sized gash where his collarbone met the left side of his neck. Blood was pouring profusely from it. He was slumped down, only held up by the strength of the soldier.

His eyes opened and closed slowly as if he was waking up from a dream or falling into one. He seemed to be trying to say something, but there was no audible sound coming from him. To Lukas, the words he appeared to be mouthing were "Kill me."

Thoughts tumbled through his head, seemingly all at once. Could he get off a clean shot at Curtas? Even if he did, was it too late for Caleb to survive? The neck wound definitely looked deep enough to infect him. Was there any chance the vaccine from Camp Tarris might actually prevent him from turning into a Fury? If not, could he potentially be turned back by some yet-undiscovered antidote?

His questions and calculations were interrupted by the voice of the man in charge across the river.

"Shoot or no shoot?" he yelled, his voice rising clearly above the rushing water, the grunting Furies, and the screams of his fellow campmates.

Lukas glanced back at the river. Behind him, Jules was wading in his direction.

"Get him," she yelled. "We can still save him if you get him back."

"It's too late," Aubrey shouted from the middle of the river. "If you go after him, they'll get you too."

Lukas glanced left and right and saw that the crowd of Furies, numbering in the hundreds, were less than fifty yards away from him now. They were an army of red-lipped scavengers, all marked by deep wounds on their faces or torsos. He had only seconds to decide. Aubrey stared him down.

"Lukas, don't," she pleaded.

Somewhere in the recesses of his mind, an odd thought occurred to him. That was the first time she'd ever called him by his first name. He looked back at Caleb, listless and semiconscious. His brother couldn't be rescued, but could he be saved? If Lukas let those Federales kill him, was he liberating him from an endless life of mindless killing?

And then, in a flash, he made his decision.

"No shoot!"

CHAPTER 56

He yelled it twice, as loud as he could. Then he tossed away his rifle, turned back toward the river, and dived in.

With his head underwater, he pumped his arms and legs as hard as possible, letting the current sweep him toward the center of the Rio Grande. He knew he had only seconds before the Furies dived into the water, oblivious to their near-certain drowning. He knew it would be worth it to them to get a good bite or two out of him before they sank to the bottom.

When he finally emerged for a breath, he saw that he was almost halfway across. Aubrey and Jules were just ahead of him. The taller older girl helped the smaller one with the sprained ankle fight through the deeper water and increasingly powerful current.

Well ahead of them, Lauren and Jamie had already reached the other side. Trevor and Javi were right behind them. Martie and Lonnie dragged Emily, who looked completely spent, out of the fast-moving water, approaching the bank.

Lukas was surprised that he didn't feel relieved watching them get to safety. In fact, he noticed that he didn't feel much of anything at all. Even the muscle-burning pain he'd come to expect, while still there, felt distant. It was all overwhelmed by a crushing, all-consuming numbness.

His brother was somewhere behind him, dead or worse, being dragged away by a shrewd, malevolent flesh-eating soldier who had tracked them all the way from camp, using Lukas as some kind of human homing beacon. He almost welcomed the numbness. It masked his despair.

"Keep swimming!" Javi shouted desperately at him, snapping him out of his daze.

Apparently he had stopped moving.

He heard a cacophony of splashes behind him, too many to count. Glancing back, he saw that dozens of Furies had already dived into the water after him. They looked like living lava, spilling into the river in one endless wave, hard to discern as individuals.

Then Lukas saw why Javi had sounded so distressed. There were so many Furies in the water now that they had started to inadvertently form a kind of human bridge. Their bodies stretched out in the water, providing the ones that followed with a path to get further toward the middle of the river before they too tumbled in and drowned.

The Fury bridge was already a third of the way across the river and showed no sign of abating. If it continued like this, some of them might actually make it all the way across.

He turned back around and resumed swimming. Within seconds, he had caught up to Jules who was struggling to both help Aubrey and move forward.

"I'll take over," he said. "Get to shore."

Jules, clearly exhausted, nodded as he wrapped his arms under Aubrey's armpits and locked his hands together, preparing to swim backwards using just his legs.

Aubrey looked at him, and on her face, he could see all the emotions that were roiling through her. There was simultaneous relief that he was there to take over, resentment at needing his help, and something between sympathy and pity over Caleb. He looked away, choosing not to address any of them.

"Hurry," Lauren shouted from the bank. "The Federales have lined the bottom of the river with wires. It's electrified for a half mile in each direction. The second you get out, they can flip the switch and fry those things."

Lukas wanted to shout that he understood but didn't have the energy to focus on anything but kicking. Swimming backwards, he could see the advancing Furies getting closer as the ones in front willingly sacrificed themselves, diving into the water, providing a solid surface for those that swarmed behind them.

Far off in the distance, Lukas could see Curtas still dragging his brother who now looked to be unconscious. The man was staring back at him. Suddenly, the soldier's body shuddered again, as if *he'd* been struck with a massive jolt of electricity. After he recovered, Curtas returned his gaze to Lukas. His lips twisted into a grotesque smile. Then he, and Caleb with him, disappeared into the trees.

Curtas might no longer be human, but he still clearly had the capacity to strategize, to ambush, and apparently even to taunt. Whatever Command Sergeant Major Curtas was now, Colonel West had been wrong. He was definitely more than just a rage-filled flesh sack.

Another large splash refocused his attention on the threat directly in front of him. The spray from the water hit him in the face. They were that close now. Another few seconds and they'd be on him.

Just then, he felt his heels hit something solid. He realized he'd reached shallow water again. He dug his shoes into the sandy river bottom and, with the last bit of strength that he had left, propelled Aubrey and himself out and upward.

With his back to the bank, he stumbled back quickly, his eyes still on the endless stream of Furies that were now less than ten feet from him. But as he thrust himself back, he lost his balance and tumbled to the sand. Aubrey fell on top of him. He tried to get up again but found that he had nothing left. His legs were putty, and his arms were like lead.

Suddenly, Lukas felt two large hands grip his underarms and yank him powerfully backward. All he could do was maintain his hold on Aubrey and let himself be pulled. The swarm of Furies seemed to be moving faster, sensing how close they were.

He glanced back and saw that Lonnie was behind him, tugging both his weight and Aubrey's, his wiry muscles taxed to their extremes. A second later, he heard Martie's voice shout out.

"They're clear! They're on dry sand!"

"*Conectar la alimentación*!" Lauren yelled. "Turn on the power! *Encenderlo*!"

The Furies were almost completely across the river now. In moments, there would be no need to sacrifice themselves. The bridge was almost complete.

Then a loud whir sounded, mixed with what sounded like radio static. Almost immediately, Furies began to collapse as they ran across the bridge, simply falling straight down or to the sides. They all trembled as if having a shared seizure. Lonnie stopped yanking as everyone watched the Furies fall like hundreds of bowling pins—all but one.

A single Fury, a twenty-something female with wild blonde hair and an open gash in her stomach below her belly shirt, had made it to the wet sand. She shivered as she advanced, clearly impacted by the electricity coursing through her system. But she had enough momentum that she didn't stop. Instead she stumbled forward, headed straight for Aubrey and Lukas.

CHAPTER 57

Lukas barely had time to think.

The Fury was only steps away, clearly preparing to launch herself at them, when something shot past them, colliding with the woman and sending her backward as they both tumbled toward the river's edge.

It was Martie.

When they rolled to a stop less than a foot from the lapping waves, the female Fury began slashing at her captor briefly before trying to break free of her grip. She seemed to somehow sense that she was in danger.

Martie, clinging to the woman's waist tightly, looked over at the group and opened her mouth. She was about to shout something when the Fury turned toward her and dove, sinking her teeth into the counselor's cheek. Martie's impending shout turned into a scream.

The Fury unclenched her jaw and again tried to rip free. This time she was successful, breaking loose of Martie's arms. She started to crawl back toward where Aubrey and Lukas lay helplessly.

After that, everything seemed to happen at once.

Lukas heard multiple clicks, indicating that soldiers had removed the safeties on their weapons. At the same time, Martie grabbed the exposed ankle of the female Fury with her left hand.

The creature glanced back, almost as if she was annoyed with the human woman clinging to her. Martie stared back at her as she raised her right arm high into the air, held it there for one interminable moment, then triumphantly flung it back toward the water. Despite Martie's mangled face, her expression was clear—she looked satisfied.

Her hand splashed into the water. Instantly her body began to convulse. A fraction of a second later, the same thing happened to the Fury.

"No!" Aubrey screamed, attempting to tear free from Lukas's arms and help. But he clung to her tightly, refusing to let her break loose.

"You can't," he whispered.

Aubrey, just as exhausted as him, soon gave up the fight. They stared as both Martie and the Fury writhed and twitched for a good ten seconds before falling still.

Then Lukas's gaze fell on the long line of unmoving Furies stretching back all the way to the other bank where hundreds more paced and growled, instinctively aware that they could not cross.

"*Disparar!*" shouted the unseen Federale leader.

Immediately a barrage of gunfire emerged from all around them. Furies on the other bank dropped like flies. The soldiers continued firing until there was no movement on the other side of the riverbank.

When the shooting finally stopped, the main Federale, still hidden by trees, said something in Spanish.

A second later, Lauren translated, "He's going to shut off the power current for a few seconds so you can get Martie. Hurry—he says he has to turn it right back on and keep it that way until they can clear away the bodies."

A moment later, the loud whir and static sounds stopped. Jamie and Trevor rushed forward. Each of them grabbed one of Martie's legs and dragged her back to the dry sand. When they were clear, the Federale leader gave the order and the whir and static resumed.

Lukas allowed himself to collapse onto his back. He could feel Aubrey disentangling herself from him as the Federale continued speaking. Lauren responded intermittently. Lukas, despite taking Spanish in school for two years now, barely understood a word of it.

Instead, he focused on catching his breath as he waited for some semblance of strength to return to his body. The tingling pain was fading fast, a clear sign that Curtas was moving away from him. But the sensation of both emotional and physical numbness that had overcome him in the water lingered, perhaps not as pronounced as before but still very much there.

Lauren walked over and stood in front of him. He realized she was preparing to address the entire group.

"Officer Hinojosa says we are safe now and can ask for asylum from the government of Mexico. There's a shelter and clinic in Piedras Negras, the closest town. They will treat our injuries and let us stay overnight. Buses will take us to our desired destination while our asylum claims are processed. He said he's sorry for the loss of our friends."

"Gracias," Lonnie said to Officer Hinojosa who had finally emerged from his hiding spot. He was a small man in a heavily starched uniform with a well-trimmed mustache.

"Lauren," Jamie said, "can you ask him if there are any others like us who safely crossed the river?"

Though the man could clearly speak some English, he appeared to prefer not to right now, so Lauren obliged. The man's long answer seemed to make her whole body sag.

"He said no," she finally said, clearly leaving a lot out.

"That's not exactly what he said," Javi noted tersely.

He was bilingual too but hadn't felt the need to speak up until now.

"What do you mean?" Trevor asked.

"He said that, in the last two days, they've only encountered four people trying to cross, all of them by themselves. But the Mexican government had already ordered the border closed and anyone who tried to cross illegally be shot."

"So what happened?" Emily asked.

"His men shot them when they tried to cross the river."

Nobody spoke for several seconds.

Finally, Jules asked the question they all wanted to. "Why didn't they shoot us?"

"Because of her," Javi said, pointing at Lauren. "They remembered her. They respected her father. They made an exception."

"So if we had showed up at the river without Lauren," Lonnie said, "they would have shot us?"

"That's right," Javi replied.

No one had any response to that.

A moment later, an engine turned over. Lukas saw a large grey pickup truck rumble down from behind the trees and park near where they were assembled. Officer Hinojosa yelled something else. Lauren translated, though even Lukas got the gist.

"This is our ride," she said. "They'll take us to the shelter now."

They stared at it. None of them seemed to have the energy to walk over and get in. Lukas sat up and took in the scene around him. The soldiers were already pulling a large boat down as close to the water's edge as was safe. In it were hooks and nets he assumed they'd use to separate the Furies' bodies and break up the human bridge that still posed a threat.

Other soldiers were helping his fellow survivors to the truck. Two of them lifted Emily up and in as she seemed completely spent. Jamie and Trevor helped the limping Aubrey over to the back of the truck where the soldiers lifted her in as well. They climbed in after her. Jules was next, gripping Jamie's hand tightly as she pulled herself up. Lonnie made his way over. His leg was dragging badly. His physical reserves appeared completely depleted. Lauren hopped in after him.

Lukas looked around. Only he and Javi were left. But then he realized that wasn't true; there was also Martie.

CHAPTER 58

Lukas looked over at Matie's unmoving body lying forlornly in the dirt.

Blood was still dripping down her mangled cheek and pooling in the dry sand. Her eyes were squeezed tight, as if she was trying to keep the pain of being electrocuted at bay. At least that was the pain he assumed she'd been battling.

He looked over at Javi who was staring at her, as well. They made eye contact, and he knew his friend was thinking the same thing. They couldn't leave her here. She had sacrificed so much for them. And in the end, just like her mother, she'd sacrificed herself to save them, to save *him*. She deserved a proper burial and a marked grave, something they hadn't been able to give so many of the others who had fallen along the way.

Lukas bent down behind her head, scooping her up under her arms and carrying the bulk of her weight. He ignored the quiet screams of his battered body. Javi grabbed her legs, doing his best to keep her upright. But she sagged badly in the middle.

And then they were there—Jules, Trevor, Jamie, and even Lauren—offering assistance, lifting Martie so that only her dangling arms were left unsupported. The others—Aubrey, Lonnie, and Emily—were too hurt or wiped out to help. But they all sat up respectfully in the bed of the truck and helped ease her in when she arrived.

They placed her in the middle of the truck bed and all sat around her. As the truck slowly made its way back up the hill, most of them kept a hand on her body so it wouldn't bounce around unceremoniously.

The truck reached the top of the hill and sped away on the dirt road leading to Piedras Negras. Lukas managed to cast one last look back across the river into the United States. Curtas was nowhere in sight. Neither was his brother.

That wasn't a surprise. The tingling sensation in his body had dissipated to a mild prickle now. At this rate, it would be gone completely by the time they got to town.

While he wouldn't miss the discomfort, the thought of losing the sensation entirely was unsettling. It was his only remaining link to his brother. If he still felt the sting, then it meant Curtas wasn't too far away, and that meant that his brother likely wasn't either. At least that was what he chose to believe.

It seemed that Curtas wanted Caleb, or at least some version of him, alive. And Lukas had to assume that was for a reason. He feared—partly hoped—that the reason was him.

After all, the soldier had followed him halfway across Texas using their unexplainable connection to track him. He had even said they'd meet again. Before, on Hollow Hill, that had seemed like a threat. Now Lukas hoped it was a promise he still intended to keep.

He assured himself that Curtas would want to keep his brother close, perhaps for intel, perhaps as bait. Whatever the reason, he hadn't killed him, and Lukas had to trust that, if he hadn't done it at the riverbank, he wouldn't now.

He held on to that hope, mostly because it was all he had left. If Caleb wasn't dead, maybe the vaccine would keep him from turning into a Fury. And if it hadn't, maybe he could somehow be returned to his former self.

He tried to remember if he'd seen Curtas spit in Caleb's eye, as he had done to Steve Sailor and attempted to do to him. He couldn't recall seeing it, but things had been so crazy that he could have easily missed it.

Lukas had never been a science guy. But this seemed beyond science. Somehow Curtas had forged a connection with him that was more than emotional or spiritual. It was physical, chemical, something he couldn't explain but couldn't deny.

A big bump on the dirt road briefly snapped him out of his thoughts, but only briefly. Within moments he was back in his head, turning over the possibilities.

It occurred to him that, if the solider could use their connection to track him, maybe Lukas could use it the other way too. If not, then Caleb was lost forever. And Lukas wasn't ready to accept that. He wasn't ready to be the last living member of the Lincoln family. He wasn't ready to give up.

He looked at the others in the bed of the truck. Like him, they were mostly just a bunch of high school kids, not yet old enough to drive, barely equipped for the normal world, much less a post-apocalyptic one.

They were nine survivors, thrown together by circumstance, hurtling toward an uncertain future in the back of a dusty pickup truck. Someone had to make sure they kept moving forward, even if everything seemed hopeless.

Lukas Lincoln settled into his spot in the truck bed, trying his best to focus on the road ahead rather than the wreckage behind them.

After all, what choice did he have?